# ASHES TO ASHES

Forthcoming books by M. Stone Mayer
(featuring Will Mercer):

Book 2: In the Crosshairs

Book 3: Fade to Gray

# ASHES TO ASHES

## M. STONE MAYER

Three Towers Press

Milwaukee, Wisconsin

Published by
Three Towers Press, the fiction imprint of
HenschelHAUS Publishing, Inc.
Milwaukee, Wisconsin
www:henschelHAUSbooks.com


ISBN: 978159598-989-5
LCCN: PENDING

Printed in the USA

*To Ella and Atticus.*
*If you dream it, you can achieve it.*
*Don't let anyone tell you different.*

*Cover concept by Ella Mayer*

# CHAPTER 1

The moon broke through the clouds, illuminating a gray mist that had formed after an evening rainstorm. Rising up like spirits, the mist moved through the dark Oregon forest before settling among the evergreens. Far below, an ancient river flowed through the hushed night. The driver of the small pickup truck took it all in.

The wind whistled in his ear, coming through the small gap of his window. Will Mercer checked his rearview mirror, momentarily blinded by bright headlights trailing close behind. He was being driven by instinct, by fear—flight winning over fight. When his eyes refocused, a yellow highway sign with a large black arrow—indicating a sharp curve—appeared out of the headlight-blinding fog. He slammed on his brakes a second too late. All four wheels locked and the truck slid sideways across the rain-soaked road, crashed through the guardrail, and plunged into the gorge.

The pickup slammed into the water, the impact sending Mercer headlong into the windshield. Instantly he was surrounded by a cold darkness trying to crawl inside his head.

*Stay awake, I have to stay awake. I gotta get out of here.* His thoughts muddled, he fought to focus on the task at hand—*get out of the truck.*

The river was deep in this place; its muddy bottom lay somewhere far below the surface. Water was pouring in through the partially opened window filling the small cab and making it sink faster. The truck had sunk fifteen feet before Mercer thought to pull the Smith and Wesson .38 from the glove box.

Fear gripping his chest, he shot out the passenger-side window—its tempered glass shattering. Cold water surged in, quickly filling the cab. He shoved the pistol into his waistband, and with one last gulp, wriggled out through the blown-out window. Halfway through, his denim jacket snagged on the door lock. Panicked, he rolled out of his jacket, leaving it to sink to the bottom.

His lungs burned. He kicked furiously for the surface but as he neared it, the current sucked him downstream. He fought hard, and finally broke through the surface to fill his fiery lungs with cool night air.

The river raged, the current growing stronger. In certain places, it cut deep into the rock that lined the banks and flowed around scattered boulders, ancient basalt rocks rising out of the water like giant chiseled teeth.

The current swept him into the first rock, hitting it hard and smashing and slicing his knee. The next few seconds were a blur as he fought to avoid dangers he couldn't see. The current spun him around and dragged him headfirst downstream. Suddenly the water pushed him headlong into a dark shape rising from the water's surface. His world went black.

\* \* \*

A large black Cadillac Escalade, fishtailed to a stop at the top of the gorge, its headlights shining on the far cliff wall. Two men and a woman jumped out and ran to the edge in time to see the truck sink into the swirling darkness, its taillights fading into nothingness.

The woman ordered her men back into their vehicle, anger flashing in her dark green eyes. They quickly obeyed. She climbed in last and slammed the door. As the Escalade turned back the way it had come, she pulled a cell phone from her black leather jacket and dialed a number. A man's voice on the phone answered, "Ms. Carson. Tell me something."

"Mercer's dead and buried," replied Carson

"Good," the man said, and then the phone went dead.

# CHAPTER 2

A thin shimmer of light pierced the forest floor, followed by another, and another. The sky east of the snow-peaked mountains glowed purple, then orange, as night surrendered to day. The silent forest gave way to the creatures of dawn, and those that ruled the night sought out darker places.

The sound of jays broke the quiet of the morning. Several of the dark blue birds had discovered a body in a place where the river slowed, forming sandbars and piles of debris. This morning, a man lay among the branches and rubble—the sand stained deep red where his head rested.

Mercer stirred slowly, the pain in his head tremendous. His mind was foggy and his world still black. His eyes flitted open. He saw a blur of water and sand. He slowly rolled onto his back. Cold and wet, he soaked up what little warmth the morning sand had to offer. He put a hand to his forehead; it was wet and sticky and came away covered in blood. He leaned over and splashed water on his face. The icy water was jolting but helped to numb the searing pain. He tried to rise, but his right knee screamed in pain and small twinkling lights exploded in the periphery of his vision. He rolled back on his side and tried to focus on his knee. A three-inch gash ran across the front of it. He cleaned the cut as best he could, then slowly checked the rest of his body.

He leaned over the water again to examine his bloody forehead. The image that stared back at him was beaten and bloodied, a four-inch gash over his left eye. The blood, which had started to congeal, was once again flowing freely. He ripped off a piece of his t-shirt and used it to swab his forehead. The bleeding slowed to a trickle.

Again, he tried to rise but his body screamed in protest. Gut-punched with a wave of nausea, he bent over and emptied his stomach onto the sand. It took several more attempts to gain his full six-foot height. His blood-soaked shirt clung to his chest and his brown hair was caked with dried blood. His bloodshot brown eyes sought out anything familiar.

Feeling a lump in his lower back, he reached back and pulled out a revolver. He opened the cylinder. Five bullets. He looked across the river, searching for something—anything—that might explain how he got here. His eyes took on a frenzied look of panic. Not only did he not know where he was or how he got here, he couldn't remember who he was. His eyes flicked from shore to shore. Fear took over his brain and his body, and the need to run somewhere, anywhere. Grabbing the revolver, he staggered from the sandbar toward the closer shore.

The water was only waist-deep but icy cold. He crossed the river as fast as he could, falling several times as his unsure feet slipped on rocks lying below the surface. He clawed his way up the bank and into the forest, half-running, half-stumbling over fern-hidden logs. Finally, with his adrenaline draining away, he collapsed under the shade of a giant fir.

Hours later, Mercer woke disoriented and sweat-soaked from a raging fever. His mind in a fog, he used the tree to pull himself to his feet. The sun blinded him, causing excruciating pain that seared from temple to temple, like lightning across a dark night sky. His body convulsed as he tried to throw up, but nothing came. Steadying himself, he limped farther into the forest.

His knee, now painfully swollen, ached making him stop every few minutes to rest. Searching the forest floor, he found a four-foot branch. He picked it up and leaned on it to see if it could support him. It held, and the pain in his knee eased slightly.

He wandered deeper into the forest and away from the river, oblivious to his surroundings. His fevered mind a swirling fog, he tried to think, to remember something about his life, but his memories began in dark icy water and the sandbar.

The sun was at his back when his head cleared enough to let him focus on the situation. *Where the hell am I? How long have I been walking?* He now felt the full force of his predicament. He was lost and he had left the basic means of being found: the river. A river served two purposes; it provided fresh water and it could lead to civilization.

Now, miles from the river, Mercer sank against a tree, his head in his hands. He was tired and hungry and starting to become dehydrated. He glanced around at his surroundings, but nothing was familiar. He tried to focus on any memory he could form, but it was like trying to hold smoke.

Finally, he stood and took inventory of himself. He had a revolver tucked in his waistband, but his back pockets were empty. He grabbed the revolver and again checked it for bullets. It felt comfortable in his hand as if he'd used it many times before. A quick search of his front pockets revealed a key and a small piece of yellow paper. His only other possession was a large Swiss Army knife in a sheath that hung on his braided leather belt.

He examined the piece of paper as though it was a thousand-year-old relic. Although damp, he could still make out the writing on it: CALL ME ASAP— SARAH and a telephone number. He had to find a phone. Maybe Sarah, whoever she was, could explain who he was and what he was doing in the middle of the forest in the middle of nowhere. He closed his eyes again, trying to imagine Sarah.

A noise startled Mercer awake. He had drifted off sitting against the tree. He dripped with a cold sweat. The loss of blood, lack of food and water, and the day's exertion had taken its toll. The sound of a branch snapping twenty yards to his right brought all his senses instantly alive. Even in his fevered state, he understood the gravity of his situation. He turned his head toward the sound and narrowed his eyes as he tried to see shapes in the gathering dusk. Whatever had made the sound was gone and Mercer let out the breath he had been holding.

He had to find water. The question was which way to go?

Mercer struggled to his feet. His legs were shaky so he leaned on his makeshift crutch. He decided to walk toward the rising moon, or at least its reflected light.

*That should be east, at least for the time being.*

After a quarter of a mile, the game trail he was following began to rise out of the valley floor. He followed the now moonlit path as it wound up the side of a ridge. After three hours of climbing, he reached the ridgeline and stepped out onto a rocky outcrop. Spread out below him was a small valley and the glimmer of moonlight dancing off water—a river.

He backtracked until he found another game trail descending into the valley—one that had seen recent use. He saw the track of an elk, a fact that reassured his unsettled mind. He could still remember some things. Given the number of tracks, he thought that a herd of elk had probably moved through earlier. As if to confirm his thoughts, the sound of bugling rose from the valley floor. The high-pitched sound made Mercer grin.

The descent became more gradual. He could hear the water now and his mind focused on reaching it. He refused to stop and rest, forcing his body forward. The trail he followed exited the forest and continued across a dark meadow. Mercer stopped at the tree line and stared into the inky darkness. Halfway across the meadow lay the river. Scattered throughout the meadow was the herd of elk.

He gave the elk a wide berth, and sank to his knees as he entered the river, cupping water to his mouth. After a few minutes of drinking his fill, he lay back on the bank and stared up at the expansive, star-speckled sky.

The sounds of night, and the animals that prowled it, became more prevalent. Feeling exposed, Mercer wandered back across the meadow. He found a large Ponderosa pine and cleared a space to lie down beneath it on the bed of soft needles. For a long time, he stared up through the dark canopy and wondered if he'd ever know where—or, for that matter, who—he was. He pulled the small key from his pocket and twirled it between his fingers, wondering what it might open.

Suddenly, a flash of memory blinded him and he saw himself running through a parking lot and into Portland's Union Station—nervously looking over his shoulder, worried that someone was following him. He was carrying a backpack. There were two sets of tickets in his hands, one for a plane headed to Minneapolis -St Paul later that night, and a round-trip train ticket to Tacoma. It seemed like a real memory, so vivid. He concentrated on trying to replay it, but the memory slipped away again. Sleep finally crept over him, dissolving and distorting his memories until he finally gave in.

He woke abruptly as a surge of adrenaline coursed through his veins. He remained frozen, though the urge to run tensed his muscles. Fighting the instinct, he lay motionless and listened to the night. It wasn't noise that woke him, he realized, but the lack of noise, an utter stillness that swept over the forest and the meadow. The crickets he had heard when he was falling asleep were now silent.

A cool summer breeze swept across the meadow and he squinted in the dim moonlight to distinguish shapes. The night was playing tricks on his eyes, creating shadows that seemed to come to life and move through the darkness.

From somewhere behind him he heard an unmistakable growl. The hair on the back of his neck stood up and fear clutched him. Wriggling free from its grasp, Mercer closed his hand around the revolver that lay next to him. He listened hard against the stillness of the night, ears searching for any sound of movement.

He closed his eyes and focused on his ears. A twig broke in the direction of the growl he had heard seconds before. His heartbeat started pounding like a jackhammer, drowning out the slight sounds he was trying to track. He tried to quiet his heart with slow, deep breaths.

Then he heard the growl again, closer this time, ten yards off to his left. He searched the darkness but the sound came from the same tree line he was using as cover. The trees hid both equally well.

Several branches snapped as a shadow burst into the meadow. A blood-curdling scream echoed across the still meadow, one no human could make. The creature that had made the sound had not seen death coming until it was too late. The sound of fleeing animals trampling grass, splashing through water, snapping branches along the way, split the night. The echo of struggle died away as quickly as it began.

Mercer again heard a growl, this time louder, no longer concerned about giving away its position. The cougar had found its meal and settled in to eat it before dragging off the rest to cache and eat later. Several smaller sounds reached Mercer's ears from where the large cat had launched its attack. Cubs born in the spring now bounded toward their mother's kill.

Unsettled by his proximity to a true predator, Mercer pulled his walking stick closer to him, tightened his grip on the revolver, and pressed harder against the trunk of the Ponderosa pine, wishing the tree could absorb him.

Mercer didn't sleep, but waited for a sunrise that refused to come. To keep his mind alert, he focused on his immediate needs. He decided to make sure he had all the necessities for surviving before figuring out what to do next. He'd need food first, then he'd focus on shelter and fire. Sometime after the first light of dawn crested the eastern ridge, he let sleep take him once more. A night of adrenaline, a low-grade fever, and fear had finally taken their toll.

# CHAPTER 3

Carson sat uncomfortably in a stiff, high-backed chair outside her boss' office. After a few minutes, a gruff baritone voice came over the intercom at the receptionist's desk.

"Ms. Carson, come." An order.

Carson stood. At five-foot-eight, with red hair and dark green eyes, her toned, muscular body shone through the cut of her clothes: black slacks, a crisp, white button-down blouse open at the neck, and a pair of black designer leather boots. She quickly slipped through the large oak door. Instantly, she was bathed in twilight, the room lit only by the slanted rays of light that leaked through the blinds and painted the Spanish-tiled floor with stripes of dull yellow light. The odors of old leather and stale cigar smoke filled her nostrils. A large oak desk occupied part of the room. Behind the desk, a high-backed leather chair.

"Yes, Mr. Ashe?"

"I want to know exactly what happened last night. Where is the body?" The chair swiveled around to reveal a large man in his late sixties, with salt-and-pepper hair and ice-blue eyes.

Carson suspected Ashe had been physically foreboding in his youth, but the years had long since given way to the pounds of affluence he now carried inside his Savile Row custom-made suit. A large diamond ring on his left pinky drew subtle attention to his wealth and power, but it only took one look into his soulless eyes to understand his nature.

"The body?"

"Yes, the body. There was a body, wasn't there?"

"Of course. It's just, well, the body wasn't recoverable."

"What do you mean, not recoverable? You told me last night that Mercer was dead and buried. Where did you bury him? Did you retrieve the information I requested?" Ashe demanded, his impatience beginning to show.

"He is dead, sir. He drove off a cliff and plummeted over fifty feet into a river up in the mountains. I never got a chance to get the information. But he's dead. No one could have survived that kind of fall. And even if he survived the fall, he'd drown in the river."

"You never actually saw the body." A statement.

Carson visibly shrank back as Ashe stared her down in his rising fury.

"Sit," he commanded, then turned his chair so that his back was once again to her.

She sat in the leather armchair opposite the large desk. After seconds that seemed like hours, Ashe spoke again. His voice was low and menacing.

"You'll do what I originally asked. You'll confirm that he is dead and you'll retrieve the information he stole from me. I don't think I need to explain to you the level of my disappointment if you fail me."

"No, sir. I'll take care of everything."

"See that you do. Now, what is the status of our disposal project?"

"It was completed today, on schedule and without any problems."

"Good. We'll need to schedule another project in a couple of days. With increased production, there'll be a need for more storage and disposal. Will there be any problem with that?"

"No, sir. I'll take care of it."

"What about the loss of our disgruntled worker? Will that slow it down?"

"No. He has already been replaced," Carson lied.

"Good. I leave it in your hands then. I'll expect to receive a report concerning the recovery operation, and I'll let you know when we need to schedule the next project. We're done."

Experience told Carson not to linger. She went to the large door, the heels of her boots clicking on the tiled floor, opened it and slid through, closing it behind her. She stepped into the reception area where Cray and Russ—the two men from the night before—now waited. They both stood well over six feet, and were muscular with broad shoulders. Russ had a full mustache that covered his upper lip and a tight buzz cut; Cray had let his hair start to grow out, and had a tattoo of a coiled snake on his neck below his right ear. Both wore black cargo pants, boots, and black T-shirts that screamed of past military service.

"What's up, boss?" Cray asked.

"Get the truck," she barked, taking her repressed anger out on them.

Seeing the fire in her eyes, they did as they were told. Carson followed, grabbing her black leather coat off the couch and checking the Beretta 9mm pistol tucked inside.

\* \* \*

The black Escalade sped south down Interstate 5, pulling off at the exit for North Wilsonville and into the parking lot of a deserted warehouse, then drove around the side of the building. Russ pressed a button on the dashboard and a large, paneled door rose, allowing him to drive in. He parked as the door, squealing on rusted springs, closed behind them.

The interior of the warehouse was two stories high. The ground level contained several hundred unmarked barrels and forklifts. There were large storage rooms in the back, each one padlocked. A stairway in the far corner led to the second story that extended one-quarter of the length of the building. A bank of windows fronted the second floor that allowed bygone managers to keep an eye on warehouse workers. Now the windows looked down on spiders and rats.

The Escalade pulled up next to a black BMW 9 series convertible. A black Chevy Silverado pickup was parked against the far wall. Carson and the two men got out of the Escalade and went up the stairs.

A long counter covered with dust ran the length of the window. The old linoleum that covered the floor crackled as the three people walked down the hallway. Carson pressed a button on the wall and a panel swung open to reveal a small cavity. Reaching inside, she pressed another button and turned off the interior security cameras that were perched in the corners of the warehouse.

Closing the panel, she pulled out a black plastic keycard and swiped it across a magnetic lock hidden in the wall. An interior door quietly swung open to a room with wall-to-wall carpeting and expensive furniture. A kitchen area off to one side was complete with a refrigerator, stove, and sink. A pool table, several couches, and a large screen TV filled the other side of the room. A door between two desks on the far wall led to Carson's private office.

Carson went to her office door; the two men hesitated.

"My office, two minutes." She opened the door and slammed it shut behind her.

\* \* \*

Russ and Cray took off their jackets and sat at the desks. While they removed their guns from their shoulder holsters, Cray said, "What the hell is going on?"

"I'm not sure, but I think it's got something to do with last night."

"I need a beer. Want one?"

He got up and went to the kitchen area, grabbed two bottles of Mirror Pond Pale Ale out of the well-stocked refrigerator, opened them, and handed one to Russ. Just as they raised the bottles to their lips, an intercom crackled to life.

"Did you two forget how to tell time?" Carson said. "Get in here. We have work to do."

The two men exchanged glances and went to her office. Carson was studying a large map and looked up as they entered.

\* \* \*

"Well, boys, we screwed up and now we have to tie up the loose ends. Russ, I need you to get your SCUBA equipment together and be ready to go tomorrow at 0500 hours. Cray, you need to scrounge enough rappelling equipment together to get Russ down that ravine and to the bottom of that river. We have to retrieve the stolen files and confirm that Mercer's dead. Any questions?" Her anger was starting to subside. "Take a look at this map. I think he went off the road here." She pointed to a curve in the thin line that defined the mountain highway that ran along the river.

"That looks right to me," Russ said. "See?" he said, pointing. "Here's that pull-off we passed. What do we do when we find the body?"

"Bring your underwater camera. We'll take a picture of the body to appease Ashe. It's the files we need. Any problems?"

"No, it should work."

"Can you get your hands on rappelling equipment?" she asked Cray.

"I have all the equipment down in one of the storage lockers. It'll take me about an hour to put the winch on the Escalade."

"Okay, get started," she directed Cray. "Russ, stay here. We haven't discussed the events that led up to the incident."

Cray smirked at Russ and left the room.

14

Carson went to her desk and Russ took a seat across from her as she opened a file.

"Okay, tell me what happened."

"Yesterday at 0900 hours, you called and told me to watch Mercer. I drove to his house. He was throwing a suitcase in his truck when I arrived. I parked on the other side of the field and watched him through my scope; he never saw me. He went back into the house and came out with what looked like an empty backpack, which he also threw into the truck and then he got in and pulled away. I followed him to his office. I was careful and stayed back because I knew where he was going.

"I arrived just in time to see him enter his office with the backpack. I waited for about an hour. He finally came out, but this time he was carrying the backpack as if it had something in it. He looked nervous—looking around and all. He got in his truck and pulled out of the parking lot. It was about 1100 hours at this point."

Russ continued. "He got on the highway and headed north. I tailed him, but he made me. I backed off because I figured he was headed to Portland, but instead he got off at North Wilsonville, so I thought he was headed here. Off the exit, he sped up and I lost him. He headed into the hills somewhere around here."

"How did you find him again? How did you know he was headed for the train station?" Carson asked.

"I put a transmitter on his truck when he was in his office. That's when I came back and picked up Cray. The same time I checked in with you."

"Okay, then what happened?"

"Cray and I grabbed the tracking equipment and trailed him to the train station. That's when we called you to meet us. Mercer must have been in there for an hour before we all got there."

"Why didn't he hop a train?" Carson asked, almost to herself.

Russ combed his mustache with two fingers. "I've been thinking about that. I checked the train schedule. There weren't any trains leaving until 1900 hours, and that train was headed to Seattle. The only train he could have used as a means of escape was the Portland to Chicago, but that didn't leave until 0500 hours this morning. I wondered why he didn't just go to the airport and catch a flight? He could have been in any state and quite a few countries before we even knew he was gone."

"I don't think he had a lot of cash on him," Carson said, "and maybe the airport security freaked him out."

"Maybe. Anyway, he saw us and bolted."

"And now we have a mess to clean up," Carson said. "Did you see him carrying anything when he ran out of the station to his truck?"

"No, he was just running."

"Alright, go get your equipment ready. There's no room for any more fuckin' mistakes. Understood?"

Carson began going through papers on her desk so Russ got up and quickly disappeared through the door. She watched the two men drive away in Russ's black pickup through the exterior surveillance cameras. She was furious but now was not the time to rip into them. She needed them at the top of their game, and she knew they had expected her to yell. By staying calm, she kept them on edge and, hopefully, alert.

# CHAPTER 4

Ted Kameron was one in a long line of ranchers trying to keep the family business going, as his parents and grandparents had before him. He raised beef cattle in Molalla, a small town in the Willamette Valley in northern Oregon, with a herd numbering over four hundred head.

Ted was a large man—typical ranching stock—and looked older than his twenty-eight years though he could outwork most men his age, and the twinkle in his slate-blue eyes reflected his youth.

It was late summer in the Willamette Valley, also known as "the grass seed capital of the world," and that meant field burning. Each year, grass farmers throughout the valley would burn their fields to get rid of insects, diseases, or weeds. Ted had spent most of the morning with bleary, smoke-filled eyes and burning lungs. It had been a hot, exhausting day, and he had been trying to herd several new cows down to pasture. It had taken longer than he had expected as none of the cows wanted to go where he was leading, or even in the same direction. The herd instinctively knew how to get out of the cloud of smoke drifting from nearby fields. That meant that first he had to find the herd, then he had to move the new cows through the smoke to join them. It took all morning but he had done it.

He'd spent the rest of the day patching holes in fences every cow seemed to know from birth. Usually, Ted worked with his ranch foreman, but today he was alone. He and his father used to work together until his dad had to give it up and retire after a tractor accident. His parents now spent their time in a cottage on the Oregon coast.

Ted snapped out of his thoughts and back to his pastures covered in a low cloud of smoke. He turned his horse and cantered out of the field, away from the cloud. He usually avoided the field burning because the farmer to the west always called to let him know when he would burn. Swearing under his breath, he was going to find out why he never got that call today.

One of Ted's other neighbors called around five o'clock in the evening to let him know that nine of his cows were heading down the road. Somehow, he'd missed a hole in the fence. He managed to get eight of the cows rounded up, but was missing one. After getting the others back in the pasture and mending the fence, Ted guided his horse out of the pasture and into a little hollow to cut across some of the neighboring fields—smoke still blanketing the ground like mist.

He headed to a watering hole at the bottom of the hollow to give his horse a drink. That's where he saw the missing heifer lying on her side. She wasn't moving and struggled to breathe.

He pulled out his cell phone and dialed his veterinarian.

"Hello, Willamette Valley Breeders. What can I do for you?" a man said.

"Is Andy around? This is Ted from the Kameron Ranch. I got a problem."

"Hold on, Ted, he's just heading out the door. Lemme see if I can grab him."

Ted heard the man yell. A minute later, Andy came on the line. "Hey, Ted, how's it goin'?"

"Had better days. I think one of my heifers is suffering from smoke inhalation, and I'm not sure what to do."

"Smoke inhalation?" Andy asked.

"Yeah. Green Grass Enterprises started burning its fields today. She must have got caught in the smoke."

"What's the tag number on the cow?"

Ted read the number off the ear tag and Andy asked him for his exact location so they could meet him.

"Is she still breathing, Ted?"

"Barely. She's probably been down for a while. Should I shoot her? I don't have a rifle with me," Ted said, answering his own question.

"No. I'll be there in fifteen minutes to put her down. Are we going to be able to get in there with a flatbed?"

"Yeah. Take the old road that heads north off River Road. There's an old fence with a gate about a hundred yards up. I'll wait for you there. Thanks, Andy. I know you were heading home."

"No problem."

Ted put his phone away and led his horse to the old road, which was slowly being reclaimed by the meadow.

Fifteen minutes later, Ted was opening the barbed-wire gate when headlights cut through the darkness. He heard the grumbling of the flatbed's diesel engine before he saw the headlights. He opened the gate and the truck passed through. It stopped on the other side of the fence.

"Ted," Andy said, "do you want to jump in here with us?" Chris, the veterinary technician, slid over on the bench seat to give him room.

"Sure. Let me tie up my horse." He tied his horse to one of the old fence posts and got into the truck. He pointed the way to the watering hole and the truck rumbled forward. The cow was still lying on her side when they arrived, her breathing strained and shallow, life ebbing away.

Andy got out of the truck, backpack in hand, and bent over the suffering animal.

"Chris, I want you to get the euthanasia ready while I get some samples."

"How come you guys are going to euthanize her? Why not just shoot her so the meat can still be used?"

"Company's policy nowadays. We don't take any chances when there might be something wrong with the cow. You should see some of the people we sell to. Your cows are always in great condition, but some people treat theirs like shit. The company decided not to take any chances or make any exceptions—you know, for liability reasons."

The Kameron Ranch, as well as almost every ranch in the Molalla area, used Willamette Valley Breeders for both their vet services and buying new stock. Ted's family had been buying heifers and bulls from them for years. It was a little strange for a company to have such a monopoly in the area, but their warranty couldn't be beat. Most places didn't offer a warranty for the stock they sold, but Willamette Valley Breeders not only fully covered their cattle, they would also come and recover the cows and pay for all disposal charges.

Andy quickly took several samples, including blood, saliva, urine, and tissue.

Ted watched as Andy handed the samples to Chris, who then handed Andy a large syringe filled with a pink solution. Ted recognized the drug, having seen demonstrations of its use in agricultural extension workshops put on by the state veterinarian. Andy took the syringe and inserted the needle into the chest of the dying cow, driving it into her heart. He pressed the plunger and the thick solution entered the cow's heart and blood stream. The last vestiges of her life drained away as her eyes turned glassy.

Chris worked the hydraulics of the flatbed. He grabbed a chain from the toolbox, wrapped one end around the back legs of the dead cow, then attached the other end to the winch and turned it on. The winch hummed to life and began dragging the lifeless cow across the grass and onto the cold metal of the flatbed. Once on, Chris worked the hydraulics to bring the bed down flat. He strapped a tarp over the cow, lashing it to the sides of the truck.

Andy finished filling out the paperwork and asked Ted to sign a form. He had signed this form before when some of his other cows had problems, usually deaths related to giving birth or stillborn calves. Andy ripped off a copy and gave it to Ted.

"Sorry about all this," Andy said. "Give me a call Monday afternoon and we'll sort out the details of the warranty. I'll try to find you a good replacement in the morning."

"Thanks, I appreciate it."

They shook hands and Andy headed for the flatbed. "You want a ride back to your horse?"

"No, I think I'll walk. I'll get the gate on my way out."

The diesel engine grumbled to life and rolled up the old road. Ted took one more look around the now-quiet hollow and turned to follow. It had not been one of his better days.

# CHAPTER 5

Cray and Russ pulled into the warehouse parking lot and opened the automatic door. It was 4:45 a.m. Sunday morning, fifteen minutes before they were supposed to leave. Carson stood inside waiting.

"Doesn't she ever sleep?" Cray muttered as they pulled up.

Russ got out of the truck and began loading his SCUBA equipment into the SUV: two tanks, a weight belt, and three full dive bags. Cray had loaded the rappelling equipment the night before. Carson walked over to where the men were working.

"Cutting it kind of close, aren't you?" she said. "Let's get going. The sun is coming up and I want to be there yesterday."

Russ got behind the wheel and Cray slid into the back seat. Russ started the engine and Carson climbed into the passenger side. As the Escalade pulled out, the large automatic door closed quietly behind them, the soulless eyes of the surveillance cameras were all that watched them leave.

It was an hour's drive back into the mountains. Russ flipped on the police scanner to monitor activity. He wanted to make sure that they weren't headed into a "police convention." So far, there wasn't any talk about a truck going off the road.

There was little traffic in the early morning hours, and the massive firs and hemlocks kept the forest dark, even as the sun started its climb across the sky.

"When we're about five miles from the turnout, I want you to stop," Carson said.

Russ nodded and fifteen minutes later, he pulled over onto the soft shoulder of the road.

"Give me a hand, Cray," Carson said. "I need the black bag with the red lettering and the laptop out of the back."

Russ shot Cray a look in the rearview mirror, unsure of what Carson was doing.

"Come on, get the lead out of your ass," she yelled.

Cray jumped out, opened the back door, and fished out the bag she wanted.

Carson grabbed it and pulled out a surveillance camera. She switched the remote sensor on and a small red light on the back illuminated. Next, she booted up a laptop and plugged an aircard into a USB port.

A look of understanding spread across Cray's face. "With the cameras, we should have enough time to prepare for any unwanted attention, no matter what direction it comes from."

"You get a cookie," Carson said, without looking up. The computer screen blinked on and after a few keystrokes, two boxes came up on the screen. One box was black, but the other showed the image of an upside-down western hemlock and the taillight of the SUV. "Okay, Cray, I want you to position that camera to look back down the road. Make sure it's hidden; these things aren't cheap. It also needs a pretty clear line of sight to the sky so it can pick up the satellites."

Cray went a few feet into the bushes. He found a young Douglas fir and positioned the camera. "How's that signal?"

"Good. Crystal-clear," Carson said.

Cray went to look at his handiwork, and watched as Carson pressed several keys and the camera zoomed in and faded out.

"Wow, that's cool."

"I'm glad you're impressed. Now let's get going. We have another one to set up," Carson said, the hint of a smile on her face.

Five miles farther up, they approached the spot where the pickup truck had gone off the road. The area was deserted.

"Why aren't there any signs of the police poking around? Like yellow tape or something?" Cray asked.

Carson studied the scene, taking in all the details.

"Take a look at the guardrail. If you didn't know something had busted through it you'd think that it's fine. The truck hit head-on in the middle, the weakest point. The impact took out the whole section. It almost looks like that's how it's supposed to look. There aren't even any skid marks. The road was wet and the truck hydroplaned. No one knows anything happened here, and unless we screw things up, no one ever will."

The two men looked from Carson to each other, broad grins lining their faces.

"Okay, let's get that other camera positioned and get back here."

A few minutes later with surveillance in place, the trio returned to the turnout and parked beside the blown-out guardrail.

"Cray, get the winch ready. Russ, get ready to dive."

Russ set up his tanks and regulators. He tested the two-tank technical dive setup to make sure the equipment was working properly. He pulled on his dry suit since the glacial water was barely above freezing, slipped a hood and mask over his head, and pulled on his buoyancy control vest or BC. He clipped neon-green flippers to one side, a dive light and camera to the other, and slipped a long dive knife into the sheath strapped to his leg.

Cray had the pulley system ready and Russ stepped into the repelling harness. Once belted in, he walked to the edge of the cliff. The metal bar of the pulley system Cray had set up extended six feet out over the edge.

Russ looked at Cray. "This is gonna hold me, right?"

"Of course it'll hold you. How much do you weigh again?"

"You know damn well how much I weigh."

"Well, it certainly wouldn't hold me, that's for sure," Cray goaded.

"Get in the water," Carson demanded. "We don't have time for this shit. If it doesn't hold you, the water will break your fall. Now go."

Shooting a look at Carson's back, Russ sat down on the cliff's edge and pulled on his flippers, then slid off the cliff wall and swung out over the abyss. The cables groaned but held. Cray started the winch and Russ began descending into the gorge. Ten feet below him, a fifty-pound anchor swayed in the wind. Forty feet below the anchor, the river churned angrily.

As Russ got closer to the river, he understood where the truck had gone in. There were rapids both upstream and downstream, but below him was dark swirling water—a deep pool.

He caught his breath as he entered the cold water, then pulled his mask over his face. His dry suit kept him warm and dry, but he could still feel the cold press of the water against his body. He looked at his dive computer; the water temperature was 38 degrees.

Surrounded by the water's darkness, Russ felt for his light, unclipped it, and turned it on. A narrow halogen beam cut through the dark water, but there was nothing to see. He had been an infantry officer in the Marines and trained in combat diving, which prepared him for diving in low visibility. He looked again at the illuminated dive computer. He was at twenty feet and descending. He felt the pull of current and wondered if he was still on-course.

He pulled two weighted glow sticks out of his pocket and cracked them. As they began to glow an eerie light green, he switched off his dive light. He dropped the glowing sticks and watched them disappear into the darkness below. He could see them for about ten feet before they were swallowed up by the black water.

Russ continued his descent. His computer displayed a depth of fifty feet. *It can't be much deeper*, he thought. The temperature had dropped two degrees from the surface and the cold was beginning to stiffen his joints. He flexed his gloved fingers a few times. Suddenly, two green specks glowed below him. He flicked his dive light back on, but he was still too far up to illuminate the bottom. The green lights got brighter and brighter as he continued down. Sixty feet flashed across his dive computer, and he noticed the line was starting to go slack. The anchor had hit the bottom.

Russ began shining his flashlight in wide swaths. When the flashlight swung to his left side, he noticed a red light that disappeared as his beam passed. He brought his flashlight back around and he saw it a second time. It wasn't a light; but the reflection of a taillight cover. Russ kicked toward the red glow and suddenly found himself behind the bed of the pickup truck.

He reached down, unclipped the anchor, and tied it to the tailgate. He swam along the passenger side of the truck, grabbing the open passenger window to steady himself. Shards of glass bit through his gloves and pierced the cold flesh of his hand. He realized it happened, but he couldn't feel anything due to the numbness. He lifted his hand and water began to leak into his glove, numbing it even further.

"Son of a bitch," he muttered through teeth that clenched the regulator mouthpiece. A cloud of bubbles escaped his regulator. He grabbed the door handle with his other hand and kicked up to the window so he could look inside. Sweeping the interior of the truck with his light, he was surprised to see it empty. The reason for the broken window, he thought. The son of a bitch had survived the crash.

Putting one foot against the side of the truck, he forced the door open. Russ then moved inside. The cab was small and with his tanks, he was forced to keep his legs outside. Again, he swept the light through the dark truck. The keys were still in the ignition and the glove box hung open. Russ quickly checked the glove box, then the floor, finally behind the seats. The truck was empty. No folder, no bag, no body. Nothing.

*Carson's gonna go ballistic*, he thought, wishing he didn't have to tell her.

He continued around the truck, inspecting the muddy riverbed, as well as the truck itself for any other signs of Mercer. Something on the muddy bottom flashed in his light. He let out most of the air in his lungs and sank the two feet to the bottom. Taking a slow, shallow breath, he maintained his position. Searching the small area, he realized he was seeing the silver button of a denim jacket. Russ pulled a bag from his BC pocket and placed the jacket inside. At least he wouldn't go back empty-handed. Russ spent another five minutes photographing the truck, inside and out, in order to show Carson what he had seen.

* * *

Carson was busy watching the computer screen. It had been an hour since Russ went into the water. The sun had climbed higher into the sky and its warmth was making her sleepy. Propped up against the rear tire, Cray had dozed off. She thought about yelling to wake him up, but she had been tough on them lately and decided to leave him alone.

The sound of footsteps on loose gravel shocked her awake. She looked at the computer screen and saw two deserted roads. Shutting the laptop, she looked up to see a backpacker exiting the forest, his boots kicking up loose pebbles as he hit the soft shoulder of the road.

Carson quietly kicked Cray. He bolted up and was about to say something when he saw the look in her eyes. She motioned with her head in the direction of the hiker.

Cray got to his feet and walked around the front of the Escalade with a map. The backpacker seemed to be alone, and was coming toward Cray. He was a tall, skinny kid in his early twenties. He wore sunglasses and a hat that hid most of his face. He grabbed a water bottle from his hip and drank as he walked.

"Hey," the kid said as he approached Cray. "Could you tell me if this is Highway 224? I tried to take a shortcut and I'm not sure where I am. My friends were a few hours ahead of me and I'm trying to catch-up."

"Yep, this is 224 all right."

The hiker turned right and started down the road. "That other trailhead should be a little west. Thanks for the help, mister."

"No problem." Cray said, watching the hiker go. He went back around the SUV.

"Hey, mister. Do you have the time?" The hiker rounded the Escalade from behind and looked at Cray and Carson, and the elaborate pulley and winch system. "So what are you guys doing?" he asked, dumbfounded. "Are you part of like a search and rescue team?"

"Yeah," said Cray, taking the hiker's lead. "We're on a practice run. We have a buddy down in the gorge on a line."

"No kidding," the kid looked excited. "I've always wanted to do shit like this."

Carson shot a look at Cray. The hiker's back was to them and she mouthed the word "Quietly."

Cray's hand slid off the grip of his pistol that was concealed in his waistband under his shirt and reached for the knife on his belt. He pulled it from its sheath and silently unfolded it with one hand. In two swift steps, he was standing next to the hiker.

"That is so cool, man," the hiker said, looking down the cable over the edge of the cliff.

"Yeah," Cray said from behind.

Suddenly, he grabbed the kid and plunged the knife deep into his side, between the ribs and into his left lung. The hiker turned to face Cray, sudden fear and pain in his eyes. Blood frothed from his mouth as he tried to gasp for air while his lung collapsed.

"Be calm, kid," Cray said. "It's almost over."

The hiker winced and coughed a few more times before he went limp. Cray held him up and pulled out his knife. It was deep red to its handle. Cray wiped the blood on the kid's shirt before folding the blade and putting it away.

"Get rid of the body," Carson said distractedly, as if telling him to take out the trash. She went back to the laptop and lifted open the screen.

Cray gave the hiker a shove, the weight of his backpack taking the lifeless body backwards over the cliff. Cray watched as the body splashed in the river below, then he saw movement and noticed the cable jerking up and down—Russ's signal to be brought up. Cray ran to the winch and started it.

Thirty minutes later, Russ broke the surface of the water into the bright sunlight. The winch continued to lift him gently out of the water.

"What the hell happened up here?" he asked after being pulled out of the gorge. "I almost got hit by a body in the water."

"A hiker came out of nowhere and saw too much. Sorry. I should have pushed him off somewhere else. You okay?"

"Yeah, just peachy. Help me get out of this thing."

Cray helped Russ get out of his dry suit. Russ carefully pulled off his glove, which had filled with blood.

"Son of a bitch," he said when he saw several small pieces of glass lodged in his hand and blood flowing freely. Russ pulled out his dive knife and used it to extract the shards.

"Cray, get me the first aid kit. I gotta get this bleeding under control."

"Well? What did you find?" Carson asked, unable to wait any longer.

Russ sat in the well of the back door and pulled a bag from his equipment with his good hand, throwing it at Carson's feet.

"I found the truck—no body. The passenger side window was smashed. I searched inside the truck, the glove box, under the seats—everywhere—nothing. Then I did a sweep of the area around the truck and came up with this. It was sitting on the bottom near the passenger-side door."

Carson bent down, opened the bag, and pulled out the denim jacket. She examined it and searched the pockets. There was a receipt for a purchase at the train station in Portland and a wallet. Carson opened the wallet and looked through it. She found a license, a couple of credit cards, and counted out a thousand dollars in cash, mostly hundreds. There was also a piece of paper with flight information for a flight leaving Portland the night before. The final destination was Minneapolis.

"He must have lost the jacket trying to get out." She inspected the jacket more closely and found several tears in the material. "Think he's dead?"

"I don't know," Russ said. "That water is fuckin' freezing and that current is pretty strong. He might have made the surface but I don't know what's downstream."

"Then I guess we had better find out," Carson shot back, her temper starting to rise again.

# CHAPTER 6

Ted Kameron woke up Sunday morning later than usual. He hadn't slept well. He'd coughed incessantly the first half of the night and then had disturbing dreams until dawn. Once he'd finally settled into a deep sleep, he'd slept through his alarm.

He pulled on jeans, a wrinkled T-shirt, his boots, and a baseball hat. He grabbed a couple of bagels and a cup of coffee and headed for his truck. He loaded an ATV into the back of the truck and closed the tailgate. It was already nine o'clock.

Ted drove to the pasture where he'd left his cattle feeding the night before. He slowed his truck and pulled across the shoulder onto a narrow two-track lane, bits of gravel sliding under the tires as he braked.

He got out, went to the tailgate, and unloaded the ATV. Driving it into the field, he topped a rise and came to rest in a spot that gave him a broad vantage point of the meadow. He got off the ATV, unlocked a large black plastic box, and pulled out a pair of binoculars. Although the cattle were used to him and his four-wheeler, he wanted to observe them while they were undisturbed so he could determine if any of the rest of his herd was sick or injured from the events of the previous night.

He scanned the distant herd; all were present and accounted for, and appeared to be fine. Ted slung the binoculars around his neck, started the ATV, and drove across the field for a closer look.

The cattle barely looked up from their grazing as the four-wheeler approached. Ted slowed the machine and eased into the middle of the herd. He turned off the engine and sat back on the seat. Two cows eyed him warily. A calf born late the previous spring moved closer to the protection of its mother, who nosed him out of her way as she ate.

Ted listened to them eat. Things seemed normal until he heard the calf wheeze. It appeared to be eating and moving all right, but he made a mental note to check on it first thing Monday morning.

He moved out of the herd, headed back toward the fence line, and followed it north. He wanted to check out where the cow had died the night before. He sped across the neighboring fields, scattering a frenzy of grasshoppers in front of him. He jumped the ATV out of a ditch and onto a dirt road, then opened up the throttle and raced down the road. He slowed as he approached a cottage slowly being overtaken by the blackberry bushes that surrounded it. Ted pulled into the graveled driveway and turned off the engine.

The brown paint on the cottage was peeling—cracked and shriveled under the heat of many summers. The roof was shingled with old cedar and Ted remembered patching it several years before. From the driveway, the cottage seemed to stare out of its dust-covered windows, resigned to its fate.

He went up the flagstone walk and tried the doorknob. It was locked. He picked up a large rock, exposing a key that lay beneath it. A thin smile crossed his lips as he picked up the key and unlocked the door. A shower of dust fell from the door as it swung open.

Ted stepped through the door and paused to let his eyes adjust to the semi-darkness. As the details of the room emerged, he saw that a thin layer of dust covered the floor and the house possessed a stale, sweet smell that Ted couldn't place. He walked through the house, soaking up details as he went from room to room. He stopped in the kitchen and tried the water faucet.

Brownish water spit from the faucet for several seconds, gradually clearing up and coming out in a strong stream. Ted's mind flashed back to the previous summer, a happier time.

He had been with Rachel then. He'd met Rachel in Corvallis while attending a workshop at Oregon State University. Rachel was an artist finishing her graduate degree. They had literally run into each other and Rachel asked him to lunch to apologize. Then, they had met later that night for drinks. That had been it for Ted. He had fallen for her quick and hard.

They dated for six months, Ted making as many trips to Corvallis as his ranching allowed. In order to find solace away from campus, Rachel started looking for a place where she wouldn't be interrupted. Ted, wanting to see more of her, knew the cottage was empty and thought it might work. It had belonged to his grandparents, who had passed away years before; his parents were just glad the cottage would be kept up and used.

Rachel accepted the offer to live in the cottage, but insisted on renting it, refusing to take charity. She loved the benefits of country living and its proximity to the Clackamas and Molalla rivers, her new kayaking playgrounds. Within a week, Ted was helping Rachel move her kiln into the shed in the backyard and putting dishes away.

He spent all his time off at the cottage, hanging out and absorbing everything he could about Rachel. They often loaded up backpacks and went to the Mount Hood National Forest on weekend hiking trips. Rachel always carried a sketchpad and charcoal and sketched everything that caught her eye. Her elegant yet simple lifestyle impressed Ted, who longed to streamline his own life. The days turned into weeks and they grew closer. Then, four months ago, she had packed up and disappeared without a word.

Ted came out of his memory, still standing at the kitchen sink and staring out the dusty window. He scanned the backyard, finally focusing on the one-room shed. He went out to the shed as though hoping to find Rachel working inside. He pulled vines from the door, oblivious to the thorns that bit into his sun-dried skin. He opened the door wide and stepped inside. A blast of hot, humid air and the smell of damp, molding woodchips met his nostrils.

He scanned the shed's interior. An old woodstove sat in the back corner, a stack of wood piled neatly next to it, now a home for spider webs. The inside was clean. Rachel had always kept it swept out in order to reduce the amount of dust that could ruin her work.

Rachel had broken his heart when she left, and to this day, he didn't know what happened or what he had done.

"God, I miss her," he said to the emptiness of the shed.

# CHAPTER 7

The Escalade sped along Highway 224 toward Estacada. Cray sulked in the driver's seat while Carson stared out the window at the trees speeding by. Russ slept in the back seat, unable to fight the exhaustion from the dive. The bandages on his hand had turned a dull red as blood continued to leak from his wound.

Cray slowed as they entered Estacada and parked near a camping store. He and Carson left Russ to sleep in the back and went inside, where a thin man with long brown hair tied in a ponytail approached them. He had a weathered look, like someone who had spent a lot of time out in the Northwest elements, and a brown goatee beginning to gray. "What can I do for you?" he asked with a broad smile.

"You rent kayaks?" Cray asked. He could appreciate the skill of these outdoorsmen, but being ex-military, struggled to get past the resentment he had been trained to feel toward any "long-haired hippie types."

"Yeah, something for running whitewater or for just paddling the flat?"

"Whitewater," Cray replied, "and I'll need the whole setup – clothes, helmet, paddle—everything."

"Okay, but we don't rent the clothes. You'll have to buy those. How many days do you want the boat for?"

"Why don't we make it three days, so I'm not in a hurry to get it back?"

"Sure. I'll get the boat and equipment together. The clothes are in the back, dressing rooms to the right."

"What else did you say we need?" Carson asked Cray.

"We need radios, a GPS, and waterproof maps," he replied. Carson nodded and they split up, meeting twenty minutes later, each with arms full of supplies and equipment.

"Okay, sir," the clerk said. "I have a boat for you. Paddle, helmet, skirt, everything you'll need for some gnarly white. I'm gonna need you to fill out these rental forms." He handed Cray the forms and a pen. "Now let me get all this stuff rung up so you can hit it."

Carson drummed her fingers on the counter, her nails clicking impatiently.

"Okay," he said, "with the rental equipment and the rest of the gear, the grand total is $2,200."

Carson handed a credit card to Cray. "Get this stuff loaded up and I'll get us some food from the coffee shop down the street."

Five minutes later, they were both back at the Escalade, Carson with a bag of food in one hand and a cardboard holder of coffees in the other. Cray finished loading the equipment and securing the kayak to the roof of the Escalade, while Carson climbed back into the passenger seat. Finished, Cray climbed in, started the engine, and pulled back onto the road heading back the way they had come.

"Hey, pal, glad you could join us," Cray said smiling, seeing Russ stir. "We have some food if you're hungry, and some coffee that should still be hot."

Carson turned in her seat and handed Russ a paper bag and a cup of steaming coffee.

"Thanks."

"You all right?" Carson asked. Russ's face was pale.

"Yeah, just worn out from being down in that cold water for so long. I'm starting to feel better already." He brought the hot coffee to his blue-tinted lips. The bag contained a couple of breakfast burritos that he hungrily devoured. "Did you get all the equipment we need?"

"Yeah," Cray said, "and the clerk at the store almost shit himself when he realized how much money we were spending."

"Where are we putting in?" Russ asked.

"There's a Forest Service road two miles upstream from the gorge. Cray will put in there and we'll drive back to the rim of the gorge for better radio transmission," Carson said.

"What about the pull-out site?" Russ asked.

"There's another road that parallels the river for a short way. We can pick Cray up there. You'll need to drive so I can run the computer to keep track of him."

\* \* \*

They turned off the highway and skidded onto the graveled Forest Service road. Immediately, they were plunged into the cool darkness of the forest. Carson rolled down her window and closed her eyes, inhaling the fragrance of the woods. She knew that she could overreact, as anger seemed to be her default emotion. She had been angry for a long time now—years—and struggled more and more with keeping her emotions in check. She could blame her childhood and the number of foster homes she had moved through, but she knew that wasn't the cause. Her childhood—one parent in jail and one dead—had taught her that she couldn't rely on anyone but herself.

She had tried the American Dream by working her way through community college with the hope of getting a decent job. She had even enlisted in the National Guard for a time to help pay her way and learn some leadership skills. What she found in the end was a male-dominated world with few options for women.

After a night of partying and getting beaten up by a deadbeat boyfriend—a pattern that had repeated itself far too often—she decided to get tough, then she got angry. The next night, while her drunk boyfriend slept, she lit his double-wide trailer on fire and walked away. She changed her name, her appearance, and her future. That was how she found herself working for Ashe. He needed a hard person willing to do whatever was needed—no questions asked—and she wanted the money and power that went with it.

The sound of the river grew as they went deeper into the forest. Carson opened her eyes when Cray pulled off the road onto a needle-covered forest floor.

"The river's right over there," Cray said, pointing. "This is probably the best place to put in."

"Okay, let's get at it. Get your game faces on and get moving."

Cray and Russ got out of the Escalade while Carson remained in the vehicle, the sound of her computer booting up emanating from her open window.

Cray wasted no time. He opened the back and stripped down while Russ worked on getting the kayak down from the roof. Once dressed, Cray leaned against the back of the truck, opened the GPS and the radios, and inserted the batteries.

The GPS was able to acquire three satellites through the dense forest canopy and Cray called the coordinates off to Carson, who entered them into her computer. A tiny red dot appeared on her computer screen next to the blue line indicating the river. She grabbed the maps and marked their location.

Cray tested the radios. "The radios work."

"Good, but take your cell phone. I don't expect you to be able to get a signal, but we should be prepared. Also, keep the chatter down. These aren't secure channels. Let's not give a reason for someone to come snooping around," instructed Carson.

"Okay, will do. Russ, give me a hand getting this stuff down to the river?"

"No problem." Russ picked up the boat with his good hand and headed into the forest along a narrow footpath.

\* \* \*

When the two men arrived at the river's edge, they noted that the river was calm, flowing over gravel and around sandbars.

"Be careful. The current is strong down in the gorge. I suspect there are some pretty good rapids downstream."

"Thanks. Just make sure you're downstream to pull my ass out."

Cray slipped into the cockpit of the boat and fitted the skirt. He clipped on his helmet and then put the radio and GPS unit into a waterproof bag and stuffed it into a pocket on his life vest. He folded the map so that it allowed him to see where he was and slipped it into a mesh pocket.

Russ handed him the paddle and Cray pushed off the sandy bottom into deeper water. He quickly angled the boat into the current. The river grabbed the kayak and pulled it downstream.

The river was cold and Cray was grateful that he had rented a short-sleeved wetsuit to go over his bathing suit. He didn't need to paddle, only steer, as the current was strong and carried him quickly downstream. He looked at his watch. He'd been at it only a few minutes, but had already covered a lot of distance.

Seeing a sandbar up ahead, he angled his boat to position it downstream. A quick, strong paddle moved him into the swirling eddy on the opposite side of the bar that kept the kayak from being pulled downstream. He laid the paddle across the cockpit of the boat and pulled out his GPS and radio. It took the GPS a few minutes to acquire a signal, then a set of coordinates flashed onto the screen.

Cray picked up his radio and flicked it on. "Base, this is Paddler. Over." The radio crackled and Cray adjusted the squelch and volume. After no response, Cray repeated the call. "Base, this is Paddler. Over."

"Base here. We read you loud and clear," Russ said. "What's your position?"

Cray read the coordinates over the radio.

"Roger that. Stand by." The radio went quiet. A few seconds later Russ said, "Paddler, be advised that you are approximately a half a mile from the place you put in, and approximately two miles from the site."

"What's your current position, Base?"

"Paddler, we have an ETA of approximately five minutes to the site."

Cray clicked his radio. "Roger. I'm on the move." He turned off the radio before receiving a reply and looked at his waterproof map. He estimated his approximate location and stowed away his equipment. In one smooth stroke, Cray moved the kayak back into the main river channel.

Cray decided not to check in again until he was past the gorge. He wanted to have a little fun, but a mile downstream, the river had other ideas. There was no shore. Canyon walls rose out of both sides of the river and squeezed the river as it coursed through the narrow gap. Cray was instantly in whitewater. He had no choice but to paddle. A thin smile crossed his lips before he gritted his teeth and entered the maelstrom.

He maneuvered around boulders, over falls, through white waves. Twice he was knocked sideways by strong waves that capsized his boat. He used the momentum of the hit to roll the kayak and pop up on the other side, paddle in hand, pushing the boat forward. As quickly as it started, the water eased, then slowed.

Cray noticed that the south canyon wall was gone and that the river made a wide turn. The current was still strong, but the water was calmer. He looked to the other wall and knew where he was.

"Touchdown!" he yelled and looked up at a figure standing at the top of the high ravine. He held up his paddle and waved it, the figure waving back. The current pulled him past the corner and then Cray noticed that the south wall began to climb back out of the river. Again, the water turned violent and Cray fought to keep his boat right side up.

"That was a quick break," he said through clenched teeth as he fought the river. "If this guy did get out of the truck, he's gotta be fish food. There's no way someone could swim this in the dark."

There were more boulders in this section of river and Cray maneuvered his boat as well as he could. After ten minutes of combat, the river once again relented. The high-walled canyons fell away on both sides, replaced by dark forests of tall firs dripping with moss. The sound of the rapids faded into the background and Cray became aware of birds and the background hum of insects.

He rested the paddle across the cockpit of the boat and closed his eyes. He took several deep breaths to slow his heart rate and relax tensed muscles. The river, which only moments before had punished him, now seemed to cradle his boat and lull him into a tranquil serenity.

Cray spied a sandbar and decided it was a good place to check in. He picked up his paddle and with one hard stroke nosed the boat high up onto the sand, anchoring it. He tossed his paddle onto the beach and unhooked the skirt. He got out and pulled the kayak farther up onto the little beach. He grabbed a Power Bar from his pocket and tore off the wrapper. When he was finished eating it and had caught his breath, he pulled the GPS and radio from the waterproof bag and turned them both on. Seconds later a set of coordinates appeared on the screen.

"Base, this is Paddler. Come in. Over."

"This is Base. We read you. Over."

Cray read the coordinates over the radio.

"Okay, Paddler, we have your position. There is a Forest Service road approximately two hundred yards to your west. We can rendezvous with you there. Over."

Cray looked to the western shore, which was farther from his location than the other.

*The road must be on the other side of those dense bushes,* he thought. "Roger that, Base. I will meet—" Cray looked at his feet. There in the sand was the perfect outline of a boot that was not his. "Holy shit!" Cray said into the radio. He stared at the boot print, his eyes moving in the direction the toe pointed. There was another. He retraced his steps back to the water's edge and carefully surveyed the sandbar.

He saw dark reddish sand near the water's edge and the impression of compacted sand. The dark sand stood out, and Cray recognized it as blood. He saw one handprint, then another. Behind the handprints were two cup-shaped depressions as though someone had been on their hands and knees. Footprints crossed the sandbar to the river's edge and headed to the closer shore—the one to the east. He bent down and pressed his hand into the dark sand.

"It's dry, probably a day," he said to himself. "Son of a bitch. That asshole survived."

The radio crackled in Cray's hand. "Paddler. Come in."

Cray came out of his trance when Carson's angry voice came over the radio. "Paddler, where the hell are you?"

"Sorry for the delay, Base, but I just stumbled across a trail. I repeat, I just found a trail. It heads east," Cray said.

The radio was silent for a few seconds then crackled back to life. Russ had been restored to communication officer duties.

"Roger, Paddler. We understand your last transmission. We'll rendezvous with you at the service road in ten minutes, over."

"Roger, Base. Paddler out."

Cray retraced his steps, carefully stepping back into his own footprints to reduce the amount of disturbance on the sandbar. He eased his kayak back into the water and slid into the cockpit. He pulled the skirt back on and grabbed the paddle.

He crossed the river channel and pulled up on the far shore. He stored his boat in the bushes lining the river and began to make his way through the forest to the road. He arrived at the road just in time to see the black Escalade speed past. He went into the middle of the road and waved his arms to flag them down, and the SUV's brake lights flared red as it skidded to a stop.

* * *

Russ pulled the Escalade onto a turnout. Cray met them in the middle of the road.

"What's going on?" Carson asked, intrigued.

"The bastard survived. I don't know how he did it because I barely did, and I had a damn kayak and daylight."

"Slow down, Cray," Russ said, "and take it from the top. What exactly did you see?"

"Right," Cray said, taking a deep breath. "I paddled the river from where you let me out, and I have to tell you that the rapids downstream of the cliffs were a killer. I beached on a sandbar lying almost in the middle of the river and then I saw the tracks and the blood."

"We should go take a look at that sandbar." Carson said

"I'll show you were it is." Cray said pointing to the river side of the road.

They followed the trail to the water's edge. Cray pointed the sandbar out to Carson and Russ. They both looked at the water.

"It looks like it's about six feet deep," Russ said. "I could swim it since I still have my bathing suit on."

Carson stripped off her clothes down to a black sports bra and panties. She walked into the water and began swimming toward the sandbar.

"Or we could all go," Russ said.

* * *

The water was cold and stabbed at Carson. She fought to keep her breath and make the short swim. *Now I understand why my men look like they're about to die*, she thought. She heard splashes when Russ and Cray dove in and started swimming across.

They all reached the sandbar together, wading out of the river and onto the warm sand. Carson caught her breath, though goose-bumps covered her arms. With very little body fat, she succumbed to the water's low temperatures faster than the two men.

"You need to lie down on the sand over there," Russ said. "The sand is warm, and you could very easily end up with hypothermia if you don't warm up."

"I'm fine. Let's find out what the hell happened here," she said, shivering.

"He washed ashore here," Cray began, showing them the disturbed sand. "There hasn't been any rain or increased snow-melt, so the water level should have been fairly constant over the past few days. See how there's no sign that he physically crawled or pulled himself out of the water? I think Mercer somehow washed up here."

"Looks like he was lying here for quite some time." Russ pointed at the sand. "See how there's a shallow impression, then a gap, then another depression a little deeper?"

"Yes," Carson said, bending down to examine the sand.

"The shallower of the two depressions was his back, the other his ass," Russ said. "And look, here are four more, probably his hands and knees. You can still make out the slight shape of fingers. And it looks like he cut his right knee, given the amount of blood in this depression."

"Or he was bleeding from more than his knee," Cray said, pointing to an area of dark sand that Russ had missed.

Russ bent down and examined the sand, then got back to his feet and took in the scene again. "He must have gashed his head, too."

Carson scanned the sandbar for other signs. "Look," she said pointing at the footprints leading into the water and toward the opposite riverbank. "He went the other way. The river is narrower on that side. We'll have to check the maps and see where he's heading."

"Exactly," said Cray.

"So we track him," said Carson, looking at Russ.

"I'm pretty good at tracking, but Cray here was in the Army's infantry. He's much better at this than I am," said Russ.

"Right," Carson said, half in thought. "Let's study the maps. We can start early tomorrow; I think you both have had enough for one day."

Back at the Escalade, Carson removed the laptop from under the seat and turned it back on. When the computer screen flicked to life, she punched a couple of the keys and plugged the GPS unit Cray had used into the USB port. She clicked on the mapping program and a map of the forest flashed onto the screen.

"Okay," she said, turning the screen so both men could see. "The red bulls-eye is our current location. Here's the cliff where the truck went over." She pointed to the narrowly spaced contour lines along the river. "This is the direction Mercer went."

"Can you zoom out so we can see the bigger area?" Cray asked.

Carson pressed a key on the keyboard. The map suddenly disappeared, replaced by one of a larger scale. All three examined the new map.

Cray was the first to speak. "Damn, that guy walked out into the middle of fuckin' nowhere."

Carson stared at the screen. It wasn't supposed to go down like this. All they had to do was pick him up. Worst-case scenario, they kill him. But it was worse than that, much worse. The fucking guy had not only survived, he escaped.

* * *

The ride back to the warehouse was somber. By the time they made it to Wilsonville, dusk had set in.

Carson went to her desk and flipped on her computer. She pulled up the surveillance tapes and watched the video footage in fast-forward, looking for trespassers. While the video played, she moved her cursor to the phone icon and a table of phone calls came up, dating back a few days. She minimized the screen, looked for new messages, and found several. She clicked on "Green Grass Enterprises" and listened to the recorded message.

"Ms. Carson, this is José from the farm. I don't know where boss is and field inspector called about burning so we go ahead and burn yesterday. I think we supposed to do it Monday. Thing is ..." there was a pause, then, "it burn really hot and fast. It no get out of control, but it smell weird. Can you call back and tell me what to do? *Gracias.*"

"Idiot," Carson said. There was a reason why he wasn't supposed to burn until Monday. She clicked on the next message, also from the night before marked, "Willamette Valley Breeders."

"Ms. Carson, this is Andy from Willamette Valley Breeders. I think we have a problem. I got a call from Ted Kameron about a downed cow. It seems to have succumbed to smoke inhalation after Green Grass burned its fields. I ran blood samples, and the cow had high levels of benzene. I thought you should know. Anyway, I'm going to need to reimburse Ted. Please give me a call back with the authorizations and settlement amounts. Thanks."

"Great." Carson said, as she absently watched a couple of kids skateboarding in the warehouse parking lot. She clicked the next message titled, "ODA."

"Ms. Carson, this is Crocker, the field inspector from the Oregon Department of Agriculture. I haven't yet received your second permit application for continued burning. The first burning window is closing and if you want to continue to burn, I will require the same paperwork as last time. Please call me ASAP. I would hate to bring an enforcement action against you. Thank you and have a wonderful day."

"Asshole," Carson said, fuming. Ed Crocker was an over-weight good ol' boy who, although raised in a farming family, could never handle the level of physical work it took to run a farm. He spent his life looking for shortcuts, no matter who he hurt in the process. He had finally landed a state job, one where he could abuse his powers and make a handsome profit on the side. He was a coward at heart, but it took a while to get past his blowing and blustering façade. Carson knew the type and had worked with Crocker for several years now.

*The bastard wants more money. Just try an enforcement action and the field won't be the only thing burning.* She looked at the last message, the one she didn't want to hear. She moved the cursor to the message marked "Ashe."

"Carson, I've been waiting. I don't appreciate your lack of communication. I'll expect a call from you tomorrow morning at nine. Do not disappoint me again."

Carson stared blankly at the computer screen. The video-surveillance had ended and the picture remained frozen on the empty parking lot. Thoughts ran through her mind as she buried her face in her hands. She was tired, but she wasn't going to be sleeping. She got up, went into her bathroom, and splashed cold water on her face.

Russ and Cray were drinking a couple of beers when Carson entered the anteroom.

"Can I get you a drink?" Cray offered.

"Yeah. Maker's. Neat. Thanks."

She took the drink from him, tossed back her head, and drained the brown liquid. Cray refilled her glass.

"Trouble?"

"That's an understatement." She put the glass on the table. "Okay, we need a plan. Any thoughts?"

Cray looked at Russ.

"I think we need a net to catch this guy. Cray can track him. We send him out to run down Mercer. We look at the maps and figure out where he'll turn up. Then while Cray is tracking him, I'll work that area. Either Cray will catch him in the forest, or I'll get him when he comes out the other side."

Carson looked at Cray, who said, "I think that's probably our best bet. Russ and me, we've been talking it over while you were in your office."

"Good. While you two are hunting Mercer, I'll sort out all the other problems that have erupted in the last twenty-four hours and brief Ashe. Let's get the maps and see where Mercer is headed." She stood and went into her office, her two men following. Everyone settled in at the conference table, and Carson spread out the maps. Russ found the spot where they had been earlier in the day.

"This is where the sandbar is." He pointed to a spot on the map. "Based on the tracks in the sand, we know he headed off in this direction." He looked at Cray. "What do you think?"

Cray studied the map. "Like I said, this guy walked into the middle of nowhere. We saw a lot of blood in the sand, and I figured some of it was from his head."

"I agree," Russ said.

"His tracks headed in the opposite direction of the road," Cray said. "If my hunch is right I think he was disoriented and confused. Everyone knows you never leave a river, but follow it downstream. Eventually you will find something—a road, a house, something. No, this guy wanders out into the forest. If his right leg has been injured then he might be slightly angling in that direction when he moved off." Cray traced his finger over the map. "That could have him over this way."

"If that's the case," Russ said, "then the next road this guy is going to stumble across is way out here, somewhere in the Warm Springs Indian Reservation. However, he could always double back and end up somewhere on the Clackamas River or farther south toward the Mount Jefferson Wilderness."

"We should cover all potential scenarios," Carson said. "Good job, gentlemen. Cray, will you be ready in the morning?"

"All my gear is stored downstairs. One quick stop at the store for rations and I'll be set."

"Good. Russ, I want you to get ahold of your contacts in those areas. Tell them that we're paying for information."

"But don't tell them where we think he is," Cray warned. "I don't need an army of yahoos running around the forest and screwing up the trail."

"Good point," Carson said. "Russ, just tell them we want any information on transients that turn up, okay?"

"Not a problem. I'll unload the SUV while Cray packs. Ready, Cray?"

"Yeah, let's get started. I'd like to catch a few winks before tomorrow. I don't think I'll be sleeping much in the next couple of days."

The men got up from the conference table and left the office.

Carson sat back and took a sip of her bourbon. She stared at the maps, wondering how this mess happened. Things had been running so smoothly. She didn't look forward to her conversation with Ashe, but at least now she had a plan.

# CHAPTER 8

Mercer woke mid-morning Sunday, struggled to his feet, and went to the stream for a drink. He cautiously approached the area where the previous night's massacre had taken place. The lions were gone but they'd left a bloody trail through the matted grass where they had dragged off the carcass.

Mercer hobbled down to the water's edge and took a long drink of the ice-cold water. He saw several fish moving around the pools and riffles, picking off insects from the surface of the water. *Protein*, Mercer thought. *That is a definite need. I could sure go for breakfast.*

He reached for his revolver and carefully aimed it at a fish swimming in the shallows of the stream. As the fish darted into a shadow, he thought better of his rash plan. Seeing some willows growing along the far bank a few hundred feet away, he set off with a new idea in mind.

The saw blade on his Swiss Army knife quickly ate through the bark and the wood of the willow saplings. He cut several three-foot switches, then closed the saw blade, opened the larger blade, and whittled the end of two of the branches into sharp points.

He slid off his belt and examined it. It was braided leather; cutting the belt at both ends freed the strips, which he quickly unbraided. He examined the eight strips and the two sharpened willow sticks. He cut two of the leather strips in half and tied the two willow sticks to his walking stick, securely attaching them in several places.

A few short minutes later, Mercer was peering into the clear water, searching for a fish. Just then, a trout fled its hiding place behind a large cobble. He watched it go and let out a slow breath. The trout hadn't gone far. Mercer slowly approached, oblivious to the world around him, focused only on the four feet of water that separated him from the fish. Three feet. Excitement and anticipation coursed through his veins. He slowly positioned his spear over the hovering fish and with one quick motion, brought the weapon down. The water splashed around him but he couldn't see through the swirling silt. When the water settled, he looked down at his empty spear.

Discouraged, he scanned the water until he spotted another fish. Again, he moved the spear to the spot where the fish lay among the cobble. Another swift movement and he brought the spear down. This time he felt it hit something other than rock. The water cleared and he saw the trout trying to escape the hold of the spear. He leaned into the spear, driving it further into the struggling fish.

Elated, he bent down and grabbed the fish with one hand. He held his new fish spear up to the sun and let out a triumphant yell. He quickly carried the fish to shore and tossed it on the grass. The fish flopped and wriggled for several minutes then, as if deciding the end was near, stopped its struggle. Suddenly, Mercer realized he had no way to cook the fish and he was not yet to the point of hunger where he would eat its flesh raw.

Inspired, he took another leather strip, looped it in through the fish's mouth, and out one of its gills, then tied a slipknot. He brought the fish to the stream and placed it in the cold water. It floated on its side for several minutes, then recovered and tried to swim away. Mercer held tight to the leather strip and after a few seconds, the fish stopped fighting and settled into the cobble, facing upstream and moving its tail with the current. With its wound, Mercer didn't expect it to last long.

He drove his fishing spear into the soft mud along the shore, and then attached the other end of the cord to the spear. Satisfied that the spear would hold, he hobbled out of the stream to collect wood, wondering how he was going to get a fire started.

*I might just have to have sushi after all.*

He pulled out the Swiss Army knife from his pocket and absently unfolded each blade, looking for anything that might help start a fire. Finding nothing, he concentrated on trying to remember anything. His memory was like a maze, some passages led to information, but the others led nowhere. The information he was able to access was more knowledge and less memory. He could read, he could identify trees and animals. He just couldn't remember anything about who he was, where he lived, or why he had woken up on the sandbar.

He was running the leather strips from his belt back and forth through his hands when inspiration decided to show up. Quickly, he stripped another long piece of leather from the belt, and grabbing the knife, got up and headed for the forest. It didn't take him long to find what he needed: two sticks and a flat piece of Ponderosa pine bark. Taking the pieces of wood back to the place he had picked for the fire, he knelt down and started the process of lighting it.

He wasn't sure if he had learned survival training in a past life, but something was helping him stay alive. He used one stick and tied the leather strip to each end making a crude bow, then wrapped the center of the leather strip around the second stick. He positioned the center stick on the Ponderosa pine bark, and putting weight on it, began using the bow like a saw, drilling the center stick into the bark. He worked at it for half an hour before he saw the smoke of a tiny red coal. He grabbed some tinder of dried leaves and pine needles and positioned the small coal in the center of it. He got down low and gently blew on the coal, making it glow red with the added oxygen, giving it life. The pile of tinder began smoking. He patiently blew on it until a small flame leapt from the leaves. He raised his hands in the air in triumph, then quickly grabbed some small sticks to feed the flame. He kept nursing the flames until he heard the reassuring crackle of burning wood.

He built up the fire so it wouldn't go out while he retrieved his meal. He cleaned his fish and then cooked it for ten minutes before hunger finally won out. He blew on it, then sank his teeth into the fleshy part of the fish and ate voraciously. He was still hungry after he had eaten the entire thing. He needed to catch more fish, but instead found himself yawning. He lay back on the ground and closed his eyes, the warms of the sun and full stomach bringing sleep like a breeze across the meadow.

The day passed slowly as the sun made its long summer trip across the sky. The temperature climbed and the creatures of the forest sought the solace of shade. Mercer woke hot and sweaty. He had fallen asleep in the sun and now suffered for his carelessness. He rolled over, got to his hands and knees, and crawled to the water's edge. The coolness of the water provided instant relief and he collapsed into the shallow water. He drank to quench his thirst. Except for the new sunburn, the pain from his other injuries had eased.

He soaked in the cool stream for an hour, and climbed out onto the shore as the sun began to descend behind the western mountains. He stood and stretched his sore body.

*Tonight will be rough*, he thought, looking at his sunburned arms. *And I need to build some kind of shelter so I'm not sleeping out in the open.*

He looked for and found the giant Ponderosa pine he had slept under the previous night. He set off to gather the material he needed to build a lean-to. He found eight six-foot branches that would provide the necessary frame. He used his knife and stripped off all the smaller branches and knobs on one side of each branch. He left the other side as it was in order to hold the cross branches. He leaned each one against the tree, then gathered pine boughs that still had needles and used them to fill in the walls of the shelter. When he finished, he stepped back to look at his creation.

"That has to be the saddest shelter ever made," he said, laughing. "I'll be lucky if the damned thing doesn't collapse on me in the middle of the night."

He crawled through a small opening and looked around the interior. It wasn't as bad as he thought. The interior was dark and cool and there was enough room for him to lie down as well as sit up. He crawled back out and collected leaves, grass, and moss. After several trips in and out, he had created a nest. The shelter complete, his mind drifted back to his stomach.

The sun had drifted below the mountains, though there was still plenty of light as day transitioned to twilight. He went back to his smoldering fire and built it up with the wood he had collected. Flames quickly spread to the new wood and the fire began to crackle and pop again.

He picked up his fishing spear and went back to the river. He walked up and down the bank, searching. Finally, he saw a silvery flash moving in the current. He waded into the stream, trying not to give away his position by approaching from downstream. He raised the spear, this time compensating for the bending effect of the water and plunged it down. He speared the fish on his first try.

The second fish was bigger than the first and more difficult to get to shore. He cleaned the fish and decided to wait for a good bed of coals. In the meantime, he walked along the bank and picked large orange berries to eat with his dinner. As dusk set in, he sat next to the fire and popped berries into his mouth while his fish sizzled over hot coals. He lay back in the grass, looking up into the darkening blue, as stars began to appear from seemingly nowhere. The moon was rising but no longer full.

Mercer was looking to the east when suddenly, a light appeared on the distant ridgeline. It wasn't moving, but remained fixed. Mercer, excitement growing, squinted to try to make out any detail. The growing darkness hid any hint of what it might be, but it was definitely a light and it hadn't been there minutes before, which meant someone had turned it on. Adrenaline coursed through his veins. Tonight he would sleep; tomorrow he would head for the light.

# CHAPTER 9

Finally calling it a day, Ted sat in his father's old rocking chair on his front porch watching the sun set behind the coastal range, a bottle of Deschutes' Mirror Pond Pale Ale in his hand. He was reliving his day and his trip to the cottage. He replayed in his mind the last conversation he had with Rachel.

"I'm going back to New England," she had told him abruptly one night.

The next day, she was gone. He never even had a chance to discuss it with her. He tried to call her, but her cellphone was disconnected. They'd been talking about marriage and having a family, maybe opening a gallery in Molalla or somewhere nearby so that she could start selling her pieces. He thought they were happy.

Where had she gone? And how hard had he really looked for her other than calling an old number? He had been hurt, which had turned to anger. He knew now how badly he still needed answers.

Ted stood and wandered into the house. He grabbed a box of cold pizza and headed for his office. Sitting behind his desk, he flipped on his computer. He opened a second beer while he waited for the computer to boot up. Once on, he accessed a search engine with a "people search" application and typed in Rachel's name and the town he thought she had grown up in. The search didn't find anything.

*What am I doing? She wouldn't be listed. She went home. I need to find her parents,* Ted thought. He tried hard to remember

Rachel's conversations about her parents. Her father had died years earlier and her mother lived alone. Rachel always felt a little guilty for living so far away.

"Beverly," he said aloud. "I think it's Beverly Mason."

Again he typed, but this time he inserted her mother's name and included the entire state of Massachusetts. Ted took a bite of pizza while he waited. The page loaded with a list of twenty names. Only four were actually "Beverly," but there were quite a few entries under "B Mason."

He focused on the four Beverly names, their phone numbers and addresses. He looked at the names of the towns to see if he recognized any of them: Norfolk, Sunderland, Braintree, and Falmouth. None of them sounded familiar. It was close to midnight on the East Coast so he wasn't about to start calling.

Ted sat back in his chair and swallowed the last of his beer, then looking at his watch, climbed the stairs to his bedroom. He would start calling in the morning.

# CHAPTER 10

All three spent the night at the warehouse. Cray and Russ slept soundly on the sofas in the anteroom. Carson didn't sleep. She spent the night combing through her files on Mercer. An alarm clock rang in the anteroom, and Carson heard movement as the two men woke. Carson took the paper she had been examining at her desk and opened her office door.

"Okay, gentlemen, I've been looking over Mercer's file because I thought there was something about him, a reason why Ashe hired him over the other candidates. Now I remember." She pointed at the sheet of paper. The two men walked over and stared at it. "The guy is an ex-Army Ranger; he served in Afghanistan," she said.

"Lovely," Russ said. "That would have been nice to know when we were tailing him. What was he doing being a farm manager?"

"I don't know," replied Carson. "All I know is that he is out there and dangerous. He knows enough about our operation to bury us."

"It will be harder to catch him," Cray said. "When I was in the infantry, I knew some Rangers. They know all of the survival skills that I was taught and then some. If this guy was any good and he's not too hurt, he might disappear like a ghost."

"I guess you'd better find him before that happens," snapped Carson.

"We're on our way," Russ said. "Come on, Cray, let's go."

The two men headed for the door.

"Cray, keep in contact with Russ. Russ, check in with me every four hours, beginning at 0800."

"Will do."

Carson took the sheet of paper back to her office and sat at her desk. She looked at it for a long time, then put it back in its folder. She had a few phone calls to make, one she wasn't looking forward to. She looked at her watch. It was only five in the morning. There were still a couple of hours to kill before she could make her calls. She tilted her chair back and closed her eyes.

* * *

Cray and Russ climbed into Russ's black Chevy pickup, a large diesel that rumbled to life when Russ turned the key. Cray studied a map. "Let's get back to that Forest Service road before the trail disappears."

Russ put the truck into gear and drove out of the warehouse. Cray studied the laminated maps of the area, tracing his finger along the contour lines and tapping his temple with a grease pencil. Fifty minutes later, they were back in the forest. The landscape was still dark with the remnants of night, though Cray could distinguish objects he recognized from the day before.

Russ flipped the CB radio to the National Weather Station. A mechanical voice said, "... the Cascade Mountains will see temperature reaching a high today of 85 degrees, experiencing 15 percent humidity and winds from the southwest. Fire danger continues to be high."

"Sounds like a good day for a hike," he said, stopping where they had parked the day before. "We're here. Get your game face on."

Cray got out, lowered the tailgate, and pulled off his boots, socks, and shirt. He stuffed them into his pack, then put the pack inside a trash bag to protect it from the river. Wearing only a pair of shorts, Cray hoisted the bag over his shoulder. He and Russ crossed the gravel road and entered the trail they had used the day before. A few minutes later, they were standing on the bank of the river, surveying the water.

"I don't envy your swim this morning."

"You sure you don't want to do this part?"

"Not on your life. You have fun doin' all your commando bullshit. I'll be sitting in the truck sipping a nice cup of coffee."

"I guess there's no time like the present."

Without another word, Cray waded into the river. He winced once from the cold but refused to admit any further discomfort. The frigid water stabbed at his lungs as he swam across, driving the oxygen from them. The water grew shallow and Cray waded out of the river onto the far bank. He gave Russ a thumbs-up. Russ waved back and disappeared into the forest.

Cray removed his pack from the trash bag, dried off as best he could, and redressed in his dry clothes. He pulled a survival knife from his pack and attached it to his waist. He took out his Glock 17 and positioned it in his back holster. He then pulled out a GPS and radio and turned them both on. He put the GPS into one of his pockets and clipped the radio to the straps of the backpack. With one fluid motion, he swung the pack up onto his back and headed downstream along the bank.

A few yards later, Cray found a boot print hardened in the mud. Then a second. They were Mercer's tracks from two days earlier, and they led into the forest—away from the river. Cray took in every detail: the broken twigs, the compacted moss, dried drops of blood here and there. Not enough blood to slow a man down but enough to make any journey painful. He also confirmed that Mercer had hurt his knee, as one track was more defined than the other, suggesting he was putting more weight on one leg.

Cray checked his watch. 0730 hours. Russ was scheduled to make his first check-in with Carson at 0800. He picked up his pace.

Cray had always been good at tracking. He was able to visualize the tracks in a way that made them seem to emerge from the forest floor. In his experience, people would usually head straight in one direction as if toward a goal. But the twists and turns in Mercer's tracks made it obvious that he was suffering from his injuries and just wandering. *Maybe he's got a concussion, even a fever.* He noticed several places within the first mile where Mercer had slept. That was a good sign. He hoped to find Mercer dead a mile or two up the trail.

He scanned the maps and GPS to see where he was headed, and as he did, his radio crackled to life. "Alpha, this is Bravo. Alpha this is Bravo. Are you receiving?" Russ's voice came over the radio.

"Bravo, this is Alpha. I'm receiving you loud and clear."

"Are you on the trail?"

"Affirmative, Bravo, and the prey seems injured."

"What is your general location?"

Earlier they had decided that Cray would give Russ the closest landmark east of his position and a number so that if someone were listening they wouldn't know where he was.

"Park Butte, 2 miles."

"That's an affirmative. I'll come around. Check in again at 1200 hours."

"Roger that. Alpha out."

Cray then switched the radio off to save power and pocketed the GPS. He packed up and moved down the trail in a slow jog. *Maybe I can catch this guy by lunch*, he thought.

\* \* \*

Carson bolted upright in her chair, her eyes darting to the clock on her desk. 7:30 am. She had only meant to close her eyes for a few minutes. She relaxed into her chair when she realized she hadn't slept through her call to Ashe. She hoped she would hear something from Russ, but first, she had to call the veterinarian and find out what was going on.

She went to a metal file cabinet marked Willamette Valley Breeders. Carson looked at the piece of paper where she had notes from the vet's call. It said "Kameron." She flicked through the files until she found Kameron, and pulled out the cattle insurance folder.

Carson quickly scanned the pages. They had made several other reimbursements in the last few years. Not enough to cause suspicion, but getting there. Still reading the file, she called Willamette Valley Breeders using the handsfree speakerphone on her computer.

"Hi, Andy. How are you doing this morning?"

"I'm doing just fine, Ms. Carson. I guess you're calling about the message I left."

"Tell me what happened."

Andy recounted the events from a few nights earlier.

"Damn," Carson said as he finished. "Let's treat this guy well. Give him an equal or better replacement if you can and the maximum amount of money, given the cow's age and breeding potential."

"The other problem I see is that this cow had elevated levels of benzene in her blood. I'm afraid there might be some water contamination spreading to Kameron's farm."

"I'll look into it, Andy. Thanks."

"Great."

"Thanks for being on top of this. Remember, don't disclose actual cause of death other than asphyxiation. And keep Mr. Kameron happy, okay?"

"Will do, Ms. Carson. Thanks again. Goodbye."

Carson clicked off the call. It was now 8 am. She flipped through the Kameron file on her desk again. Unfortunately, the property abutted Green Grass Enterprises on the downwind side in several places.

The ringing from her computer brought her back to the present. "Carson."

"This is Russ."

"How's the search going?"

"Cray is on the trail and moving fast in a southeasterly direction. It appears that Mercer is hurt, but he's got a two-day head start."

"Where are you now?"

"I'm headed out to Highway 22. I'm gonna drive east toward Bend and angle back in to where I think Mercer might be heading. I've made a couple of calls to some informants. They're on the lookout. I hope to hear something soon. I have a chopper standing by in case Cray has problems finding him."

"Good. I'll talk to you again at noon."

Carson checked her watch. Half past eight. She had half an hour to figure out what she was going to say to Ashe.

She ran through her report in her head several times. She contemplated how much of yesterday's events she would tell him. She wouldn't bother to tell him about killing the young hiker. That was the kind of thing she was just supposed to take care of—Mr. Ashe didn't want to know the dirty details.

It was five minutes to nine when she dialed his direct line using her computer. He answered after several rings. "Carson, I hope you're going to make me happy. Right now, I'm not happy."

Ashe's words caused her rehearsed report to slip from her memory like sand through her fingers. One moment she was full of confidence, the next she was backpedaling—all before she even said a word. That was Ashe's talent in manipulating people. With a single word or sentence, he was able to make them feel worthless, like they would never measure up to his expectations—and they never did.

"Mr. Ashe, I want to apologize for not responding to your calls earlier. We were still in the mountains and the cellular coverage was horrible."

"Ms. Carson," Ashe said with a sigh of impatience, "I do not care for excuses or the pathetic state of cellular communications. What I do care about is knowing that our problem has been taken care of. Can you at least tell me that?"

There was silence as Carson regrouped. She decided the best thing was to be direct.

"No, sir, I can't. We haven't recovered Mercer's body."

"Explain."

"As you know, we ran him off the road Friday night. His truck plummeted off a cliff and into a deep section of the river—"

"I already know this."

"Right. We attempted a salvage mission early Sunday morning. The truck was right where it had gone in the river, but Mercer and the documents were gone. We searched downstream and found where he washed up, but there was no body. Somehow, it seems Mercer survived and wandered off into the forest. We think he's badly hurt, given the amount of blood and erratic tracks."

"Unbelievable," Ashe said. "What are you doing now?"

"Cray is currently tracking Mercer through the mountains on foot. Russ has set up a safety net with his contacts to prevent Mercer from eluding us if he comes out the other side."

There was a long pause after Carson finished. She waited for Ashe to re-engage.

"Okay," he said finally. "Keep on Mercer. I don't think I need to tell you what he could do to us. Is there anything else I need to know?"

She hesitated. "Well, sir, there has been another complication. José, the assistant farmhand at Green Grass, burned the fields a day early."

"Son of a bitch! Why the hell did he do that?"

"It seems that the state field inspector was pressuring him, and José thought they could burn anytime. He was clueless. No one lower than the farm managers know what's going on. Anyway, he burned the fields but didn't make the courtesy call to the adjacent landowners, and a rancher lost a cow," Carson said. "I spoke to the vet this morning, and authorized him to take care of the problem. I pulled one of our other farm managers from down south to come and handle things. We still have a few weeks of burning left. I'll also have a chat with the field inspector. If he gives me too much trouble, I'll have Cray pay him a visit."

Carson hoped Ashe didn't realize that she was making some of this up on the fly.

"Good," Ashe said. "Check in at the same time on Wednesday, unless something develops."

A click through the computer speakers and the conversation was over. Carson slid down in her chair, exhaling long and slow. It could have been worse.

She stretched to get rid of the tension and then called Green Grass. The phone rang for a long time, then a man answered with a thick Hispanic accent.

"*Hola. Como esta? Perdón*, Green Grass Enterprises. How I help you?"

"Hello, José. This is Ms. Carson from headquarters. How are you doing today?"

"Oh, Ms. Carson!" José said, "I happy to hear your voice. I call you the other day but you were no home."

"It's okay, José, I got your message. I just wanted to call you and talk to you. How are you doing?"

"Not good, Ms. Carson. I burn like Mr. Crocker say but it *no bueno*. The fire, it was hot and we almost lose it."

"Why did you burn early, José? The farm wasn't scheduled to burn until today. Why did you burn without Mr. Mercer?"

"Mr. Mercer was *no aqui*. Mr. Crocker, he tell me if we no burn, we miss monitoring period and it affect data so we no can burn over next few weeks. He also say he call immigration if I not do as told."

"Mr. Crocker said that? I don't want you to worry about anything, José. I talked with Mr. Mercer and he had to leave unexpectedly due to a family emergency. He's okay, but he won't be back for a while," she lied. "I'll be sending another farm manger to take his place. I hope to have him there soon. I'll talk to Mr. Crocker today. He won't bother you again. If he even talks to you, you call me right away, okay?"

"*Sí*, Ms. Carson, *gracias*. I no want to be in charge. I like my job. I need my job."

"I know, José, and you do a fine job. Like I said, I'll have a replacement manager there in the next day or two. You take care. Also, remember that we are now planning to burn again on Wednesday, and not before."

"*Sí*, Ms. Carson. I understand. *Adios*."

Carson dialed Crocker on his cell phone, so their conversations could not be easily recorded on his end. She knew there was technology on the market to record it, but Crocker wasn't that smart.

Crocker's phone rang. "Oregon Department of Agriculture. Ed Crocker here."

"Crocker, this is Carson from Green Grass Enterprises. I think you remember the last time we met." The last time they had met, Carson had ordered Cray to break one of Crocker's fingers for trying to extort more than his usual kickback. Carson could almost see him nervously running a hand through his oily, slicked-back hair, coming to a stop on the bald spot on top of his head. "I'm not happy."

There was silence on the other end, broken only by the soft wheezing of someone who smoked too many cigarettes and ate too many doughnuts.

"Ms. Carson, I'm not sure I know what you're talking about," Crocker finally said.

"That's funny," Carson said, adding a menacing note to her voice, "I think you know exactly what I'm talking about. So why don't we cut through the crap, Crocker? If you're unhappy with our current arrangement, then we need to talk. Now, what's all this shit about applications and extensions?"

"The late-summer burning season ends in a couple of weeks, and I don't know how many more times you want to burn this year."

"We let you know when we are going to burn and I'm well aware of the burning schedule. I appreciate your concern for the welfare of our business, but I don't appreciate it when you try to shake down one of my employees by threatening him. Your arrogance is costing me money and I am not happy. I think I really need to emphasize this point to you: When I'm not happy about it, you are not happy. Do you understand me, Crocker?"

"Yes, Ms. Carson, I understand what you're saying."

"Good. I don't expect to hear any more about this until the burning season ends. Do you have any more questions for me?"

"No. I understand everything clearly. I'm real sorry, I don't know what I was thinking. Please don't hold it against me."

"Relax, but not too much. We'll be burning again soon. I'll let you know when. Goodbye."

Carson disconnected the call, then stood up and stretched her tight shoulder muscles. She went to the far wall and studied a map of the Pacific Northwest. There was a variety of colored pins fixed to different places on the map. Some were red, some black, some green. She traced a finger down the map to a green tack near the town of Molalla, where Green Grass Enterprises was located. Then, scanning the map again, she looked for other green tacks and found them in Yakima, Ellensburg, and Wenatchee, Washington. There were also pins in Vale, Burns, Redmond,

Sweet Home, and Klamath Falls, Oregon. Her finger came to rest on Klamath Falls. Looking back at the maps, she saw many more black tacks.

*I should get a jump on coordinating the winter work. What a nightmare that's going to be,* she thought. She went back to her desk and sat down. She moved her mouse across the pad and after a few clicks, she opened a map of the Pacific Northwest, similar to the one on the wall but this map was linked to a database. Like the map on the wall, there were red, green, and black dots on the computer map.

She clicked on the green dot near Klamath Falls, and the computer dialed the number for "Klamath Falls Ag Enterprises."

"O'Neil," a man said.

"Hi, O'Neil. This is Carson. Have you had a nice vacation?"

"Vacation, my ass. I hoped you'd forgotten about me since we weren't burning this summer. What's going on, Carson?"

"I need you to get up to Molalla. It's time you earn all that money I've been giving you."

"You never give me anything," he said gruffly.

"I had a manger jump ship and I still need some burning done. I also have a field inspector who likes to intimidate the farmhands. I thought you'd be a good replacement."

"Okay, I can be up there tomorrow night. Where am I headed?"

"Green Grass Enterprises. The assistant farm manager's name is José Garcia. He's a good worker, but like all the assistant managers, he doesn't know what really goes on there. I'll let him know to expect you. Thanks, O'Neil. I appreciate it."

"Did you just thank me? You must be in quite a pinch."

# CHAPTER 11

Mercer lay on his grass and pine-needle bed and listened to the world as it came awake. He thought about his situation and the light on the eastern ridge. His leg was healing, the pain nearly gone. His fever had broken and his head had been clear for at least a day.

Mercer rolled out of his shelter and stretched his muscles. He stared at the dawn sky and the mountain ridge that lay to the east. He squinted trying to see the source of the light that was now dark. He wondered if the top of the lower ridge would reveal its source and the way back to civilization. He'd leave this morning to avoid the heat of the day and climb the lower ridge. If there was nothing there, he could always come back to the little river valley to regroup.

He shoved his hands into the pockets of his jeans to warm them from the brisk morning air. The fingers gripped the piece of paper. He pulled it out and looked at it again. CALL ME ASAP— SARAH (503) 555-7789. *She can sort this out, tell me who I am. I just gotta find a phone.* He shoved the piece of paper back into his pocket and started for the river, wondering about Sarah, trying to picture her in his foggy mind.

The grassy meadow was wet with dew, but there were still some hot coals in the fire pit. He added some dry grass and leaves from his bed. Along with the hot coals, a flame soon leapt from the dew-dampened wood he had collected the day before. The fire smoked for a while before it took hold and soon a warm blaze spit a shower of sparks into the morning air.

Warmer now, Mercer wandered down to the water's edge with his fishing spear. His legs were stiff, though a vast improvement from the previous day. He set about fishing and after an hour, had landed two fish. He cleaned them, then hung the larger one over the fire. The trout would cook a little more slowly and he could pack it with him on his hike. He cooked the other fish the way he had done the day before and ate it for breakfast.

# CHAPTER 12

Cray slowed his pace to keep from losing Mercer's tracks. Most of the morning, he had followed a trail that meandered through the forest unsure where it would lead. Then the trail straightened out and went directly to the base of a ridgeline that curved around to the southeast.

He looked at his watch. 1130 hours. He wasn't due to check in until 1200 hours. Deciding that he could reach the top of the ridgeline in half an hour, he checked his pack and started to climb.

It was tough going, steep and rocky. Cray continued up, slipping several times. Twenty minutes later, he was on top of the ridge in a clearing that looked out to the east. In the valley below, he saw the long, meandering shape of a river. His eyes followed it south until they stopped on something out of place. A wisp of smoke rose from a clearing near the western bank of the river. Cray tried to control his excitement.

He concentrated on the place where the smoke was rising, but he couldn't make out anything else. He sat down and pulled out his maps, GPS, radio, and water. He turned on the radio and GPS. The GPS flashed Cray's location.

Cray took a long drink from his water bottle while he looked at the map. He compared his location with the larger map and found his position. The river he was watching was a tributary to the Whitewater River that later merged with the Metolieus—this little stream dumped into the world-class trout river twenty miles downstream. He decided he would have to search the clearing for Mercer's trail to determine if he was heading for the Metolieus.

Cray chewed beef jerky and scanned the river and the meadow with his binoculars. Someone was definitely down there. No tent and they'd done a half-ass job of banking the fire. Suddenly, the radio crackled to life.

"Alpha. Alpha, come in."

Cray picked up the radio and fingered the handset. "Alpha here. Over."

"What's your status? Over."

"I'm still on the trail. My current position is roughly six miles to the southeast of my last position. I'm about two miles west of the Whitewater River and headed that way. Over."

"Affirmative. Do you have cell phone reception?

Cray took out his cell phone and checked. "That's an affirmative. I'll wait for your call. Alpha, out."

A minute later, Cray's phone rang. "Hey."

"Hey. I'm headed to Redmond to talk to a few guys. I have a chopper waiting in case we need it tomorrow to fly in and extract you and Mercer. How's everything on your end?"

"Everything's fine. I'm still on Mercer's trail and it's starting to take shape, like he's come to his senses or something. I've spotted some smoke along the river that I'm going to recon. It could be hikers, but it could be him. I'm gonna go down and check it out. I'll check back in at 1600 hours, earlier if I find him. That should give me time to get back down there before dark so I can camp near the river."

"I'll let Carson know."

"Good. Later."

Cray packed up his equipment, hefted his pack onto his back, and headed down the rocky trail toward the river below. Every now and then he spotted a boot print.

# CHAPTER 13

**M**ercer quickly ate his breakfast of roasted trout and berries he had collected. He stowed the remaining berries and second fish in a makeshift bag he made from his shirtsleeves, tying off each end with a couple of strips from his leather belt. Hoisting it to his shoulder, he grabbed his fishing spear and set off. He crossed the stream and made his way across the meadow toward the eastern ridge.

Traveling was much easier now that his body had had time to heal. His knee felt almost good as new, only hurting slightly when he walked. He made good time hiking up the eastern ridgeline. Numerous game trails cut along the slope. He used them as much as he could to make the going easier. After hiking steadily for two hours, he slipped on a rock and fell. He got to his knees and rested for a few minutes to catch his breath.

*Pace yourself. Go slow.*

His injured knee ached when he tried to get back up. He had been so excited at how little pain he'd felt earlier but now it was back. He looked around for a suitable walking stick, refusing to use his fishing spear for fear his weight might break it. Quickly, he found one and hobbled farther up the hill.

The sun was overhead when Mercer stopped again. His face was hot and red from exertion, even though the day wasn't. Too much, too fast. He brushed the sweat from his brow with his forearm, then checked his surroundings. He hadn't seen much in the way of wildlife during his climb, but based on the number of game trails, the nightlife was probably busy.

A well-traveled trail broke off to the south and paralleled the ridgeline above. He decided to keep moving, but needing a break, turned onto the new trail. He saw tracks made by deer, elk, and maybe a coyote or cougar. *Was that one a bear?* His mind was busy as he limped along, studying the tracks, recognition firing in his brain. But still only revealing facts and not memories.

Mercer turned once again upslope, pushing to reach the crest of the ridge. It was an arduous climb, his muscles starting to complain with each step. He looked up with relief several times expecting to see the top, only to be fooled by a false summit and the continuation of the slope. Finally, after two hours struggling up the trail, be broke through a choked stand of young fir trees and onto a precipice that looked on a valley below and across at the higher ridgeline. Exhausted, be sat down on a boulder. Suddenly a flash of metal caught his eye. He quickly scanned the opposite ridgeline and saw its source. There, sitting above the trees, was a fire tower. He hadn't seen it originally, as he had been scanning the southern portion of the ridge, but now that he saw it, the fire tower stuck out plainly.

Excitement coursed through his veins, along with a heavy dose of adrenaline, as the first sign of civilization and rescue showed itself. The fire tower at least meant a road or established trail to somewhere, and since he had seen the light the night before, he knew someone was up there. He only hoped they were still there.

He got to his feet feeling renewed and started to pick his way down from the top of the ridge. The trail he took gradually levelled out as he entered a gully, the beginning of the small valley between the two ridges.

Giant firs blotted out the sun, dropping the temperature. The ancient trees that had escaped the logger's axe stood as a reminder of an era long since passed. Large sword ferns grew in their shade, and a bed of fallen needles softened the ground under his boots.

He heard the stream before he saw it. The high use of the game trail he was traveling on now made sense: it led to water. He quickened his pace. The stream appeared a few more feet down the trail. Several bushes with plump, bluish-purple berries grew along the trail.

The water bubbled up from the earth not more than fifty feet away. He limped up the stream and knelt, greedily drinking the ice-cold spring water. His thirst quenched, he turned his attention to the nearby berries. He picked one and squished it between thumb and forefinger, then licked his finger. A sweet tartness hit his taste buds that made the juices run in his mouth. *Edible.*

Recovering from his morning hike, he spent a few hours picking berries along the stream. He wandered fifty yards downstream and discovered that the stream emptied into a small lake another hundred feet down.

When he reached the lake's edge, a giant trout leapt into the air. *Holy shit. That was a big one.* But it was too far out for him to catch.

He scanned the shallows for fish he might be able to spear, but saw none. The lake was deep, the water growing dark a few feet from shore where the bottom dropped off. He saw some water bugs and stoneflies in the water, as well as a couple of salamanders, though he couldn't remember their names. *Maybe I never knew them to begin with.*

Sudden movement caught his eye. A large crayfish emerged from under a submerged log. *That looks like dinner.* He dropped his makeshift pack, the remnant of a trout still inside, and took off his boots. He put his revolver on a rock, stripped down to his boxers, and stepped into the lake. The cold water bit his ankles and stung his toes.

The crayfish, sensing Mercer's shadow, quickly scurried under a submerged tree limb. The clarity of the water gave Mercer the false impression that the lake was shallower than it was. When he bent down to grab for the crustacean, his arm was too short to reach the bottom without his head getting wet. Refusing to let food escape, he dove under the water and grabbed at the clawed creature. His numb fingers fumbled over the crayfish. The crayfish fought back by nipping them while backing further under the log.

Mercer's lungs began to burn and he surfaced empty-handed. But the day was warm and he was determined. He floated in the shallows, scanning the bottom, until he found a submerged log with two claws and antennae protruding from beneath it. He kicked for the bottom, lifted the log with one hand, and snatched the crayfish with the other. The small creature fought valiantly but it did little good. The cold water had numbed Mercer's fingers and he didn't feel the crayfish pinching. He spent an hour searching for more crayfish, and stopped when he could no longer bear the cold. By then, he had collected seven.

It was late afternoon so he decided to make camp along the lakeshore. He gathered wood and scraped an area near the shore to build a fire. His spirits were high and he hummed a tune that his fragmented mind drew from somewhere. He pulled out his sticks and leather for making the fire and knelt by the pile of dried leaves and twigs he had collected. He had grown skilled at using the bow and drill to get an ember started and before long, he was blowing gently on a small coal.

Something triggered a memory deep within Mercer's mind. A fleeting image of standing in a grassy field. Beyond the field, forested hills to the east. The setting sun elongating his shadow, distorting it. Then the image was gone and he was once again kneeling by the lake, his body trembling.

Mercer dropped his head into his hands and tried to bring the memory back, but nothing came. The unexpected memory had caught him off guard, but his spirits rose when he realized that maybe his mind still contained them, and that somehow he could get them back.

Smiling, he went back to the task of lighting his fire. A few minutes later, the heat from a roaring fire warmed him.

He ate the last of the roasted trout while he cooked the crayfish in the coals. The crustaceans cooked quickly, turning a bright red. He decided to eat two of the seven crayfish and save the remaining five for his hike the following day. He wasn't sure how long it would take to reach the fire tower, and he needed all his strength to climb up the ridge to where it was perched.

After eating, he leaned back against a decaying log. Chunks of reddish-brown wood had flaked off and settled on the needle-covered ground. The warmth of the fire and his full stomach soon persuaded him to sleep.

Night had settled in when he woke abruptly. His senses were on alert and the hairs on the back of his neck were standing up. The warmth from the fire was gone; only the faint glow of smoldering coals remained. But it wasn't the cold that woke him. *What was it?*

He scanned the area from his position against the log, trying not to move. His ears burned trying to listen, then he heard it—a very real, very audible, growl, quickly followed by the sound of blowing. *A bear*, he thought, seconds before he saw it.

Frozen with fear, he looked around for a stick or something to use to defend himself. His fishing spear was leaning against a tree near the water's edge ten feet away. His pistol still lay on the rock where he had left it earlier in the day, also out of reach.

Then he saw it—the reason for the bear. He had fallen asleep with the bones and skin of the trout and shells from the crayfish lying next to him. Now he smelled the remains of his dinner, the same smell that had reached the bear.

\* \* \*

A 400-pound male black bear had smelled the fish. He was a common nighttime visitor to the campsites of lazy hikers who ate where they slept, failed to bring bear-safe storage containers, and forgot to hang their food away from their campsite. This bear had grown fat during the summer.

With a vision of fish in his mind, the bear approached the smoldering fire. The bear's eyesight was poor and he relied primarily on his sense of smell. He usually smelled a combination of clean humans and food, but here, he smelled only fish and smoke. Assuming the campsite was abandoned, the bear entered the area with little apprehension.

\* \* \*

Mercer's eyes were fixed on the approaching shadow. His brain raced through his options. He pressed his body up against the giant log, trying to disappear into it. The bear continued toward him. Unaware of Mercer's presence, it ambled toward the source of the smell. Unfortunately, that source lay right next to Mercer.

An idea suddenly flashed across Mercer's brain. He carefully reached out a hand toward the fire and grabbed the rock he had used for roasting the crayfish. It was hot and he grimaced as it burned flesh.

Slowly, he brought his arm back and threw the rock over the bear's head. It landed several feet away and rolled into the underbrush.

The bear jumped at the unexpected noise so close to him and spun around to investigate. Mercer took the opportunity to fling himself over the log and lie quietly on the other side. Straining to listen, he heard the bear moving around in the area where the rock had landed.

As quietly as possible, Mercer crawled along the log toward the water's edge. He heard the heavy footfalls of the bear's approach. He mustered all of his courage and stood, then dove into the lake. Fighting for breath, he forced his arms and legs to move, and swam.

The bear charged after him, splashing into the shallows and roaring angrily, incentive enough to keep Mercer moving. He swam to the opposite shore and pulled himself out. Squinting, he tried to see if the bear was still around his camp, but the only thing he saw was a faint glow of coals smoldering in his fire pit. A fear more powerful than the bear began to develop. After fighting for his life in the wilderness for so many days, he was going to die of hypothermia. He frantically rubbed his arms and legs to warm them.

The night was still and the temptation of the fire too much. Having made his decision, he waded back into the shallows of the lake. As cold as the water was, it would allow him to move quietly. His walk around the lake was free of any incident. An hour later, Mercer was back at his campsite. He knelt in the water and strained his ears for even the quietest sounds. All he heard was an insect chirping and the slight rush of the wind through the alders that lined the lake.

The bear was gone and Mercer didn't delay in building up the fire. Soon he had it roaring. He wanted assurances that the bear would think twice before approaching again. Warmed by both the fire and the exertion of rebuilding it, he sat down against the log where he had slept earlier. This time he was fully dressed, his pistol and fishing spear by his side.

The bear had rooted around where Mercer had eaten his dinner, spreading the fish bones across the carpet of evergreen needles. All that remained of the five roasted crayfish he had left near the fire were a few bits of red shell. He'd have to figure out what to do about food in the morning. His exhaustion after such a prolonged adrenaline high was more powerful than his fear, and Mercer sank into a fitful sleep, waking every hour to the sound of ghost bears.

# CHAPTER 14

Russ pulled off Highway 97 onto a gravel road heading west. He wanted to meet with Sully, an ex-Navy buddy, who now led organized hunting trips in the area. John Sullivan, whom everyone called Sully, owned a helicopter, and there was some speculation that he used it to track wildlife and let hunters illegally shoot from the air. So far he hadn't been caught.

Russ turned onto a dirt driveway that headed south and disappeared into a stand of trees. He had been here many times and had once even stayed here when he and Sully were dishonorably discharged from the service. For a time, they worked together for a private security contractor before eventually going their separate ways.

The road dropped down over an old dried-up riverbank and led to an aircraft hangar, a machine shop, and a one-level, ranch-style house. A large satellite dish stood next to the house, and all the buildings were painted to camouflage with their surroundings.

A large sign between two fence posts read Wildlife Tours. Russ chuckled, knowing the different legal and illegal "wildlife tours" his buddy offered to the right customers.

Russ stopped the truck next to the house, got out and stretched his stiff legs and back. A large black dog ran toward him, teeth bared, snarling. The dog wasn't any recognizable breed; but given its size, and the size of its teeth, it really didn't matter.

"Bear!" Russ commanded. "I know you aren't snarling at me."

The dog stopped when he heard his name, the large chain around his neck clinking to a stop a second later. Bear lifted his nose and smelled the air, then dropped his head. Bear's eyes were not yet convinced whether Russ was friend or foe, but he cautiously approached. Russ extended his hand palm down to allow Bear to properly identify him.

Bear sniffed Russ's hand twice, then licked it with a sloppy, saliva-covered tongue. Bear sat at Russ's feet and allowed him to stroke his head and scratch behind his ears. Russ found the right spot and Bear's hind foot began thumping the ground.

"Oh, hell," a deep voice said from inside the hangar, "you've ruined my dog!"

"Sully, how the hell are ya?" Russ said, walking to the hangar entrance.

"I'm not dead, so I must be doin' something right," Sully said, laughing. "Money comes in and the law hasn't caught me yet, so I can't complain. Good to see you, man. It's been a while."

Sully was in his late thirties, a few years older than Russ. His white T-shirt displayed the remnants of a powerfully muscled body, one not made from hours in a gym, but from hard work and sweat. Lately, his middle had begun expanding, falling from the unforgiving force of gravity and beer. His hair was a reddish-orange and his skin was fair, which this time of the year was a similar color to his hair. He wore camo fatigues and heavy work boots.

"You hungry? I was thinking about grilling up some elk steaks. They're fresh," Sully said, a grin cutting across his unshaven face.

Russ raised an eyebrow, knowing elk season wasn't for a couple of months yet.

"Well," Sully said in a tone Russ recognized as the beginning of a tale that would be far from the truth, "you see, I took my

Cessna up for a little early morning recon flight of a fire the Forest Service put out a week ago. They contract with me to do some fire spotting. Early morning is the best time to fly because you can still see the glowing embers in the dark."

"Anyway, I was done surveying the fire and was landing when out of nowhere this bull elk steps out onto the runway. I didn't have time to react and that bastard jumped up into my landing gear. I thought I was gonna die, if not for my nerves of steel. The dumb animal broke its neck, so I brought it up here, butchered it, and was planning to grill up a couple of steaks. You in?"

"Sure. Throw a couple of beers in there and I won't tell the game wardens that if they look real close they won't see any damage to the underside of your plane."

Both men laughed and finally shook hands.

"So what do you have going on? What can I do, and how much are you paying?" Sully asked.

"I'll explain over those beers."

Sully nodded, clapped Russ on the back, and led him around the hangar to a covered patio area that looked out onto Mount Jefferson. Two lawn chairs sat under the overhang. A refrigerator with a tap sticking out of the door had a stereo on top of it. A large barbecue grill sat out in the open, a little way from the chairs. A screen door led into the back of the hangar where Sully had a large freezer.

"Pour us a couple of cold ones, Russ. There are frosted glasses in the freezer compartment. I just hooked up that keg yesterday so there's plenty to drink. I'll go grab those steaks."

Sully disappeared while Russ found the glasses and poured two frosty beers. Sully returned carrying a platter of large, bloody steaks in one hand and a couple of foil-wrapped potatoes in the other. Sully went to the grill and turned on the gas. After a few seconds, he hit the electronic ignition button and a large ball of fire jumped from the grill. "Now we're ready to cook!" He put the foil-wrapped potatoes on the grill and turned to Russ, smiling broadly.

"Nice," Russ said, handing Sully his beer. "How many eyebrows have you gone through just for that fireball effect?"

"More than you'd believe. It seems I lose more after I've been drinking, but what the hell." He took a couple of long draws from his beer. "Ah, nothing like a cold beer on a hot day."

"You can say that again."

"Come on and have a seat, pal," Sully said, pointing to the two lawn chairs. "Food won't be ready for a while so let's talk business while we're still sober."

"So what's the gig? Wait a second!" he said, suddenly remembering something. He grabbed a remote control from a side pocket attached to his chair. He hit the power button and the stereo on top of the refrigerator began to play a country song Russ didn't recognize. He noticed that Sully had set up a surround-sound system.

"What's up with the music?"

"The surround-sound makes it real hard for people of the law enforcement persuasion to listen in. I know my compound is bug-free cuz I check it every night, but I worry about those damn bionic ears."

"Aren't you a tad bit paranoid?"

"You might think so, except I found a few bugs two weeks ago and there have been people snooping around by the tree line. Bear senses them but I keep him back. I went out last night and looked for myself. There were boot prints all over the place, the kind three out of four law enforcement agents prefer," said Sully smiling.

"Maybe I shouldn't be here. In my line of work, I really don't need any kind of legal heat."

"Don't worry. These are just local yokels playing with their new equipment. But if it makes you feel better, I'll make sure no one is out there." Sully turned and yelled, "Bear!" The dog came bounding around the corner. "Patrol!"

The dog growled once and ran off toward the tree line. "No sane cop will hang around out there with Bear sniffing around."

"Thanks, Sully. Let's get to it then. The issue is that one of our farm managers got greedy and went AWOL with enough information to bury us. So he makes a break for it and we lose him on the other side of the mountains when his truck went off a cliff into the river, but the bastard survived. Right now, my partner is tracking him, trying to catch up to him. You remember Cray, right?"

"Yeah, I like Cray."

"Anyway, Cray's dead on his trail but a couple of days behind. We figure the guy is headed this way. So I need your chopper on call to give support to Cray if he needs it. Usual price."

"Done," Sully said, smiling.

At that moment, barking erupted from the tree line, where two shapes were moving fast through dense brush. A man's scream indicated that Bear had caught up. The pursuit continued for a few more seconds, then the dog turned and ran back along the tree line to where he had flushed his quarry. A few seconds later, a victorious Bear trotted from the trees, dragging some very expensive listening equipment behind him.

Sully looked at what Bear dropped at his feet. He picked up the surveillance equipment. "I always wondered what kind of stuff these guys could afford. Not quite state-of-the-art, but close," he said, inspecting the equipment. He found the playback button and pressed it. "Let's see how the surround sound works, shall we?"

There was only a few minutes of recording, and it was all country music from Sully's stereo. "Good," Sully said, a triumphant smile on his face. He tossed the listening equipment on the workbench at the back of the hangar. "How about a refill, Russ?"

People thought Sully was just happy and stupid, a good ole boy to get drunk with but not much else. Having served with him, Russ knew better. It was all part of Sully's nature; he made people underestimate him so he would have an edge. Obviously, these cops had no idea who they were messing with.

"I should throw those steaks on."

Russ looked at his watch. 1558. "Damn, I almost missed Cray's check-in. You got somewhere I can make a cell phone call and not be overheard?"

"Where you're sitting is probably the best spot. I'll have Bear do another run through the woods to make sure it's cleared out. I wouldn't worry about it, though. Those last guys are long gone." Sully whistled for Bear, who had taken to a dirt patch under the shade of the workbench. Bear, knowing what to do, ran toward the woods, his head low, sniffing the ground.

Russ pulled his phone from his pocket and conferenced in a call with Cray and Carson.

"Cray, you start," Carson said.

"Sure. I saw smoke along the river and went down to check it out. Found a well-used fire pit. The coals were still hot so he hasn't been gone long. His tracks are all over the place. He's been eating fish, given all the bones I found near the fire pit. Something else, though. I searched around the tree line and found a lean-to he built to get out of the weather at night. He had been sleeping in there, covering himself with leaves for warmth."

"Where did he go?" Russ asked.

"I found some fresh tracks, maybe from this morning, on the opposite side of the river heading east toward the next ridge. I think he went off exploring. It would be dumb to leave the river for too long. I thought I'd stay here until morning to see if he comes back. If he doesn't, I'll start after him tomorrow. What do you want me to do with him if I do catch him? Do you want me to drag him back?"

The phone was quiet, then Carson said in a low but firm voice, "Kill him. First, use any means necessary to find out what he did with the files he stole. Then kill him and leave his body for the coyotes."

\* \* \*

After hanging up, Cray hiked back down to the base of the ridge and made camp at the edge of the woods. He picked a spot where he could see across the river and all the way to the far tree line. He had a great view of Mercer's fire pit as well as the tree where Mercer had his shelter. Cray watched the meadow while he ate the dried food he had packed. Just then, a cold breeze cut across the valley and Cray shivered. He hoped it wouldn't keep up all night or it was going to be miserable. He pulled his sleeping bag around him and hoped Mercer would return soon.

Cray was up most of the night checking the meadow every half an hour, first with an infrared scope, and then with night goggles. He saw a few deer, a cougar with a couple of cubs, and an elk. It would be a great place to hunt.

# CHAPTER 15

Jessie O'Brien, a U.S. Forest Service fire tower observer, couldn't remember the last time she had slept. She was working toward a graduate degree in natural resources management, and was hoping that work with the Forest Service during the summer might help her find a full-time job when she graduated. She also figured she'd have a lot of free time to work on her thesis. Now she was experiencing writer's block, and hadn't done anything other than surf the internet and refill the coffee pot.

Jessie was a computer nerd by birth. Programming and hacking came easy to her, as if computers were a language she'd always known. None of the fire towers had internet access, but instead relied on short-wave radios and satellite phones for communications. But Jessie had rigged her fire tower, using a satellite uplink, to get on-line. She was also piggybacking on someone's signal down in the valley, making it free, though not quite legal. No harm, no foul. Besides, she had used the signal to update and optimize the signal owners' system, free of charge.

Even with her highly lucrative computer skills, Jessie was drawn to nature and wanted a profession where she could do good for the planet. Idealistic, yes, but pragmatic too was her response to questions about her future. Her thesis was looking at climate change and modelling fire intensity through time to help better predict catastrophic forest fires. It used both her computing skills and her love for the outdoors.

The fire tower was one large square room that sat aloft four steel legs about thirty feet in the air, perched atop a rocky outcrop. This made the tower approximately ten feet above the tops of the trees. The room was divided into thirds. One third was where Jessie had her bed, a reading lamp, a bookcase, and her trunk. A pole hung over her trunk, which allowed her to hang some of her clothes. Another third of the tower was her kitchen area that consisted of a two-burner hotplate, a washbasin, a coffee maker, a small refrigerator, and a number of shelves and crates for food and cooking utensils. The final third was her makeshift office that consisted of a large table that held her computer, the radio, and another bookcase. She'd pinned a large map of the forest to the wall, covering one of the windows.

Jessie knew it was a violation of the rules to cover the window, but she used the map, as well as some others, to give herself some privacy. Though she knew she was out in the middle of nowhere, she still had a hard time changing her clothes in a room full of windows perched up above the trees.

Jessie scanned the western horizon through her binoculars. She thought she'd seen smoke early in the morning between her tower and the far ridgeline, but it had disappeared. Now night was settling in and she hoped that it would not be another sleepless one. She had one more day in the tower until she would be relieved for two days, and she was looking forward to being back in civilization, sleeping in a real bed, and restocking her food.

Sitting back down at her computer, she looked at the screen of words, hit Save, and opened up an internet browser. *I wonder who's on-line and ready to play some War of Worlds*, she thought, distracting herself again.

# CHAPTER 16

Morning came early and Ted fought through the urge to stay in bed. Slowly he dragged himself to his coffee maker. After the first belt of coffee, his world began to come into focus. He ate a light breakfast and poured another cup of coffee into his travel mug. He met his farmhand, Miguel Ramirez, out in the barn, where he was busily collecting the equipment they would need for building fence.

"Morning, Miguel. How are you doing today? Did you enjoy your day away from this place?"

"My wife is glad I have to work," Miguel said. Miguel was married, with a couple of little ones. He had worked for Ted's father and Ted kept him on when he took over the business. Miguel knew everything about the ranch, and Ted relied heavily on him. Miguel was also willing to try Ted's new ranching ideas, which helped Ted's confidence. "She says that I'm worse than the kids when I'm home. I guess I pester her too much."

"Good. Maybe you won't take time off," Ted joked, and the two of them laughed.

"We had a cow die yesterday," said Ted.

"What? Why didn't you call? What happened?"

"It died from smoke inhalation. Green Grass Enterprises burned and never called to tell us. Luckily, we only lost one. Besides, the vet came out and took care of it. I didn't do much of anything. In fact, they've already replaced it with another heifer and wrote me a settlement check."

"They did?" Miguel said, a little suspicious. "I don't know how they stay in business."

"What do you mean?"

"Do you know how many cows they replace? Quite a few by my count, and I probably don't even know half of them," Miguel explained.

"What are you talking about, Miguel?"

"This farm has had ten cows replaced in the last eight years. A couple of heifers that died from miscarriages, a couple of bulls that turned out sterile, a few calves born with life-ending deformities. I always thought it was just bad luck, but that vet's guarantee is a little too good. My friend, Felipe—he works for the Martensen's—and we were talking about it once. He said that they also had a number of similar problems. All of them insured and replaced."

Ted nodded slowly, dazed by what he'd just heard. If Miguel was right, than the vet's business should fail, but it seemed to flourish.

Ted and Miguel got into Ted's truck and drove down the lane to the main road.

"We need to head over to that field by the cottage," Ted said. "We'll park there and work up the cattle."

"Whatever you say, *jefe*."

Ted thought about what Miguel had said to him. He had wondered why the deal the vet offered was so good. At first, he'd been swept away by the service and the compensation. He thought it was too good to be true but he was told it was just business. Ted was pulled from his thoughts when the truck bounced from pavement to the gravel lane that led to the cottage. He pulled the truck onto the driveway.

"This place is really starting to fall apart," said Miguel breaking the silence. "Look at all that dust."

"That isn't dust, it's ash."

Miguel only shook his head. "You know there've been sick workers too."

"What? What do you mean?" asked Ted.

"My niece, Dia, she works for an organization that helps sick migrant workers. She said there were quite a few from around here."

"How many? What kind of sickness?"

"Don't know. That's the hard thing about migrants. They tend to just disappear as they move from farm to farm. I can call Dia if you want to talk to her," offered Miguel.

"Yeah, maybe," said Ted. "Let's get the four-wheelers unloaded," Ted said lost in thought, his gaze still on the grimy windows.

They got the ATVs unloaded and drove them back down the lane to a gate that was installed in the fence.

"Okay," Ted said, "here's the plan. I want to move the cattle up here, near this gate. Then we'll go for the stragglers. Okay?"

Ted and Miguel expertly herded the cattle and moved them up through the gate. Both counting the cattle as they moved through the pasture. After ten minutes, Ted asked Miguel how many he had counted.

"A hundred fifty."

"Sure?" Ted said, rubbing his forehead. He had counted 149.

"Positive. How many are there supposed to be?"

"A hundred fifty. I must have missed one. Let's move them to the other pasture."

It was a beautiful day. The sky was blue with a few wispy white clouds to the north. Ted scanned the skyline and soaked in the warm summer sun. They worked through the morning and then took their lunch break back at Ted's house. Miguel ate on the front porch, while Ted went to his office, sat at his desk, and looked at the sheet of paper with phone numbers on it.

*Get on with it, Ted*, he told himself. He grabbed his cell phone and dialed the first number. Beverly in Falmouth. Ted had a website showing a map of Massachusetts. He scanned the map, looking for the town. It was on Cape Cod. The phone rang several times before Ted realized he was holding his breath. Finally, an answering machine kicked in. "Hi, you have reached Matt and Bev. We can't come to the phone ..." Ted hung up mid-sentence— she's a widow.

He dialed the next number, the Beverly in Norfolk, a small town in southeastern Massachusetts. Ted waited as a phone rang on the other side of the country.

"Hello?" came a crackly, older woman's voice.

"Hi," Ted said. "I'm trying to reach a Rachel Mason."

"Rachel? No Rachel here."

"Oh, so sorry, ma'am. I must have the wrong number. You have a nice day."

"I will. You, too. Bye-bye now."

Smiling, Ted looked over the two remaining phone numbers. He settled on the Braintree number, a town to the south of Boston. He dialed the number but again, there was only a machine. One more number remained for a Beverly Mason in the town of Sunderland. Ted looked at the map. Sunderland was located along the Connecticut River in west-central Massachusetts.

He dialed the last number on the list. After a few rings, a woman picked up. Her voice was older.

"Hello?"

"Hi. I'm trying to reach Rachel?"

"Rachel isn't home. Is there something I can do for you?"

"I'm a friend of hers from Oregon," Ted said, his stomach summersaulting, "and I'm trying to get in touch with her. I haven't spoken to her in a while."

"Oh," the woman said, "Rachel is sick. She's been in and out of the hospital for the last few months. In fact, ever since she came back from Oregon."

"Oh, no," Ted said, dumbstruck. "What's wrong?"

"There have been quite a few things, but cancer seems to be the toughest one to beat. She's in chemotherapy today." The woman paused as though uncertain to say more. "What did you say your name was, dear?"

Ted froze. Not sure what to do or how to answer. Panicking, he clicked off his phone. After a few minutes, Ted's present came back into focus. He checked his watch and left to get Miguel and finish his day. He met Miguel at the pickup truck.

"What's wrong?" asked Miguel, seeing a shadow across Ted's face.

"Huh? Ah, Rachel's sick," Ted replied quietly, kicking some gravel with his boot. "Cancer."

"*Mis dios,*" replied Miguel quietly.

"So, your niece is working with sick workers from around here?"

"*Si.*"

"Think she'd be willing to meet with me and talk about what she's seeing?"

"I'll call her now and see if she can come over after work," said Miguel, pulling his cellphone from his pocket.

"Thanks."

Miguel wandered around the back of the truck, speaking Spanish rapidly into the phone. The conversation was soon over and Miguel walked back.

"She'll be here at five o'clock. Now let's get back to work."

"Okay, *jefe,*" said Ted smiling, appreciating Miguel snapping him out of his mood.

They spent the rest of the day laying out a new fencing system that Ted had wanted to try. The sun was hot, but the work felt good to Ted and took his mind off Rachel for a few hours. However, soon it was half-past four and they were loading up their tools and getting ready to leave the pasture. They were back in the barnyard by quarter of five and putting equipment away when a red Chevy Colorado pickup truck pulled into the driveway. Ted watched as the woman behind the wheel parked the truck closer to the house. She quickly got out and walked toward the two men.

"*Dia, mi sobrina,*" said Miguel smiling. "Thank you for coming. It's nice to see you."

Dia hugged her uncle and then looked at Ted, who felt like he was being measured.

"Ah, yes, this is Ted," said Miguel.

"Hi,' said Ted. "I really appreciate you coming over tonight."

"Sure, nice to meet you. My uncle didn't say much. Maybe you can fill me in on what's going on."

"Well, let's get out of the heat. I could use something cold to drink," suggested Ted, leading the way for Miguel and Dia.

They reconvened in the kitchen, taking up seats around Ted's table. Ted grabbed a pitcher of iced tea from the refrigerator and put some ice and tea into three glasses. After sitting back down and taking a long, thirsty drink from the cold glass, Ted put the drink down and leaned back in his chair.

"So, your uncle tells me that you're working on a health initiative with migrant workers?"

"Yes, workers that come in on temporary visas for working the fields and the harvest usually don't have access to health care like the rest of us. If they get injured on the job, they are usually taken to the hospital, but would rather avoid any place that is going to ask for their names and addresses, even if they're sick. So, we run a mobile clinic that makes house calls to certain places when they have time off, usually in the evenings, to provide them access to health care," Dia explained.

"Wow, how does something like that get funded?" asked Ted.

"We have a grant from the World Health Organization and one from the state. We aren't rolling in money, but we have enough to get buy during the harvest season."

"That's good. So, I wanted to talk to you about whether you have noticed any patterns with farm workers getting sick, especially around here," began Ted.

"Dia, tell Ted what you told me about those sick workers," interjected Miguel.

Dia took a long drink from her tea, thinking about how to begin.

"Well, we've had a number of young men come down with some strange illnesses—like cancer."

"What kind of cancer?" asked Ted.

"Well, it's really more a blood disease, like leukemia. We have been trying to figure out if these men were exposed to something prior to coming to Oregon or if it's a hazard from the work here. Can I ask you what your interest is?"

"Well, someone close to me has gotten sick. She is being treated for cancer, or at least going through chemotherapy. I don't know much more about it. But I've also had some cows die from what the vet says is smoke inhalation, but I'm not so sure. It all seems to be timed with field burning."

"Hmm, that is interesting. Tell me a little bit about your friend," said Dia.

"Well, she was my girlfriend at the time and we were getting pretty serious. She lived in a cottage on the farm down by the river. One day things were fine, the next she said she was moving home and then left."

"Her name was Rachel," offered Miguel.

"How was Rachel right before she left? How did she look? Was she sick?" Dia probed.

"She was fine, I think."

Ted thought hard. "She seemed tired. I remember that she said she had been working hard to get pieces ready for an art show. I thought she was just burning the candle at both ends. And I think she had a stomach virus. It always seemed to get better at night, but then she'd relapse in the morning. She finally went to the doctor. She took off a few days later."

"*Mis dio,*" said Miguel rubbing his eyes.

"What?" asked Ted.

"She was pregnant, my friend."

"Wait. What? Pregnant?" said Ted. Dia only nodded her agreement with her uncle.

"She was having morning sickness and was probably early in the pregnancy. A month or so," suggested Dia.

"I'm a fucking idiot. How did I not see the signs?"

"Well, women are pretty good at keeping that secret until we want to share it. Usually, we want to make certain we're pregnant before telling anyone. How did she leave?" Dia asked.

"Abruptly. I put a lot of her stuff in storage. She only took her clothes and personal stuff. I still have her furniture and other things stored in the barn," replied Ted, still stunned.

"Where did you store all the artwork she'd been working on?"

Ted thought back to that painful time. "Now that you mention it, I don't remember storing any artwork. I never saw any of the pieces she was working on for that show."

"So," Dia said, "whatever happened, it was serious enough for her to run home. And that's when the doctor discovered the illness."

"I guess so. But why would she take off like that? We could have talked about it. Unless...," Ted began, something catching in his throat mid-sentence, "unless she lost the baby."

Dia and Miguel exchanged glances.

"Ted, you have a lot to process. What I can do is look at my records and see if I have any clusters of patients around here or around field burning season. Maybe there's a connection there. I'll go back through the lab results and see what I can find out. Have you tested the water from the cottage?"

"No," said Ted. "I will. I have a friend at the university who can run some tests for me."

"Any way you can talk to Rachel and see about getting more information about her condition?"

"You should go see her," said Miguel.

Ted thought about that. "Go out there? I don't know that I could. I mean, I have a ranch to run."

"*Mierda*—bullshit," said Miguel translating his own words. "I can take care of things here. That's not a good excuse. You would not forgive yourself if you could help her and did nothing."

"Okay, okay," said Ted, raising both hands. "It looks like I'm heading out there. I'll see about flying out there on Friday for the weekend."

"Let me give you my cell number, so you can call me if you learn anything," offered Dia. Ted entered her number into his cell phone, and gave his number to Dia. "I'll call you as soon as I learn anything. Maybe this is something we can fix."

"Thanks. I really appreciate your help," said Ted.

The three rose and Ted led Dia and Miguel back through the house to the front door. He thanked Dia again and watched her walk to her truck. Miguel lingered behind.

"*Amigo*, I want you to get your tickets to go. I'm serious about what I said. You need to help her if you can and get some answers yourself. Okay?"

"Yeah, thanks, I'll do it tonight," said Ted, shaking his friend's hand.

Miguel gripped Ted's hand firmly and then stepped down from the porch and headed for his own truck. Ted watched him go and then sat in the old rocking chair and stared out toward the western hills. As he sat there, his mind slipped into a memory.

\* \* \*

It had been a cool day the previous July and Rachel was living at the cottage. The forecast was for rain the following day and

Rachel had wanted to get some sculpting in before the humidity rose too high. Ted was working in a nearby pasture, moving a few cows and their calves. He was riding his horse down a draw when his cell phone rang.

"Did the weatherman call for snow today?" Rachel asked.

"I can't imagine he did. Why?"

"It's snowing over here. Come take a look for yourself."

"Snowing in July? I'll be right over." Ted kicked the sides of his horse, urging it into a gallop, and headed to Rachel's.

He realized what she was talking about when he got closer and saw ash falling from the sky. It looked like gray snow drifting down and blanketing the grass. Ted found Rachel standing outside barefoot and in a thin, pale blue denim dress, watching the ash fall.

"Hey, honey," she said. "Do you like my little snowstorm?"

"Sorry about that. I guess they're burning fields today. No one called me. Are you okay?"

"Yeah, I'm fine. Kind of tickles my throat, though. I don't think I'll stay out in it too long. Are you hungry? I wouldn't mind having a snack."

"That sounds great. Let me put the horse in the shed so he doesn't have to breathe this. I'll tie him up in the corner away from your work."

"I'll meet you inside," Rachel said, then coughed a few times. "It's starting to come down a little heavier."

Ted watched her run across the yard and into the cottage.

# CHAPTER 17

**M**ercer bolted upright, his hand reaching for his pistol. He whipped his head around, seeking the noise that woke him, still too groggy to register what he had heard. He smirked when he saw the ripples in the lake, the fading sign of a leaping fish and the orange sky of the rising sun.

He rubbed his eyes and stretched, his muscles aching from the previous day's hike and his midnight swim. He shuddered at the thought of the bear ripping apart his camp and finding his cache of food. *Food.* His stomach rumbled. *It looks like it's berries for breakfast.*

Mercer got up, testing his muscles, hoping they would cooperate. He snatched up his few belongings and wandered down to the water's edge. The berries were thicker on the far side of the lake, so he'd hike that way, then continue east toward the fire tower.

He began picking his way around the lake, eating berries wherever he found them. By the time he got to the east side of the lake, he had eaten his fill and began collecting berries for the hike. He hoped he'd make it to the fire tower by midday.

Before leaving the shoreline, he looked back across the lake at the place where he had spent the night. Wisps of smoke rose from the still-smoldering fire. A cold breeze hit him as he turned and started back into the forest, sending a chill through his body.

\* \* \*

The strong blast of wind swept across the little lake and funneled through the place he had spent the night. It was so strong it scattered the poorly banked fire and spread hot coals over the forest floor. The weather had been hot and dry and the dying coals found new life in the dried leaves and needles of the forest. Small spot fires began to burn. The wind died down as quickly as it had come up. The small fires continued to burn slowly, eating, and growing. Every now and then, two fires ate their way to each other and met, creating a new, larger fire.

Mercer, unaware of the small fires now burning, hiked east away from the lake. He found a game trail and followed it to the base of the next ridge, the one where he hoped the fire tower sat. He rested a few minutes before getting the itch to move on again, his excitement barely containable.

The southeast wind began to blow again. This time, the fire was ready to take full advantage of it. It moved faster, eating more and growing larger. It moved to the northwest, spurred on by dry southern winds visiting from California. The winds had now grown warm and the fire sent sparks out in front of it, as though scouting ahead. Before long, a wall of flames marched steadily out of the area near the lake and headed for the western ridgeline.

* * *

Cray woke up and scanned the river valley for signs of Mercer. He hadn't returned to his camp so Cray decided to pack up his gear and move down to the river to eat breakfast before climbing back up the ridge for his check-in. He packed quickly and searched the valley again in case he had missed Mercer during the night.

Around mid-morning he began his hike back up the western ridge. He climbed steadily, though his muscles were stiff. He was thoroughly enjoying himself and promised to do more backpacking in the future. He had started late and was going to be late for the check-in, but he wasn't worried about it. He didn't have anything to report.

Cray was approaching the top of the ridge when he thought he smelled smoke. He froze in his tracks and sniffed again. This time he was certain. Somewhere, the forest was on fire. He turned to look down the ridge he had just climbed. The valley was still and looked as it had earlier that morning. Cray's eyes wandered across the meadow and up the opposite ridge. He narrowed his eyes, trying to distinguish the top of the far ridge. He struggled to focus, realizing a second before it turned orange with fire that he was looking through a haze of smoke. Moments later, the ridge was ablaze and the fire was surging down toward the valley.

"Shit. That must be a half-mile wide and moving fast."

He noticed that the wind had picked up and was blowing in his direction. He sprinted for the top of the ridge. He pulled out his cell phone as he ran and yelled "Russ" into it to activate the voice dialing system.

\* \* \*

At quarter-past twelve, Russ's phone chirped to life.

"Russ, I need an evac fast!"

"Slow down, pal. What's going on?" Russ sat up, his muscles tensing.

"You know that ridge I called from yesterday? In fifteen minutes, it's gonna be on fire. I really don't have time to slow down."

"Sully, fire up the bird!" Russ yelled. "We have an extraction, and I mean yesterday."

Sully disappeared into the hangar and reappeared with a red duffel bag. He sprinted to the helicopter and climbed in.

"Cray, read me your coordinates, and we'll be there as fast as we can."

"One step ahead of you." Cray read a series of numbers and Russ pulled a pen from his pocket and wrote the numbers on his arm.

"We're on our way," Russ said, running to the helicopter.

"Be quick. That fire isn't slowing down for anything."

Russ clicked off his phone and climbed into the helicopter that already hovered a foot off the ground. Sully flew the chopper over the field and above the trees while Russ strapped himself in and pulled on the headset. He read the coordinates and Sully punched them into his on-board navigation system. Cray was forty miles away. Sully increased the speed and corrected the heading.

\* \* \*

Jessie looked up from her computer. She had finally been inspired and had been typing frantically for the last hour. It was mid-morning and another beautiful day in the forest. Suddenly, she realized the small ridge to the west was clouded in.

"Shouldn't be any fog this time of day," she said to herself standing and grabbing the binoculars. It was smoke and a lot of it. She peered through the binoculars and was able to pick out small fires burning in the forest. Quickly, she grabbed her radio handset.

"Headquarters, Tower 256, over. Headquarters, Tower 256, over."

"Go ahead, Tower 256," came a man's voice through the radio's speaker.

"Headquarters, I have a fire," said Jessie, reading the coordinates of the small ridge.

"Affirmative," said the man on the other end of the radio. "We just received another report of it from a helicopter in the area. Which direction is the fire moving? Over."

"Appears to be heading due west. The wind is pushing it up the ridgeline. Over."

"Affirmative, Tower 256. Please provide status updates every fifteen minutes. We are dispatching the incident management team to ascertain the situation, over."

"Affirmative, headquarters, I will report in every fifteen minutes, over," said Jessie marking the fire on the map and pulling down a green ledger to start taking notes.

\* \* \*

Cray could only wait. He searched the top of the ridge for a clear spot where the helicopter could land and pick him up, but everywhere he looked, he saw ten-foot tall or taller spruce and fir trees. He found an area where he could watch the quickly advancing fire—now almost to the edge of the east side of the river—and have the best chance for the helicopter to get to him.

The river didn't slow the fire down. Cray watched as spot fires leaped to life yards ahead of the main firestorm. Soon, the entire meadow was ablaze. He lost sight of the frontline of the fire as it approached the base of the ridge below where he now sat and waited, helplessly. The thought of running had crossed his mind though he knew it would do him no good. The fire was moving too fast and the winds were against him. It would overtake him before he made it down the opposite side of the mountain.

Smoke was the first sign that the fire was quickly approaching. Cray coughed before he noticed it. White wisps, like early morning fog, were beginning to spread along the ground and limit Cray's vision. Thickening smoke now obscured trees he had seen moments before. Sweat beaded along Cray's brow as the temperature—and his panic—rose. Suddenly, flames jumped to life 50 feet from where he stood.

He reached for his water bottle and wet his bandana. He tied it around his face like a bandit from a western movie and breathed in the moistened, somewhat filtered, air. The wet cloth also gave him some comfort as the heat of the fire washed over him. He reached for his radio and tried calling Russ, but he was unable to hear anything over the sudden rushing sound that was getting louder.

Cray, trying to keep his nerve, put his hand on his gun. The feel of cold metal against his sweating palm calmed him. He knew that if it came down to burning to death, he would put a bullet in his head first.

Small fires were starting all over the forest floor. Cray watched one erupt next to him, and he quickly stamped it out. He would not be able to keep that up for long. Smoke began to swirl around him as the wind changed direction and the air was forced down.

Cray looked up through the thick smoke and saw what he thought was a red light. Comprehension instantly spread across his face. Rotor wash. He snatched the colored smoke grenade from his pack, pulled the pin, and tossed it a few feet away. In a fraction of a second, red smoke poured out of the little device.

* * *

"There!" Russ yelled, pointing at the red smoke rising out of the white. From the helicopter, the entire mountain appeared to be on fire.

"Get in the back," Sully ordered. "There's a duffel bag with rope and harness. Attach the carabiner and toss Cray the harness."

Russ quickly did as he was told, while Sully tried to get the chopper lower, fighting the fire-created winds. As the chopper leveled out, Russ leaned out and dropped the harness into the swirling smoke.

Cray looked up just in time to see the harness falling toward him. He stepped to the side to give it room. The fire was now all around him and he had only seconds to react. He quickly stepped into the harness, secured it around his waist, then yanked hard on the rope.

Russ felt the tug and yelled for Sully to pull up. The chopper rose in the air and Cray was yanked off the ground as the chopper continued to gain altitude. When Sully was sure they were high enough, he tipped the nose down and forced the chopper forward. Cray just cleared the trees as they began their retreat.

Cray looked back toward the ridge where he had been seconds before and watched as a wall of fire completely engulfed it. The chopper continued west, away from the fire. After a few minutes, Sully turned north. Cray saw a large meadow and realized they were headed for it. Once over the meadow, Sully lowered the chopper until Cray was once again on the ground, setting the chopper down next to him.

Cray collapsed, his adrenaline-drained body and shaky legs unable to support him. Russ jumped out of the chopper with a first aid kit as soon as he was within a few feet of the ground and rushed over to Cray, who had multiple second-degree burns.

"Nice hike?" Russ asked, smiling at his friend as he pulled the burn cream from the first-aid kit.

Cray smiled weakly and slumped back to the ground, exhausted.

"He okay?" Sully asked, coming up to the two men.

"Yeah, we made it just in time. Thanks, man."

"No problem, I haven't had this much excitement in years."

Just then, Russ's phone rang. Carson. It was one o'clock, and it appeared that he had missed five earlier calls.

He answered, and gave her the update on Cray and the fire.

"I know," she said, "I'm watching it. A news helicopter in the area, somewhere near Camp Sherman, was doing a story on fishing, and is now showing footage from the east side of it," she told him. "See to Cray, then call me back. I have a feeling that our missing person problem is solved."

# CHAPTER 18

The going was easy though Mercer's leg throbbed with pain. After half an hour, he stopped to catch his breath and rest on the soft cushion of the forest floor covered with decades of evergreen needles. He sat on a steep hillside where he could see the shape of the fire tower in the distance. The shadows of the forest were starting to grow long in the late afternoon sun. He hoped to make it to the structure in the next few hours while he still had light.

After only a few minutes of rest, a sudden desire to get to his goal pushed him forward. He rose and picked his way down the slope. A quarter-mile later, Mercer stumbled out of the brush and onto a marked hiking trail. He collapsed against a rotting log, his emotions catching up to him as he sobbed, overtaken by the joy of finding a trail that he knew led somewhere.

The trail climbed, turning into a set of steep switchbacks, each one more brutal than the last. Every time Mercer thought he was getting near the top, the trail cut back sharply in the opposite direction. More than once, he attempted to bushwhack his way straight up the side of the mountain, but the terrain was too steep. The physical exertion was taxing, requiring him to take breaks, slowing his progress. After nearly two hours of hiking, Mercer suddenly broke out of the forest into a small mountain meadow. The fire tower stood near the middle of the meadow on a rocky outcrop.

Mercer started to run, then stopped, unsure how to proceed. Ever since he had spotted the tower, he had assumed someone was there who could help him. Now he wasn't sure, for some reason he felt wary of it. He watched the tower for a few minutes, and then remembered he was armed. He stepped back into the shadows of the trees and unloaded the revolver. Stuffing the bullets into his pants pocket, he took the revolver and hid it under some rocks along the tree line. Then he stepped back out into the clearing and slowly began working his way toward the tower.

* * *

Jessie checked the clock on the wall, jotted notes down in the green ledger that lay open on the desk, and then scanned the distant fire until the crackle of the radio interrupted her thoughts.

"Tower 256, headquarters. Tower 256, headquarters. What is your status?" a man's voice crackled over the radio.

Jessie brushed a long strand of black hair out of her face as she picked up the handset. "This is 256. Status is the same. No sign of the fire advancing to the east. Over." This had been the same report she had given for the last four hours. She was tired from being tense.

"Received, 256. Be advised we are shifting to four-hour status reports."

"That's an affirmative."

"We'll talk to you around 2000 hours. Headquarters out."

Putting the radio handset down, Jessie went to her bed. She grabbed her alarm clock and set it for ten minutes of eight— enough time to check the forest before giving her status report.

She sat down behind her computer and ran her fingers through her hair, then pulling it back, made a tight ponytail. She yawned, and stretched her arms up over her head. There was no way she'd be able to focus on her writing now. She surfed the internet to see pictures of the fire that the news helicopter had captured. She was glad it had moved west and not east. Suddenly, her stomach growled and she realized she hadn't eaten anything since breakfast.

She looked through her food stores to see what she could scrounge up for dinner. After a quick assessment, she decided on gourmet macaroni and cheese with a little broccoli so there'd be something green on her plate.

After wolfing down her dinner, she decided to shower. The tower's bathroom facilities were on the ground, so she grabbed her things and opened the trapdoor that led down from the tower.

The afternoon was still warm from the heat of the day but it was beginning to cool as the cold air from the mountains worked its way downslope. She followed a well-worn path to the building near the edge of the trees. The building had several rooms. One contained the hot-water heater, one a toilet and sink, and one a shower. The last room housed the electrical equipment for the complex. A large water cistern sat outside the building—still three-quarters full. In the summer, the Forest Service brought a water tanker up every few weeks to fill it.

The water was hot and Jessie let it roll off her skin. She sighed as her tense muscles began to soften. She stayed longer than normal, but she felt that she had earned the luxury of a long, hot shower. Half an hour later, she was back in the tower, her nose buried in her laptop, working on her thesis.

The excitement of the fire had left her with a lot of untapped energy and she had refocused it on her research. The sun was dropping toward the trees and its rays cut below the eaves of the tower and blinded her. She looked up, annoyed, and squinted. She froze as something in the meadow caught her eye. A man was limping toward her tower. She grabbed her binoculars and focused them on the figure. He looked injured, his face unshaven, and his clothes tattered.

Jessie leapt to her feet and immediately locked the trap door. Then, taking a 12-gauge shotgun out of a locked cabinet, she loaded it. She grabbed a pistol from the same locker and loaded it as well. She placed the pistol in the top drawer of her desk and then picked up the shotgun. The shotgun was Forest Service issue, the pistol was hers. Unlatching the door that opened out onto the tower's catwalk, Jessie stepped outside and leaned against the railing. The man hadn't noticed her, and continued to limp toward the tower. Suddenly, he looked up and froze.

"What can I do for you?" Jessie called to the man.

He said nothing for a long time, just scratched his head and face nervously.

"Sir, can I help you?"

This time, Jessie raised the shotgun up across her chest. Suddenly, the man collapsed onto the ground.

"Oh, shit!"

Jessie climbed back into the fire tower, grabbed her binoculars, and studied the unmoving man. He appeared to be breathing. She grabbed the pistol from the drawer and tucked it into her waistband. Then, trading the shotgun for a first-aid kit and water bottle, she unlatched the trapdoor and climbed down from the tower.

The man lay motionless as she approached. She stopped a few feet away and called out again.

"Sir, are you okay?"

No response. She slowly approached him. He appeared to be unconscious. She bent down and examined him. All that she could be sure of was that he had been through a rough time. Jessie unscrewed the lid of the water bottle and splashed some water on his face. His eyes flickered a few times, then slowly opened.

"Don't move," Jessie said in a firm voice. "Drink some of this. Slowly."

He opened his mouth and allowed her to pour water into it. He sputtered as he choked on it. Jessie did a quick assessment to make sure there wasn't anything seriously wrong with him. He was dehydrated and sunburned, but since he had been walking, she assumed nothing was broken. His face and arms were bruised, there was still the remnant of a cut across his forehead, and it looked like his leg had a cut that had recently been bleeding. His clothes were ripped, but it appeared to Jessie that much of it had been torn on purpose.

"What's your name?"

The man shook his head and lowered his eyes.

"Are you okay? Can you talk?"

"Yes …." he croaked.

"You look like you got into a fight with the mountains and lost. Let me take a look at that leg."

The man tried to get up on his elbows, but quickly sank back down.

"You just lie still. You've been through an ordeal but you're safe now."

He closed his eyes and let his body relax while Jessie examined his leg. The wound was infected but it was something she could patch up.

"Okay, mister, let's get you back to the tower where I can treat your injuries and we can figure out what to do next. Give me your hand and I'll help you up."

Jessie took his arm and helped him to his feet. It took a couple of tries to get him up, but soon they were working their way across the meadow toward the tower. As they approached the stairs, he seemed to get some of his strength back.

"Do you have a phone here?" he asked suddenly, an urgency coming through in his tone.

"Yeah, but right now we need you to get up those stairs where there's a cot and a hot meal. Do you think you can do that?"

"I'll give it a shot."

After a painstaking few minutes of lifting and pulling, Jessie finally hoisted the man through the trap door. She sat him down in a chair and went to her cot. She took her bedding off and spread a new sheet and blanket over it, then helped him to the cot to lie down.

"Don't go to sleep on me yet. I need you to drink a quart of water and eat something." He nodded and closed his eyes. Jessie filled a bottle of water and handed it to him. "Drink all of this, okay? And do it slowly."

Jessie started up her cook stove. A few minutes later, she had a can of beef stew heating in an old blackened pot. Once hot, she ladled some into a metal bowl and took it to the man. She helped him to a sitting position and handed him the bowl and a couple pieces of bread.

"Now eat this slowly," she instructed.

He nodded as he scooped a spoonful of stew into his mouth. As he ate, Jessie tended to the cut on his leg.

"Now, how about we get to know each other a little? My name is Jessie and I work for the Forest Service. What's your name?"

He stopped eating and concentrated. Finally, with a shaky voice, he said, "I don't know. I can't remember."

A cold chill ran down Jessie's back. "Okay, what do you remember? Let's start there."

"I remember a river and almost drowning, but I'm not sure if that was real. I remember trying to get to this tower. I remember the bear, but I can't remember anything about myself. I remember certain things, like what berries are edible, how to light a fire, and how to clean a fish, but no memories of my life," said the man, starting to show his frustration.

"Okay, try to relax. You've been through a major trauma and it's your brain's natural reflex to bury the memories. I'm sure it's not permanent. I'll call you in and see if anyone knows anything. At the very least, we'll get you some medical help, okay?"

The man nodded, then sat straight up. "Did you say you have a phone here?"

"I have a radio and a satellite phone. Why?"

"I have this," he said, shaking again and drawing a carefully folded piece of paper out of his pocket. He unfolded it with the utmost care and showed it to her.

Jessie took the piece of paper and looked at it. The paper read: CALL ME ASAP- SARAH (503) 555-7789.

"Based on the area code, this seems to say that you're either from the northern part of the Willamette Valley or at least Sarah is. Somewhere north of Corvallis," Jessie said.

"I need to call her."

"Okay, but how about you get some sleep first? It doesn't seem like anything but your memory is in bad shape and I'm scheduled to make a trip to town tomorrow. How about you call your friend tomorrow morning and I'll take you in? I'll also call into the ranger station in case someone is looking for you, okay?"

"Yeah, that sounds okay. I haven't slept well in a while," said the man slowly, thinking through the proposition.

"Then it's agreed. Now finish that water and get some shut-eye? When you get up, we'll give your friend a call."

The man gulped down the remaining water and lay back. Jessie pulled a blanket over him and then pulled the privacy curtain across the front of the cot, separating it from the rest of the tower. Within minutes, Jessie heard his breathing grow slow and steady as he fell into a deep sleep. She went to her desk, switched on the desk lamp and sat down. Turning up the radio and grabbing the handset, she called the ranger station.

"Headquarters, Tower 256. Headquarters, Tower 256."

"This is headquarters, over," crackled the radio.

"Jimmy, is that you? I thought you'd be out on that fire."

"The one and only. Nah, got stuck on the bench at the District Office for this one. Wish I were, though. So what's up?"

"I have a situation. Over."

"Is it an emergency, 256?"

"Negative. A lost hiker stumbled across my tower. He's dehydrated and a bit banged up, but otherwise physically okay. There is one slight problem, though. He's seems to have trouble remembering how he got here, even his name."

The radio fell silent before crackling to life again. "Can you repeat that, 256? It sounded like you said he has amnesia."

"That's affirmative. I always get the interesting ones. He does have a phone number of a friend to call. The plan is to call her in the morning and have her come pick him up in town. I'll drive him out when you relieve me."

"Affirmative. Are you sure you'll be all right?"

"He seems pretty harmless. I expect him to sleep straight through till morning."

"Received," Jimmy said. "Let me know if you need anything. I'll see you in the morning. Headquarters, clear."

"Thanks. 256, clear." Jessie put down the handset and leaned back in her chair. She looked out across the darkening field. A coyote broke from the woods and moved through the grass in search of a meal.

"It looks like we're both in for a long night."

# CHAPTER 19

The two men helped Cray out of the helicopter and into Sully's house where they set him down on the couch. Russ found some water and forced Cray to drink. Sully, feeling slightly helpless, opted to cook. A few minutes later, Russ smelled steak, eggs, and bacon coming from the kitchen. Sully had also brewed a pot of coffee, its aroma just beginning to infiltrate the house and mix with the smell of bacon.

"Russ, come here. That fire footage is on the TV."

Russ went into the kitchen and found Sully leaning back against the counter, watching a small television. The pictures splashing across the screen showed the fire's utter destruction of the forest. Increased winds out of the southeast had stoked the flames, and it was growing.

"He's really lucky," was all that Sully could say.

Russ nodded and looked back into Sully's living room to see Cray fast asleep.

"Cray's exhausted. Let's eat outside and let him get some sleep."

Sully loaded the plates with food while Russ filled two mugs with coffee. They went outdoors and sat where they had the previous evening. Russ was exhausted too, but decided that food would do him good.

Sully finally broke the silence. "By the looks of that fire, it seems like your little problem might have gone up with the rest of the forest."

"It doesn't seem like anything could have survived that blaze. Heck, Cray almost bought it."

"Do you think you're going to need to find the body?"

"Not sure at this point."

"Do you need to get your buddy to a doctor?"

"No, he seems okay. Just superficial wounds. I think he just needs some sleep and to rehydrate. If you don't mind us crashing here, I'd appreciate it."

"Hell, I hardly ever have visitors, especially old buddies. The visitors I usually get come bearing handcuffs and usually want to arrest me."

They finished their food, recounting old war stories, most of which had taken place in South American jungles where the United States had never been officially at war. Bear sat by Sully, nuzzling his hand with his nose.

After catching a couple of hours of sleep himself, Russ checked on Cray, who was still asleep, and shook him awake. He would need a briefing before he called Carson to report.

It took a few minutes to rouse Cray. He wiped the sleep from his eyes and tried to sit up.

"Stay down," said Russ. "I need to ask what you found, then I want you to go back to sleep. Here, have some more water." Russ handed Cray a glass, which he drained. "I'll get you something for the pain after we talk, okay?"

"Sounds good," Cray replied, exhaustion evident in his voice.

Cray took a deep breath and told Russ what he had seen on the trail through the woods. He spoke of the valley with the river and the shelter he had found—the place where Mercer had evidently been holed up, recovering. Finally, he told him about the fire.

"If Mercer was in that fire, he's dead," Cray said. "It was moving too fast to outrun. Hell, I had a head start but I wouldn't have made it out without you guys."

"So do you think he's dead?"

"Yeah."

"Good. I'll let Carson know. I'll wake you up again in a few hours and we'll get something to eat. Here, take these," Russ said, handing Cray a couple of pills. "Oxy, best thing for pain."

Cray swallowed the pills and Russ stood and quietly left the room. He went outside and looked toward the trees, wondering if he was being watched. He went to the stereo and flipped it on. A Jimmy Hendrix song flowed out of the speakers. Russ, comfortable that his conversation wouldn't be overheard, sat in a folding chair and pulled out his cell phone. The phone rang once before he heard Carson's voice.

"How's our hiker?"

"Alive. I just gave him some pain meds and he's sleeping."

"Good. Did he brief you?"

As Russ retold Cray's story, Carson listened without interrupting. Russ finished by asking, "Do we know how this fire started? What are they reporting?"

"So far they seem to be saying that it was a lightning strike. The federal administration had scheduled a press conference to talk about forest management and they're using this as their case study."

"Lightning? Can we confirm that? It was clear last night, not a cloud in the sky. I'm curious as to how there could have been a lightning strike."

"Interesting. I'll call my contact at the weather service and see if he has any information. Either way, I feel pretty comfortable that our problem's been solved."

Russ hung up and looked at his watch. It was 1830. He looked out to the tree line and studied the forest. He relaxed against the chair and closed his eyes. A few minutes later, he felt cold glass against his cheek. He opened one eye and peered up at Sully, who was holding out a cold beer. Russ smiled and took it.

The two men sat and watched Bear run across the field toward the forest to see if he could find anything, or anyone, to chase.

* * *

After hanging up with Russ, Carson stood and stretched. She had been up most of the night before and had spent the day catching up on work and waiting for news.

"Not quite time to relax," she said aloud, once more manipulating her computer to dial Ashe. The sound of a ringing phone slipped from the computer's speakers, breaking the silence of the afternoon.

"Report," was the only word she heard.

Carson cleared her throat and sat up at the sound of his voice. "Yes, sir. There is a large forest fire burning where we tracked Mercer. We're confident that he's perished in the fire. I will receive a full debriefing tomorrow. O'Neil is now running Green Grass Enterprises and they are back on schedule."

"Good," Ashe said and hung up.

Carson sat back in her chair, feeling once again in his good graces. She was about to turn off her computer when she remembered Russ's question. She found her contact with the National Weather Service. The computer dialed the number and after a few seconds, a man's voice answered.

"Jackson here."

"Hi, Steve. This is Carson. How are you?" Carson said in one of her sweeter voices.

"Holy shit! I'm good. How are you? It's been a while."

"Yes, it has. I'm doing well."

"Great. We should get together sometime. I'm still stationed in Seattle, but I make it down to Portland every now and then."

"Definitely. Hey, the reason I called, other than to talk to your charming self, is to ask you a weather question. I was wondering if you had heard about the forest fire down here in the Mount Jefferson area."

"Yeah, I was actually working on some information for the Forest Service when you called. What's up?"

"How many lightning strikes did you record last night in that area?"

There was a long pause. "Good question. Do you want the official story or the actual data?"

"Is there a difference?"

"Our instruments didn't pick up any lightning strikes last night. However, the Administration determined there was one in the Mount Jefferson Wilderness area. I guess it made better press for their 'healthy forest initiative' than a careless hiker, but you didn't hear it from me."

"Hiker?" Carson repeated, the veins in her neck tensing. "Do you really think a hiker started it?"

"I don't think it was a raccoon, if that's what you're asking. There's a fire ban in that area because it's so dry. What we did pick up were some high winds yesterday morning out of the southeast. It would have been easy for a spark from an unbanked fire to jump into some dry fuel. I know it wasn't lightning so there aren't a lot of other alternatives. I told them that the lightning story was weak, but no one wanted to hear it. Why the big interest?"

"I have an employee who's out hiking in that area and he hasn't called in. I'm concerned. Do you know exactly where that fire started?"

"Pretty close," he said, and read off some coordinates.

After hanging up, Carson sat back in her chair, deep in thought. Suddenly she rose and went to the table where a large map of the Mount Jefferson area lay open. She grabbed the ruler and attempted to find the coordinates Steve had given her. The fire's location was in a depression where several small lakes dotted the landscape. There was a ridge directly to the east, and to the northwest was where Cray had been.

"Damn," she said, shaking her head. "No way. The odds are too crazy." She desperately wanted to believe her own words. Lost in thought, she went to the dry bar in the corner of her office and poured a whiskey, swallowed it, and poured another. "No," she said finally. "As far as anyone knows, he's dead and that's how he's going to stay."

# CHAPTER 20

Ted Kameron stood on the porch, breathing in the morning air, and watching Miguel's pickup truck turn up his driveway and head toward the barn. He jogged over to greet Miguel. "*Hola*, Miguel. *Como estas?*"

"*Bien*. How are you today, Ted?"

"Okay. Just a lot on my mind."

"I know. Let's see if we can't work it out of you," Miguel said. "Let's string some fence."

"Sounds good. I could use a little workout this morning."

The morning's work went smoothly and Ted was happy with the progress. As they broke for lunch, Ted's gaze wandered to the southwest, where a gigantic plume of smoke was rising. The smoke was white and close, different from the dark smoke rising from the forest fire reported in the Cascades.

"Hey, I'm gonna check on the herd," Ted said absently to Miguel, heading for the pickup truck.

"You want me to come?"

"Nah, eat your lunch. I'll be back."

Ted drove to the pasture where the herd they had moved the day before was now grazing. He contemplated how big the fire was in the nearby fields versus the one burning in the mountains. He unloaded the four-wheeler, opened the pasture gate, and sped across the pasture to where the herd had congregated. Ted urged the four-wheeler forward, separating cows out from the herd, counting as he did. Some of the herd was on the far side of the pond.

"130 ... 142," Ted said aloud. "145, 46, 47, 48 ... 49." Ted scanned the area for the remaining cow. He had definitely counted 149 cows this time.

After an hour of looking, Ted was convinced that one cow was missing. He swore under his breath as he sped back to the truck. He loaded his four-wheeler and drove back to his house to pick up the cattle trailer.

After hitching up the trailer, he was struck by an idea and ran into the barn. From a wall cabinet inside his workroom, he pulled out a box full of medical supplies he used on his animals. He also grabbed a cooler and some dry ice packs, and loaded everything into his truck. He ran into the house and emerged a few minutes later with a respirator he had used when painting his dining room. He pulled out of his driveway and drove toward the large plume of white smoke.

Ted arrived at the edge of the smoky pasture fifteen minutes later. The missing cow was nowhere in sight. If it was in the pasture, it might have gone down to the creek. He loaded his equipment and cooler onto the four-wheeler. The air smelled sweet. He began coughing almost the moment he arrived. Ted pulled the respirator over his nose and mouth and put on a pair of goggles to protect his eyes. Ready, he drove the four-wheeler toward the drainage at the far end of the pasture. He saw a large shape lying near the edge of the creek. He hoped the sound of the four-wheeler would cause some kind of reaction in the cow, but it didn't move.

Ted stopped the four-wheeler next to the cow and got off. He quickly checked it and saw that it wasn't breathing. His heart sank.

The smoke grew thicker and the respirator was starting to fail. He pulled the medical equipment from his four-wheeler and opened the bag. Pulling out a syringe and needle, Ted drew several samples of blood from the cow and put them in the cooler.

He took out a scalpel and began cutting away pieces of flesh. He removed several samples of the cow's tissue, put them in different bags, and labeled them.

When he stood up to put the tissue samples in the cooler, he was hit hard by a dizzy spell. He reached for the four-wheeler and held on to the handlebars until the spell passed. He realized that he was coughing, even with the respirator. He only wanted a few more samples.

Ted sprinted to the creek and filed two vials with creek water. He ran to a pool, detached from the running creek, and filled a third vial. His eyes were stinging now and streaming with tears, even with the googles. Stowing the vials in the cooler, he leapt onto the still-running four-wheeler and sped toward fresh air, his coughing subsiding as he approached his truck.

A few minutes later, he was driving down the highway with his windows wide open, sucking in as much fresh air as he could.

Suddenly, a thought leapt into his mind and he slammed on the brakes, his truck and trailer fishtailing to a stop. He quickly turned the truck around and sped back toward the smoke. He turned onto the familiar dirt road with Rachel in the forefront of his mind. The smoke was thick again, but not as bad as it had been in the pasture.

Fresh ash was falling from the sky, enough that Ted made footprints as he went to the house. He fumbled with his keys, then entered the deserted cottage. He turned on the tap at the sink and took two water samples, one of the brown stuff that always bubbled up first and one of what most people considered water. Once the vials were full, Ted went back to his truck. He stopped to stare at the ash floating down and decided to get a sample of that as well. He pulled a Zip-Lock bag from his pack and scooped up as much ash as he could, then sealed and labeled the bag. He got back into his truck and once again drove out of the smoke.

His mind raced as he drove back to his house. He felt like he was breaking the law or doing something dangerous. "All I did," he reassured himself, "was take samples from my own property." But for some reason, the self-talk wasn't helping. The water and ash samples wouldn't be hard to analyze. He still had a friend at Oregon State University who could analyze them for him. He hoped Dia could analyze the tissue and the blood. He'd have to get Miguel to help bury the carcass.

Once home, Ted placed the cow tissue and blood samples in the refrigerator and called Dia. She answered on the second ring.

"Hi Dia, it's Ted from yesterday. Sorry to bother you but I had another cow die from what looks like smoke inhalation. It's smoke from the burning of my neighbor's field."

"Did you take blood samples?" interrupted Dia.

"Um, yeah. That's why I'm calling. I have both blood and tissue samples, I was wondering..."

"I'll be over in an hour. Keep them cold," said Dia.

"Okay, yes. I put them in the fridge."

"Good. See you soon," said Dia, clicking off the phone.

Ted, remembering he had left Miguel, called him and explained. He said he'd have Dia pick him up on her way to the ranch and would just keep working until she arrived. Ted then went to his desk and flipped through his address book. Finding what he was looking for, he called his friend who worked for the soils lab at the university in Corvallis.

"Soils lab, this is Sam," a man said, his voice sounding like he was more at home on a surfboard than in a laboratory.

"Sam, this is Ted. Ted Kameron," he said. They hadn't talked since before Rachel had left.

"Hey, Ted Kameron," Sam said formally, a smile in his voice. "How the hell are you?"

"Good, good. How are you doing?" Ted said relaxing.

"Oh, you know, wishing I was half as baked as my soil samples. It's way too nice a day to be stuck in my lab. When are you and Rachel coming down for a visit? Katie was talking about you guys just the other day, saying how it's been ages."

"You're right. It's been too long. I'm real sorry I haven't called before now."

"Ah, forget it, man. You know, the phone works both ways. So, how are you doing? How's Rachel?"

"That's kind of why I'm calling." Ted recounted what had happened over the last year and how Rachel had left. Then he told him what he had found out the day before.

"Cancer, huh? Leukemia even?" Sam said in disbelief.

"Yeah. Anyway, I'm going out there on Friday to talk to her and offer any support that I can. But I need your help."

"I thought there might be a reason you called me."

"Yeah, I'm worried that something environmental caused Rachel's cancer and that it had something to do with where she was living. You know that cottage my grandparents had? Well, the farm to the west burns its fields, and I've lost two cows in the last week, maybe due to smoke inhalation, maybe not. I went out there today and took some samples of the ash, and water from the creek and well."

"Get them to me. I'll analyze them tomorrow."

"Really? Thanks, Sam, I appreciate it."

"I have an officemate here who does water quality testing. I'll tell him it's my sample and get him to run the tests. That way, I can coordinate the tests we run so if I find something, I can have him look for the same compound."

"Sam, I don't know how I can thank you."

"Same as always, Ted. I work for beer. If you can be down here by six, I'll start running tests tonight."

Ted's spirits rose higher. "I'll be there by six."

"Good. I'll see you then."

Ted hung up his phone and went back to his truck to retrieve the water and ash samples. He was organizing them when Dia and Miguel drove up. Both got out of Dia's car and walked over to Ted.

"Your day got crazy, eh?" said Miguel raising an eyebrow, trying to lighten the mood.

"Just a little," replied Ted, smirking.

Ted explained everything that had happened since he had left Miguel at lunch. Miguel and Dia listened without interruption.

"I'll take care of the cow. I'll take the backhoe down there tonight and bury her," offered Miguel.

"Where are the blood and tissue samples now?" asked Dia.

"I put them in the refrigerator, like you said," replied Ted.

"Good, let's get them. I can take them to the clinic and start running some tests. If we could prove that whatever is in the blood and tissue samples is also found in the water and ash, we'll be able to nail these assholes," explained Dia. "Once I know what kind of poison we are dealing with, I'll start pulling migrant worker medical files, and see if anything turns up. Once I do, *Tio*, I'll need your help to see if you know any of them or their families."

Miguel nodded. "You're doing the right thing here Ted, now get down to Corvallis. I'll take care of everything here."

Ted nodded, and got into his truck, the ash and water samples in the small cooler next to him. Miguel closed his door.

"Be careful," replied Dia. "I'll call you as soon as I know anything.'

"Thanks," Ted said the words seeming not enough. "Really."

"I know," replied Dia.

Ted started his pickup, smiled at both of them, put it in gear, and drove down the driveway.

# CHAPTER 21

**M**orning came early. Jessie had only dozed off once or twice during the night. The man never budged. Jessie stood and stretched, then went to her coffee-maker and started a pot. The sounds of her movement woke him. Jessie heard him turn over, then sit up.

He pulled the curtain out of the way. "What time is it?" he said, wiping his eyes.

"It's about seven. Coffee?"

"Please. It sure smells good. Is there some place I could wash up and ...?"

"Of course. Just climb down the tower and go into the brick building. That's the bathroom. There should be a clean towel down there and some soap. If you open the trunk in there, you might find some clothes."

"Thanks," he said, rising to his feet.

He swayed slightly and Jessie wasn't sure if he was going to remain upright, but he soon got his balance and moved toward the trapdoor. She watched him as he went.

He returned fifteen minutes later, his face clean-shaven and wearing a red T-shirt and a pair of army-issued green shorts. He looked ten years younger.

"Wow! You look a hell of a lot better."

"Thanks. That felt great. I hope you don't mind but I used a disposable razor I found in the bathroom."

Jessie smiled and held out a mug of steaming coffee. "Not a problem. I see you managed to clean up some of your wounds and find some clothes."

"Yeah, quite the collection of clothes in that trunk, but they sure beat the rags I was wearing." He took the cup of coffee from Jessie's outstretched hand.

"I was just about to make some breakfast. Today is the day I get out of here for 48 hours to refill my stores, so it's kind of a buffet-style breakfast of whatever I have left."

"Anything but trout," he joked. "I've been eating a lot of fish."

Jessie laughed and went to her cupboards. She pulled down a can of corned beef hash, then reached into her refrigerator and came out with some eggs and cheese. "Okay. I'll get right on it. Do you want to try calling your friend?"

The man stared at the wrinkled piece of paper with the phone number on it. "I guess I'd rather wake her up than miss her."

"Let's turn the phone on, acquire some satellites, and give her a call." Jessie turned on the phone and held it out.

"Thanks." He reached for the phone, hand trembling, and dialed the number.

"Hello?" came the voice of a woman over the phone.

He fumbled with the handset before answering. "Is this Sarah?"

"Yes. Who is this?" Jessie could hear the woman ask from where she stood.

"This is going to sound crazy, but I don't know who I am. I've been lost in the woods for a few days and can't remember anything, who I am, where I come from. All I have is a piece of paper with your name and phone number on it. Can you help me?"

"Will?" Jessie heard the woman say, surprised. "Is that you?"

* * *

His head spun. *Will.* His name was Will? It sounded familiar. "Is my name Will?"

"Yes," she said, louder than before. "Your name is Will Mercer. Where are you? I'll come pick you up."

"Right now, I'm in a fire tower in the forest, but I can get a ride into town and meet you," he said. Turning to Jessie with a broad smile on his face. "Hi! My name is Will Mercer. Where and when do you think you can drop me off?"

Jessie smiled. "How about noon at the Raven Knot Café in Sisters?"

"Okay," Mercer said. "Sarah? I can meet you at the Raven Knot Café in Sisters at noon."

"Wonderful. I'll bring you home and get you checked out."

"Great. Thanks, Sarah. I can't wait to see you. I hope you can recognize me because otherwise it might be a little awkward."

"I remember what you look like," reassured Sarah.

"Okay, I'll see you soon. Goodbye." Mercer sank back onto the cot and smiled. "How about that breakfast?"

* * *

Sarah Carson hung up her phone, smiling to herself. "That son of a bitch is alive." She dialed the phone again.

"Russ here."

"The bastard is alive. I just talked to him. He called me," Carson ranted.

"Slow down. Who are you talking about?" Russ asked, wiping the sleep out of his eyes.

"Will Mercer just called me. He lost his memory in the crash and doesn't remember who he is. He thinks we're friends. Anyway, I told him I would meet him at noon. I'm going to need you and Cray before that. Is Cray ready to work?"

"He looks pretty good this morning. You're sure he lost his memory?"

"Russ, he didn't even know his own name. But I recognized his voice at once and he's the only person I know who's been lost in the woods."

"Right. Where and when?"

Carson quickly explained the plan and set a meet for eleven o'clock.

"I'll be damned," Carson heard Russ say as she hung up the phone.

# CHAPTER 22

The morning seemed to crawl on forever, as Mercer watched the minutes on the clock in the fire tower tick away at glacial speed. Jessie sat at her desk, typing, looking up every time he checked the clock. She would have taken him into town sooner, but she had to wait for her relief and a truck. Around ten o'clock, she heard the sound of a pickup bouncing around on the poorly maintained gravel road leading up to her tower.

"Our ride's here."

Jessie powered down her laptop and stowed it away in her backpack, which lay in the corner. Then, swinging the pack onto her shoulder, she stood and went to the trapdoor. Mercer quickly followed. She picked up a duffel bag of clothes to be washed and dropped it through the trap door.

Jessie descended the tower stairs just as the truck pulled up next to it. A young man in his early twenties and dressed in a Forest Service uniform got out from the driver's side and reached for a backpack in the bed of the truck.

"Hi, Jimmy. How ya doing?"

"Doing just fine. Glad to get out of the radio room, even if it's just for a couple of nights. How are you and your guest doing?" Jimmy asked.

"We're fine. He called a friend to pick him up in Sisters, so I'm gonna drop him off." She turned to Mercer. "Will, you can go ahead and get in the truck."

Mercer smiled and nodded at Jimmy, then got into the passenger side of the truck.

Jimmy smiled back, then looked at Jessie and raised an eyebrow.

"He's harmless. Just lost."

"If you say so."

"I'll see you in a couple of days," Jessie said, stowing her duffel in the bed of the truck and sliding in behind the steering wheel, placing her backpack between her and Will.

"Let's get you back to civilization," she said to Mercer as she started up the truck.

Mercer looked out the window and smiled as they headed into town. The drive took almost an hour and they arrived in Sisters around eleven o'clock.

Sisters was a quaint small town on the east side of the Cascade Range, which tapped into the tourist trade since it was the first town when crossing the mountains from Portland to Bend. Jessie dropped Mercer off at the restaurant where he was to meet Sarah. They were an hour early and Jessie offered to wait with him, but he told her that she had helped enough and that he didn't want to take up any more of her day off. Jessie gave him her number in case he needed anything and a couple of dollars for a cup of coffee. He thanked her for all of her help and said goodbye.

After watching her drive away, Mercer wandered down Main Street for a while to kill time, looking through shop windows at nothing in particular. Finally, he decided to head back toward the restaurant. He went inside and chose a table along the front windows, in order to see if he could recognize Sarah before she came in the door. When the waitress came over, he ordered a cup of coffee. Sipping his coffee and looking out the window, he wondered how the day would unfold.

\* \* \*

At five minutes of eleven, Sarah Carson pulled into a gas station past the turn off for Camp Sherman, just west of Sisters. She parked behind the building at a truck stop diner, next to Russ's pickup truck. Russ and Cray got out of the truck, and the three went inside. The diner was dim and occupied by a couple of rough -looking men. It was the kind of place where tourists didn't stop or, if they did, left very quickly.

Carson directed them to a table in the corner. Once seated, she took a long look at Cray. "You look like hell."

"Thanks. Good to see you, too."

"I'm glad you're okay. Now to business. As I told Russ this morning, Mercer is still alive. He survived the accident, the river, significant injury, exposure to the elements, and a rather large forest fire. Today his luck ends." Carson spoke in a low voice so only Cray and Russ could hear her.

"Why is Mercer coming in voluntarily?" Cray asked.

"Oh, that's the beauty of it. Head injury. He can't remember anything, not even his name. But he had a slip of paper in his pocket with my name and number on it. He called hoping I could help him," said Carson wryly, a smirk replacing the usual tight lines of her mouth.

"You're shitting me?" laughed Cray. Russ just looked on incredulously.

"So here's the deal. Russ, you and I will go into the restaurant but sit in different places, so he'll think I'm alone. Cray, I want you to wait in the truck. I'll approach him, and Russ will come up behind and we will escort him out of the restaurant, quietly."

\* \* \*

Mercer had drunk a pot of coffee and it was finally having an effect. He went to the restroom, located toward the back of the building. Returning a few minutes later, he stood at the entrance of the hallway to the restrooms to see if he recognized anyone. He was about to walk back to his table when the front door opened and a woman with red hair pulled back in a tight ponytail walked through the door. She scanned the room, looking for something or someone. Suddenly their eyes met, and she smiled.

Mercer felt like he'd been punched in the gut. His head spun and he felt faint. He reached out to the hallway wall to brace himself as memories flashed through his mind—green fields, fire, and smoke. His life came back to him with a tremendous flood of fractured recognition and comprehension. He recognized Sarah Carson and knew that he had to run.

The door opened again and a tall man walked in. Mercer knew him, too—one of Sarah's enforcers. His heart raced as he tried to figure out what to do. Time slowed and seconds lasted minutes. Then a voice deep within his head screamed, "RUN" and he listened.

\* \* \*

Carson saw Mercer standing near the restrooms when she walked in. He looked like a deer frozen in the headlights. Seconds later, Russ walked in. She thought she had seen Mercer flinch. Then he turned and ran.

"What the hell is he doing?" Russ asked.

"I think he just remembered everything. Get him."

Russ pushed past her and ran toward the hallway. Carson stepped back outside and yelled to Cray.

\* \* \*

Mercer, not knowing exactly what he was doing, ran for the men's room. Once inside, he locked the door, then ran for the window on the back wall, opened it, and threw himself through. He crashed into the ground, rolled, and quickly scrambled to his feet. Forcing the renewed pain in his leg back into the recesses of his mind, he ran for the forest that rose up behind the restaurant, knowing only that he had to escape or he'd be dead.

\* \* \*

Cray rounded the side of the building in time to see Mercer disappear into the trees. He ran after him, but his injuries from the fire slowed him down. He pulled the pistol from his jacket and pointed it at the fleeing man. The pistol's silencer tracked the man's retreat and Cray squeezed the trigger several times, but none of the bullets found their target.

Carson and Russ came up behind Cray, who quickly holstered his gun. "That way."

"Russ," Carson said, as if unleashing her hound.

Russ ran toward the tree line in the direction Mercer had gone.

Turning back to Cray, Carson said, "Mercer remembers who we are."

"Aw, hell."

\* \* \*

Mercer ran as fast as he could through the forest. He knew they were chasing him. He thought he heard the soft sound of bullets piercing trees he had passed moments before. His legs burned and his knee ached, but he continued deeper into the woods. Then the survival training that had kept him alive kicked in—*evade*.

He came across a stream that ran perpendicular to the way he was heading. Jumping into it, he ran downstream as fast as he could. His tracks would stop at the water's edge and his pursuer would know he was running the river. He hoped they would guess the wrong direction.

\* \* \*

Russ chased after Mercer, following his trail deeper into the woods. Mercer's tracks stopped at the edge of a stream. Russ searched for any sign of Mercer, but he couldn't tell if Mercer had gone upstream or down. He pulled out his cell phone and dialed Carson.

"I lost him," he said when she answered. "The little fucker is smart. He's running a stream. I can't tell which direction he went. I need Cray, if he can run."

There was a pause, then Carson came back on the line. "Cray's coming. Find Mercer, Russ. Find him and kill him."

"It will be my pleasure."

Russ was kneeling along a stream, examining the ground, when Cray arrived breathing hard.

"Can't tell if he went up or downstream, Cray. Which one do you want?"

"You know me, man. I always go with the flow. I'll take downstream," said Cray trying to catch his breath.

"Okay, stay in contact and be careful. This asshole was a Ranger. And I think he remembers his training."

"Don't need to tell me twice."

The two men split up.

* * *

Mercer ran downstream for what seemed forever. The going was slow as he crawled over downed logs and scrambled over boulders that lay in his way. Willow and other brush scratched his arms and face as he moved. The stream suddenly emptied into a small lake. Mercer's mind worked overtime, his flight response pumping adrenaline into his blood.

Memories were coming back to him like waves crashing against rocks. He remembered his days in the military, his time in Afghanistan, and his years of struggling after being discharged. He remembered being a farm manager in the town of Molalla and that Sarah Carson was his boss. He also remembered running from her men on the night he had his accident, but a lot of that detail was still missing. He hoped it would come to him soon so that he could make sense out of why they were trying to kill him.

He took off his boots and tied them together. With the boots over his shoulder, he dove into the chilly lake. He swam for the far shore, hoping to make it across before his pursuer caught up to him. The swim reminded him of the night he had escaped the bear. The water was warmer than it had been that night, and he had more strength now.

Time was crucial as he pulled for the far shore. He reached it five minutes later and crawled onto the sandy bank. Looking across the lake, he marked the spot where the stream emptied into it. No one was there. He got to his feet and pushed through the thick underbrush that lined the shore, once again disappearing from view.

\* \* \*

Cray struggled to work his way downstream. He wasn't at full strength and was beginning to tire again. He stopped several times to catch his breath and cough up black mucus, a remnant of his flight from the fire. After thirty minutes, his cell phone rang and he sat down heavily on a log to answer it.

"Any sign of Mercer?" asked Russ.

"No, nothing I can say for sure is him. Just seeing a few things that make me think he went this way: a scuffed log, some broken willow branches, and what looks to be recently shifted rocks."

"That's more than I'm finding. I'm going to turn around and head your way."

"Good. I'll keep going. I'm sure you'll catch up." Cray slowly rose to his feet. Muscles aching, he was moving even more slowly now.

A half-mile farther downstream, Cray came to the lake. His heart sank when he saw the expanse of water and no sign of Mercer. He swore under his breath and again sat on a log along the bank. He scanned the distant shoreline for any sign of movement, but saw nothing. The air was still and growing warm.

\* \* \*

After her two henchmen had sprinted off into the woods, Sarah Carson went back to the truck and grabbed several maps of the surrounding area, then returned to the diner. She sat down in a large booth and ordered a cup of coffee, then spread the maps out on the table and tried to figure out where she was, and where Mercer was heading.

An hour passed while she studied the map, tracing with her finger where Mercer had gone off the road and into the river, where Cray had escaped the fire, and where the closest fire tower east of the fire was. Between the tower and Sisters was the fly-fishing village of Camp Sherman. Carson circled the tower and the town.

Her phone, which had been lying on the table, vibrated to life. She picked it up. "Talk to me."

"We're both on his trail. He seems to be heading north-northwest."

"Where are you now?"

"About a mile north of the diner, near a lake."

Carson traced her finger from the approximate location of the restaurant north until it came to rest on a small lake. She circled it, then drew a line from there to Camp Sherman. "Okay, I think I know where he's going. Tell Cray to get back here; he's only going to slow you down. You track Mercer. Call me if he changes direction. We'll meet you on the north side of the forest."

A half hour later, Cray arrived at the diner where Carson was finishing a cup of coffee. A grease-stained brown paper bag and Styrofoam cup of coffee sat on the table. She looked at Cray as he approached. "Here, I got you something to eat," she said, tossing the bag at him.

Cray caught it against his chest. "Thanks." He unwrapped a grilled cheese sandwich and bit into it hungrily.

"Come here and look at this map. This is where I think we can cut him off. Based on the direction he's heading, I think he's trying to make his way back to that fire tower here," she said, pointing to a red circle on the map. "We can cut him off here." She pointed to another red circle around Camp Sherman. "Okay? Let's go."

She folded her maps and stood up. She pulled out some money and threw it on the table, then went to the door. Once outside they climbed into the truck, Cray started the engine and the truck roared to life. He pulled out of the diner's parking lot and sped off to the west.

\* \* \*

Mercer ran for what seemed like an eternity. He was tired and dirty, but he kept his legs moving all the same until he pushed through some dense brush and found himself standing on a gravel road. He took a second to catch his breath, bending at the waist, his hands on his knees. Remembering that south led toward Sisters, Mercer turned and went north. Soon he came across a deserted Forest Service campground. He saw a pay phone, a dinosaur of a bygone era, on a post next to the information sign. He ran to it and picked up the receiver—a dial tone. He fished the piece of paper with Jessie's cell number out of his pocket and dialed the operator. A nasally voice answered.

"I need to make a collect call," Mercer panted into the phone. A few seconds later, the operator connected him to a ringing phone.

"Hello?" A woman answered.

"Is this Jessie?"

"Yes. Who is this?"

"Will. From the fire tower."

"Oh, yeah," Jessie said, her voice softening. "How's everything going? Did you meet up with your friend?"

"I'm in trouble," Will began. "It seems my friend wants to kill me. She just had two guys chase me through the woods."

Jessie was silent.

"Are you still there? I'm sorry, but I don't know who else I can call."

"I'm here. Why is your friend trying to kill you?"

"I'm don't know. I mean, I've been trying to think it through, but just need a safe place to sit and think. I don't want to get you involved, but I don't know what else to do. I don't think I can go to the police. I don't know what I'd say."

"Let me make a few calls. Maybe we can stay at the fire tower again."

"I'm not so sure that's a good idea," explained Will. "Sarah knows I called from one. She'll search all the nearby ones."

"Okay, let me think. I have a friend in Salem I can call. Let me see if we can stay there. Where are you now? I'll come get you."

"I'm somewhere northwest of Sisters in a Forest Service campground. The sign says Riverside Campground," Mercer said, reading the sign in front of him.

"I know exactly where that is. I'll be there in half an hour."

"Thanks. I owe you."

"I'll see you soon," Jessie said, ignoring his last comment.

Mercer stood motionless as the dial tone buzzed in his ear. Finally coming to his senses, he hung up and took in his surroundings. The campground was deserted for the middle of summer, but he couldn't risk being seen. He went back across the road and worked his way through the brush that lined the opposite side. He found an outcropping of rocks a few yards into the woods and decided it would be the safest place to wait for Jessie and still watch the road. He knew that men were still on his trail and hoped Jessie would get there first. He had no idea where Sarah was. He remembered that she was the one to fear.

He crawled onto the outcropping and found a place where he could sit, hidden from view from almost every direction. He needed time to think, time to sort out why they were trying to kill him. He remembered his childhood, doing chores on his parents' hobby farm and growing up running around the forests of northern Minnesota. The farm and his parents had died years ago. He remembered enlisting in the Army and becoming a Ranger. He was sent to the mountains of Afghanistan to fight a new enemy, one more extreme than he had been prepared for. He had put in his time, but had become weary of risking his life to take targets that did little to help the people of Afghanistan or win the war. They took villages from the Taliban, liberating the locals, only to leave the area and let the Taliban back in, punishing the locals for siding with the infidels. He remembered being dishonorably discharged.

He remembered being a transient up and down the West Coast, following the seasons and trying to find some kind of purpose in all of it. It was during this time that a bitterness toward life had taken root like a cancerous cell growing into a debilitating tumor. He met Sarah Carson after responding to an ad for a farm manager in the newspaper. Now she wanted to kill him.

He shifted his weight and a sharp pain jabbed his leg. Wincing, he reached into his pocket and pulled out the key. He had almost forgotten about it until now. It had held no meaning for him when he was lost in the forest, but he had kept it. Now he remembered—the locker at the train station.

His plan had been to take the train to kill time and avoid his pursuers until he could get to the airport and take a flight out later that night. Sarah and her men were too close—Russ and Cray, mean sons of bitches. They had caught up with him at the station. Thinking fast, he had hurried over to some rental lockers, dropped some coins in one, opened the door, and thrown his backpack inside. He looked over his shoulder to make sure no one was watching, took the key, and walked away.

The memory left another clue to his life. The backpack. *If I can just get the backpack, it will tell me the rest.*

Movement in the forest broke his concentration. He craned his neck to get a better view. A man moved stealthily through the trees. "Damn it," Mercer said under his breath.

* * *

Russ had moved quickly through the forest. He stopped when he came to the brush that lined a road and looked around. Seeing nothing, he crept quietly through the undergrowth and knelt so he could scan up and down the road unseen. Confident he was alone; he stepped out onto the hard-packed gravel. He pulled out his phone and called Carson.

"I just came out in some kind of campground. The sign says 'Riverside Campground.' Any idea where the hell I am?"

"Yeah, we know where you are," Carson said, testily. "It looks like Mercer is headed back to the fire tower. It's north of your position."

"What do you want me to do? I don't have the gear to keep this up."

"Okay, head south along the road. We'll pick you up. Then we'll try to cut him off."

"I'm not sure that's the best approach. Asshole's moving fast, but carelessly now. He's leaving a pretty good trail. If we give up that advantage, we might lose him. How about I just hike up the road until I see you, get some gear from the truck, and start back on his trail here? You and Cray can drive around and still cut him off at the tower."

"Fine," replied Carson curtly.

Russ put away his phone and started jogging up the road, away from the campground.

* * *

Mercer watched from his hiding place as Russ pocketed his phone and started up the road away from him. He couldn't hear the conversation but wondered why Russ would abandon the chase. His trail was obvious and he knew it. In fact, had Russ looked around at all, he would've seen footprints leading to the phone, then back across the dusty road.

Feeling like he had a little room to breathe, Mercer leaned back and absorbed the coolness of the rocks through his warm skin. He closed his eyes and settled in to wait.

\* \* \*

Russ had been running for ten minutes when he finally met up with Carson and Cray. Cray saw him coming and pulled off to the side of the road. Russ collapsed up against the truck, trying to catch his breath. Cray offered him a bottle of water, which Russ quickly drained.

"How mad is she?"

"She's fine now. She knows you were right. That was the problem."

"I figured that. It's just that we're so close, we can't make any mistakes."

"I totally agree, partner." Cray opened the back door of the truck and pulled out a bag of food. "Here, picked up some grub for you."

Russ looked in the bag and pulled out a couple of energy bars. "Thanks. From the smell I was afraid you got me a greasy burger."

"That's what I had for lunch. That and a grilled cheese sandwich at the diner."

Carson appeared around the driver's side of the truck. "Did you catch your breath yet?"

"Yeah, what's our next step?"

Carson pulled out a map and unfolded it. "We're right here," she pointed to the intersection of two roads. "You called us from here." She traced her finger across the map until it came to a rest on 'Riverside Campground.' The fire tower is here." She moved her finger north on the map to a red "x."

"That's a ways away," Russ said, almost to himself.

"Yes, it is," Carson snapped, "but it's the only place for him to go."

"I'm not disagreeing with you," Russ said, backpedaling. "It's just an observation, that's all."

"We have company," Cray said. His two comrades looked in the direction he was motioning and saw a green pickup truck coming around the corner and into view. Carson quickly folded the map, grabbed a bottle of water, and leaned up against the truck as though taking a break after a hike. The truck slowed as it approached them. They could now see that it was a Forest Service vehicle. The driver, a young woman, waved as she drove by. Carson, Cray, and Russ waved back. Soon the truck disappeared down the road leaving a small trail of dust.

"Okay, where is that tower again?" Russ asked after the truck disappeared.

"It's near Shitike Butte, to the northeast of Lionshead," Carson said, pointing to the map again.

"Cray, what do we have for equipment?"

"My pack's in the truck. You can travel light but well-equipped. This food and water should restock the rations." He handed Russ another paper bag.

"Good. I only need two more things: more rounds and a spare cell phone battery."

"I'll get them together while you change into some better clothes," Cray said.

"You have five minutes and then we're on the road," Carson barked.

* * *

Jessie pulled the light green Forest Service truck right up to the pay phone, got out, and looked around. A second later, she saw Mercer step from the brush.

"Am I glad to see you," Mercer said in a loud whisper when he finally got to the truck.

"What's going on? Why are you whispering?"

"He was here, no more than a few minutes ago. I don't know where he went."

"Get in. Who's 'he'?" Jessie asked. "How many people are looking for you?"

"There are three of them. The one chasing me is tall, strong, and has black hair."

"What does Sarah look like?"

"Compared to her thugs, she's shorter and has red hair."

Jessie had turned the truck around and was heading south, when it hit her. "Get down" she yelled at Mercer. He obeyed, instantly recognizing the fear in her voice.

Just then, a black truck came into view, heading toward them. It was the same one she had passed fifteen minutes earlier.

"Stay down and don't move."

Mercer did his best to dissolve into the truck's floorboards.

The black truck slowed as it approached but did not stop. Jessie politely waved to the driver, who waved back. She accelerated as soon as they passed. Within minutes, Jessie was out on the main road, heading southwest. She kept looking for the black truck in the rearview mirror, but it never appeared. Feeling safe, she told Mercer he could get up.

"Those were your friends we just passed," she said, answering the puzzled look on his face.

Mercer turned around and looked behind them.

"They aren't there," she said. "We have about an hour's drive, so why don't you do a little explaining?"

Mercer took a few minutes to gather his thoughts, then told Jessie everything he could remember.

* * *

Cray dropped Russ off at the campground, then he and Carson headed back the way they'd come. Russ retraced his steps to the last point where he had seen Mercer's trail. He followed the prints to the pay phone and his stomach tightened as he saw fresh footsteps stop at the pay phone, then double back across the road. Russ followed the trail like a bloodhound after an escaped convict. He saw the outcropping and the disturbed ground where Mercer had hidden.

"That son of a bitch watched me."

He followed Mercer's trail back out to the road where it stopped at a set of tire tracks. "That woman in the Forest Service truck. Shit. She drove him right past us." He pulled out his phone and dialed Carson. "Turn around. The bastard just drove out of here, right past us," Russ said through gritted teeth.

"We'll be there in five minutes," she said.

A few minutes later, the black truck roared up the road, skidding to a stop a few feet from Russ. He climbed into the back, then Cray turned the truck around and they raced back up the road.

"Where are they headed?" asked Cray.

"Who the hell knows," Russ roared. He was more enraged at himself than at Cray.

"We stick to the plan and head to the fire tower," Carson said. "We can assume that woman driving was his contact and she's taking him back there."

# CHAPTER 23

A million thoughts ran through Ted's mind on the drive back from Corvallis. He wondered what his neighbors were burning, if it was the reason for Rachel getting sick, and if she'd be happy to see him.

As he pulled his truck into the driveway, he saw a red Ford pickup he didn't recognize. It looked as if it had just arrived. Ted pulled his truck up to its usual spot and got out. His dog, which had been barking at the strange truck, ran to him, barking over his shoulder. Ted ran his hand over the dog's head to calm him.

"It's all right, boy," he said as he walked up to the pickup. The driver's window rolled down and Ted saw the two men inside.

"Is he friendly?" the driver asked.

"He is now. What can I do for you?"

The truck doors opened and the two men cautiously got out. Ted recognized José from Green Grass Enterprise, but he didn't recognize the driver. "Hey, José. *Como esta?*"

"*Bien, y tu'?*"

"*Bien.* Who is your friend here?"

"Tom O'Neil," the driver said. "I'm the new farm manager at Green Grass. José says that you're an adjacent landowner. I thought I'd come over and introduce myself."

Ted's stomach suddenly dropped. "Nice to meet you. What happened to Mercer?"

"He quit," O'Neil said curtly. "I heard that you lost a cow a couple of days ago. Just wanted to make sure that everything was fine today with the burn."

Ted nervously looked over at the backhoe parked near the barn with fresh dirt still clinging to the teeth of the bucket and thought of the buried carcass in his field.

"I did lose a cow on Saturday, but everything was fine today. José gave me enough notice to move my cattle to another pasture," Ted lied.

"Good. I think we can work together so that those kinds of incidents are avoided in the future."

"Good," Ted said.

"All right, José, let's go. Thanks for your time, Mr. Kameron. It was good to meet you," O'Neil said without the slightest hint of sincerity. He turned and got back into the truck. José looked at Ted with a face that expressed an apology.

Ted watched the truck turn around and drive back down the driveway, before he turned and walked to his house. Once inside, he saw a handwritten note on the table from Miguel letting him know that he had buried the cow. Ted pulled a cold beer from the refrigerator and sat down at his kitchen table, thinking about the note, the samples, and his upcoming trip to Massachusetts. It was still a couple of days away, but already Ted's stomach was tying itself in knots. A few hours and a few beers had past when suddenly, Ted's cell phone rang.

"Hello?"

"You owe me a case of beer, and the good stuff, not that watery crap" came Sam's surfer voice on the other end.

"You already ran the tests?"

"Yep, I scored big time on the first one. The luck of the Irish, I guess."

"Too bad you're a Swede. What did you find out?"

"Benzene."

"What? Are you sure?"

"Yeah. No way to miss it. The levels are off the chart in the ash samples so I had my friend run the water samples for benzene, and he came up with the same thing. I mean, they're a hundred times what the Environmental Protection Agency lists as acceptable. What's going on up there? What are you into?"

"Sam, I'm still trying to figure that out, but I can't thank you enough for this. I don't know what I'm going to do with it, but thanks."

"Not a problem, buddy. Call me in a few days and I'll have the official results by then but I think benzene's your problem. I'll email you what I do have in the morning." The phone clicked off as Sam hung up.

Ted sat in silence, looking at his phone. Then snapping out of his mood, he quickly called Dia.

"Benzene. They detected large amounts of benzene in the ash and water," Ted said when she answered the phone.

"What? How did you get the results so fast?"

"My friend said he got lucky on the first test. Is it something you can test the blood and tissue samples for?"

"*Si.* I started running some comprehensive tests this afternoon, but we'll start analyzing them for benzene first thing tomorrow," replied Dia.

"Thanks. I should get the official results from the water and ash samples in a couple of days. But I think tonight, I have some research to do."

"Send me anything you turn up, okay?" said Dia.

"I will," said Ted thanking her again for her help and hanging up. Then he grabbed his half-ful beer and quickly went to his office. Powering on his computer, he sat down in front of it and started working.

He Googled the term "benzene." Almost immediately, he was directed to the EPA's home page. A few seconds later, the search engine logged a number of hits for the substance.

"Okay, here we go," Ted said aloud.

"Benzene is a clear, colorless, highly flammable liquid. It's used for making plastics, rubber, and resin, among other things. It's a known carcinogen and a mutagen. Exposure to benzene can irritate the eyes, nose, throat, and skin. It can also cause dizziness, lightheadedness, headache, and vomiting. At high levels of exposure, it can cause convulsions, coma, or sudden death from irregular heartbeat. Short-term effects include nervous system disorders, immune system depression, and anemia. Long-term effects include chromosome aberrations and cancer. There is some evidence that benzene might be a reproductive hazard as well. There is also evidence that it is teratogen in animals—a substance that can cause birth defects, including miscarriages."

Ted finished reading and hung his head in his hands.

"It's my fault."

Ted rose from the computer, and this time grabbed the bottle of Knob Creek bourbon from his dry bar. He wandered downstairs and back outside where the night was warm and frogs and crickets sang to the stars. Ted sat on the porch and looked out into the darkness. His thoughts drifted to earlier that morning and the smoke, then to Rachel. He woke up several hours later, still sitting on the porch, the bottle half gone. The cold night air was beginning to stiffen his joints. He got up and went to bed, not bothering to undress, and fell into a fitful sleep filled with fire and smoke.

# CHAPTER 24

Mercer explained as much as he could while Jessie drove. There were large gaps in his story. A lot of his recent past was still a blur. He explained his time in the army, how he had worked as a farm manager, and that Sarah Carson was his boss. He seemed fuzzy on this point because he was sure that she didn't own the farm; she just oversaw operations. She was one step above him. He also told Jessie how they would always burn the fields this time of year, whether they needed to or not. He jumped forward in time to his run from Carson and her thugs, his trip to the train station, and the attempt to outrun them in the mountains.

"Why are they trying to kill you?" asked Jessie, deadpan.

He pulled out the key and showed it to her.

"I think I took something. I'm pretty sure that whatever's in the backpack in this locker is what they're after." He looked out his window at the passing forest. "Who did you say we were meeting?"

"A friend of mine. Jeffrey Pennoyer. Most of his friends call him Pen. Everyone else calls him Jeff."

"What do you call him?"

"Let's just say I'm the one who started calling him Pen."

"I see," Mercer smirked.

Jessie saw his reaction. "No, it's not like that. We were an item a long time ago but we both went our separate ways. Now we're just friends." The words seemed awkward. "He has a place in Salem. Don't worry, I trust him completely."

"What does he do?"

"He's an environmental attorney. Just graduated and passed the bar in February. He might be of some help to you."

Mercer nodded and turned to look out the window. Soon Jessie noticed that he had drifted into a restless sleep. She could only imagine the dreams and nightmares he was struggling through. She wondered whom she had picked up in the woods. She felt safe with him, but his story didn't make sense. How did this guy get messed up with people trying to kill him? She also wasn't sure what mess she was getting her friend into. She fought the urge more than once to drive him to the nearest police station. An hour later she caught movement out of the corner of her eye.

"Where are we?" Mercer asked groggily, wiping the sleep from his eyes.

"Just turned onto Interstate 5."

"I really appreciate everything you've done for me. I can't begin to repay you."

"You were in trouble. What was I gonna do? Leave you there? We'll be at Pen's in twenty minutes. Don't worry. There's no way your friends are going to find you. Then we can all figure out what to do next."

A little while later, Jessie's cell phone rang. "Pen?" she said, answering it. "We should be there in a minute. Where are you? ... Is the key in the same place? ... Okay, we'll see you then. And thanks." She hung up her phone.

Jessie pulled her truck off the main road and into a cul-de-sac lined with single-family homes and row houses. A new development, everything clean and fresh.

Mercer got out of the truck and Jessie found the spare key, unlocked the front door, and went inside. Mercer followed, looking over his shoulder across the quiet street.

Jessie fumbled around in the house turning on lights. Soon they heard a car pull up. Mercer half-stood at the sound.

"Relax. You're safe here. There's no way they could find you," Jessie reassured him.

Jessie, hearing a car door slam, got up and went to the front door. She opened the door and the man on the porch smiled broadly at her.

"Jess, it's been a while."

"Too long. How are you?"

He flushed a little under her gaze but managed to keep his composure. "I'm good. I have some groceries in the car. Give me a hand?"

She followed him out and helped him unload his Subaru.

Mercer waited and held the door open for them. Pen smiled and said hello as he passed, working his way to the kitchen.

"I picked up a couple of frozen pizzas and some salad fixin's. I figured you, of all people, would be tired of canned food and might want something green and fresh."

"Thanks," said Jessie.

Pen pulled the pizzas from the bag and set them on the counter. "These should be ready in about twenty minutes," he said, reading the directions on the box. He turned on the oven to preheat it. "In the meantime, how about a beer?" He reached into another bag and pulled out a six-pack of beer. He handed one to Mercer and one to Jessie, then pulled one out for himself.

Jessie opened her bottle and took a long drink. "That's good."

Pen lifted his bottle for a drink while eyeing Mercer. "So, what's going on?"

"It's a long story," Jessie said, looking toward Mercer. "I found Will wandering toward my fire tower yesterday, pretty dehydrated and beat-up," she began.

"You mentioned on the phone that someone was after him and you needed a place to hide out," Pen interrupted. "I think I need the whole story, and I need to hear it from him." Pen turned to Mercer. "You see ... Will, right? You see, Will, Jessie is a very dear friend so I need to know what kind of trouble you are in and whether or not you have put Jessie in harm's way."

Mercer had been looking at Pen, but quickly found a more interesting spot on the floor.

"Cut out that macho, protectionist, Neanderthal bullshit," Jessie said. "You're not my guardian."

"You're right. I'm not, but I care about you. You're a friend and you are now in my house, so I need to know what we're facing."

"Listen," Mercer said, cutting off Jessie, who was about to verbally slap Pen, "I'll tell you everything I know. And you have to believe that if I could have avoided getting any of you involved, I would have."

\* \* \*

Mercer retold his story, as much as he could remember from the time before the accident to his journey through the forest to his latest encounter with Carson and her thugs. When he finished, he pulled out the locker key and set it on the table.

"I didn't have much on me and my memory still has holes, but I think that whatever is in this locker will help me piece things back together."

Pen sat in silence for a long time, analyzing the tale he had just heard. The timer on the stove went off, breaking his concentration. Jessie rose and went to the kitchen to take the pizzas out of the oven.

"Okay, so you need to stay here for a few days," Pen said. "I'm going to take that key and go check out the locker. You and Jessie sit tight and I'll be back in a few hours. I agree that we need to know what's in that locker," Pen said as Jessie came back with plates of pizza.

"Wait a minute," she protested. "Those thugs could be watching the locker."

"I don't think so," Pen said. "If what you both said is true, and I tend to think it is, they're still somewhere down by Sisters. If that's the case, then no one is watching the locker and I should be able to slip in and out. I'll be back in two hours, tops."

"I really can't ask you to do that for me. You've both already risked enough just letting me be here."

"I guess it's a good thing you're not asking, then," Pen said wryly. "Give me the key."

Pen took a couple of slices of pizza for the road, then drank the last two swallows of his beer. Mercer handed him the key, to which Pen winked and gave a half-smile. "Just save me some beer, okay?" Then he turned around and headed for the door.

Jessie followed Pen out onto the porch, closing the door behind her. She grabbed his arm as he headed for the stairs. "Be careful, okay? I'm not sure what I think anymore, but I do know that he has crossed some very dangerous people."

"I'll be careful. I'll call you when I get to Union Station and when I'm headed back." He pulled Jessie close to him and whispered, "You be careful, too. Something isn't right with him and I'm not sure what it is. There's a shotgun upstairs in the back of the closest in the master bedroom. Shells are in a box on the shelf above it." He turned and went down the stairs.

* * *

The black pickup skidded to a stop along a graveled Forest Service road. Carson had ordered Cray to stop and he had hit the brakes too hard.

"Jesus! Whose side are you on?" Carson yelled. She had bounced off the dashboard and her computer slid off her lap.

"Sorry. Sorry. The brakes are a little touchy."

"Why are we stopped?" Russ asked from the backseat.

Carson gathered up her computer and maps and settled back onto her seat. "The fire tower is about a mile up this road, but it looks like the road is visible once we make the next bend. I want you two to go the rest of the way on foot and find out if he's up there."

The two men nodded and got out of the truck. Grabbing his pack from earlier, Russ started up the trail. Cray followed, checking the weapon holstered under his arm. They stuck to the tree line. Several times the tower came into view, but was too far away to see anything in detail, even with binoculars.

Twenty minutes later, they approached the end of the gravel road. They scanned the area but didn't see any sign of the green pickup truck. Russ searched the road for tracks and discovered a set of tire tracks heading toward the tower and then back down the road from where they had just come.

They knelt by the side of the road. "I think they've been here and left again," Russ said, pointing to the road. "Tire tracks coming and going."

Cray fixed his binocular on the fire tower. "He's in there, Russ. He's in the tower. I just saw a guy walk in front of the window."

Cray tossed Russ the glasses and Russ held them up. A smile broke across his face when he saw the man's back through the binoculars. "I'll be damned."

The two men worked their way back down the road to where they'd left Carson.

"What did you find?"

"He's up there," Cray said, excited.

"We think the woman might have dropped him off and headed back to town," Russ said. "Maybe for supplies or something, but we saw him walking around in the tower."

"Good," she said. "Let's wait until dark, take the rifle up there, and finish the job. Russ, I want you to take the shot."

"With pleasure, this guy has been a pain in my ass for far too long."

They waited in the truck for the sun to set. Nerves tightened and adrenaline seeped into Russ and Cray's bodies as darkness began to edge its way into the forest.

Finally, Carson broke the silence. "Time to go. Take the bastard down."

Russ and Cray got out and went to the backdoor of the truck. Russ pulled out a rifle with a noise suppressor screwed into the end of it.

"Got the night scope?"

Russ tapped the scope attached to the rifle. Cray nodded and the two men began to move silently up the gravel road. They covered the distance quickly this time with darkness eliminating their need for caution. As they rounded the final bend, they could see the fire tower lit from within and heard the dull hum of a generator.

The two men, no more than shadows, crouched behind tall bushes lining the road. They watched the tower for movement, but the man that had been inside wasn't visible. Then they heard what sounded like a wooden door shutting and a shadow move from the brick building back toward the fire tower. As the man began to climb the tower stairs, his silhouette was visible in front of the rising moon.

Russ raised the rifle and targeted the man. He could see the shape of the man through the scope, but because of moonshine, his features were not distinguishable. He held the outline of the man in the crosshairs as the target climbed the tower stairs. Then Russ relaxed his finger and lowered the rifle.

"Bad angle. See if you have a better shot." He handed the rifle to Cray and moved a little further away from him.

Cray took the rifle and aimed at the man now standing at the top of the stairs. Cray squeezed the trigger and a muffled shot hissed through the air. Instantly, the man on the tower crumpled and slid backwards down the stairs.

"Never knew what hit him," Cray said proudly as he watched the now motionless man on the tower through the scope.

"Let's go check it out."

Cray shouldered the rifle and the two men cautiously approached the tower.

The man had fallen down one flight of rusted metal stairs and lay on a landing. Russ was the first to see him.

"Shit."

"What?" Cray asked, catching up. Suddenly, the dead man's features were visible. "Who the hell is that? And where the hell is Mercer?"

Russ rolled the body over and as he did, both men got a glimpse of the Forest Service uniform and badge. Russ was silent for a few seconds until a thought finally hit him. "He's the replacement. We just killed the replacement fire spotter. They never came back here."

The two men stood over the body, wondering what to do next. The faint ringing of a phone broke the silence. Russ was the first to recognize the sound. He sprinted up the remaining stairs and burst up through the tower's trap door. He scanned the square room and spotted the phone sitting on a long table. Grabbing it, he clicked it on.

"Yeah," Russ said softly.

"Hi, Jimmy. It's me, Jessie. Listen, I'm not going to be able to get back tomorrow. I have an emergency I need to deal with. Can you cover?"

"Yeah. Where are you?"

"Jimmy, are you okay? You sound kind of weird."

"Just tired from working that fire," Russ said, trying to make a good story. There was silence on the phone. Jessie spoke again, but this time more slowly.

"Tired from being out on that fire-line?"

Russ answered before he could stop himself. "Yeah, it was a bad one."

"Who is this?" Jessie suddenly demanded. "And where is Jimmy?"

Russ instantly realized the game was up. "Was that his name? Your friend is dead, and you're next if you don't give up Mercer." Then he was listening to a dial tone.

* * *

Jessie dropped the phone and it clattered on the hardwood floor. Mercer grabbed her as she swayed on her feet and guided her to a chair. The blood drained from Jessie's paling face and her hands trembled.

"What happened? Who was that?" Mercer asked, kneeling in front of her, but Jessie was in shock and just stared at the floor. "Jessie. Jessie," he said in a sterner voice, trying to pull her from herself and the emotional blow she was experiencing.

"Jimmy," she finally said in a quiet voice.

"What about Jimmy?" Mercer asked, his voice turning soft, but Jessie was replaying the phone conversation over and over in her head, trying to sort out the insanity of the situation.

"They ... they killed him." she finally blurted out. "They must have thought he was you." She dropped her head into her hands and sobbed.

"Jessie, what did they say?"

"They said that if I didn't give you up, I'd be next."

"We need to call the police. They are probably still out at the tower," said Mercer.

Suddenly a fire from somewhere in the bottom of Jessie's stomach started to burn. She wiped her eyes and grabbed her computer, booting it up. Quickly hacking into Pen's internet network, she placed a call to the Sisters' police department.

"Why not just use your cell phone?" asked Mercer, a look of confusion on his face.

"Traceable. Not taking any chances," Jessie said as she typed.

Suddenly a voice came through the laptop speakers. "This is the Sisters Police Department. How can I direct your call?"

"There has been a shooting at Forest Service Fire Tower 256. The Forest Service employee's been shot. Shooters still on-site," Jessie said quickly into her laptop's microphone.

"Excuse me?" came the female voice of the dispatcher. "Who is this?"

"Forest Service Fire Tower 256. Get units there now," demanded Jessie, who then cut the connection.

\* \* \*

Pen headed north on Interstate 5. Then a quick exit in the Rose Quarter and he was driving through Portland, heading for the Broadway Bridge, over the Willamette River, and to Union Station on the other side. Traffic was light and with the window down, the cool summer night air felt good on his face.

Pen heard Jessie's warning that the locker might be being watched and was taking it seriously. He had called the station on the way into Portland and found out that a train from Seattle was due in at 9 pm. It was the last one for the night, and no outbound trains were scheduled. He thought if there were people in the station when he went to retrieve whatever was in the locker, he was less apt to be spotted or confronted.

He checked his watch as he waited for a traffic light to turn green. It was ten minutes of nine and he was three minutes from the station. Plenty of time to get a parking spot and scope out the locker.

A few minutes later, he pulled into the parking area for Union Station. There were a few people hanging around outside Wilfs, the restaurant that abutted the train station, but the station itself seemed deserted. He wandered inside and as aimlessly as he could strolled toward the row of lockers. Leaning against the closest one, he looked at his watch, then scanned the interior of the building.

Pen hoped to look like someone's partner who was there to pick up a passenger. A young couple stood against the far wall and an older couple sipped coffee on one of the long benches. The only other people in the large, cavernous room were a woman in shorts and T-shirt and what looked like a homeless man sleeping on one of the benches.

He reached into his pocket and fished for the key. He pulled it out, read the number on it, and then balled it in his fist. He was counting lockers when a man's voice came over the loudspeaker announcing the arrival of the Seattle train. Just a few more minutes. Pen slowly worked his way down the row of lockers, his back to them, trying not to draw any attention, until he was near the one he hoped to open. He leaned against the lockers and quickly scanned their numbers. The one he wanted was one to his right.

People began to trickle in from the platform. When the room had finally filled, Pen made his move. Key in hand, he turned and slipped the key into the lock, opened the door, and grabbed the backpack stuffed inside. He quickly slung it over his shoulder, and headed for the exit. He looked over his shoulder once but no one appeared to be following him. Slipping into the crowd exiting the building, Pen was just another traveler arriving home. He walked briskly back to his car and got in.

\* \* \*

Russ was still in the fire tower thinking about their next move when his cell phone rang. "Yeah."

"It's me, Connor. You told me to call you if someone opened the locker. I've been sitting in this train station for a week, acting like some homeless son of a bitch, watching a stupid locker. I'm calling to tell you that some guy just walked in here, opened it, then left with a backpack. I expect to see the money wired into my account within two days."

"You'll get your money, you little weasel. First, tell me what the guy looked like. Was he with a woman?"

"No, he was by himself. He was about six feet tall and pretty thin, like a runner or something. He had black hair and glasses."

"That's not the guy we're looking for," Russ said, his mind racing. *Who the hell was this?*

"I followed him outside and got a photo and a partial license plate. Sorry if this isn't the news you wanted, but it's all I have."

"Text me the picture. I need to know who this guy is." He hung up and stared out the tower's window into the darkness. "I think things just got worse."

\* \* \*

Pen didn't completely trust Mercer and he wanted time to look at what was in the backpack. He turned onto Natio Parkway and drove toward Interstate 5. It was a quick drive to Lewis and Clark College's law school, where he had spent the last three years of his life. Ten minutes later, he pulled into the law school's temporary parking area and turned on his flashers. He went to the library and found a desk hidden behind the long rows of books. The library, deserted this time of year, contained only a few people enrolled in summer classes.

Pen sat at the desk and unzipped the backpack. It contained a number of manila folders and a couple jars of what appeared to be soil. He left the jars in the bag and pulled out the stack of folders. Flipping open the first one, he scanned the pages.

The first folder contained fertilizer invoices for a farm in Molalla. The invoices looked fine at first glance, but then Pen noticed that the fertilizer listed did not have a name brand or chemical breakdown associated with them. He noticed something else as well: The dates these fertilizers were delivered—although spanning several years—began in mid-summer. He didn't know much about farming, but wasn't the time to apply fertilizer in the spring, during planting?

Pen closed the folder and opened the next one. Field burning applications, permits, and inspection reports covering the last ten years, filled the folder. They looked to be standard state forms. However, there was something very peculiar about the dates. He pulled out the first folder again and opened it. A burn inspection report was issued five days after every shipment of fertilizer was received. He wasn't sure if there was a connection yet, but it piqued his interest.

The next folder contained only a map of the region. The map was marked with a number of different-colored dots. The map didn't have any kind of legend to explain it, and it wasn't detailed enough to provide any specific locations.

The fourth folder contained water quality and soil analyses, but Pen didn't understand what he was reading so he closed that folder and opened the last one. The last folder contained a single sheet of paper, a typed letter.

> Ms. Carson:
>
> I have worked for you for five years now and in that time have come to understand your operations. I have waited for the promotions and raises that I was promised over that time, though I have not seen any additional benefits. I have sufficient information that the authorities might be very interested in reviewing. My demands are simple: I have reviewed the law and fully understand how much chemical disposal would cost and how much fines and penalties would be if caught. Therefore, I feel that $500,000 is a fair price for my silence, my information, and my resignation. I await your response.
>
> Will Mercer

Pen read the letter several more times before sitting back and removing his glasses. He rubbed his eyes, then checked his watch. It was time to get back to Jessie. He didn't know for sure whether or not Mercer was telling the truth about his memory, but he was sure there were very dangerous people after him.

Gathering up all of the papers, Pen stuffed them back into the backpack. He got to his feet, suddenly exhausted. He was halfway out the door when a thought crossed his mind. Turning around, he went back to a stack of books and searched for one on hazardous waste law that he had read before in a class taught by the author, a local professor. Pen checked it out and left the library.

The drive back to his rowhouse in Salem took an hour. He parked the car, grabbed the backpack, and went inside. Seeing him, Jessie ran into the living room from the kitchen and threw her arms around him. He saw that she had been crying. She held him as though afraid to let go. Then Jessie began sobbing. Pen tried to comfort her as best he could.

"What happened?"

"Jimmy. It's Jimmy. They killed him," she said between sobs. The pain was still too fresh. "It's my fault."

"Wait, what? Who's Jimmy?"

"He was my replacement at the fire tower, a friend of mine, and they killed him," choked Jessie.

"Are you sure? Start at the beginning. What happened?"

Jessie shuddered from her sobs. "I called Jimmy to tell him I wasn't going to get back tomorrow and another man answered the phone. He said he had just killed Jimmy and that I was next if I didn't give Will up."

"What did you say?" asked Pen.

"Nothing, I just hung up. Then I called the police in Sisters."

"Good, maybe they'll catch them. It's not your fault, Jess," Pen assured her. "It's not your fault. You couldn't have known."

He looked around and noticed for the first time that Mercer was nowhere to be seen. "Jess, I have a very important question to ask you. Where is the shotgun?"

"What?" Jessie asked, still overwhelmed by emotion.

"The shotgun. Is it still upstairs?"

"Yes."

"I'll be right back."

He broke their hold, ran up the stairs to the master bedroom, and opened the closet. Reaching into the back of the closet, he pulled out a Mossberg twelve-gauge shotgun. He grabbed a couple of shotgun shells off the top shelf, and quickly loaded the gun. Then he turned and went back downstairs.

"Where is he, Jess?" Pen asked softly.

"He went out on your back deck to get some air, right before you came back. What's going on? What's that for?" Jessie said pointing at the gun, her voice rising.

"I got his backpack, Jess. I'm not so convinced our friend is innocent in all this."

Just as he finished speaking, Mercer came in through the back door. Pen raised the shotgun level with Mercer's chest. Mercer froze in his tracks, his eyes growing large.

"I got the backpack, Will. I've read all of the papers. You have some explaining to do, whether you can remember or not. Sit down over there." Pen motioned to a chair with the barrel of the shotgun.

Mercer did as he was told.

Pen tossed the backpack onto Mercer's lap and told him to take out the folders. "I'm going to give you time to read through them, but I'm particularly interested in your explanation regarding the last folder."

\* \* \*

Mercer pulled the folders out and began opening them. He read the letter in the last folder first. Then he flipped through the remaining folders before returning to the letter. He read it again. He held his head in his hands, rubbing his eyes and rocking slightly back and forth. Memories flashed through his mind. He remembered being in the Army in a special unit that went out for weeks at a time, traveling light, tracking and attacking Taliban positions regardless of the casualties, enemy or civilian. It had hardened him, killed the good-natured man he was and reduced his morals to a pile of kill or be killed ashes. He watched his friends die around him on ill-planned missions to take and secure targets that high command would just give back a week later.

Returning to base, to a more normal military life, proved harder and harder—as did following the orders. Finally, he couldn't take anymore, hit a superior, and was dishonorably discharged, allowing his military life to come to an end. Disenchanted with life, he sought to take from the world what he felt was owed to him. It had been a dark time, drifting up and down the West Coast, bouncing drunks at biker bars, enforcing for petty criminals, and all the time looking for a big score.

Waking up one morning in a run-down motel outside of Bakersfield, California, bloody, bruised, and nursing a knife wound from a bar fight the night before, he decided it was time to move on and find something more permanent and honest. He headed north to Oregon.

He knew something wasn't quite legitimate about Green Grass Enterprises when he responded to the advertisement and interviewed for the job. The money was a little too high for a farm manager, and the expectations were low. He had been around farms growing up in rural Minnesota, but he wasn't a farmer. That didn't seem to matter to Carson. She wanted someone who could keep things moving and quiet and she would pay for it.

He knew they were breaking the law after the first season, but he stayed. They over-applied what they called fertilizer and then burned it off. He and his men had to wear full hazmat suits, which they had been told was just company policy. Mercer knew better. He saw his golden ticket, and approached Carson more than once on advancement into her inner circle. Each time, he was met with empty promises. Finally, he decided it was time to take what he thought was his.

Mercer shook the memories from his head and looked up. He didn't recognize the man in those memories, even though deep down he knew he had done those things.

"I have no explanation," he said, his eyes dropping to the floor. "All I know now is that I brought this trouble on myself and not for any reason other than greed."

"What is he talking about?" Jessie asked.

"Why don't we let him try to explain it to us? I think I have a pretty good idea, but I want to hear it from him," said Pen.

Mercer tried to start a sentence, then thought better of it. Finally, he found a way to begin his story.

"I'm not sure where to start," he said, "My memory has started coming back in bits and pieces, and I'll try to string as much of it together as I can. I don't recognize who I am, was. This isn't me," Mercer started holding up the folder, a pleading look in his eyes. "I was in a car accident Friday night. I woke up in the forest and couldn't remember anything. I remember things now. I'm an ex-Army Ranger, and my survival training that had been drilled into me so hard it became instinct kept me alive and led me to Jessie.

"I had no idea someone was trying to kill me. Seeing Sarah today brought my memories crashing back, but I'm still trying to get things in the proper order. I'm still struggling with the idea that I'm the man who wrote this letter and who was knowingly involved with these people. I have memories of being mean and cruel, but I don't feel like that's who I am. It's like watching someone else's life.

"Okay," said Mercer taking a deep breath, "I was the farm manager for Green Grass Enterprises in Molalla, Oregon. We were a grass farm, or at least that was how we were set up, though as you can tell from these financial records we never made a profit. Hell, we didn't even cover the salaries of the employees.

"I'm not sure who paid the bills," Mercer said replying to the unasked question on Pen's face.

"My job was to run operations at the farm. The bulk of the work came during the summer field-burning season. We would burn all of our fields during the open-burn windows, often when the fields didn't need it. Sometimes even after they had already been burned, which was kind of a neat trick. Before each burn, we would get a load of fertilizer treatment to apply to the field a few days prior.

"For a long time, I wondered why I had gotten the job. I didn't have any real farming experience, I was ex-military. Like I said, an Army Ranger, and a pretty good one. I just got tired of taking orders, watching my buddies die, and seeing others profiting from my loyalty. After my discharge, I was in a downward spiral. Maybe it was a little PTSD, I don't know. After drifting a bit, I saw this job and thought it would be a good opportunity to do some clean, solid work."

"When they hired me they told me there was room for advancement. It turns out it was just an empty promise. I quickly realized that I was just back to taking orders without question, though what I was ordered to do in my new job was never legal."

"Did you ever try to get out?" Pen asked.

"I think that is what I was trying to do, but by blackmailing them. Not the smartest idea I've ever had."

"So you're saying that you're the good guy here?" Pen asked.

"No. I'm not. At least, wasn't. That's not me. I know you have no reason to believe me. I know that I'm better than that." Mercer mumbled staring at the floor, ashamed.

* * *

They sat in silence for a long time until Jessie finally spoke.

167

"So you were a good guy, then an asshole, and now a good guy again? You sound like half the men I date."

"Jessie, this is serious," said Pen.

"You don't think I know that," scolded Jessie. "My friend was murdered because they thought he was Will. Yeah, I get that it's serious. But, I also believe Will. I have a pretty good asshole-meter and if he was still the guy he's describing, all my alarms would be going off. They aren't. I think he's being earnest. Maybe the accident knocked some sense into him. Who knows? But I want to deal with what's in front of us and not behind us."

Pen began to speak and then thought better of it.

"Let me see the folders," said Jessie.

Mercer handed them over, refusing to meet her eyes. Jessie took the folders and began flipping through them.

"What's this map?"

Pen sat up. "I forgot about the map. It lacked any written information so I only scanned it."

"I think it's where they have other operations," Mercer said. "My farm is a green dot, but I'm not sure what the other colors mean."

Jessie studied the map. "Pen, look," she said, pointing to a place on the map. "This is in the middle of Gifford Pinchot National Forest. And this one is in the Ochoco." She traced her finger along the paper.

"Are you sure? How can you tell?"

"Look at the major highways. They're pretty much the only thing on the map. They kind of mark national forest boundaries. These sites are either in the forests or on property adjacent to the boundaries."

"I'm guessing that our friend here might be a little fish in a big, nasty pond," Pen said, motioning to Mercer. "Okay. I'm not sure how I feel about this. It doesn't sound like you were the greatest guy. And I have to tell you that I'm not too keen on polluters. But if we turn you in, then those in charge might be able to slip through the cracks, and if they catch you, they will kill you. So it seems like we don't have a lot of options."

"I'll just go. I'll take my chances on my own. You've already done too much," Mercer got to his feet as though to leave.

"Sit down," Jessie said. "You're not going anywhere. First, your old co-workers just killed a friend of mine, and they need to pay for that. Second, Pen is going to need your help to break up this ring, or whatever it is they're doing."

Pen and Mercer looked at Jessie upon hearing reason number two.

"What are you talking about, 'breaking up their ring'?" Pen asked.

"They're breaking I don't know how many environmental laws," Jessie said. "And you, my friend, just happen to be an environmental lawyer. And as of this moment, I'm your client. They are ruining the forests and God knows what else, Pen. We need to stop them. I'm so tired of Big Business' belief that public resources like air, water, and forests are here for their personal gain. It seems clear that the federal government isn't going to take a hard line with these companies so it falls to the courts to fix it. In order to do that, I need an attorney. And you're him."

"Twenty-four hours," said Pen quietly.

"What?" asked Jessie.

"I said, 'twenty-four hours' then we turn him and everything we have into the police. I will spend that time trying to sort out the legal issues. Will, I'm not sure what to think about you, but what I do know is that they're trying to kill you, and now Jessie. We can help stop them, so no matter what your intentions are, or were, I think we need each other."

Mercer looked up for the first time in almost an hour. "I can't explain or expect forgiveness for my past actions. All I can do is make sure I don't make the same mistakes and try to make things right. I'll do whatever you tell me."

"How about making a pot of coffee?" Pen said. "I'm gonna be up late."

Mercer nodded, a smile spreading across his face.

"Thanks, Pen. What should we do while you're working?" Jessie asked.

"I want Will to write down everything he can remember about the operations and who was involved. I'm also really interested in some of the coinciding timelines that seem apparent from the documents in the folders. See if you can chart them out. Then, get on-line and see if you can't pinpoint with a little more accuracy where those colored dots are located."

"I'll be upstairs." Pen shouldered the shotgun and grabbed his own backpack, which housed his computer and the book from the law library. He stopped halfway up the stairs. "I think we're going to need to move into my office tomorrow so I have better access to resources."

Jessie and Mercer nodded in agreement and Pen disappeared up the stairs.

Jessie made a work area at the kitchen table while Mercer made coffee. "I'm really sorry that I got you into this. I never meant for anyone to get hurt. I'm really not that guy."

Jessie stopped what she was doing. "I believe you, but you need to prove it. We have some work to do, and you need to focus on putting your memories back together."

# CHAPTER 25

The walk back to Carson was a slow, quiet one. Cray still wasn't sure exactly what had happened, and Russ was wondering how he was going to spin it. Seeing them approach, Carson got out of the truck and met them in front of it.

"Success?" she asked curtly. Seeing Cray look to Russ for the answer, Carson knew something was wrong. "What happened?"

"They weren't there," Russ said.

"What do you mean? You said that someone was up there?"

"Yeah, but it wasn't Mercer," Russ said.

"Do we have a problem I need to know about?" Carson asked crossly, but before Russ could say anything, the sound of distant sirens answered Carson's question. "Let's go."

⚔ ⚔ ⚔

The headlights from Carson's BMW illuminated the unlit parking lot of the abandoned warehouse. The large garage door slid open, allowing her car passage into the darkness. She pulled in next to Russ's truck, which he and Cray were unloading. She got out of her car and climbed the stairs. The two men continued to put the equipment away, avoiding her eyes.

"My office in five minutes," she yelled from the top of the stairs, then entered the anteroom and slammed the door.

Carson went into her office and closed the door. She poured some bourbon into a glass, then opened a recessed cabinet and took out a bottle of pills. She popped two into her mouth and chased them down with the bourbon. It had been a long time since she had resorted to the pills, but the pressure of the last few days had taken its toll. She refilled her glass and went to her desk. She sat in her chair, took another swallow of her drink, and closed her eyes as the liquid burned its way down her throat.

Her mind had been in a fog all the way back while she tried to understand what had happened. Everything had gone wrong. They had lost Mercer and killed a federal employee, which would mean federal investigators. Russ had assured her that they wouldn't be able to trace anything back to them, but she didn't believe him. She was pulled from her thoughts by a knock on her door.

"Come!" When the two men entered the room, she said, "Sit," as though commanding trained dogs. "Explain it all."

Cray looked to Russ, but Russ continued to stare at the floor. "Everything was going according to plan ...." Cray began trying to fill the silence.

"Yeah, right up until you shot the wrong guy," Carson said. "Russ, I want you to explain it to me, since you changed my orders. I remember telling you to take the shot."

Russ raised his eyes and met Carson's. "I had a bad angle."

"You had a bad angle? That's why Cray took the shot? Did it ever occur to you that maybe you had a bad shot because the two of you were not in a good position? Did it ever cross your tiny brain that maybe, just maybe, two supposedly highly trained mercenaries could, under the cover of darkness, get a little closer to the target? Maybe even close enough to confirm the target before taking the shot? Or maybe you lost your nerve."

"No," Russ said.

"Ms. Carson," Cray began, "Russ did have a bad shot—"

"Your friend set you up," Carson said, cutting him off. "The blood of this guy is on your hands, Cray. You took the shot. You killed the Fed. I want to know why."

"No, that's not what happened," Cray said. "Russ just didn't have a good shot."

"That's what he told you," Carson said, "but I want to hear it from him." She turned to Russ. "So, did you have a bad shot?"

"Yes."

To Cray she said, "I need to talk to Russ alone. Go grab a few hours of sleep. We start the hunt again in the morning."

Cray did as he was told and left the office. Once Carson and Russ were alone, Russ raised his eyes to look squarely at Carson.

"Now tell me what happened," Carson said.

"Cray made the original call that it was our guy in the tower. When we got back up there, I couldn't tell if it was Mercer I was looking at or not. I thought about getting closer to identify him, but we didn't know what, if any, security they had up there. Most of the occupied towers have motion-sensor lights around the tower, and some have them around the parking areas. Cover up there was sparse to begin with so I wasn't going to go out under a spotlight. I figured since Cray identified the guy earlier, he would know if it was the same one he was taking down."

"Are you sure that's it? Or are you just making sure you don't have any blood on your hands if this goes south?"

"Both. If we ever find Mercer, then mission accomplished. If we don't, then I'm not going down for any collateral damage."

"Get out," Carson said coldly. "We aren't done, but for now, just get out of my sight."

Russ shot her a look of disdain and left the room.

Carson closed her eyes and leaned her head back against the chair. Mercer was in the wind, and they had no idea where he was. Carson felt like her world was slowly falling down around her. Given her handling of the Mercer problem, she fully expected one of her men to kill her on the orders of Ashe. She hadn't spoken with Ashe recently and decided that she wouldn't take his calls until she either had Mercer in hand or dead.

# CHAPTER 26

Ted woke up late Thursday morning, pulled from sleep by the ringing of his cell phone. Rolling over, he grabbed the phone. "Yeah?"

"*Hola, mi amigo,*" came the familiar voice of Miguel. "Rough night? I'm on the front porch. We working today?"

"Yeah," Ted said, still groggy. "Listen, I have some errands to run today before my trip tomorrow. Can you run the show?"

"*No problemo.* I'll talk to you when you get back. You okay?"

"Yeah, just a lot on my mind."

"I know, *mi amigo.* I'll check in with you this afternoon."

"Thanks."

Ted turned off his phone and rolled out of bed. It had been a long night, and he thought the knot in his stomach was only going to get worse. He went to the kitchen to start coffee. While it was brewing, he went into his office and picked up the stack of papers he had printed out the night before and checked his email. A new message was in his inbox.

> Ted,
>
> Attached are the preliminary results from the samples you brought me. I'll have the complete analysis for you sometime next week. I thought this might be helpful to have when you go east. Good luck.
>
> Sam

Back in the kitchen, Ted poured himself coffee and sat at the table to look through the papers. He wondered how long Green Grass had been burning. He wasn't sure what was going on while he was away at school but thought he could find out from the State Department of Agriculture and his dad. His farm should also have records of livestock losses. He already knew of two and Miguel had mentioned the problem as well. His farm was also not the only one in the valley that could be affected. Putting the papers together, Ted slid them into a folder. He had a little digging to do.

The County Planning Office was housed in an old brick building just off Main Street. Ted had been there a few times before and it always reminded him of an office time had forgotten. An old wood and frosted-glass door led into a larger room with a long counter. The smell of burnt coffee permeated the air and seemed to leave a yellow hue on the walls.

Ted smiled as he walked through the door. The office was exactly how he remembered it. An older woman with a gray beehive hairdo stood behind the counter and looked down her horn-rimmed glasses as he entered the room.

"My, oh my," she said when she saw Ted. "Little Teddy Kameron. How are you? How are those parents of yours?"

"Hi, Mrs. Clark," Ted said. "I think you were here the last time I came in, five years ago."

"Yep," Mrs. Clark said, winking. "Some things never change."

"To answer your question, my parents are both doing well. How are you doing?"

"Oh, you know. Some days my bones hurt a little more than others, but that's why they invented aspirin. So what can I do for you?"

"I was hoping to take a look at the plats—land maps—around my place."

"You looking to expand?"

"Maybe. Just not sure who owns what anymore."

"You don't need to tell me," Mrs. Clark said, waving him off. "Nowadays you never know who owns what, or if they even live in the state. Heck," she whispered, "there's a piece of land here, which I can't tell you about, that belongs to an actor from California."

Remembering Ted's request, the woman caught herself and said, "How about I just get you those maps and stop chewing off your ear?"

"I'd sure appreciate it. If it wouldn't be any trouble, could I get a copy of the maps from ten years ago as well? I'd like to see who has bought or sold what."

"No trouble at all," she said, as she went down one of the rows of map drawers. "I think they're over here. Ah, here they are. So you wanted a current one and one ten years old?"

"Yes, please."

Mrs. Clark came back with two large maps. "You can look at them over there," she said, motioning to a large table in the corner. "You just can't take them out of the office."

"Thanks so much."

Ted took the maps, went to the table, and spread them out next to each other. His property was clearly marked near the center, but the surrounding landowners had changed. Ted looked at the names on the old map, many of them he remembered from his youth. Most of them were now gone, replaced with Green Grass Enterprises. He wondered if they had all been willing sellers or if any of them had gotten sick. He pulled out a notebook and wrote down the names of the previous property owners.

He examined the maps for a long time. Green Grass had never approached his family other than buying a parcel from his grandparents. Based on the current map, though, if they were looking to expand, Ted's farm was a much better prospect than some of the land they had recently purchased along the river bottom. Ted couldn't figure out why they were buying up those strips. They weren't going to be good for growing anything because they always flooded.

Ted went back up to the counter, "Mrs. Clark, do you know who the contact person is for Green Grass Enterprises?"

She thought for a moment. "There should be a record around here somewhere. Let me cross-reference that with the property tax information."

She busied herself in another file cabinet. Computers had not yet taken over her filing system, though a brand-new one sat in the corner gathering dust.

"Got it," she said triumphantly holding up a piece of paper. "Okay, the name I have here is S. Carson. The address is a PO Box in Wilsonville. There isn't any phone number."

"Thanks." Ted returned the maps to the counter. "Here you go. Thanks so much for all your help."

"Not a problem, and do say hello to your parents from me."

"I sure will."

Ted drove back to his house, a list of questions running through his mind. One of the first things he decided to do was to read up on the state field-burning program. Settling back into his office chair, he turned on his computer and pecked at the keys. When he found the Oregon Department of Agriculture page, he began reading. He discovered that in the Willamette Valley, the state oversaw the burning of about 65,000 acres of grass fields. He printed pages as he read.

Based on a summary of the program, the state had allowed field burning since 1948. In order to be enrolled in the program, a farmer needed to obtain a permit after filing an extensive application. Field burning typically took place from mid-June through the end of September, with the Department of Agriculture setting daily restrictions and monitoring burns. Ted thought they might know whether or not Green Grass Enterprise had a permit and their burn monitoring information. He reached for the phone.

"Hi," Ted said when he connected, "I'm trying to contact the smoke management coordinator for the Molalla area."

"You want to talk with Ed Crocker. One minute and I'll connect you," said a voice on the other end of the line. Ted heard a click, another ring, then, "Ed Crocker."

"My name is Ted Kameron. I run a farm in Molalla and want to ask you a couple of questions about the field-burning program up here."

"You say Molalla?"

"Yeah. I was wondering if an adjacent farm had a permit and how many times they are allowed to burn under it."

"What farm?"

"It's owned by Green Grass Enterprise."

"Yes, they have a permit. I oversee those burns myself from the state side of things. Right now they don't have any limitation on the number of times they can burn."

"Oh, I see," Ted said. "You said you monitor it? What kind of things do you monitor?"

"We monitor issues related to field burning," Crocker said. "And if that is all, I'm on my way out the door. If you have complaints, call the smoke complaint line."

Suddenly, Ted was listening to a dial tone. He slowly put the receiver down, not sure what had just happened.

* * *

Ted spent the night thinking. He tried several times to sleep, but it never came. He talked to Dia and Miguel earlier in the night and told them everything he had learned. He just couldn't get the conversation with the field inspector out of his head. When morning finally came, so did the butterflies in Ted's stomach. He had effectively forgotten that he was going to see Rachel. He had focused his attention on the fires, but today was the day he would see her again. The day stretched out before him like a long graveled road disappearing into distant hills. He wondered if he could even get himself to the airport, let alone knock on Rachel's door. He was still working on what to say to her. *I just have to remember that she left me. She'll probably be more uncomfortable than me.* Patting his dog's head, he grabbed his suitcase and headed for the door. Moments later, he was driving toward the airport.

# CHAPTER 27

Pen rubbed his weary eyes as he watched the sunlight filter through the window. He had been up all night reading hazardous waste case law. He thought they might be dealing with violations of at least three federal laws, maybe more, not to mention a variety of criminal charges. He was able to research only so much before it became apparent that he didn't have the resources he needed.

"Okay," he said aloud to himself, "I'm going about this the wrong way. I need an ordered, systematic approach. Right now, I'm approaching it shotgun-style and I'll miss something."

Standing, he stretched, and then went downstairs.

Mercer had fallen asleep in the armchair, while Jessie slept on the couch. Pen went to the kitchen table, where they had worked most of the night, and looked at the documents spread across it. It looked as though they had made progress coordinating timelines between periods of burning and claims for livestock damages, but not enough to be considered proof of a crime—correlation was not causation. He sank wearily into one of the kitchen chairs. He turned to see Jessie rise from the couch and wipe sleep from her eyes.

"Morning," she said.

"Morning. How ya doing?"

"I'm okay. Still pretty shaken about Jimmy. I'm not sure what I should do. Whether I should call into work or what. I'm sure all hell has broken loose."

"Call in. If these people are connected in any way to the national forest, they might figure out who you are, especially if you become a missing employee."

"Yeah, but if they do have connections, they can probably figure out that I was assigned to the tower anyway."

"Good point. But they'll have to at least use their contacts to figure that out versus the evening news reporting a shooting and a missing employee. You can't go back there, Jess. Besides, I'm going to need help if we're going to work this case. What's your procedure for calling in?"

"Usually, I'd call the tower and coordinate what time I need to be back."

"Do that and play dumb to the murder if anyone answers."

Jessie nodded and picked up her phone from the table. Dialing, she waited for an answer. She was caught off guard when a man answered.

"Yeah?"

"Hello. Who am I speaking with?"

"Ben Sharp, District Ranger. Who's this?" the man demanded.

"Ben, it's Jessie. What's going on there? Where's Jimmy?"

"Jessie?" the man's voice grew softer. "Am I glad to hear your voice. There's been an incident here. Jimmy was killed. Shot by someone. Where are you?"

"Staying with a friend in Bend," Jessie lied. "What are you talking about, shot?"

"Someone shot him with a high-caliber rifle. The police think it's some random act, but we won't know until they finish processing the scene. I'm waiting for the FBI to get here. Listen, stay put. We aren't putting anyone in this tower who isn't law enforcement, and you're not. I'll gather your things and drop them off at the district office in Bend so you can pick them up. Give me a call in a few days or so and we'll talk about reassigning you. Are you okay?"

181

"Yeah. Thanks, Ben. I think I am just in shock. I saw Jimmy yesterday. Okay. I'll give you a call next week."

"Good. I have to go, Jess. Be safe."

"Thanks," Jessie said, clicking off her phone. She looked at Pen as she put her phone back on the table.

"Okay, you're with me this week," he said.

* * *

Mid-morning Pen, Jessie and Mercer drove the short distance to Pen's office in downtown Salem. Jessie looked out the window. They had pulled up in front of an eclectic coffee house.

"So you're a barista now?" asked Jessie, smiling.

"I wish. I end up spending half my salary on coffee," replied Pen, winking. "Not really. They actually treat me pretty well. No, my office is upstairs. Come on, the door is right there," Pen said, pointing to an inconspicuous door beside the coffee house.

The three got out of the car and headed for the door, Pen leading the way and Mercer looking over his shoulder.

"Relax," Pen said. "There's no way your friends are going to find you here. If anything, they're watching the train and bus stations and the airports. I can't imagine they are scoping out coffee houses in the Pacific Northwest. No one has that many hired guns."

Mercer cracked a smile. "Good point," he said, as he followed Jessie up the stairs, which ended at a single landing with one door. Pen unlocked the door, and entered his office.

"Come on in."

The office was immaculate. Beautiful Persian rugs covered the recently restored hardwood floors. A waiting area with a large window on the far side of the room provided a view of the Willamette River. The main room contained three doors. Pen went to the far door and opened it. Flicking on the lights, Pen stepped inside. His two companions followed closely behind. Pen went to a large oak desk and put down his backpack. A state-of-the-art computer with a flat-screen monitor sat on his desk. On one side of his office was an enormous bookcase that held a number of legal books and case reporters. Pen caught Jessie looking around his office.

"Impressed? My dad insisted on buying me the books for a graduation present. A subscription to a legal database would've been more practical. The other doors are for the bathroom and a kitchenette. The kitchenette is stocked, so go help yourselves. I want to get my computer up and running and start working."

Jessie led Mercer back to the kitchenette. The room had a full refrigerator and stove. There was a closet pantry and a table with four chairs.

"Kitchenette, my ass," said Jessie loudly, laughing. "This room is bigger than my entire fire tower."

"Your friend's got money," said Mercer, looking in the refrigerator.

"Yeah, but he doesn't flaunt it. Sometimes I think he's oblivious to it. Did you find any coffee?"

"Nope," Mercer replied, checking the small freezer for a bag of beans.

"I think Pen will want coffee," Jessie said. "Will, can you whip something together for food? I'm starving. I'm going down to the of the coffee shop, want anything?"

"Just some black coffee," replied Mercer.

"How cosmopolitan," replied Jessie with a crooked smile.

Walking into the coffee house, Jessie realized why Pen had chosen this location. The place was an eclectic-hippie ish caffeine heaven or, more accurately, Shangri-Latte. She went to the large glass counter and ordered an Americano for Pen, a black coffee for Will, and for herself, a mocha. Just as she was about to hand the money to the woman behind the counter, Pen walked in.

"Hi, Rose," he said to the barista.

"This for you?" Rose, a pretty, curly red-haired woman, asked. She turned to Jessie. "Pen doesn't pay for his coffee here," she said, handing Jessie's money back. "We kind of barter coffee for legal work and we totally take advantage of it, too."

"I don't know about that," Pen said, laughing, "I drink a hell of a lot of coffee."

"True. Can I get you anything else, sweetie?" she asked Jessie.

"No, that's good for now. Thanks, though."

"We should get back upstairs. Thanks for the coffee, Rose. I'll see you later." As they climbed the stairs Pen said, "Looks like Will is up there making a feast."

"Good. I'm starving."

They walked into the kitchen and saw a table full of food.

"I wasn't sure what y'all wanted so I made a couple of things."

"It looks great," Pen said. "Let's talk and eat. I have some preliminary thoughts about the situation we're in."

Once they had loaded their plates with food and sat down, Pen explained what he had found.

"There are three federal laws that your company has probably violated right off the bat. First, there is the Resource Conservation and Recovery Act, or RCRA. This act regulates the generation, transport, and disposal of hazardous waste. Second, is the Comprehensive Environmental Response, Compensation, and Liability Act, or CERCLA. A lot of words so most folks just refer to it as Superfund. Superfund is a clean-up kind of law. It also focuses on hazardous waste disposal. Finally, there's the Clean Water Act."

"Clean Water Act?" questioned Jessie.

"Let me explain," Pen began. "The Clean Water Act covers the release of a pollutant into navigable waters. This means that you can't dump crap into the river. This might be a harder one to prove, but it should be on the table. There are a number of other laws that might also be implicated, but I'm going to need to do a lot of research."

"You said there might be other laws?" Jessie asked.

"Just off the top of my head there are likely issues concerning the Clean Air Act, the Toxic Substances Control Act, Safe Drinking Water Act—and those are just the federal laws. There are usually corresponding state laws. Then there are the criminal offenses, like conspiracy, attempted murder, and murder. We'll have to figure it all out and see where we go from there. At some point soon, I want to call in the authorities, but first I want a better picture of what's been happening."

"Wow," Jessie said after hearing Pen's list of violations. "Where do we even start?"

"I start by locking myself in my office for the next few hours. What would be helpful is if you two went through Will's paperwork to see what else you can do with it. See who is doing what and by whose authority. Try to work out some kind of timeline; anything you think will be helpful. I'll start asking you to pull together information if we have it, so it would be best for both of you to be familiar with the documents."

"Sounds like a plan," Mercer said. "I'll get started." He cleared his dish and went into the main room.

# CHAPTER 28

Russ entered a seedy tavern in northeast Portland. It took a few seconds for his eyes to adjust to the darkness and soon he was able to see the two men sitting at the bar. It was 9 a.m. and the bar wasn't officially open, though that hadn't stopped the creatures who were sipping beer. Men who frequented this bar at this time of the morning were there for three reasons: to conduct business that couldn't be conducted in the light of day; to cure their hangovers; or to live out their existence on the margin of society, not quite part of it but merely observing it through bleary eyes as the days marched past. Russ was there to conduct business.

The bartender poured a cup of coffee and slid it to Russ as he walked up to the bar. "He's in the back booth," the bartender said before Russ asked the question.

Russ picked up the steaming mug of coffee. He took a sip of the burnt water as he went toward the back of the bar. Connor sat in a dark booth, lit only by an oil candle. He was drinking a Bloody Mary.

"You're not actually drinking Han's coffee, are you?"

"Did you get the money?"

"Yeah, thanks." Connor took a sip of his drink.

"You got the picture?"

"Yeah, though I have no idea how he's connected to your world." Connor took a sheet of paper out and handed it to Russ. It was a standard license printout with an address in Portland and a picture of a man in his late twenties.

"Did you dig up anything on this guy?" Russ asked, studying the printout.

"Maybe, but it will cost you. It's more info than you originally contracted me for."

"Fine. Now, who is this guy?"

"As I'm sure you have read, his name is Jeffrey Pennoyer and he lives in John's Landing, that neighborhood in southwest Portland. He is or was—I'm still not sure about this—a law student at the local law school up by Tryon Creek State Park. His father is a local businessman and his mother is on the city council. They're loaded."

"Is this address good?"

"I haven't checked it out, but I assume it is."

"Where do his parents live?"

"The West Hills." Connor pulled out another sheet of paper. "Here's the address."

Russ took the sheet and studied it. Connor, happy with himself, slid down in his seat and took a long drink of his Bloody Mary. The two men were quiet for a long time. The only sounds in the bar were the tinkling of glasses and bottles as the bartender got ready for the day and the almost imperceptible groans of the two men sitting at the bar, their bodies tired from life.

Russ put the papers down. "This is good. I'll wire your account another grand."

"Sounds good," Connor said, smiling.

Russ grabbed up the papers. "I need to check this address out."

He slid out of the booth, pulled a couple of bills from his wallet, and threw them down on the table.

Russ was temporarily blinded when he stepped from the dimly lit bar into the bright summer sun. He shielded his eyes as he climbed into his truck and headed toward John's Landing, the address on the slip of paper Connor had given him.

John's Landing was a residential neighborhood in southwest Portland, wedged between the Willamette River and Interstate 5. The houses were quaint, but like most housing in the area, expensive. The drive from northeast Portland took ten minutes. The house he was looking for was on Viewpoint Terrace, a street on the north side of the neighborhood. Russ decided that he would first drive by the place before taking a closer look. His heart sank as he pulled past it. A large For Rent sign sat in the front yard. Turning his truck around, he decided to head back to the warehouse to see if he could track down this Pennoyer on his computer.

Two hours later, Russ' eyes were still glued to the computer monitor. He had been searching for any information he could find on Jeffery Pennoyer, with very little success. The name was more common than he'd thought, and with the guy's parents so success-ful, most of the search hits were about them.

"Damn it," Russ said, and slammed his fist on the table.

"That kind of day, huh?" Cray said. Sitting in the armchair near the sofa, he put his feet up on the coffee table and closed his eyes. "What's the plan?"

"We need to come up with one. We seem to have a lot of information but nothing solid. We need to find this guy before someone comes looking for us."

Carson came through the door. "Gentlemen, tell me what we know."

"Okay, it turns out that the guy who went to the locker was not Mercer but a Jeffrey Pennoyer. He's a recent grad from the local law school in Portland and we think a friend of the woman from the Forest Service. He comes from a wealthy, politically connected Portland family. I think our priority should be Pennoyer," Russ said. "We find him, we find Mercer and the woman."

"Any ideas on how to do that?" Carson asked.

"No. I've been trying everything I can think of but I haven't had any luck. I checked his last residence in Portland, but it's abandoned and looks like a rental. I've searched the internet for any current listings for this guy and can't find an address."

"Try the Oregon Bar Association," Carson said. "Check to see if they have a website with an attorney locator. If this guy is licensed to practice in Oregon, he's probably listed."

"I'm on it," Russ said sitting up. A few minutes later, he found what he was looking for. "Bingo. The guy has a practice in Salem."

"I want you two to stake it out."

The two men nodded.

"Stay there until he turns up. If this guy leads us to Mercer, then we take care of everybody. Understand? And no one ever finds the bodies."

Russ and Cray nodded again.

# CHAPTER 29

The flight was crowded and long. When it finally landed in Hartford, Connecticut, Ted went straight to the rental car counter, though his anxiety over the trip was almost debilitating. He was torn, one part of him wanting desperately to see Rachel, the other afraid of what he might find. Half an hour after landing, he was heading north on Interstate 91 toward Massachusetts.

He finally reached the exit for Sunderland around 7 p.m. and checked into the Motel 6 just off the interstate. After showering and changing, he opened his backpack to make sure he had all of the papers. He decided to go to Rachel right away, around 8 o'clock. Otherwise, he would be awake all night.

"Just get 'er done."

Sunderland was not a large town. In fact, it was a small farming community with large apartment developments providing housing to students and faculty from the University of Massachusetts, located a town over. While it was a short drive to her house, he drove past it along the giant oak-lined road several times before getting up the nerve to park. All of the lights were on in what looked like a well-maintained, turn-of-the-century, three-story, Foursquare house. Two cars sat parked in the driveway—one was Rachel's Subaru.

Working up his courage, Ted got out of his car and went to the front door. It took several times before his knocking actually made any sound. And the last knock seemed too loud and forceful.

His palms were sweaty, even though the evening air was cool. Finally, an older, gray-haired woman dressed in a paisley house coat answered the door. Ted assumed she was Rachel's mother.

"Can I help you?" Her smile putting Ted's nerves slightly at ease.

"Is Rachel home?"

The woman quickly measured Ted. "Yes. Let me get her. Won't you come in?"

Ted stepped inside and waited nervously, pacing. He saw Rachel's familiar artwork adorning the entryway and extending into the house.

"Ted?" A surprised voice said from above him. "Is that you?"

Ted looked up to see Rachel standing at the top of the large wooden staircase in a robe and slippers, her mother beside her, quizzical looks on both of their faces.

Leaning heavily on the railing, Rachel walked slowly down the stairs as Ted moved to the bottom of the staircase. The last year had not been kind to her. The Rachel Ted remembered had a young, energized face and eyes that twinkled with a mischievous light. The woman coming toward him now was older and tired, a look of pain endured and hope dissolved. Someone cheated by life.

As she got closer, though, Ted saw a flash in Rachel's eyes— eyes that were alive and excited. She reached him seconds later and wrapped her arms around his neck, burying her face in his chest. Ted returned the embrace, trying to absorb her and all of her pain. Emotion welled up inside of him and caught somewhere in his throat. He blinked back the tears that were trying to force their way out while Rachel let hers go freely.

He held her for a long time, both forgetting there was a third person in the room. The time and space that separated them seemed to dissolve.

Rachel was the first to break the hold, wiping tears away from her eyes and cheeks. "It's so good to see you. How are you here?"

"You, too," Ted said, fumbling for words.

They heard a noise behind them. Rachel blushed.

"I'm sorry. I'm being rude. Mom, I'd like you to meet Ted Kameron."

"I've heard a lot about you. I'm glad we finally get a chance to meet."

"It is very nice to meet you, ma'am. I sure wish we had met earlier."

"Have you eaten?" Rachel's mother asked.

"Yes. I grabbed something on the road."

"That doesn't sound good. I'll put on a pot of coffee and maybe entice you with some fresh apple pie."

"That sounds wonderful, ma'am."

"One condition, though. No more of this 'ma'am' stuff? Call me Connie."

"Sure, Connie." Ted gave her a grateful smile.

"Come into the kitchen so we can talk," Rachel said, following her mother.

She led Ted through an archway that opened into a soft yellow kitchen with white accents. It seemed like a warm, happy place, full of good memories.

Ted sat in one of the chairs around an oval dinner table. Rachel took up the chair directly across from him. They stared at each other for a long time.

Rachel broke the silence. "Ted, I'm so sorry I left the way I did. A lot of things went wrong and I didn't know how to even start to explain."

"It's okay, Rach," Ted said, reaching across the table and taking her hand. "I won't lie to you, I was hurt and confused, but I think I've managed to piece together why you left. I just want you to know that I love you. And I want to help you fight this thing."

"Oh Ted. I still love you too. I never meant to hurt you, and I know I did. And once I left, I couldn't find the courage to call you.

This is not going to be easy for you to hear, but I have to get it out," Rachel took a deep breath. "I was pregnant. But before I could even tell you, I got sick and miscarried. I was ashamed. I hid it from you, but I couldn't bear losing the baby, so I came home. When I got home, I went to the hospital because I was still really sick. The doctors told me I had some kind of blood disorder and that it was likely the early stages of leukemia. I needed extensive chemotherapy. I've been fighting it ever since," Rachel explained.

Ted had prepared for the news, but hearing it from Rachel's lips stunned him. "I wish you had told me about it," he finally said. "Do the doctors know what caused the miscarriage and the leukemia?"

"No, they thought if they could pin it down, they would have a better idea how to treat it. I'm so sorry I didn't tell you. It wasn't fair. I know that."

"It's benzene," Ted blurted out abruptly. "It was in the water and the air. The ash that used to cover the old cottage when the neighbors burned their fields was loaded with it."

He waited for the information to sink in before he started again. Rachel's mother stopped working at the sink and turned to listen. Rachel looked at him dumbfounded. Ted could see her processing the information.

"Rach, you have to believe I didn't know anything about it."

"Yeah, I know you wouldn't. Benzene?" she asked, still stunned.

"Yes. I think it was the reason for the miscarriage," Ted said. "I recently had some cows die and started taking samples from them, the stream, and the ash and water from the cottage. I sent them to Sam. Do you remember him from Corvallis? Anyway, he ran the analysis. He said the levels were off the charts. So, I did some research. A miscarriage is one of the results of high benzene levels. Another is leukemia." Ted paused to let this information sink in, but couldn't hold back the tears any longer. Rachel sank into her chair as if defeated.

"It's all my fault. I asked you to live there. I put you in harm's way."

"I don't understand," said Connie in a guarded voice. "How did Rachel get exposed to benzene?" Her protective instincts took over. She was standing behind Rachel, her fingers white from her grip of the chair. "I need to know how this could even happen."

"Mom," started Rachel.

"No, Rachel, we need answers," her mother said, cutting her off. "Ted?"

"It's okay, Rach. I'd be pretty mad too. I mean I've been beside myself since I found out. So, farmers in the Willamette Valley can burn their grass field in order to get them ready for planting. The grass seed business is really big there. There's a grass farm that is adjacent to mine that seems to burn its field a lot. When they do, if the winds are right, the ash and smoke blows onto my farm. There is also a stream that runs across their property and through mine before it empties into the Molalla River."

Ted continued. "Whatever it is that they're burning, they must be adding something to it, because it's not just normal smoke. When my cows died, I started looking into it. Miguel, a friend who works with me is checking to see if any of the migrant farmworkers in the surrounding area have become sick. His daughter works with migrants on health care. I tried to get answers from the state, but was told to mind my own business. Once I found out, I knew I had to come out here to see you," finished Ted.

"It's all my fault," he mumbled and dropped his head to stare at the table.

"Oh, no," Connie said. "You're not the one at fault, and it seems to me that we now have some answers. We'll tell the doctors and maybe there's something else that can be done. But right now it looks like Rachel needs you and since you flew all the way here, I'm thinking that you need her too. So let's focus on that." Then she sighed and let her grip on the chair loosen. "Okay, now how do you take your coffee?"

There was silence as Rachel and Ted sat in their respective states of shock. Then Rachel squeezed Ted's hand. Ted looked up into her eyes and smiled, the guilt suddenly being washed away by a wave of relief and happiness.

"Cream and sugar," he said, starting to laugh.

They picked up where they had left off. Old feelings buried under time and distance emerged as though recently experienced. Rachel and Ted talked long into the night about their time together and apart. Rachel told Ted about her struggles with the miscarriage, her medical tests and treatments, and the regret she felt for leaving him. The love they had felt for each other was still strong. Eventually Ted caught a glimpse of the clock on the wall. It was one in the morning and fatigue from his travel was taking its toll. Rachel also looked exhausted, given the hour and her condition.

"Listen, I should probably get going. It's really late and I think we could both use the rest."

"How long are you staying?"

"I have an open-ended ticket. I'm staying as long as you want me to."

Rachel's eyes welled up with tears again, her emotions close to the surface. One broke loose and trickled down her cheek.

"Ted, will you stay with us while you're here? I really want you close."

Ted got up from his chair and went to her. Crouching so that they were at eye level, he wiped away the tear and kissed her on the cheek. "I'm not going anywhere, if that's okay with you."

"It's okay with me." Rachel's tears flowed freely down her cheeks.

Ted lifted her to her feet and hugged her for a long time. It felt like home to him.

# CHAPTER 30

P en worked through another night, claiming to be on a roll. Jessie had finally given in to exhaustion, and crashed at his house. Mercer slept on the office's leather pull-out couch, dropping from exhaustion around two in the morning. Pen had Mercer working on putting a timeline together about when the farm burned its fields and when the veterinarian paid out compensation. There was some information that pointed to a connection, but not enough.

Pen came out of his jurisprudence prison as the eastern sky began to brighten. He saw Mercer still asleep on the couch. He checked his watch; it was still early. He'd have to wait for the coffee house to open. He decided he needed a key to the place so he wasn't restricted by their hours. *I guess I could always buy a coffee maker.*

He had finally made it to the end of his legal goose chase for one of the laws. He was sure they had a solid case against the farm for violations of the Resource Conservation and Recovery Act, a law that regulated the transport and disposal of hazardous waste. What he really wanted was to prove that a parent company was involved. If his instincts were right, this farm was a tax write-off, a loser company designed not to make any money. Green Grass Enterprises was likely some kind of shell company with a ghost staff and no assets, therefore no money for remediation or damages if they were ever taken to court. The key was to determine if there was a connection to a parent company and find out exactly who it was.

He was also sure about Superfund claims, but again, it came down to who owned the waste being burned. Superfund, as well as some of the other laws, would require testing soil, water, and air samples to figure out if they were polluted and how far the pollution went. As far as the criminal issues, Pen could only try to pull together notes from what had occurred over the previous week. Once he felt there was a solid case, he would send it to the District Attorney's office to see if they would move on it.

Pen didn't try to be quiet as he scrounged in the kitchen for something to eat. A light sleeper, Mercer got up almost immediately.

"Sorry, didn't mean to wake you."

"No problem. I needed to get up anyway. I want to talk to you about what I found out last night, but maybe we should wait until Jessie gets back, so we're all on the same page."

"Yeah, good idea. Besides, I'm not sure I could actually carry on a coherent conversation right now."

"Did you get any sleep?"

"Not last night. Got a lot of good work done, though."

Pen checked his watch; it was now 7 a.m. and the coffee house was open.

"How about I buy you a cup of coffee?" Pen offered, closing the refrigerator in slight disgust.

"Sounds good to me."

Pen led him out of the office, down the stairs, and into the subdued atmosphere of the coffee house.

The cool morning summer air hung in the sleepy coffee house like a blanket. The door was open and a few early risers were drinking their morning no-nonsense coffee, green teas, and lattes. Pen strolled up to the counter with the familiarity of someone who had spent many hours there.

A bleary-eyed woman in her twenties appeared behind the counter. She had short black hair and a variety of tattoos.

"Hi, Pen. What are you doing here so early? I thought you lawyer types took weekends off."

"Very nice, Suzette," Pen said. "And I thought you Goth types couldn't come out during daylight hours."

"I try not to. Judy's sick this morning, and I was already up. Anyway, what can I get for you?"

"I'll have the usual, and my friend here will have a—?" Pen waited for Mercer to order.

"Coffee, black. Thanks."

The barista moved down the counter and made the drinks.

"Been here a couple of times?" Mercer asked.

"That obvious? Even before I rented the office upstairs, I spent a lot of time here studying for the bar exam. I like it here because I can fade into the background."

Suzette delivered their coffees and disappeared to help a new customer.

"Come on, let's grab a seat before they're all gone," Pen said smiling, looking at the mostly empty restaurant.

A number of old tables and chairs lined the room, flanked by several old second-hand couches that gave the place a comfortable feeling. Behind the coffee bar hung a number of antique coffee grinders. Along the far wall, art displays from local artists.

"So what's the plan for today?" Mercer asked as they settled into their seats.

"Not sure yet. I thought we'd wait for Jessie before deciding."

"Wise decision, Counselor," said a familiar voice from behind them. They both turned to see Jessie standing there.

"I didn't even see you come in," Pen said, yawning.

"If you were any closer to that cup of coffee, you'd be drowning," Jessie said, sitting down. "What are we doing today? I mean Will and me, because you, my friend, are getting some sleep. You look like shit."

"Thanks for sugar-coating it."

"She's right, man."

"Mutiny this early in the day?" Pen asked pretending to be hurt.

"I was thinking that Jessie and I could try to track down some of the issues we've come up with. It seems to me that you have a lot of the legal stuff going, but we need to track down some of the facts."

"Good. At some point I'll need to file a complaint, and to do that, we need a basis for the claims. Right now, we have a lot of holes in the story we're going to tell, and we need those holes plugged. We at least need to know the claims that we are going to bring. If we miss some of the big ones, we might be out of luck. Any ideas on where you two should start?"

"A couple," Jessie said. "We need to go to the Molalla Town Hall and look at landowner records. We're going to need information from the state on the burning program and how often Green Grass Enterprises burns. We also need some information from that veterinary group regarding its livestock warranties." Will just nodded his agreement.

"Good," Pen said. "That would help answer a lot of questions. How's your memory doing, Will?"

"It's slowly coming back. Kind of spotty with some of the details, but I'm actually hoping that working today will help bring things into focus."

"Good. I might need you and your memory on the witness stand, and I need both of them intact so be careful. Those killers are still out there somewhere, so be alert and keep me posted."

The three finished their coffee, chatting about different things. Mercer told them about the part of his life that he could remember. When they finally had finished their coffee, they went outside. The sun had risen high in the sky and the cool morning air was getting warm.

Jessie took Pen aside. "Go get some sleep, okay? We need you at the top of your game. This isn't a sprint."

"Yeah, I know. I'm just a little excited. I'll get some sleep."

"We'll probably be out all day. How about we plan on meeting you back at your place for dinner?"

"Good. I'll pick up some food later and we can barbecue out on the deck," Pen said, yawning.

"Come on, Will," Jessie said, motioning to the car, then stopping.

"I'll grab a cab," Pen said, reading her mind. "Don't worry about it."

"Let me go grab some papers," Mercer said. "I'll be down in a minute."

A few minutes later, they were pulling away from the curb heading for Interstate 5 and Molalla. Five minutes after they left, a cab pulled up and Pen climbed in. Fifteen minutes later, he was asleep.

* * *

Mercer spent the time on the way to Molalla trying to piece together more memories. If he could just fill in the holes from the last few weeks, he could put together a better picture. He saw himself walking across a field of grass and working with a Mexican, whose name he couldn't remember. He remembered the slow winter when there wasn't much to do, and thinking to himself that he was actually being paid to watch the grass grow. And he remembered smoke.

Jessie took the Molalla exit from the Interstate and was headed toward the center of town when something clicked in Mercer's head.

"Turn here," he said.

Jessie hesitated for a second, then followed his direction. "Do you remember something?"

"Yeah, but I can't put my finger on it. It's more like habit or instinct. I just feel like this is where I always turned," he said, feeling as puzzled as Jessie looked.

"I've learned not to mess with instinct," Jessie offered, shrugging.

The road went south for a few miles and then turned to the west. The tree-lined street they had been following opened up to miles of agricultural fields. Trees lined rivers and acted as windbreaks. The view of the foothills to the east and the large snow-capped mountain rising out of the clouds was a startling contrast to the flat farmland they were driving through. Soon the farmland was broken up more and more with smaller woodlots and pastures.

"Bear left," Mercer said when they came to a fork in the road.

Jessie did as she was told and a few miles up the road, they passed a sign that read Green Grass Enterprises. "Here?" Jessie asked, alarmed. "Aren't these the same guys who are trying to kill you?"

Suddenly memories flooded Mercer's brain, unlocked from the dark place they had been imprisoned. The memories came back in such a rush that he was hit by a sudden wave of nausea.

"Pull over, quick."

Jessie pulled to the shoulder. Mercer opened the door and vomited into the dust and gravel that lined the sunbaked asphalt.

"You okay?"

Mercer only nodded, his head still hanging out of the car. He looked around. The road was deserted. A gravel road led into the distance, away from the farm's sign. The farm buildings were out of sight, but the road looked well maintained. The fields adjacent to the asphalt were planted with grass. Slowly, Mercer pulled himself back into the car.

"Feel better?"

"No, I don't feel well at all, and I'm not sure that I ever will."

"What are you talking about?"

"I remember everything. Everything. You and Pen shouldn't be getting yourself mixed up in this," he said, staring out his window at something far away. His mood suddenly dark.

"Take a deep breath, Will. We need to talk through this and a pity party isn't going to help. Let's go get something to eat and talk about what you remember."

They headed back to Molalla, where Jessie pulled into the parking lot of a diner and turned off the car. It was eleven in the morning and the lunch rush hadn't started yet.

As they entered, a woman behind the counter said, "Take a seat anywhere you like and I'll be right with you."

Jessie led Mercer to a booth in the back. A few minutes later, the waitress appeared.

"Here are your menus," she said. "Can I get you something to drink?"

"Coffee," Mercer said, avoiding the woman's eyes.

"I'll have a Diet Coke."

"I'll get those right out." The waitress looked at Mercer as if trying to place him. Finally, she turned and went back to the counter.

"I know her," Mercer said after the waitress had left. "I've never eaten here but I know her from town."

"Is she connected to the farm at all?" Jessie asked, leaning across the table.

"No."

"Then don't sweat it. As far as she knows, you just haven't been around. It's only been a few days."

Will nodded. "I guess I'm starting to get paranoid."

"You should be paranoid. Someone is out to get you, but not everyone. You just need to apply your paranoia correctly. What did you remember in the car?"

Mercer stared into his coffee before answering. "Everything. All of it. Burning fields. Paying off the state inspector. Hurting people. I know who I am now and I'm not a good person."

"Come on, how bad could it be? We already know about the blackmail plan."

"I knew what was going on and I let it happen. Hell, I helped it along. That was my job. I helped them squeeze out surrounding farmers and make them sell. When they wouldn't do it willingly, I helped convince them, and not in a nice way. Sarah Carson told me what to do and I did it. I knew if I disobeyed, her men would pay me a visit. She reminded me all the time how expendable I was. But I bought into it. The money was too good to be true for such little work. In fact, the farm never made a profit. I was actually encouraged to lose money. A larger tax deduction or something. Maybe I was bored and wanted more action, or I'm just not a good person, I don't know, but I wanted to be in Carson's inner circle."

"You're not that person anymore. Do you feel like that person? Because I don't see that in you. Whatever happened to you in the accident and in the forest changed who you are. You get a do-over, a chance to set things right. Not many people get that chance in life."

He thought about what she said and nodded his head slowly.

"The important thing is that now you nail the bastards."

"I'd like to do that," he said with a self-satisfied smile. "Let's look over this menu and get some food, then I will spill my guts again, but this time it will be a bit more productive."

They ordered lunch and ate quietly. Mercer, still buried deep in thought, reflected on his past. He took one last bite of his sandwich, wiped his mouth, and cleared his throat. "Okay," he said, "how much do you want to know? Where do you want me to begin?"

"Begin at the beginning. I want to know everything."

"Get comfortable." He cleared his throat one more time and took a swallow of coffee. "As you know, I was born in a small town in northern Minnesota. I had a pretty normal family; a mom and dad and a sister. We lived on a hobby farm, though my dad was a forest engineer working for one of the national forests. From the time I could walk, I was out in the woods, running around.

"I camped, fished, and hunted most of my childhood. But I didn't know what I wanted to do with my life. My parents tried to expose me to the world but it was only through the lens of Minneapolis. So I joined the Army. It seemed like a good deal at the time. I excelled at it and eventually became a Ranger and was deployed to Afghanistan. The thing was, my moral compass was set differently than my superiors. I kept being ordered to do thing that ran counter to how I was raised. The things I saw, and the orders I was told to follow—none of them seemed right, seemed just. I probably could have kept moving up in the Army if I could have kept my mouth shut and done what I was told. One day I had seen too much and when ordered to stand down, took a swing at my commanding officer. He had it in for me anyway and the dishonorable discharge was an easy way to get rid of me.

"When I got home, I was rudderless. I was depressed and struggling with assimilating back into life here. I ended up falling in with the wrong crowd. I turned to drugs and booze, drank too much, broke some laws, wound up sleeping in a cell a few too many times. I started to hate things—authority mainly. During my time in the Army, I was working hard and not getting any-where and watched other guys being handed promotions based on who their parents were or how they were connected. So I decided I needed to look out for me.

"The problem was that I still didn't know what I wanted to do, other than live the American dream—be a millionaire by the time I was thirty. You know, the dream that creates an entitle-ment based merely on your citizenship. Anyway, I knew I couldn't live under my parents' roof again, so I hit the road. I wandered quite a bit until I ended up in Oregon.

"I was working as a bouncer in one of the local bars and just getting by when I saw an ad in the paper for a farm manager. It paid a lot more than what I was making, so I figured I'd go for it. I should have known something was up when I passed the security clearance they required. No one in their right mind should have hired me based on a background check. I couldn't figure out why a background check was even needed. Anyway, Sarah Carson interviewed me and I got the job."

"Who is this Sarah Carson anyway?" Jessie asked.

"She was my boss. I never understood if she was Green Grass Enterprises or part of some other company. All I knew was that there was absolutely no doubt she was in charge. Her two henchmen backed her up all the way. And if she didn't like something you were doing, she told you and then had her boys remind you.

"I got the job. It was easy work and I knew from the beginning that it was a cover for something. I called her one day, concerned with the condition of the grass crop and how it wasn't growing well. I was concerned that we wouldn't meet any kind of expected revenue. She told me that the farm wasn't expected to have revenue, or even meet its operation costs. I suggested that the poor growth might have something to do with over-applying the fertilizer treatments. She told me to do what I was told. From that point on, I figured one of two things: either we were a loser business, a tax write-off, or we were doing something illegal. Over time, I figured out that it was both.

"That's when I got greedy. I suggested to Sarah that I could help if they wanted to buy more property or intimidate people. She took me up on it. I did whatever she told me without asking for anything in return. I had hoped that she would pull me onto her team. I knew both of her men and one of the guys, Cray, is dumb as a tack. I figured I could do the job as well as him.

"When I approached her on it, she turned me down flat. She told me that everyone was expendable. Then she had her two boys remind me by giving me a couple of broken ribs. As I lay there in the parking lot of a local biker bar spitting up blood, I decided I needed to get out. But I would take them for as much as I could. I wasn't interested in bringing them to justice. I wanted to hurt them and I wanted cash. That's when I started pulling together the paperwork in the backpack."

"And that's when they tried to kill you," Jessie finished. "Have you ever been to their office?"

"No. We always spoke either by phone or at the farm office."

"Do you know what they were applying as fertilizer?"

"No idea. It came in unmarked barrels and there was a special team that applied it. The farm staff wasn't involved with the application. Our role was to light the fires and control the burns."

"Do you know where it was coming from?"

"No, it just rolled in at night. They applied it and we burned a few days later. I do know that it was really flammable. When we lit the fields, they went up like a torch, even if it had rained the previous night."

"You said that you were acquiring property?" Jessie asked. "What was that all about?"

"We wanted to reduce the number of complaints from adjacent land owners. I think there was a fear that the smoke and ash were affecting local crops and livestock. They wanted more of a buffer for their activities. We had a deal with that local veterinarian about replacing livestock. Anyone who complained was pushed out. There is one rancher left nearby. We convinced the grandparents to sell a piece of their property, but the grandson still runs the larger operation. Ted Kameron. We never had a problem with each other."

"Sounds like a place to start. Do you think you could find your way over to his ranch?"

"Sure."

\* \* \*

A half hour later, Jessie pulled the car onto the driveway of the Kameron ranch. It was mid-afternoon and the ranch was deserted. A large dog met the car as it slowed to a stop near the house. Jessie and Mercer looked at each other and frowned.

As they brainstormed about their next move, an old Ford pickup came bouncing down the gravel driveway behind them. It pulled up next to the car and the driver got out. He yelled something to the dog in Spanish and the dog moved back toward the porch that lined the front of the house. The man walked around the truck to Jessie's side of the car.

"Hi," Jessie said cheerfully. "Is this the Kameron ranch?"

"Yes, ma'am," the man said, bending down so his face was even with hers.

"Miguel? Is that you?" Mercer asked, leaning over toward the driver's side.

"Will?" Miguel said, surprised. "Where have you been?"

"Long story. Is Ted around?"

"You just missed him. He left yesterday for a few days. Is there something that I can help you with?"

"Can we talk inside?"

"Okay, come in," Miguel said warily.

Mercer and Jessie got out of the car and followed Miguel into the house.

\* \* \*

"Here, have a seat," Miguel said, motioning to the kitchen table. He introduced himself to Jessie. "I'm Miguel Riveria, the foreman on the farm."

"My name is Jessie. I'm a friend of Will's."

"It's nice to meet you," he said, smiling with his eyes. "So," he asked, turning to Mercer, "What can I do for you?" The smile left his eyes.

"I don't know if you heard, Miguel, but I left my job at the farm rather unexpectedly."

"*Sí*. José told me that you left because of some family emergency."

"So that's the story," Mercer said, almost under his breath. "Miguel, it's crucial that you don't let José know you saw me. It would put you and your families in danger."

"What do you mean?" Miguel said, his eyes narrowing. "Does this have something to do with the dying cows? It doesn't take an accountant to figure out that vet is over-paying on his livestock policy. No one complains when they get paid off, right?"

Miguel watched Mercer look down at the table, unwilling to meet his eyes. He could only nod in response.

"Why can't I tell José?" Miguel demanded, his tone going cold.

Mercer exhaled through his mouth and his shoulders dropped. "I left the farm, but it wasn't because of any family crisis," he began. "I was running. I tried to blackmail the owners with information about what we were burning. They decided to kill me instead. I barely escaped with my life. Jessie here found me and is trying to help me set things right. But if these people know you talked to me, they'd use every means possible to find out exactly what you know. They don't mind hurting people, Miguel."

Miguel sat in silence for a few minutes, mulling over what Mercer had just said. He had never really trusted Mercer. Mercer had come across as someone out to make as much money as he could without caring whom he hurt, or how he got it. He was certainly no farmer and not respectful of the land.

"What are you burning?" asked Miguel through gritted teeth, his anger growing with each second.

"I don't even know," replied Mercer. "They had a special team that applied what they were calling fertilizer right before we burned. I was just supposed to manage the farm and the burns."

"And that never struck you as odd—burning off the fertilizer you just applied?" said Miguel roughly, his anger bleeding through.

Silence crept into the kitchen. Miguel was fuming at what he had just heard. He inhaled deeply through his nose and slowly let out his breath, trying to regain his calmness. After several minutes, he lay his hands palms down on the table and looked from Mercer to Jessie.

"Cows aren't the only things getting sick around here. Old people and kids have been getting strange diseases. Not so many that anyone would notice, but enough. My niece works for a group that helps provide health care to some of the local field workers. They've been getting sick. We don't even have the same number of neighbors. Most have sold to you and moved away, many to treat illnesses they couldn't explain. You need to talk to Ted. He's headed to the East Coast to see his old girlfriend. He doesn't know I know, but she's sick, really sick. I think it's from living in that old cottage near your farm."

Miguel watched as the last comment hit Mercer. He seemed to deflate even more as realization sunk in. Miguel knew that Mercer had met Ted's girlfriend a few years back.

"What happened to her?"

"Ted's not sure. He thinks that whatever was in that ash was toxic," Miguel said, watching Mercer's face for any signs of guilt. "He also thinks she had a miscarriage."

Mercer was visibly shaking now.

"Do you know what Ted's girlfriend is sick with?" Jessie asked.

"Her name is Rachel," Mercer said suddenly, anger in his voice.

Miguel looked at Jessie and leaned back in his chair. "I think she has cancer. I don't know if Ted knows for sure, but there were a lot papers about cancer lying around this table a couple of nights ago, right before he told me he was going on his trip."

Jessie nodded. She reached down and pulled a notepad and pen out of her bag.

"Miguel, you said that there were other people who have gotten sick. Some kids and older folks. Do you have names?" Jessie asked.

"Yeah, I could probably name a few, but I'm not going to, not now. My niece is looking into it. I'm sorry, but I know these people, and I don't know you. You have to understand that some of these people we'll never find again. They don't exist, at least not in any books. They do the work no one else wants and live on the edge of society trying not to be seen."

When Jessie looked at him, puzzled, he said, "They are migrant workers. Illegals. The ones I knew moved on, looking for work that wasn't as strenuous when they first started getting sick. The names they had weren't their own. Just realize that quite a few people have gotten sick."

Jessie looked up from her pad, which already contained a half a page of notes.

The sun had moved far across the sky while they talked and now it beamed through the back window of the kitchen, casting light around the room.

Miguel looked at his watch and swore in Spanish under his breath. "*Perdóneme*," he said to Jessie. "*Pero*, I must get back to work. I have a lot of chores to do before I can call it quits."

"Miguel," Mercer said, rising and extending his hand. "Thank you so much for your help. I'm going to make things right, I promise."

Miguel measured the man now standing in front of him and finally took his hand. "I hope so, Will. This place needs some healing. Keep your head down," he said, cracking a smile. "It was nice to meet you as well, *Señorita.*" He extended his hand to Jessie.

"Thanks. You, too," Jessie said. "Oh, one more thing. Can we get Ted's cell phone number?"

Miguel thought about the request "Just be sensitive to his situation. He is going through a very difficult time and might not be very responsive."

Jessie nodded her understanding and thanked him again.

They drove in silence for a long time—Mercer lost in his thoughts and Jessie trying to organize hers. Miguel had given them a lot of information that they would need to follow up on, but now it was time to meet Pen and regroup. The day had been hot and Jessie looked forward to drinking a beer and watching the Willamette River flow by.

# CHAPTER 31

They spent the morning packing Russ's truck and were now speeding down Interstate 5, heading south to Salem. It was dusk by the time they pulled up across the street from Jeffery Pennoyer's office. Neither man was happy with what they saw. The office was merely a door that led to a second-story office suite, and the door was next to a coffee house full of people enjoying the summer evening.

"Not sure we could slip in there without being noticed," Cray said.

"We'll see what the morning crowd brings," Russ said. "Let's look for a hotel."

Fifteen minutes later, they were in their room creating a surveillance plan. Russ offered to take the first watch. They agreed they needed to get into the office to look around and see who they were dealing with. After developing a plan, the two men drove back to a place across the street from the office where they could watch without being conspicuous.

Wanting to check out the coffee house, Russ got out of the truck and went in. It was brighter than he had expected and full of people. Most were college age, though there was a mix. Russ grew uncomfortable almost instantly in the young crowd, with their multiple body piercings, dreadlocks, tattoos, and baggy, second-hand clothes. He soon realized that no matter how he dressed, he still stood out like the neo-conservative militant he was.

A blonde-haired, unshaven twenty-something was playing an acoustic guitar in the corner, singing a ballad of his trip along the Pacific coast. Russ paused to listen, acting as casual as he could. Most patrons were either watching the guitarist or talking quietly. One guy, who looked to be in his early thirties, was tucked back in the corner working on a laptop, earphones in his ears.

Russ feigned interest in the food on display in the large old-fashioned glass counter as he stood in line for coffee. The line moved in front of him, and he was soon next. The woman behind the counter was striking, with black hair and tattoos on her arms. She smiled at Russ and asked what he wanted.

"Ah ... two large house coffees to go, please."

"Okay, that'll be three bucks, even."

While Russ waited for his order, he read some of the posters and advertisements that lined the counter. Most of them were critical of the government. Some spoke of international atrocities, while others discussed local issues. All of them were "calls to arms" for the politically motivated. Then a business card caught his eye. He leaned in to read the print: Jeffrey Pennoyer, Attorney at Law. Specializing in environmental and natural resources law. *just upstairs* was added at the end in black marker.

"Here're your coffees, sweetie," the black-haired woman said, tapping Russ on the shoulder.

Russ nodded and picked up the two cups of coffee. Then he surveyed the place one last time. When he turned to leave, he noticed a back hallway that led to the restrooms and the alley. He made a mental note of the exit and headed for the front door.

"See anything interesting?" Cray asked, when he returned.

"Definitely the right place. The guy's business card is on the wall."

They sat and watched the office while they drank their coffee and Russ described the exit to the alley. Both were on edge because this was their only lead. They knew that instead of just killing Mercer, they would need to kill the woman and the attorney as well.

"This is great coffee," Cray said after taking a swallow.

"It's probably the first organic, shade-grown, fair-trade coffee you've ever had," Russ said, taking a sip.

After finishing their drinks, Cray got out of the truck and closed the door. "So I'm back to relieve you at 0200?"

"When you come back, we'll break into the office. Keep your phone on in case someone shows up."

"Sure. Good luck." Cray turned and walked off down the street.

Russ settled in for a long sit. He watched coffee patrons come and go. He noticed the clash of cultures as patrons from a sports bar at the end of the block left the bar and walked past the crowd of coffee drinkers. It was NASCAR meets Nietzsche.

The night dragged on as the street became more and more deserted. Panhandlers stalked pedestrians trying to make it from a restaurant or bar to their car without being accosted. Most simply pulled dollar bills from their pockets and handed them over so that they could pass unmolested.

The streets were soon deserted. The night sky clouded over and a light drizzle fell. It was a little after 1 a.m. and Russ was restless. He stretched, then decided to get out and look around. He walked up the block and headed for the alley behind the coffee house. All the businesses were closed for the night.

He slipped into the alley and looked for the back door to the coffee house. Instead, he discovered a rusty fire escape—a way into the office. Smiling, Russ jogged back to continue watching the front of the building.

Russ jumped as he opened the car door, Cray sitting unexpectedly inside. "Jesus, you're early," Russ said, his heart pounding.

"I thought you might need a break. Didn't know you were out bar-hopping."

"Very funny. Now that you're here, stay here. I'm going in. The place is deserted."

"Okay, I'll get comfortable. Have a good time breaking the law."

Russ pulled a bag from behind the seat and backtracked to the alley. He jumped up and grabbed the bottom rung of the fire escape. The ladder slid to the ground, the rusted metal grinding against itself, creating an eerie metallic scream. Russ looked over his shoulder to make sure he was still alone.

He climbed to the roof to see if there was access that might be easier to break into. A typical flat tarpaper-and-gravel roof, with vents poking up in different places, but no access to the building beneath. He went back to the fire escape.

Climbing back down to the second story, Russ examined the windows and tried to decipher structures in the dark rooms. He tried the window. It was unlocked. He slid it open and slipped inside.

The room was dark and quiet. Russ pulled a flashlight from his pack and flipped it on. The narrow beam cut across the office waiting area, illuminating the entrance door on the other side of the room. He moved around the room and entered the kitchen. It had been used recently as there were dishes in the sink and the trashcan was full.

Russ tried the closed door off the main room, which led to an office. One look at the shelf of legal books and he knew he was in the right place. He swept the room with his flashlight and froze when it hit a map tacked to the wall. It was a map of Molalla, one that Russ knew well. He examined the recent scribbling and drawing that overlaid the map. A cold sweat washed over him when he realized what he was looking at. He frantically searched the office for other papers, but it had been cleaned out. Russ turned on his phone and dialed Carson.

"Yes."

"We have a big problem. You know how we thought the attorney with Mercer was probably just a friend?"

"Yeah?"

"It looks like he's acting like an attorney. The stakes just got a lot higher."

* * *

Jessie and Mercer returned to Salem just as the sun was dipping behind the mountains. Pen was outside on the deck, reading and grilling steaks. He looked up when they entered and waved them over with a large grin. He pointed to the bucket of chilling beer and motioned for them to join him. Mercer grabbed two beers and handed one to Jessie.

"What are you all happy about?" Jessie asked, taking a sip of her beer.

"Just thinking through this entire case. I think we've got a chance here. You said you got some good information on your trip today. Let's sit down and compare notes."

The three sat at the outside table. Jessie reported what they had learned on their trip. Mercer related how his memories had returned and what they consisted of. Pen discussed the legal ramifications of the Green Grass company and the potential laws that had been broken. He had made a list of the information they would need to file a complaint.

"I don't need all the specifics for filing a complaint, that all comes during discovery. What I need are all of the players. So far on my list I have this Green Grass company and probably the state Department of Agriculture. Can you think of anyone else?"

"Sarah Carson gets her orders from someone else. Someone very powerful," Mercer said. "I never got close enough to find out who."

"So where does that leave us?" Jessie asked.

"I think you and Will need to get a hold of this Ted Kameron guy. We need to know what he knows. I'll see what I can find out about Green Grass and whether or not they're affiliated with anyone." Pen got up to check the steaks. "I have a friend with the District Attorney's office. I'll give him a call. In the meantime, Will, I want you to tell me everything you remember about the farm operations. But first, let's eat."

\* \* \*

"What do you want me to do?" Russ asked, an uneasiness permeating his gut. He had phoned Carson again after he had thoroughly searched the office. "I didn't find anything else, just the map."

"The map is plenty. It looks to me like we have an opportunity to make our entire problem go away—kill them all. Did you bring a silencer?"

"Yeah. I'll make sure Cray blocks them from leaving and all the loose ends will be wrapped up by noon."

"Good. Call me when it's done."

Russ dialed Cray and explained the plan. Cray understood his orders and checked his watch to make sure it was in sync. It was four-thirty in the morning.

\* \* \*

Daylight came too early for the late night Pen had spent going over civil procedure codes, environmental statutes, and recent case law before putting his legal complaint together. It was 6 a.m. and he found his two compatriots sound asleep in different rooms. He didn't want to wake them so he decided to go get his District Attorney friend's contact information from his office. Coffee, however, was the first priority of the day. He left a note and headed for his office.

There was a light crowd at the coffee house. A few regulars sat at tables reading books and newspapers. Pen was greeted by a yawning black-haired woman.

"Morning, Suzette," Pen said in response to her yawn. "Rough night?"

"No, I was here late—pulled a double shift. We had a band and the crowd hung around," she said, rubbing her eyes and stretching. "What can I get you, sweetie? The usual?"

"Yeah, but also give me two house coffees to go. So, were all of the usual suspects here last night?"

Suzette laughed. "So I'm guessing that I fall into the 'usual suspects' category, given the number of my tattoos and piercings? Am I a suspect now, Counselor? Who are you, 'The Man'?" she said, laughing. "Actually, I think 'The Man' was in here last night, trying to narc on my customers."

"What do you mean?" Pen asked.

"Just some guy who definitely did not fit in. He was tall. Big mustache. Looked very military. Drove a macho truck. We don't get that kind too often. Anyway, I think our clientele may have scared him off."

At mention of the man's description, alarms went off in Pen's head. He went to the large front window and looked across the street.

"Suzette, come here. Is that the same truck?"

"That's the same truck, but not the same guy."

"Hold my coffee for me? I'll be right back."

"Sure thing. Is anything wrong?"

"I'm not sure." Pen went to the back exit and the alley. He slowly opened the door and looked down the alleyway. It was deserted. He turned and his blood froze. There, almost touching the ground, was the fire escape ladder that led to his office. He knew it could be down for a couple of reasons, but he didn't buy any of the innocent ones. Pen backed into the coffee house and quietly closed the door. He dialed 9-1-1 and reported a break-in. He explained that he thought the intruder was still inside.

The operator told him that units were being dispatched to his location.

\* \* \*

Russ's cell phone rang. "Yeah," Russ said, adrenaline coursing through his body.

"The lawyer just walked into the coffee house. He's alone. Should be headed your way anytime. Keep the line open. I'll let you know when he's on his way up."

"Okay. Let's get this over with."

\* \* \*

Cray noticed the cruiser pull up to the coffee house, but figured they were stopping to get a refill. It was a coffee house, after all. He watched as the cop in the cruiser got out and went inside. Within a minute, two other cruisers had boxed Cray in and he barely had a chance to yell to Russ with a warning before he saw the cop from the coffee house exit and head for the law office. Three minutes after the first cruiser had pulled up, Cray found himself handcuffed and leaning face down on the hood of the truck.

"What are you arresting me for?"

"Loitering," answered one of the cops. "We'll see what else in a second." The cop frisked Cray. "Weapon," he reported when he felt the outline of Cray's Glock.

"I have a permit for that," Cray protested.

"Search the truck," he directed one of the other cops. "I think we have reasonable cause here. Don't you?"

"Fuck you," Cray spat.

\* \* \*

"Get out!" That was all Russ heard in his ear as Cray yelled the warning. Russ ran to the window he'd entered through. He grabbed his bag and stepped out onto the fire escape, just as a police car turned into the alley.

Russ scrambled up to the roof. He watched the cop in the cruiser jump out of the car, head for the ladder, and start climbing. He had no intention of waiting around. Russ ran along the roof, out of sight from the road, toward the entrance of the alley. Russ hoped this cop was alone. He made it to the far end of the building, which ran almost the entire city block. He could hear shouting from the street.

Russ smiled and waited. The young cop chasing him had finally made it to the roof. Russ watched him come, even putting up his arms in surrender, then he sprang into action. He pulled the gun from his bag, the silencer already attached, and fired two quick rounds toward the cop. Russ didn't intend to hit him; he just needed a distraction. The young cop saw the movement and jumped behind a vent, drawing his weapon.

Once the cop rolled out of view, Russ jumped off the building and dropped fifteen feet to a lower roof. The jump to the street was just as easy. He sprinted for the police car back in the alley. The cruiser door was still open, the keys in the ignition. Russ got into the car and started the engine. He pulled out of the alley, driving away from the commotion, and saw the young cop in his rearview mirror make it to the edge of the roof just in time to see his cruiser disappear around the corner.

Russ knew the police would be after him in a matter of minutes. Working from instinct, he turned on the lights and siren and sped onto a ramp to the highway. Cars pulled out of his way as he drove across the Willamette River. He took the first exit, turned off the lights and siren, and headed north.

Apartment complexes and strip malls lined the road. He looked further up the road and saw his escape. A city bus was approaching, though it was still a couple hundred yards away. He spotted the bus stop between him and the bus and pulled into the parking lot of an adjacent apartment complex. Getting out of the car, Russ tried to look as natural as possible. He looked into a couple of cars as if reporting to a call, then casually strolled to the main road.

The bus was just pulling up to the stop when Russ got there. He climbed aboard, paid his fee, and went to the back of the deserted bus. The driver never looked up; he just closed the door after hearing the change drop into the ticket machine. The bus pulled back into traffic and headed back the way Russ had come, over the river and toward the downtown bus depot. Russ watched as two police cruisers, lights flashing and sirens blaring, raced across the bridge toward the place where he had just abandoned the cruiser. He smiled.

\* \* \*

Pen entered his office after the police secured the area. They asked him to look around to see if anything was missing. Pen checked his desk and files, but everything seemed to be in order. The police finally sat him down on the couch and started a barrage of questions. His thoughts were spinning. Suddenly Pen's thoughts went to Jessie and Will.

He flipped open his phone and dialed Jessie. She answered with, "What's up?"

"Listen very carefully. Get all of our stuff together and get out of the house as fast as you can. They know where we are."

"What are you talking about?" Jessie asked, fear creeping into her voice.

"They were here at my office. They might know where I live. You have to get out now. Come to my office. The police are here. I'm going to call my buddy with the District Attorney's office. Move fast, Jessie. I don't know how much time you have."

"We'll be out of here in five minutes," Jessie said.

"Be careful. I'm sending the police to pick you up." Pen had written his address on a slip of paper while he was talking to Jessie and handed it to the cop who had been questioning him.

After getting off the phone with Jessie, Pen dialed the number for Josh Benjamin, his contact with the District Attorney's office. Pen had been enrolled in an attorney-student mentoring program while in law school and his mentor was the District Attorney for Marion County. The phone rang a few times before it was answered.

"This is Josh," said a groggy voice.

"Hi, Josh. Jeffrey Pennoyer. I'm really sorry to call you at home this early, but I'm in serious need of your help." Pen explained his situation, the case he was working on, and the recent developments while the D.A. listened silently on the other end.

Once Pen had finished explaining his situation, Josh said, "Let me talk to the officer in charge. Stay where you are. I'm on my way."

"Yes, of course. Thanks, Josh."

Pen handed the phone to the officer. The large man took the phone and listened in silence. He only spoke two words to Josh: "Yes, sir."

Handing the phone back to Pen, he said, "Mr. Benjamin will be here in ten minutes. I'll post a man up here, down at the door, and across the street."

"Thanks for all of your help," Pen said. "I can't tell you how much I appreciate it."

"This is what we do. I need to go question the suspect we have in custody. I'll send an officer up here as soon as I can."

\* \* \*

Russ got off the bus at the depot in the center of town, roughly three blocks east of where his partner was in police custody. A few cars lined the road. They would be easy enough to steal but they were too visible. Then he saw the sign for the parking garage and smiled. Ten minutes later, he pulled out of the garage in a beat-up Chevy pickup truck. Reaching for his phone, he dialed Carson.

"Tell me it's good news."

"We've had a security breach."

"How bad?"

"Bad. Cray's in custody. I'm on the run."

"Talk to me," she said, her voice full of stress.

"I'm not going down for this. I'm out," Russ said.

"What?" he heard Carson scream as he hung up.

Russ got back on his phone and dialed Sully. It rang for a long time before Sully finally answered.

"What?"

"It's me. I'm in a jam. I need an extraction."

"Where are you?"

"I can be out at Silver Falls State Park in half an hour," Russ said.

"I'll meet you there. Be safe."

Thirty minutes later, Russ pulled his stolen truck off the road. He got out and scanned the sky for Sully. Over the cool breeze, he heard the sounds of rotors, then Sully's chopper came into view, flying low over the treetops. It circled Russ, then hovered twenty feet away. Russ ran to the chopper and climbed in next Sully.

Sully guided the helicopter back up, turning east and once again flying just above the trees, the helicopter soon disappeared into the morning mist.

* * *

Carson was enraged. Her blood pressure and cortisol levels were spiking almost at the same time. *What the fuck is going on? How dare Russ just bail like a coward. And where the hell was Cray? He was in custody?* As she replayed the short conversation with Russ over in her head, her rage started to turn to panic. She never panicked. The feeling was alien to her. She planned, executed, and enforced, but never panicked. She could see everything unraveling, as if someone had just pulled a thread on a rug. She needed to get out. If Cray talked, the police would be showing up sooner or later. Calling Ashe was out of the question unless she wanted to die young. Her eyes darted around her office. It was full of incriminating evidence. The maps, the files, not to mention the laptop that sat on her desk—all implicated her. She needed to get rid of as much as she could and fast. She grabbed a stack of files from one of the file cabinets and ran to the shredder.

\* \* \*

The police officer in charge of the situation at Pen's office was Captain Murphy, a large man with bushy eyebrows and a nice smile. He had been on the police force for many years but this was the first time he had ever been involved with a hired hit. His officers had performed nearly flawlessly, though the rookie losing his cruiser wasn't good.

Captain Murphy left Pen to go take a look at the man his officers were holding down on the street. The man sitting in the back of the cruiser looked military or ex-military. Murphy went to the other cruiser to see what his officers had found in the truck. The items were laid out on the hood of the car, one of his officer standing guard.

"What do we have here?" On the hood lay a pistol, its clip of bullets and silencer lying next to it; a high-powered rifle with some kind of fancy scope; a couple of IDs for two men, one of whom sat in custody, the other on the run; $5,000 in cash; and a picture of the attorney with the office address scrawled on the back.

"I've never seen one, but this looks like all of the ingredients of a contract hit. What do you think, Joe?" Murphy asked the officer standing guard.

"That's what it looks like to me, Cap."

"Tag them and put everything in your trunk, Joe. I want to go have a chat with our friend."

Murphy went back to where Cray was sitting and opened the door. Cray looked at him for a second, then turned his head and stared straight ahead.

"You know you're in a lot of trouble, son. I got enough from your truck to charge you with conspiracy to commit murder. But it doesn't have to go that way. Maybe all I have you on is unlawful possession of a loaded firearm. So, what do you say, pal? Gonna help me out?"

Cray turned toward Murphy, a smoldering fire in his eyes. "Charge me or let me go. If you charge me, then I want to talk to my lawyer. Otherwise, shut the fuck up."

Murphy laughed. "Ah, spit and vinegar, huh? Okay, tough guy, we can play it your way. You're under arrest for conspiracy to commit murder, unlawful possession of a weapon, possession of a concealed weapon, and whatever else I can think of on the way back to the station."

Murphy pulled his head out of the cruiser and stood up. "Hey, Joe, read this jackass his rights for me, then take him to the station, book him, and find him a nice cozy holding cell. I'll be down later."

Murphy closed the car door and went back across the street to Pen's office.

"Hi, there, Murph," Suzette said, coming out of the coffee house with a cup of coffee. "Here, just the way you like it."

"Thanks, honey," Murphy said in a fatherly tone. "Are you doing okay?"

"A little shaken up, but I'm alright."

Suzette disappeared back into the coffee house. Murphy took a deep breath and went up the stairs to Pen's office.

\* \* \*

Murphy was standing talking to Pen when two people carrying large boxes entered.

226

"Captain, this is Jessie, this is Will," Pen said.

The D.A., Josh Benjamin, arrived a few minutes later. At sixty-two, he was the oldest man in the room, even though his tall, slim stature made him appear younger. His hair, which had been black in his early days, was now salt and pepper, with more salt than pepper.

They all sat or stood in the waiting area. Pen thanked them all for their help and explained what had transpired in the last several hours.

"We've been working on a case for the last few days, trying to figure out how to approach it. I would like you to hear the story that Jessie and I heard. This gentleman is Will Mercer," Pen said, pointing to Will. "It's his story that resulted in the events that transpired this morning."

Mercer took his cue and began to tell his story, and this time his memory was complete. He explained about the events that led up to the car chase, his struggle in the wilderness, Jessie's help, the second attempt on his life, his memory returning. Several times, Murphy's jaw dropped as the story progressed. When Mercer finally finished, an uneasy silence spread through the room.

Josh broke the silence. "That's unbelievable. Where are you going with this case, Jeffrey?"

"I started researching the environmental laws that this company broke. I realize a number of criminal charges can be brought as well, which is why I was going to contact your office. We are also going to follow up leads on the potential health issues of residents living near the farm, but we're just starting on that."

"We have one lead that we were going to check out today," Jessie offered. "His name is Ted Kameron."

"And there's something going on with the state field inspector who covers this area."

"We need to think about next steps here," Josh said. "Captain Murphy, what's the status of the two men involved this morning?"

"We have one in custody. The other fled the scene and we haven't picked him up yet. We issued a BOLO for him. The guy in custody isn't talking. They were serious, though. They had a high-powered rifle with a fancy infrared scope, pistol with silencer—the works."

Murphy saw Jessie stiffen.

"Excuse me, did you say they had a rifle?" asked Jessie.

"Yeah. Pretty fancy, too," Murphy said.

"You need to contact the state police in Bend," Jessie said. Murphy could almost see her mind working. "I think these guys were responsible for the forest ranger shooting out there a couple of days ago."

"What?" Murphy asked, surprised.

"I think they thought they were shooting Will, but we had already left and my replacement was in the tower."

Murphy turned to his officer. "Get on it. I want to know if the same weapon was used in that shooting before I talk to this guy."

"Yes, sir," the officer said, calling in to dispatch to get patched in with the state police as he left Pen's office.

Josh finally sat down on the couch and sighed. "Okay," he said, "we might need to move fast here or else these people are going to run. And for you three," he said, turning to Pen, Jessie, and Mercer, "you are coming with me to my office. There's a little more room to spread out there, not to mention additional security."

"And we're already packed," Pen said, motioning to the boxes.

"Good. Let's go, then. Thanks for all the help, Murph," Josh said. Pen, Jessie, and Will nodded in agreement.

"I'll be in touch as soon as possible with any new information," Murphy said.

# CHAPTER 32

Ted woke up early after a solid night of sleep. Even though it had been late when he finally drifted off, he realized that he hadn't slept well in a long time. He lay in bed remembering the previous night and how wonderful it had been to find Rachel and realize she still cared for him.

He pulled up to Rachel's house at 8:30 and they walked to a local restaurant just down the street for breakfast. Ted was only too eager to stretch his legs after a full day of traveling. The morning was still cool but starting to get humid, a well-known trait of New England summers.

The restaurant was excellent, and Ted ate well, enjoying the company. Thoughts of his farm and responsibilities drifted away, replaced with what seemed like a new life. The conversation at the table was vibrant and Rachel broke out in laughter more than once. Each time she did, her mother looked at Ted and gave him a little wink.

As they walked back to the house after breakfast, Ted's cell phone sprang to life. The caller ID said it was Miguel. "I'll catch up. I have to take this."

"Okay, but don't you disappear on me."

Ted threw her his keys. "This should guarantee that I'm staying." He answered the call.

"*Hola, amigo. Que tal?*"

"*Bien.* How are you?"

"I'm doing great. Having a good time," Ted said happily. "Everything okay with the farm?"

"The farm is fine. But I had two visitors come looking for you yesterday with some interesting information. Will Mercer showed up on your doorstep with a woman," Miguel said.

"Mercer? I thought he had gone home or something? What did he say?"

"He says there are some men out to kill him; that he's been on the run. They were talking about the field burning and people getting sick. Anyway, I gave him your phone number."

Ted's mind raced to process what he had just heard. "I'm glad you did. Any news from Dia?"

"Yes, I just spoke to her. She said she tested the blood and tissue samples. They were off the chart for benzene—her words. She has also been tracking down workers who had sicknesses similar to what benzene could cause. She came up with a list of about twenty people so far."

"Who?" asked Ted.

"Let's see," Miguel said. "There is a Señor Bouche, little Isa O'Sullivan, Señor and Señora Calderon, Señorita de la Pena, little Josh Evans," Miguel began. "I will have her email you the list."

"Okay, good. I know a couple of people on that list," replied Ted sighing.

"*Amigo*, how is Miss Rachel?"

"She's really sick. I'm sure it's connected to the shit they're burning."

"What are you going to do?"

"I can't leave her. Not until she's better. I want to talk to Mercer. The vet is involved somehow as part of the payoff to keep ranchers quiet." Anger rose in Ted. "Miguel, I need you to take over operations until I return."

"*Amigo*, I will take care of everything," he said proudly. "Tell Miss Rachel that we are praying for her."

"I will. Thanks," Ted said, and hung up.

Rachel and her mother had stopped to wait for Ted, who trotted up beside them.

"Everything okay?" Rachel asked.

"Yep. That was Miguel. I needed to give him a promotion because he will be running the farm until I get back. So now you know I'm here indefinitely."

* * *

Cray was taken to the police station, fingerprinted, and booked. All they had him for were a couple of firearm infractions, and he had legitimate permits for the weapons. Since Cray had not seen Russ at the police station, he figured Russ had slipped away. They couldn't prove anything. But as Cray talked himself through the events that had taken place, fear tugged at the back of his mind.

After what seemed like hours, an officer came into the general lockup area and called his name. Cray rose from the bench.

"Time for you to make your call. This way." The officer opened the cell and pointed Cray in the direction of a phone on the wall.

"About time," Cray mumbled.

The officer glared, unmoved by Cray's attitude, but walked down the hallway to allow Cray some privacy.

Cray grabbed the receiver and dialed Russ's cell phone. It switched to voicemail automatically. Frustrated, Cray dialed Carson.

"It's me, Cray. I got picked up. I'm gonna need some help."

"Help, huh?" Carson spit. "Seems to me that you made your bed. You're the one who got caught, not me. And your friend ran. That asshole called and told me he was 'out.' Just like that. So consider yourself on your own. And, if you think about talking, remember how much I can pin on you," Carson said, and then hung up.

Cray stood with the receiver in his hand, shaking with fury. Taking a deep breath, he hung up the phone and looked toward the officer.

"I'm going to need the name of a public defender."

* * *

Captain Murphy arrived at the police station after Cray had been booked. So far, his morning had seen more action than almost his entire career. One of his officers waved at him as he sat down at his desk. "Line two, Captain," he yelled across the room.

Murphy looked at the blinking light on his phone. He sighed and picked up the receiver. "This is Captain Murphy."

"This is Trooper Johnson out of Bend. I got a call from one of your officers about a shooting. He said you might have picked up the guy? I want to fax the ballistics information to you."

"Yeah," Murphy said, "this morning. I haven't had a chance to talk to him yet."

"Just a heads up. The FBI is involved on this one since the guy who was shot was a federal employee. You should be hearing from them too."

"We're still trying to sort it all out on this end. I'd appreciate the information." Murphy gave the trooper the fax number.

Murphy hung up and the fax machine jumped to life a couple of minutes later, spitting out several pages. Murphy scanned the information. The type of rifle matched. He would be able to confirm once they ran their own test, but he had enough to start turning the screws on the suspect. He took a folder from his desk and placed the papers inside, then went to the holding area.

"Bring Mr. Cray Warren to interview room two, please," Murphy said to the officer in charge.

Murphy went to the observation area for the interview room and waited for Cray. It was his first chance to get a good look at the guy.

Cray walked into the room with purpose and sat down. He was obviously military, though Murphy figured he was now more mercenary. He looked very calm and Murphy figured this wasn't his first rodeo. After making Cray wait ten minutes, Murphy walked in.

"Has he asked for his attorney yet?" he asked the officer standing guard inside the room.

"Yes, Captain, though he wants a public defender. Someone should be here in an hour."

Murphy sat down and turned his attention to Cray. "Okay, Mr. Warren, do you understand your rights as they were read to you?"

"Yes," Cray's eyes fixed on the wall straight ahead.

"We can wait until your attorney gets here or I can tell you what I have on you right now. I want you to understand I'm not looking for a confession and I would advise you not to make one until you consult your attorney. Understood?"

"Yes." Eyes still fixed on the wall.

"Good. As you know, we have you on several weapons charges, including a loaded weapon in a vehicle and carrying a concealed weapon. But those are small fish compared to what I think I have you for." Murphy opened the folder in front of him and watched for a reaction.

"You see, these are ballistic reports from the state crime lab. Someone shot a Forest Service employee a couple of nights ago with a high-powered rifle, a rifle just like the one I found in your possession. Now rifles in Oregon are not unusual. The thing that caught my attention was your scope. What kind of settings does that thing have? Night vision? Infrared? Where do you even get something like that?"

Cray didn't respond, though Murphy noticed his eyes now focused on him.

"I need to run some tests, but I think I'm going to find that your rifle was the same one that killed that poor kid in the fire tower. What was he, like 22 years old? The thing is, once I find that out, this whole thing will be out of my hands. The FBI is heading the investigation because a federal employee was murdered. And I have to tell you, those special agents are tough. Anyway, think about what I said. Think about why no one would take your call or help you out this morning. I heard that you made two calls before asking for a court-appointed attorney. Sounds to me like you're being set up. Talk to your attorney, and I'll come back down to discuss this with you again."

Cray's eyes had dropped to the floor.

Murphy stood and gestured to the officer to follow, then walked out of the room. He turned to the officer once they had closed the interview room door.

"Okay, I am going to get in touch with the FBI and then head over to Josh Benjamin's office. Call me when his attorney shows up," directed Murphy.

"Sure thing, Captain."

Murphy returned to his desk and dialed the FBI field office in Portland.

\* \* \*

Pen, Jessie, Mercer, and Josh entered the government building and went to Josh's office. The room held a large worktable at one end and the walls were lined with legal textbooks. Pen's boxes were put on the worktable. Pen, Jessie, and Mercer took seats, still recovering from the morning's events.

"Captain Murphy should be here soon," Josh said. "Let's review what we know before he gets here so we're clear. Will, much of this will fall on you because you're our primary witness and have been involved since the beginning. What I'd like to do is put together a timeline starting with when you first began working for Green Grass Enterprises."

Josh turned to Pen. "You've done this kind of exercise before. How about taking notes?" Josh prompted Mercer to begin his story.

Will began with the time he was hired. Josh interrupted a few times as he probed for more information. The exercise also helped Mercer. Retelling his life over the past few years helped him to examine his memories and strengthen his ability to recall them. An hour later, they had sketched out a rough roadmap of events that led up to the attempted murder that had occurred hours before. They had just finished when there was a knock on the door.

"Come on in," Josh said as Captain Murphy entered. "Welcome, Murph. Glad you could join us."

Murphy sat down and Josh summarized the salient points of Mercer's story, and Murphy filled them in on the FBI's interest in the rifle.

"The suspect also made two calls from the station. I don't know who those calls were to; however, I do know that one call lasted five seconds and one lasted one minute. Typically, a five-second call means that he never got connected or it went straight to voicemail. But what I find interesting is that after the one-minute call, he requested a public defender. That suggests to me that he's been left to take a fall," Murphy said. "He likely called his boss. If they were going to protect him, then a high-powered attorney would've showed up. Instead, he's asking for a public defender, indicating that his boss is cutting him loose. I find that very interesting."

"So where do we go from here?" Jessie asked.

"We need to follow the evidence," Josh said. "If we make too many assumptions, it could come back to haunt us in court. I'll call Judge Simpson and get a search warrant for this guy's residence," Josh said. "We have probable cause to justify a warrant at this point. Hopefully, we will find some evidence there to point us in another direction. I'll explain to the judge that there was another man involved who escaped and we're trying to find any connection that might help us apprehend him. Do you have this guy's home address, Murph?"

"Yes." Murphy flipped open his notebook. "I'll coordinate with the FBI and get the locals to secure the scene until we get up there."

* * *

Mercer had been quiet for the last half hour, attempting to put together an idea in his head that Murphy triggered when he reported on the status of the suspect. Suddenly it clicked.

"Captain," Mercer said, catching everyone off-guard, "you said the guy made two calls. What if I could tell you the second number?"

"I guess I would find that very interesting."

"So would I," Josh said.

"The number he called was (503) 555-7789. That's the number for Sarah Carson of Green Grass Enterprises, his boss," Mercer said.

"That might change everything," Josh said. "Murph, can you get an address on that place? A physical one? There have to be tax records or something that lists a physical address."

"I'll get someone on it right away. In the meantime, we'll check out the home address." Murphy got out his cell and dialed.

"I know I'm the novice here," Pen said, "but if this Cray guy called his boss and she knows he's in custody and decided not to help him out, isn't she going to destroy every piece of evidence she can?"

"Excellent observation," Josh said. "Murph, the home address can wait. We need this work address ASAP."

Time passed slowly while the group waited for information on the address. Pen sat with Jessie and Mercer huddled together over the information they had already pulled together.

"The thing I keep going back to," Pen said, looking up at Josh, "is that we're only talking about the storage and disposal aspect of this operation. There has to be a source of the chemicals, like a parent company. That's the big dog we need to take down."

"I agree," Josh said, "though proving that might be very difficult. We need to prove that there was, or is, sufficient oversight of the parent company for liability to transfer to them. If this Green Grass was acting on its own, or if they were disposing for several companies, we might not be able to get there."

"I would bet this Green Grass group has no assets and therefore no injured party can recoup damages," Pen offered.

"Got it," Murphy said, hanging up his cell phone. "It's a warehouse up in Wilsonville, right off the Interstate."

Josh dialed the judge, who granted the search warrant.

"Murph, I want us all there," Josh said. "We'll stay out of the way, but Will can help decipher anything you might come across. Also, based on the insight just displayed by these kids—and I don't mean that in a derogatory way, I'm just old—it's critical that they be there to walk us through it. They seem to know what's going on."

"You'll need to wait until we secure the scene," Murphy said. "I need to coordinate with the Wilsonville PD and the County Sheriff."

"Perfect," Josh said. "Let's get moving."

As they drove north on Interstate 5, Pen recounted to Josh everyone he thought was involved: Green Grass, State Department of Agriculture, and a parent company. Josh winced at the naming of the state department.

"Can you confirm the state's involvement?"

"No, not at this time. The guy who heads up the burning program was just extremely unhelpful. His name is Crocker."

"I'll get someone to look into that," Josh said. "Anyone else of interest?"

"There's a local rancher?" Jessie said. "His girlfriend got really sick. His property is adjacent to the Molalla farm."

"Have you spoken with him yet?"

"No," Mercer said. "We spoke with his farmhand. He's out of town, but we have his cell phone number."

"See if you can get him on the line," Josh instructed. "See what he knows, if he has any names."

Jessie flipped through her notepad until she came to the number for Ted Kameron.

\* \* \*

Ted's phone buzzed to life on Rachel's kitchen table. They had been drinking coffee and catching up.

"Hello," he said, answering the unfamiliar phone number.

"Mr. Kameron?"

"Yes, this is Ted Kameron. Who is this?"

"My name is Jessie O'Brien. I got your number from Miguel. I'm working with Will Mercer regarding what's been going on at Green Grass."

"Miguel told me you might call."

"Oh, good. How's your girlfriend doing?" Jessie asked, compassion coming through in her voice.

"We're trying to figure that out."

"Mr. Kameron, may I call you Ted?"

"Heck, yeah. Mr. Kameron's my dad," the strain in Ted's voice easing.

"Thanks. The reason I'm calling is that things have passed a tipping point here. We are putting together a case with the District Attorney's office and right now we're on our way to search the Green Grass office. I don't have a lot of time to talk right now, but I do need two things from you. The first is if you know of anyone else involved. We are trying to figure out how deep this conspiracy goes."

"Who do you have so far?"

Jessie read off the short list of suspects.

"I hate to do it because they're nice guys, but I'd add the veterinarians to that list."

"Miguel mentioned something about that but he didn't go into any detail."

"Miguel is a pretty tight-lipped guy. Anyway, the outfit's name is Willamette Valley Breeders. The thing about the company is that they sell livestock throughout the valley but they have to do it at a loss, given the kind of insurance and warranties they provide. Their payout for down or dead animals is so high they pretty much have the entire business. And because they pay so well, no one questions why the cows are dying or why there are so many miscarriages."

"Why do you think their pay-out is so high?"

"To hide evidence and keep the locals quiet. I took samples from where the last cow died and had a buddy run some tests. The benzene levels were off the chart for both the ash and water samples we tested. Benzene is a carcinogen, among other things." Ted's chest was getting tight with anger. "You said there was a second thing?"

"You just covered it. Do you think we can get copies of those reports?"

"Give me your email address. I'll email copies to you. By the way, you might also want to look at the local property maps. I was doing some of my own research and it looks like Green Grass bought up a lot of land around their original farm. My farm was one of the hold-outs."

"Thanks," Jessie said, writing down everything he said. "You should have my number on your cell phone if you think of anything else. Are you coming back soon?"

"No, but I'm available to talk. I really need to be here right now."

"I understand," Jessie said. "Thanks so much for your help. I'll be in touch."

"No, thanks for your help. Let's get these bastards."

\* \* \*

"We have another player," Jessie announced. "Willamette Valley Breeders in Molalla." She recounted what Ted had told her.

"Okay, good," Josh said. He flipped open his phone and dialed the Molalla Police Department. "Yes, hi. This is District Attorney Josh Benjamin. May I please speak to the officer in charge?" Josh explained to the officer on the other end exactly what was going on. "I need a couple of cruisers to babysit a couple of places for me. The first is Willamette Valley Breeders. Make sure they don't run. The second is a farm in Molalla, one Green Grass Enterprises. Don't let anyone on or off the property. Thanks, I'll be in touch."

\* \* \*

Two police cars and an unmarked sedan were in the parking lot of the deserted warehouse when they pulled in. The passengers peered out at the empty parking lot, their hearts sinking. The doors were locked tight, a No Trespassing sign posted in the parking lot.

"I'm not sure we're in the right place," Murphy said, getting out of the cruiser. The local cops approached him. "Thanks for meeting us here," Murphy said. "You guys know anything about this building?"

Two of the cops were Wilsonville police and the third was FBI special agent, Lynn Brewster. Agent Brewster was a six-foot-tall black woman in a sharply cut navy pant suit, her weaved hair pulled back in a ponytail.

"It used to be a computer component warehouse, but that was probably ten years ago," one cop said. "It's been empty ever since. I think they pretty much gutted the place before they left."

"I'm not so sure it's abandoned," Pen said, stepping out of Josh's car and pointing to the lower corner of the roofline. Everyone turned to see a surveillance camera sweeping the parking lot. "Not sure why you'd need surveillance on an empty parking lot for an empty warehouse."

"Let's find out." Josh said, pulling out the search warrant.

"Okay," Murphy said. "I want anyone who is not law enforcement back behind the cruisers." Murphy opened his trunk, pulled out a shotgun, and asked one of the younger cops, "Will you grab my door knocker?" His "door knocker" was a sledgehammer. "The rest of you follow me."

The cops quickly approached the door, weapons drawn. Murphy tried the metal doorknob, but it was locked. Motioning for the cop with the sledgehammer, Murphy moved aside to give him room. One hit popped the locks, and the door swung open into darkness. Cops, weapons drawn, stepped inside.

The interior of the expansive warehouse bay was as dark as night. The only light that pierced the interior came from the open door that backlit the police, making them easy targets.

"Get away from the door!" Murphy barked, seeing their vulnerability. He ran his hand along the wall until his fingers found a light switch. He flicked it on.

Murphy stepped into the large bay and scanned the room. It appeared deserted except for a red Mustang and a black Cadillac Escalade. The Mustang looked like it hadn't been driven in a while compared to the mud-caked Escalade.

The cops cleared the large room, methodically searching it. The contents of the warehouse, other than the vehicles, consisted of a few empty wooden pallets and some locked storage lockers. Murphy moved up a staircase to a room lined with old computer monitors and dust. It, too, was empty.

Murphy went back down to the door that led to the parking lot and motioned for everyone to come inside.

"We didn't find anything. It looks like someone might just use it for vehicle storage."

"Someone uses this place. The mud seems pretty fresh on this SUV," Agent Brewster said, inspecting the large Escalade.

\* \* \*

Jessie went up the staircase to the second story and watched through the large windows as the cops tried to get into the locked Escalade. Her gaze dropped to the floor where something caught her eye. She looked down the length of the floor, then went back down the stairs to Murphy.

"I found something, maybe. Can I show you?"

Murphy nodded.

"Look at the counter, then look at the floor," Jessie said.

Murphy moved past her and examined the countertop. It was covered with a thick layer of dust, except for several square panels. His eyes dropped to the floor where dust had piled up against the walls. The main walkway was clean, with a few muddy prints. Like a bloodhound on scent, Murphy followed the muddy prints across the floor to a place along the wall. Murphy went back to Jessie, who was still standing at the top of the staircase.

"Good job. Now get back downstairs and tell the other officers to come up here," Murphy whispered.

Adrenaline coursing through her veins, Jessie ran down the stairs to the other officers. They pulled their weapons and moved past her toward the staircase.

* * *

While he was waiting for them to arrive, Murphy went back and examined the floor. He noticed what appeared to be a hidden doorway, the thin lines invisible to the casual onlooker. He stepped back and motioned to the other officers. The young officer relegated to battering in doors, moved forward and swung the large sledge, smashing what seemed to be a solid concrete wall. The force of the strike and the lack of resistance sent the officer through the hidden doorway, splintering it under the force.

The officers rushed into the room, weapons pointing in different directions. The difference between the warehouse floor and this hidden room was unnerving. Motion-activated lights flicked on as they burst into the room. As their eyes adjusted to the brighter lighting, they found themselves in a large luxurious room with a pool table, a TV, a couch, a couple of desks, and a kitchen off to one side.

Another closed door was set in the far wall between the two desks. The officers once again made sure the room was clear before coming together at the closed door. Murphy tried the doorknob. It was unlocked. Slowly turning the doorknob, Murphy pushed the door wide open and the other officers swept the room.

The office had been ransacked. Shredded papers were strewn everywhere. Wires once connected to a computer lay across the otherwise empty desk. The room was deserted However, the activity that had taken place had been recent.

"All clear, Murph," shouted one of the officers.

"Good. Bring everyone else up here," he said over his shoulder. Murphy examined some of the shredded documents to see if he could make out any words. The rest of the group entered the outer room and went straight to where Murphy stood.

"Nobody touch anything," Murphy said. "I'm treating this as a crime scene."

The rest of the group nodded, shocked by the condition of the inner office.

"Looks like we missed them by an hour or so," Josh said.

Murphy turned and looked at him, shaking his head. "Yeah, we were close."

Pen entered the office with the rest of the group and went to the desk. He saw a printer lying on the floor next to it. He sat in the chair and took in the surroundings. It was the wires on the desk that caught his attention. Something was off but he couldn't put his finger on it.

"Hey, Jessie, come here for a sec."

Jessie went to where Pen was sitting. "What a mess."

"Yeah, we were so close. But I have a question for you. Something here is bugging me and I can't figure out what it is. I can't seem to account for all the cables on the desk. There are too many. One for the missing computer, one for the printer, what are the rest?"

Jessie examined the cords. "These two look like network cables. One connects to that router, so it's the internet connection, but the other network cable goes into the floor. Typically in businesses, they go to a server, which is used as a shared backup hard drive. That hard drive should be somewhere nearby. My guess is that it's somewhere in this office."

"Okay. So what do we do?"

"I'm gonna go get my laptop out of the car and see if I can hook into the network. You should brief the rest of the group. The cable runs under the floor; we need to find the physical drive in case I can't get in."

Jessie heard Pen explain her theory to the others as she left to retrieve her laptop.

# CHAPTER 33

The BMW sped along the country road, Carson in a state of panic. She had fled the warehouse just in time. There were loose ends she needed to tie up. No one she had been calling had answered their phones, and she wasn't sure where to go.

"Damn it!" she yelled as she got voicemail again. She pulled into the parking lot at Willamette Valley Breeders, but her blood ran cold as a police cruiser pulled in behind her, so she continued through the parking lot and exited back onto the main road. In her rearview mirror, she saw the police car pull into a parking spot and two uniformed cops get out.

Carson stepped on the accelerator and sped down the road, then her muscles froze. She heard the siren before she saw the cruiser. It came up behind her fast. Within seconds, it would be on her. She quickly turned into a side street. The cruiser sped by, siren wailing and lights flashing.

She pulled off the road and rested her head on the steering wheel in an attempt to calm her nerves. She was at the end of her rope, but knew that if she could just keep it together, she might get out of this mess. She was a survivor. Carson had loaded her trunk with enough evidence incriminating Ashe that even if she got caught, she thought she could plea bargain her way out. It was unhealthy to cross Ashe, but at this point her choices were pretty slim. Talking herself down, Carson regained control of her nerves. She pulled the car back onto the road and drove toward the farm.

The five-minute drive seemed to take an hour. As the car climbed a rise, Carson slammed on her brakes, seeing a police cruiser at the end of the driveway, blocking the entrance to the farm. They had everything locked down. Carson drove carefully past the cruiser, the cops paying little attention as she passed.

She drove toward the Interstate. She needed to get some distance, but she wasn't sure in which direction. Canada was closer than Mexico, but fleeing the country wasn't yet a solid plan. First, she needed to get her things and pick up some traveling money. Turning onto the on-ramp, Carson sped north on Interstate 5 toward Portland.

* * *

Sully flew Russ back to his compound. During the flight, Russ tried to figure out his next move. He was now on the run, with no safe harbor. He had crossed Cray and Carson for self-preservation but in doing so, he had also crossed Ashe. He was playing a dangerous game. The only way out of this mess was to turn on Carson again and tell Ashe about the current situation. By turning on her, Russ might enter the good graces of the man himself.

"Sully, I need to borrow your satellite phone," Russ said as they sat in Sully's backyard.

"Sure, but I gotta ask, what kind of trouble are you in? You know the law has been watching this place. All they need is a reason and I'm screwed."

"Relax. I'll get you out of this mess. I have a plan. That's why I need your phone."

"The other thing, buddy, is the money. We're friends, but this is business."

"I'll get the money."

Sully threw Russ the phone and went inside. Russ looked after him, wondering if his old friend was going to be a problem. Russ dialed Ashe's office.

The phone clicked as it connected and rang somewhere on the other end. Finally, Ashe said, "Yes?"

"Mr. Ashe," Russ said, no longer confident, "this is Russ Miller. I work for Sarah Carson."

"I know who you are. I don't know why you're calling me," Ashe growled.

"Have you, ah, heard from Carson?"

"No, it seems as if she's avoiding me. Is there something you wish to talk to me about?"

"Well, sir, all hell's broken loose."

"Be clear, man," Ashe growled.

Russ took a deep breath to regain his composure. "Yes, sir. Here's the situation. One member of her team, Cray, has been apprehended by the Salem Police Department. He will likely be charged with the murder of a federal employee, which will pull in the FBI. The last I knew, Carson was in the office in a state of panic. Will Mercer—the farm manager—is still alive and is teamed up with an attorney. I have gone into hiding after barely escaping the police. I believe Carson cut Cray loose. Sir, I'm sure Cray will make a deal if he can. I thought you should be informed of the situation."

Ashe was silent. When he finally spoke, his voice was low and dangerous. "I wasn't aware of any of this. Ms. Carson will be handled. Her disloyalty to me will be repaid. Are you loyal to me, Miller?"

"Yes, sir."

"Good."

"But I don't have access to any assets," Russ said.

"Be at my office. Three o'clock. We will discuss your continued employment," Ashe said, and the connection went dead.

Russ smiled and let out a long breath.

Sully wandered back into the yard, a couple of cold beers in his hands. "I know it's early, but I figured you've probably already had a long day. Sorry about before."

Russ nodded. "I made a deal, buddy. I'll get the money I owe you, but I need a ride to pick it up."

"When do we go?"

"Around 1300. Do you have a backpack I can use?"

"Sure." Sully looked oddly at him.

"And how about some food?" Russ was beginning to feel good.

"Now we're talking. I'll throw on a couple of steaks," replied Sully.

"You might also want to pack some things. You know, the incriminating stuff."

"Yeah, yeah. I know. I'm on it." Sully seemed annoyed but he was still smiling.

At 3:00 p.m., Sully's helicopter landed on the heliport of one of Portland's Westside skyscrapers. Russ slid from the passenger side of the helicopter and went to the rooftop entrance. Once inside, Russ went down the short flight of stairs to a landing that contained only an elevator door. Pressing the down button, the door opened and Russ entered.

His hands were sweaty and he tried to gather himself. He took a deep breath as the elevator door opened to marble flooring and dark wood walls. Russ stepped out and began walking down the long hallway. A receptionist at the end of the hall looked up as Russ approached.

"Go in, Mr. Miller. He's expecting you."

Russ went to the large wooden door. Entering, he was met by the bluish fog of cigar smoke. He closed the door behind him. The room was dark; it was always dark. Russ waited for his eyes to adjust. He had been here before, but never as the center of attention. Ashe waited in his chair, his back to Russ.

"Sit."

Russ sat.

"I must tell you that I am disappointed and deeply troubled, Mr. Miller. I thought I had hired professionals. I was obviously wrong, since only you return. And I'm confident you're here to convince me not to kill you."

Ashe turned his chair around to face Russ. "I guess you are the smartest of the three." He tapped cigar ash into a large crystal ashtray on his desk. "We spoke of some business. Operations in this part of Oregon will have to stop until I assess the status. I assume the authorities are now involved, given the incarceration of your friend."

Russ nodded.

"I have a job for you. We need to tie up the loose ends and do damage control. How many know of the operations?"

"There's the vet, the state guy, the farm employees, among a few others."

"Fine, how many of them can tie operations back to this office?"

Russ thought for a minute. "Only two: Cray and Carson. The rest can only link the operations back to Green Grass."

"Good. You will take care of Carson. I'll look into the Cray situation. Do you have a problem with that?"

"No, sir. I'll take care of her."

"Son, I have heard that guarantee before so you can understand my lack of confidence. I want you to fully understand the consequences of failure."

Ashe pushed a button under his desk and Russ watched as an oak panel slid sideways to reveal a hallway and two large men in dark suits.

"Mr. Miller, if you fail me or cross me, these men will protect my interests. Do you understand me?"

"Yes, sir," Russ said, his brow sweating in the cold room.

"Good. See the receptionist for the money you need. She will also give you a new cell phone. That is the only phone with which you are to contact me," Ashe said turning his back to Russ, indicating the meeting was over.

Russ stood and quickly left the room.

* * *

The two large men remained standing in the dark office.

"Take care of this Cray issue. He is being held at the Salem Police Department. I am sure the FBI are on their way. Get there first."

# CHAPTER 34

Jessie returned to the ramshackle office with her laptop, red-faced and breathless. The group had converged on the desk and were examining the various cables. She plugged a network cable into her computer and turned it on. Crossing her fingers and holding her breath, she clicked on the message that popped up on the screen describing the presence of the network.

"I'm in," Jessie yelled.

"What do you have, Jess?" Pen asked, excited.

"Don't know yet. It's going to take some time. I'm going to need the same software to open up the files."

"Good work, Jessie," Agent Brewster said. "You work on this for now to see what's there, then we'll get our IT folks involved. Right now, the rest of us will try to find that hard drive."

The group split up and began searching. Jessie dug into the hard drive's directories, trying to find files she could open. Scrolling through the lists she clicked on one called Cattle Policy. The document opened and she scanned the pages, not quite believing what she read.

"Agent Brewster, I think you should read this."

Lynn went to the laptop and looked at the open document, her eyes growing wide. "Captain Murphy, come here, please," she said, her eyes not leaving the screen.

Murphy went to her and read over her shoulder. "Damn."

"Yeah, I know. Did you get local law enforcement over to Valley Breeders?"

"They're standing by there now."

"Get over there and call back with their fax number. I'm going to have a search warrant faxed over there. We're going to be looking for blood and tissue samples, reports, and insurance claims for cattle."

"Will do." Murphy started for the door.

"We'll be in touch if we find anything else," she said, then turned back to the computer screen. "Let's see what else we have here."

Pen went back to Jessie. "Jess, will that thing tell us anything about where this stupid hard drive is hidden?"

"No. All it contains are the files." Jessie said, her brain churning. "Wait a second and I'll check something." She worked back through the directories, reading folder names. There were two additional folders in the main directory, one called the Marine and the other simply "R." Jessie accessed the first folder. It contained mostly porn. The second folder was password protected.

"Pen, the hard drive is located in the closet," Jessie said, pointing to the open closet door. "My guess is that it's on the back wall, maybe behind a panel or something."

"How do you know that?" Lynn asked, surprised.

"Check the outer office. If I remember right, there were two desks out there. So there are two additional network cables. See, here's the thing: two other users were on the hard drive besides the user in this office. I figure that they didn't share a computer. So, then the hard drive is likely somewhere between the network cables. The only place in this office that might have room for it is that closet."

Jessie watched Pen go into the closet and start pulling out the file cabinets that lined the back wall. "Found it!" he yelled as he opened a panel and stared at the hard drive.

"Let's take that into evidence," Josh said. "We'll get it back to Salem where we can really get to work on it. I'll call in one of our computer specialists to help. Jessie, do you mind staying on this? You seem to know your way around these things and understand what we're looking for. You can bring my staff up to speed."

"Sure thing."

"What's next, Agent Brewster?" Josh asked, leaning against the desk.

"We probably have two more stops today: one at the vet and one at the farm. Will, I'd appreciate your help but it's probably not appropriate for you to be on site. I'd like Pen and Josh to come with me. We'll need to see if there's anything that ties all of these businesses together. Will, I'd like you to work with Jessie. I believe there are still a number of leads we'll need to work through."

Josh turned to the officers. "Please help Will and Jessie get back to my office, and tag this hard drive. I'll have my computer specialist meet you there."

He turned to Pen and Lynn. "Let's go meet Murphy at the vet's."

The party split up in the parking lot. Lynn, Josh, and Pen left for the vet's office, while Mercer and Jessie were escorted back to Salem, hard drive in tow.

* * *

"What kind of stuff are we looking for?" Pen asked as they drove to Willamette Valley Breeders.

"We need evidence that implicates a bigger fish," Josh said. "Like you thought, there has to be a parent company somewhere behind everything. I agree with your summation that what we have now is a skeleton company. I'm sure when we look closely at this Green Grass Enterprises, we'll discover it has no assets. If there are people out there who are sick, we want to find the parent company with the deep pockets. This is going to get sticky, Agent Brewster, because we have a potentially corrupt government employee on our hands. This might get political quick if we're not careful."

"You mean the Department of Agriculture employee?"

"That's the one," Josh said. "We need to make sure he doesn't get wind of this until we have something worth bringing him in for."

"You're right. We can't go after him without strong evidence. We'll have to wait and see what is on that hard drive," replied Lynn.

They rode the rest of the way in silence, each person wondering what they would find next. There were two police cars parked at Willamette Valley Breeders when Murphy stepped out of his car to meet Josh, Lynn, and Pen.

"How's it look in there?" Lynn asked as she got out of the car.

"We caught them sleeping," Murphy said, smiling. "They hadn't been warned yet. One of the officers first on the scene remained inside to make sure they didn't destroy anything."

"Did the warrant come through?" asked Josh.

"Yep, a couple of minutes ago," Murphy said. "I guess it's time to get to work."

Willamette Valley Breeders owned the building that served as its offices and a number of garages and barns with livestock pens. The office was larger than it appeared from the parking lot. Large examination rooms led out the back to holding stables and corrals. Three people sat at a table drinking coffee. A Molalla police officer sat in a nearby chair, flipping through a magazine. He stood when the group entered.

"Officer, I'm Special Agent Brewster with the FBI and this is District Attorney Benjamin. We appreciate your assistance." Josh shook hands with the officer. "Okay, ladies and gentlemen, we're looking for the manager of this business," Lynn said to the people at the table.

One of the men stood up. "My name is Andy Walters, and I'm the manager here. This is Chris Chambers, my technician, and Sally Michaels, my office assistant. Could you please tell me what's going on?"

"Sure, Dr. Walters," Lynn said. "We have a warrant to search your premises. We have evidence to suggest that your company has been part of a conspiracy to commit fraud and extortion. We're working on a list here, so we're sticking with the fraud charge right now. I'm sure there will be more."

"What's he talking about, Andy?" asked the office assistant.

Andy ignored her. "Am I under arrest?"

"Not yet."

"Do I need an attorney?"

"They're always a good idea," Josh said. "This warrant allows us to look at all of your files, including computer files. Can you point my team in that direction?"

"Sure, anything we can do to help. Chris can take your people to the files and Sally can get you going on the computer. May I call my attorney?"

"Sure, Dr. Walters. I will make note of your cooperation in all this," replied Lynn.

Andy pulled out his phone and dialed a number. They could hear a phone ringing on the other end. The normal voicemail never clicked on. Finally, he hung up.

Lynn raised an eyebrow. "Your lawyer not around?"

"Yeah ... No. She isn't available. Agent Brewster, can we talk privately? I want to make sure my people aren't implicated in anything."

"Let's go into your office and you can tell us what you think we might find."

Lynn waved Josh over and they followed Andy inside. Andy sat at his desk, his head buried in his hands.

"Dr. Walters asked us in here to talk about why he thinks we're here," Lynn said to Josh.

"I want to be crystal clear on this, Dr. Walters," Josh said. "You are not under arrest so your Miranda rights have not kicked in. You do not need to talk to us and if you do, you should have an attorney present. Do you understand?"

Andy nodded, a resigned look on his face.

"Do you want to have an attorney present?"

"No."

"Okay."

"Dr. Walters, we are here about your business relationship with Green Grass Enterprises," Lynn began. "I have to warn you: we have been to their office headquarters and it has been abandoned. However, we found some computer files that link you directly with the work they were doing. We also have a witness, an ex-employee who tells a very strange story of hazardous waste dumping, cover-ups, extortion, attempted murder, and finally, murder. We have another witness with samples that would suggest his cattle were poisoned. We also have a woman who fell seriously ill from what we think was occurring on the Green Grass farm. The thing is we want the entire story, and your part in it."

Andy slumped a little lower in his chair. "You've talked to Ted Kameron?"

Lynn checked her notes. "Yes."

"I figured. Ted's a smart guy. It was only a matter of time before he got suspicious. I didn't think anyone else would question the insurance policies, and no one ever did."

"Dr. Walters—Andy—why don't you start from the beginning?" Lynn suggested.

Andy dropped his shoulders, his eyes fixed on a spot on his desk, and then began his story.

He had been approached a year after graduating from veterinary school. He had developed a gambling problem and owed a lot of money to the wrong people. Then one day, a woman showed up at his job. Her name was Sarah Carson. She told him that her boss had bought his gambling debt and that he had to work it off. She made it very clear that the job was not an offer but a requirement. He asked about the specifics. She told him that all he had to do was run a large animal veterinary clinic in Molalla. Her company would pay for setting him up. The salary she offered was competitive with other clinics, even with the debt.

Carson told him he could operate the clinic however he chose, except for a few conditions. The first condition was that he would be established as the sole provider and vet for cattle in the area. In addition, his office would offer an insurance policy on the cattle he sold, which would compensate local ranchers in a way that would not only guarantee their business but also their silence.

"What did she mean by silence?" Lynn asked.

"I asked the same thing. She told me it was related to the second condition. Any animal that died, had deformities, miscarriages, whatever, would be collected and disposed of. The rancher would not be given the test results or the cause of death."

"What if the rancher asked?" Josh asked.

"Given the insurance payments and replacement cattle, they wouldn't. But I had a canned answer if they did."

"How much did your company make a year?" Lynn asked.

Andy looked up and chuckled. "We never made money. I don't think I was ever supposed to make money."

"When was the last time you talked to Mr. Kameron?"

"I don't know, a week or so. He had a cow die."

"Ted told one of our investigators that he thought his cow died from acute benzene poisoning," Lynn said, looking for a reaction.

"Benzene … Yeah, that's what I confirmed, too. I knew they were burning something at that farm, but for a long time didn't want to know what it was."

"What do you mean?"

"This whole business was established to cover the field burning going on by one of Carson's company farms. Cattle were always getting sick and dying around the same time they were burning their fields. And benzene ... well, the effects of benzene are consistent with what the cattle were dying from. But my response was always smoke inhalation."

A quiet settled over the office for a few minutes as Lynn and Josh tried to absorb what they had heard and wondered where to take the investigation next.

# CHAPTER 35

Cray Warner fumed. Carson had made him kill a hiker. Russ had him shoot a federal employee he thought was Mercer. Russ could have taken that shot—should have taken the shot. Now Cray was on the hook.

He knew that the ballistics tests on the rifle would link him to the murder of the ranger. He had only two options: make a deal or take the punishment. At best, the punishment was life in jail. At worst, the death penalty. He tried to remember if Oregon had the death penalty.

He needed to deal.

"Guard. Guard. I want to talk," he shouted to the cop guarding the holding cells. "Get me someone who can deal."

\* \* \*

Sarah Carson's BMW continued to speed north. She drove around the outskirts of Seattle and onto Route 2, heading east into the Cascade Mountains. Her destination was a cabin near Stevens Pass, nestled deep in the forest off a quiet gravel road. It was only fifteen minutes from the Interstate, but felt like it was out in the middle of nowhere. She had kept it a secret from just about everyone in her life. Every now and again, when the stress of her job got to be too much, she would disappear for a few days to recharge.

Carson finally began to relax when her cabin came into sight. She pulled her car into a shed. Parking it, she grabbed her bags and headed for the side door. She paid a local to keep the place up, and once inside, she found that it was clean and ready for use.

Quickly, she turned on the cabin's security system. Though the cabin looked rustic, it was equipped with all of the modern amenities, including the best security and surveillance system money could buy. An infrared motion detector located at the end of her driveway would alert her to approaching vehicles. Coupled with infrared cameras mounted around the area, she would be able to see if anyone was coming. She always knew someday someone would.

She unloaded the bags, including a number of groceries she had purchased on her way. She was on edge and more than once found herself jumping at normal forest noises. She hoped it would rain and quiet the woods, at least for a time. Once unpacked, she fell into a large, overstuffed chair. Soon she drifted into a restless sleep, exhaustion finally overtaking her stressed body.

Hours later she woke abruptly, feeling vulnerable, her senses tingling. The sun had set behind the trees and the forest was filled with the graying light of dusk. The forest noises had grown hushed. She looked toward the door, which she had left open, only the thin metal of the screen door keeping her safe.

Pulling her 9mm from her bag, she grabbed her pistol and swept the house to make sure she was still alone. She crept through the cabin, checking every room, every closet, every shadow. Empty.

Checking the security system, Carson saw that everything was in order. She went to the refrigerator, put the pistol down on the counter, and pulled out a bottle of vodka from the freezer. Pouring herself a glass, she downed it in one pull. She poured a second, sat down at the table, and began to appreciate the magnitude of the mess she was in.

\* \* \*

Russ climbed back into the helicopter and tossed an envelope to Sully. He smiled as the chopper lifted off the skyscraper. Russ settled into his seat and pulled on his headset. "That envelope is yours," he said. "In addition, I've retained your services for the foreseeable future. You've been paid in advance."

"So where are we going?" Sully asked as he maneuvered the helicopter.

"I need a rifle," Russ said. "A sniper rifle—high power, good scope, with some kind of silencer or noise suppressor. Can you do it?"

"When do you need it?"

"Yesterday."

Sully thought a long time before answering. "Johnny D."

\* \* \*

Murphy's cell phone rang while Josh and Lynn continued interviewing Andy. He stepped outside to take the call.

"Cap, I need to talk to you," said his second-in-command.

"What is it, Bill?"

"That prisoner we got; he wants to cut a deal."

"Has he spoken with an attorney yet?"

"The Public Defender hasn't arrived yet, but the guy says he's declining representation."

"Interesting. Okay, let me talk to the DA." Murphy hung up his phone and went back into Andy's office. "Josh, we need to talk. Some new information has just come to light."

"Please excuse us for a second," Josh said to Andy, rising and stepping out with Murphy, who explained his phone conversation.

"Good," Josh said when Murphy finished. "Sounds like we need to get back there. I think we know everything we can from the owner here. I'll have Pen and your officer work on pulling the files together."

\* \* \*

Back in Salem, the computer specialist had shown up and was working through the recovered files with Jessie. For a long time, they seemed to be either looking at mundane information or files they weren't sure about, but they hit gold when they discovered the audio files of Carson's phone calls. The computer specialist ran from the room to find another laptop with the right software. He came back in, breathless from his sprint down the hall.

"Okay," Jessie said. "Let's see what this will do for us." She hit a couple of keys. Suddenly, the speakers on the new laptop crackled to life.

"Oregon Department of Agriculture, Ed Crocker here."

"Crocker, this is Carson from Green Grass Enterprises. I think you remember the last time we met. I hear you're up to your old tricks again. I'm not happy."

"Ms. Carson, I'm not sure I know what you are talking about."

"That's funny. I think you know exactly what I'm talking about..."

"Damn," Jessie said, "we got them. Get a printer. We can print transcripts." She slapped the computer specialist on his back.

"Be right back," he said, grinning.

They listened to each file and printed out the conversations. Mercer highlighted some of the more incriminating details of each conversation and put the printouts into different piles.

"We need to call Josh," Jessie said. She pulled out her cell phone and dialed. "Josh, it's Jessie. We have a breakthrough. It appears that this Sarah Carson recorded all of her phone conversations. She may not have meant to, but she used her computer as a speakerphone and it saved back-up files. You really need to see these transcripts. I think she reported to some guy named Ashe."

\* \* \*

Cray pondered what he'd say when he got a chance to deal. He'd give up Carson, but wasn't sure what to do about Ashe. If he turned on Ashe, he would be a dead man, whether killed in prison or on the street. He sat in his cell and stewed.

\* \* \*

A large black sedan pulled into the police station parking lot. Two men in dark suits with FBI badges got out and went to the building's entrance. They informed the officer on duty that they were there to talk to a prisoner.

"Agents, my captain's not here, but he'll be back soon. I'll radio him and tell him you're here."

"We'd like to see the prisoner in the meantime."

"Yes, sir. You'll just need to check your guns and I'll have him brought into an interview room." The officer directed the two men to where to check their guns and instructed another officer to retrieve the prisoner.

"I'll give the captain a call after you two get settled in," the officer said.

Within a few minutes, they were directed to an interview room. One agent remained outside, behind the one-way glass, while the other entered. The duty officer went back to his desk to call Murphy.

"How are you doing, son?" the agent asked Cray across the table as he entered and was led to a plastic chair. The officer leading Cray in turned and left the room, closing the door behind him.

"Seems to me that you're in a heap of trouble."

Cray nodded and leaned forward in his chair, examining the man. "And you are?"

"A friend of Mr. Ashe."

\* \* \*

Cray's face went gray as he realized what was happening, but it was too late. The man grabbed Cray's arm and pulled him forward. With a syringe in his hand, he plunged it into the eye of the coiled snake tattooed on Cray's neck. The drug felt hot as it entered his bloodstream and worked quickly. Darkness closed on Cray's world and his lifeless body slumped back in his chair, his head dropping to one side.

* * *

The man smiled and arranged Cray to look as though he was resting his head on the table. Then the two men went back to the officer on duty.

"I just laid it on the prisoner," the first man said. "He's pretty upset. I want him to stew on it for a while, so leave him until we get back. Is there a place around here for coffee?"

"A couple of places on the main drag."

"We'll be right back."

They walked outside to their black sedan. The man who had just killed Cray popped the trunk and threw the used syringe on the bodies of the two FBI agents inside. He closed the trunk and slipped into the driver's seat. The black sedan slid out of the parking lot and headed back the way it had come, north toward Portland.

* * *

"What the hell are you telling me?" Murphy roared, running toward the interview room.

"Sir, I have no idea what happened," the duty officer said. "He was alive when we left him with the FBI agents. Then they left and when we checked on him, he was dead. No sign of a struggle."

Murphy entered the room. Cray's body was now on the floor.

"Tell me exactly what happened here," Murphy said through gritted teeth.

"Yes, sir. The two FBI agents came in to interrogate him. We had received word from the Portland office that they were coming. They checked their guns. They were only in there for a few minutes before they left to go get coffee, but they never came back. They said they wanted this guy to stay in here and stew. When we checked on him, he looked like he had his head down on the table—not an uncommon sight for this room, sir. Anyway, after half an hour, I went in there to check again. When he didn't respond to my commands, I physically checked him. That's when we realized he was dead."

"Who moved him?"

"We did, sir, to better examine him. But we didn't find anything," the duty officer said.

Murphy went to the body and felt Cray's hand. It was cold. Cray was dressed in a standard prison jumpsuit, only his hands, neck, and head were exposed. He turned Cray's head and examined his neck.

"There's a tiny puncture in his tattoo. Hard to see but it's there. Get the coroner over here. Have him run a tox screen and look for fast-acting poisons. What about our surveillance cameras? Did we catch those guys on video?"

"Not much, sir. They seemed to know where our cameras were in the office, and they turned off the one in the interview room."

"Shit. Get me everything we have on this guy, and I mean everything. And I want it yesterday," Murphy didn't wait for a reply. He marched off to his office and slammed the door.

Josh listened as Murphy relayed the bad news. When he finished, Josh said, "It appears that someone didn't trust Cray Warren to keep his mouth shut. A professional hit in a police station? Whoever is at the top of this pyramid is starting to get nervous."

"Any idea who the top dog is in all of this?"

"There seems to be this Ashe fellow. Ever heard of him, Murph?"

"Can't say I have. I'd know him if he were from Salem. Most likely he's up in Portland or Seattle."

"I'm going to have Pen look into it since he's halfway to Portland already. Anyway, there are quite a few phone calls from Ashe to this Ms. Carson, directing her to do particular tasks, one of which was to take care of our friend Mr. Mercer."

"Interesting," Murphy said.

"We also have some pretty incriminating evidence against a Mr. Crocker from the State Department of Agriculture. I'm thinking about having you pick him up. Can you get over to my office? We still need you on this."

"Let me call my chief and bring him up to speed, and then coordinate with the FBI. Then I'll call you back."

"Thanks, Murph. Call me when you're done."

Murphy hung up and dialed the Chief of Police. Murphy recounted all that had happened. After hanging up, Murphy sighed and dialed the FBI field office. He assumed that Lynn would brief her boss, but wanted to be the one who delivered the news.

"Agent Naum? Yes, this is Captain Murphy in Salem. I want to know if the agents you assigned to our case are still in the office. If so, I'd like to talk to them. We've had some events occur down here."

"Captain, those agents left two hours ago."

The hair on Murphy's neck tingled. "Can you track their car?" he asked, tension in his voice.

"Yes. Why?" Naum asked.

Murphy explained what had happened at the station.

"Holy shit, Captain, I'm gonna have to get back to you. I will coordinate through Agent Brewster. We need to make contact with our agents."

The phone went dead and Murphy was once again alone with his thoughts. Would this Ashe guy be so brazen as to kill federal agents? Who is this guy?"

* * *

Pen had pulled together as much information as he could at the vet's office when the call came for him to drive to Portland and track down information on a guy named Ashe. He quickly loaded the trunk of his car and headed north. Pen called his father, a businessman in Portland, to see if he had ever heard of Ashe.

266

"Ashe?" Pen's father asked. "Can I ask what this is all about?"

"Not right now, Dad. We're in the middle of an investigation."

"Okay. I'll tell you what I know. But first I need to warn you. Ashe is a very dangerous man. You need to be very careful."

"So you know him, then?"

"No, I don't know him, only of him. He's very much a shadow. No one really seems to know him. He has no known partners. He's in the manufacturing or a textile business or something. Not even sure which company is his. I think he has his hands in a number of businesses."

"Do you know the name of at least one of the companies he's involved in? We need a place to start."

"I think he's involved with a company called ChemTech. It's on the north side of Portland. The company got nailed a few years back as a responsible party in the Superfund status of the Willamette River. I remember seeing a picture of Ashe in the newspaper."

"Great. Thanks, Dad."

"Be safe, son. This guy's dangerous."

"I will."

* * *

Josh, Lynn, Jessie, Mercer, and Murphy sat around a large conference table eating pizza. The computer specialist had gone home after realizing that Jessie had everything under control. The FBI field office had contacted them and told them that they had located their agent's car in a nearby state park. Both agents were dead in the trunk, shot execution-style.

"We need to pull together the rest of the pieces. We know there's a major conspiracy that includes a minimum of five parties: this Green Grass Enterprises, an employee with the Department of Agriculture, the farm, the vets, and Ashe. We can prove they've broken a number of laws, the probable murder of three federal employees, and the attempted murder of two other people. Then we have the question of extortion, bribery, intimidation, fraud—the list just goes on. Right now, we have a stakeout at the farm and warehouse, and police presence at the vet," finished Josh, recapping the day's events. The only thing we turned up at the farm was a very scared farm hand named Jose. It appears the new manager was away."

"What do we do next, Josh?" Mercer asked.

"I think we start making some arrests."

Everyone turned to Josh, their eyes widening.

"What do you think, Murph? I figure with this Carson woman is in the wind, the communication link to Ashe is temporarily severed. We could pull people in quietly for questioning."

"I like it. Can we get some arrest warrants?"

"I just need to make a couple of calls and talk to the judge," said Josh.

"Let's do it," Murphy said.

"Good. I need you two," Lynn said turning to Mercer and Jessie, "to make sense of this information. Find out where there are gaps, where we need more info—anything that jumps out. It's gonna be a long night."

"Lynn, there's a call logged in the files that doesn't make sense," said Jessie.

"What you mean?"

"Carson called a Steve Jackson with the National Weather Service. It seemed like they dated. She asked him about the fire down in the national forest, and lightning strikes."

"I want to interview him. I'll have the Seattle field office bring him in."

\* \* \*

Steve Jackson lived in Seattle, near the University of Washington. He was watching a baseball game and yelling at the television and didn't hear the first set of knocks on his door. The

268

second set made him jump. He quickly got up and went to the door. He was shocked to see a pair of FBI agents.

"Are you Stephen Jackson?" one agent asked.

"Steve, yeah. Can I help you?"

"We need to ask you a few questions. Your name has come up in an investigation involving the murder of three federal employees."

"Are you sure it's me you want?" Steve asked, his mind racing. He had never gotten as much as a speeding ticket.

"Mr. Jackson, you're not under arrest and you're not a suspect. We just hope you can shed some light on a few things," explained the agent.

"Sir, do you know a Sarah Carson?" asked the second agent.

"Yeah, kind of. We're friends." Steve shifted his weight.

"Are you sure you were just friends?"

"Okay, I was pretty into her, but don't think she was into me. I kind of felt like it was nothing more than a hookup. In fact, we only spent one weekend together, and then I didn't hear from her for a year."

"Mr. Jackson, where did you spend that weekend?"

"She owns a cabin east of Seattle, in the mountains. Pretty rustic place, but it was nice there."

"Could you locate that place again?"

"Probably. I can show you on my computer and get you pretty close."

"That would be great, sir."

The agents stepped into his house and Steve led them to his computer. After only a few minutes, he was able to locate the area of Carson's cabin. He couldn't quite pinpoint it because of the tree cover, but he was sure he was close.

The agents wrote down the coordinates and called Agent Brewster directly.

* * *

"The helicopter will be at the airfield in five minutes," Murphy said, hanging up his phone.

"Good." Lynn didn't look up from the printouts she had been flipping through. "Let's get ready to move, Murph. We need a four-person team. Me, you, one of your men—preferably one good with a rifle—and Will. We'll rendezvous with agents from Seattle on-site."

Mercer sat up at hearing his name. Lately, he had felt more like a nuisance than a help in the investigation. "Why me?"

"You're the only one who can identify this Carson woman. That makes you a necessary member of the team. You aren't scared of flying, are you?"

"No, ma'am. I was an Army Ranger in a previous life. Dropped into a lot of places by helicopter."

"Jessie and I will keep poring through these phone records and follow up on anything we come across," said Josh.

"Okay, let's move," Lynn said, gathering up some notes and heading for the door.

"Be careful," Jessie said, her eyes fixed on the computer screen.

Mercer smiled as he left the room. He had been in the back seat for far too long and had never been very good at paperwork.

* * *

Carson wasn't planning on staying long at her cabin, just a few days. She sat by the fire, trying to sort out everything that occurred in the last 72 hours. Knowing that there was no going back, she began to formulate a plan. The first step was to change her appearance. While fleeing north, she first stopped at her condo in Portland and grabbed all the documents she needed for her new identity—the woman on the passport was named Natalie Barton, who had short brown hair and wore glasses.

Downing another shot of vodka, Carson got up and went into the kitchen. She pulled a brown hair-dying kit and scissors from a paper bag.

*No time like the present.*

Methodically, Carson began her transformation into Natalie Barton. Every now and again, she took another shot of vodka. She felt the numbness of the alcohol and made a conscious effort to slow down. She needed to stay alert.

*I'll get good and drunk when I'm the hell out of this place.*

After a few hours, she looked into the mirror at a person she didn't recognize. She still needed to get the glasses, but they would have to wait for a trip to town. Tonight, she would plan the rest of her escape.

Carson figured the easiest way to get out of the country was by ferry to Vancouver Island, Canada. If Ashe was searching for her, he'd be watching the airports, train, bus stations, and the Interstate border crossing. She hoped that the ferries into Canada would be an oversight. Once in Canada, she would hop a flight to somewhere in South America, probably Venezuela because of the lack of U.S. extradition. She had wired enough money to offshore accounts to lay low for a while.

She smiled at the thought of new life somewhere warm and dry. The next day was Saturday, and crowds of sightseers would help camouflage her escape. That was only 12 hours away.

She pulled her things together. She had a backpack and a duffle bag for the trip. She had to travel light, so she only grabbed a couple sets of clothes and some toiletries, which she threw in the duffel bag. In the smaller backpack, she stored her new identification, her remaining cash, and the files she had taken from her safe. Stowing them by the back door, Sarah Carson—now Natalie Barton—picked up a book on South America and sat down on the couch, her 9mm lying next to her.

\* \* \*

Russ and Sully were headed back north after meeting up with Johnny D to buy the rifle. The transaction had gone smoothly, though Russ had been worried that Johnny D might shoot down the helicopter, thinking it was some government agency coming for him. He was crazy that way.

Sully landed the helicopter in an empty field so Russ could figure out their next steps. Russ opened up a map of Washington and traced his finger over the lines until he found the small dot representing Skykomish.

"At least there won't be any witnesses out there," he said looking at Sully, then placed another call, this one to Ashe.

"What?" Ashe's tone was far from welcoming.

"Carson has a place up near Skykomish, Washington. She mentioned it a couple of times, even bragged about it to me and Cray. I'm headed there now."

"Good," was all Russ heard before the phone clicked off.

"Let's move, Sully."

* * *

Ashe, sitting in the smoky twilight of his office, pressed a button on his desk. Once again, the hidden door opened and the two large men entered the room.

"It's time," Ashe grumbled. "I want you to take care of all of them: Carson, Miller, the pilot, anyone who's there. Nothing points back to me. Understood?"

The two men nodded.

"Good. They're headed to Skykomish, Washington. They won't move on the woman until dawn. Activate the homing device in the phone when you get close. No one ever finds the bodies. Call me when it's done."

The two men quickly left the room.

* * *

Pen had been on the phone all afternoon, following up leads. It appeared that Randall Ashe had financial interests in a number of companies that produced chemical waste. Pen discovered that Ashe had permits for the storage and disposal of the waste, though he couldn't get the numbers to add up. He uncovered that a single chemical waste disposal company serviced all of Ashe's companies, but he couldn't figure out who owned it. He called Josh to let him know what he had discovered.

"Hold on, Pen, I want to call a guy I know." Pen heard Josh click the buttons on a speakerphone.

"Matt? ... Yeah, it's Josh. Josh Benjamin. How are you? ... I'm okay. I actually called because I'm in the middle of an investigation and could really use your help. I'm trying to find out who the owner/operator is for a company called CD, Inc. I'm pretty sure it's privately held. It's a hazardous waste disposal and possible storage company ... Yeah. Call me back at this number. Thanks, Matt, I appreciate it."

"Okay. Pen, you still there?"

"Yeah, so what we have, based on Jessie's research," Pen said, flipping through his legal pad, "is that Ashe had control over Green Grass Enterprises. I think we can pretty much prove that Sarah Carson was Ashe's employee, not an independent contractor. If that's the case, then we can link Ashe to not only chemical dumping, but murder, attempted murder, extortion, bribery of a state official, and any toxic torts we can pull in. The only hole is linking Ashe to the disposal company. That's where there's a gap."

"That would be the final nail," Josh said.

A few minutes later, Josh's other phone rang.

"Just a second, Pen," Josh said as he picked up the other phone.

"This is Josh ... Yeah, interesting. Are you sure? ... Can you fax the information to me? ... Great. Thanks, Matt, I really appreciate the help." Josh switched back to Pen. "Did you get that?"

"So, is it Ashe?" Pen asked, sitting on the edge of his seat.

"No."

"Damn it, that would have wrapped it up with a bow."

"It isn't Ashe," Josh said again. "It's Ms. Sarah Carson."

"What?" Pen said, jumping up. "It's Carson? Well, if it's Carson, then we have proof she ran it under Ashe's direct oversight, just like Green Grass Enterprises."

Josh smiled broadly. "Exactly."

* * *

Sully landed the helicopter in a deserted, dirt-covered baseball field on the outskirts of Skykomish. Sand whipped up in Russ' face as he exited the helicopter and ran toward the rusting metal bleachers, the large rifle cradled in his arms. The helicopter lifted back off and flew toward the forest surrounding the small park. Russ slung the rifle over this shoulder and left the ballfield and cautiously crept through the shadows of the evergreen forest that lined the highway, trying to stay concealed from anyone moving through the area.

A half-mile down the road, he could see the unmistakable neon of a motel. He covered the distance in four minutes. As he surveyed the rundown motel from the edge of the parking lot, his eyes focused on several cars parked in front of the different rooms where their owners were presumably sleeping. Russ crept up to the cars, looking for the right one. One of the rooms was lit, so he quickly stepped away from Honda Civic parked in front.

He checked the doors on the other two vehicles. The pickup truck was locked, but the big navy blue Buick Park Avenue wasn't. He crept to the door in front of the car and listened. He couldn't hear anything from inside the room, no television or voices, so he crept back to the driver's door and opened it. He slid the rifle across the large seat and then pulled some wires from under the dash. It was an older-model Buick, before everything had gone electronic and he was quickly able to hotwire it. The engine purred to life. Climbing in and quietly shutting the door, Russ put the big car in reverse, backed up, and then pulled away from the motel, driving east toward Carson's cabin.

He drove the Buick past the entrance to the driveway where Carson's cabin was supposed to be. He didn't see any signs of life, though the cabin was hidden from the road. He turned the car around, made another pass by the driveway and then abandoned the car on the gravel road a half-mile north. He grabbed the rifle and stepped from the car. The night was quiet except for the open-door chime from the Buick. Russ gently pushed the door close to avoid slamming it. Entering the woods, he moved parallel to the road to avoid making contact with passing cars. He carried the large rifle, a 9mm pistol with a silencer, and his pack.

He moved quickly through the darkness. He planned on taking a distance shot from the cover of the forest. He hoped that he was right about it being Carson's cabin. He made it to the driveway without incident, quietly stepping onto the gravel. He was far enough down the driveway where he could see both the driveway's entrance and the outline of the cabin and shed. He unslung his rifle and peered through the scope, switching it to night vision. He smiled when he saw signs of an overly paranoid Carson. An infrared security system had been mounted along the driveway to detect the approach of cars. Switching the scope to infrared, Russ could clearly see the beam that stretched across the driveway.

Re-slinging the rifle, Russ moved back into the woods to approach the cabin from the side. He moved into the cover of the trees where he could still see the driveway, but had a direct line of sight to the front windows of the cabin, a perfect position. Russ unslung his rifle once again and sat down against a spruce tree to wait for dawn.

\* \* \*

An hour away, a black Cadillac cruised up Interstate 5. The two men weren't talking; they were watching a blinking light on a computer monitor. One man pointed to the turn-off for Highway 202, the route to Skykomish. The other man merely nodded.

* * *

Two unmarked black SUVs left the Seattle field office of the FBI at midnight. Six people were split between them. The vehicles followed each other in convoy, navigating the quiet city streets and entering the network of highways. Before long, the city slipped into a short stretch of suburbs, then dark forest. The SUVs muscled up the incline of the foothills of the Cascade Range without struggle. The lead SUV held Murphy, Lynn, Mercer, and Murphy's officer. They had called ahead and made arrangements to use the King County sheriff's offices as a staging area to coordinate the operation. It was where their chopper would be waiting. It was due in at 4 a.m. Once they arrived at the offices, all they could do was wait.

It was 2:30 in the morning and the order came for everyone to get into their tactical equipment. Each wore a Kevlar vest, and had their service-issued pistols and either a rifle or a shotgun. They looked like a SWAT team getting ready to storm a house with their wireless communication earpieces, military pants, and combat boots.

"You look ready, Murph," Lynn said when he entered the room.

"Yeah, a little tight, though," he said with a wink. "Need to lay off the scones at the coffee house. If the bullet penetrates the vest, it still has a good layer of blubber to get through before it hits anything vital."

Mercer and the remaining agents entered the room ready to go. As a civilian observer, Mercer was only equipped with a Kevlar vest.

"Okay, why don't we run through it?" Murphy said.

The officers and agents took seats around Lynn and Murphy.

"Just to be clear, this is an FBI operation. Salem PD is assisting. We don't have jurisdiction in Washington, but the FBI has been coordinating with the local county sheriff and state police. Clear?" Murphy asked.

Not waiting for a response he continued, "We're going to have two primary teams. The first team will enter the property along the main road. That team will be Agent Brewster, Officer Sykes, and me. The second team will approach the cabin along this overgrown trail. That team will be agents Stone and Adams. Will stays near the main road in the SUV. He will be on site for identification purposes only. The King County sheriff's office is on standby if we need additional support."

"I want everyone in the right frame of mind," Lynn said. "Sarah Carson and her associates are killers. We think Carson might be holed up in her cabin. She's definitely on the run, so she's going to be desperate. We also know one of her thugs evaded police capture in Salem and is on the loose. Her associate might be with her, so we need to be cautious because there might be more than one person in the cabin. And we know that Carson was taking her orders from someone higher up. Someone we think ordered two men to murder our agents and a suspect in custody."

"I want them alive. If you need to shoot, aim to wound. I want to bring down this whole ring and get justice for all the folks these assholes have hurt. Be careful, and good hunting," said Lynn.

"Okay, it's about that time," Murphy said. "Let's pack up and head out."

The group gathered their belongings and began filing out to the parking lot of the sheriff's station. The moon had long since set, but the stars still lit up the darkness. They climbed into the SUVs and left the parking lot once again in their convoy. It took an hour to reach the area where the cabin was located. The two Seattle FBI agents parked their SUV on the shoulder of the road at an intersection with an old, unmaintained road, and quickly disappeared into the dark woods. It would take another thirty minutes to approach the cabin from the front.

* * *

The black Cadillac passed the sign for Skykomish, the passenger once again pointing to the digital map with the blinking light. The driver nodded and made a right-hand turn. They were close. The cover of night was being pushed aside by dawn, though still too far east to brighten the woods.

"Take the driveway up on the left," the passenger said. "We're just about on top of the signal. It hasn't moved in a while."

The driver nodded.

"Remember, we kill everyone."

"I remember," the driver growled.

The passenger pulled out his handgun and checked to make sure it was loaded as the car swung onto the gravel driveway. The driver stopped the Cadillac a few yards in from the main road before he put it in park and turned off the engine.

* * *

Carson woke up in a cold sweat, the stillness of early morning pressing down on her. She had fallen asleep on the couch reading. Groggily, she pulled herself into a sitting position to get her bearings. She stood up and went into the bathroom. She jumped as she caught a glimpse of herself in the mirror. She didn't recognize the person staring back. The short brown hair of her alias would take some getting used to.

She checked her watch. 4:30 a.m. She scanned the cabin. Something wasn't right, she could feel it. Her eyes stopped on the blinking red light of her security system and her stomach dropped. Someone was out there. Carson ran to the screen that displayed the surveillance cameras. A car sat at the far end of her driveway, its headlights out. It had tripped the infrared warning system.

* * *

Russ heard the car pull onto the driveway. At first, he thought it was Sarah. Then he heard two car doors quietly opening and closing.

* * *

"The signal is coming from over there, just off the driveway."

"Yeah, but it looks like there's a cabin up ahead," the driver whispered back.

"Two birds—one stone," smiled the passenger.

It was 4:30 a.m.

* * *

Carson kept low, away from the windows. Her best way out was through the back. She kept a mountain bike in the shed. Fear clutched at her. Her backpack and duffle lay by the kitchen door. She pulled her pistol from the backpack, then slung the pack over her shoulders. The duffel would stay behind.

She edged up the wall alongside the kitchen door and peeked around the corner. Nothing. She crept back to the security monitor. Her blood froze when she saw two large men now standing in front of the car. One began walking toward the house while the other left the driveway and entered the woods.

She crept back to the kitchen door. Opening it slowly, she winced at the creak from the old hinges. It was ten steps to the shed. She made a break for it, covering the distance in a few seconds. Slipping inside, she met the odor of decaying wood, sawdust, and old oil but nothing else.

* * *

Russ watched the house through his infrared scope. He thought he saw movement inside, but no clear shot. He lowered the rifle when he heard the car doors. Throwing his rifle over his shoulder, he pulled out his pistol and turned toward the sound. Dropping his pack, he crept through the woods, staying low and using the fallen logs and ferns for cover.

The forest was starting to brighten. From his new vantage point, he could see the road and the place where he had been hiding. A large figure appeared out of the trees. He had a pistol in one hand and was moving toward the place where Russ had just been.

Russ unshouldered his rifle and peered through the scope. One of the men from Ashe's office. Laying the rifle down, Russ grabbed his pistol and moved cautiously toward the man. The man reached Russ's earlier location and picked up Russ' backpack. Dropping it, he looked around. Their eyes met across the short distance of forest that separated them.

"What are you doing here?" Russ hissed. "I told Ashe I would take care of it." The man moved a few feet closer to Russ. "I have Carson in this cabin. I'll take care of her."

"I am not here to take care of the woman," the man said in a low growl. A smirk crossed his lips as he leveled his pistol.

A shot rang out through the early morning air, followed by a second muffled one.

* * *

"Shots fired? What the hell was that?" Murphy said as their SUV pulled over near the driveway to the cabin.

"Agent Adams, report in," Lynn ordered.

"Adams and Stone here. We heard it, too. It wasn't us," replied Agent Adams.

"Okay, everyone move!" Murphy ordered.

Murphy rammed the shifter into drive and gunned the engine. The large vehicle covered the distance to the driveway in twenty seconds. Murphy pulled in behind the black Cadillac, blocking it. A bullet ricocheted off the front of the SUV as it skidded to a stop.

"Out, out, out!" Murphy said. "Remember, we want these guys alive. Will, stay down!"

Murphy, Lynn, and Officer Sykes sprang from the SUV, each taking positions behind the Cadillac while Mercer ducked down behind the seat as ordered.

\* \* \*

Sarah Carson heard gunshots in the woods. Then more shots from the driveway. She grabbed her mountain bike, peered out the shed door, and, not seeing anyone, wheeled the bike around the back of the shed. She looked toward the old path leading away from the house but movement caught her eye. She ducked down behind a long, rusted propane tank and watched as two men in full assault gear moved alongside the end of the cabin and out of sight. Swallowing the burning panic rising in her throat, Carson wheeled the bike around the far end of the tank, into the woods, and out of sight of the cabin.

Several more shots rang out as she pushed the bike as fast as she could through the log-strewn forest. Finally, she came out on an old road. She looked back toward her cabin. Not seeing anyone, she climbed on her bike and pedaled hard, putting distance between her and the assault taking place not far behind.

\* \* \*

Murphy and Agent Brewster were pinned down, not knowing exactly where the shots were coming from. Every time Murphy peered around the Cadillac, another shot ricocheted off the side panel of the car.

"Anybody see these guys?"

"This is Agent Adams. We are moving up from behind. Give us a second and we'll take care of it."

Two shots rang out from further down the road, followed by a groan of pain. "You're clear," Adams said over the radio.

"Okay, let's move in," Agent Brewster said. "How many men did you see, Adams?"

"We only have one, ma'am."

"Be on guard because there's at least one more guy out there, maybe more. Stone, Adams, secure the cabin. Anyone have eyes on Carson?" Lynn asked.

Murphy was kneeling on the man groaning in the driveway. The man had taken a shot through each leg. He quickly disarmed and cuffed him. Agent Brewster and Officer Sykes spread out and headed into the forest lining the driveway. Sykes found a backpack lying on the ground at the same time Lynn found the two men.

"I have two here."

Sykes ran to Lynn's position. One man, a look alike of the one on the driveway—large and muscled and in a suit—lay dead on the ground, a bullet through his throat. The other man was trying to crawl away.

"Don't move," Lynn ordered.

The man stopped and looked back over his shoulder. Using most of his energy, he rolled onto his back. Lynn could see that he had taken a shot in the shoulder. She kicked the pistol out of the man's hand.

"This is Agent Brewster calling the King County sheriff's office. Do you receive?" Lynn said into her radio.

"This is the sheriff's office. Over."

"We are going to need an ambulance on site. We have several men in custody who have sustained gunshot wounds."

"Affirmative. We're sending the paramedics now."

Lynn instructed Sykes to secure the area and search the assailants. She met Murphy back on the driveway and they both headed toward the cabin. Agent Stone came out onto the front porch as they approached.

"What did you find?" Lynn asked.

"My guess is that she was here. We found a packed duffel bag by the back door. There was hair dye in the sink and a book on South America on the couch next to a half-empty bottle of vodka.

Receipts for groceries dated yesterday. Adams is checking out the shed."

Adams came back a few minutes later. "We just missed her. I'm guessing by minutes. Her car's still here. My thought is that she slipped out on foot when the shooting started."

"So where the hell is she?" Lynn asked, looking into the woods. Sirens brought Lynn back from her frustration. "Agent Stone, I want you to head back down the path to your vehicle. If she's close, see if you can find some sign of her. The rest of us will figure out what we have here. It looks to me like we weren't the only ones trying to find Carson. I'm going to get Will. Maybe he can identify one of these guys."

They went back up the driveway toward the flashing of ambulance lights. The paramedics were already working on the two wounded men, and Officer Sykes was laying out the weapons and items he'd found on them, including a large rifle.

"Hey, Murph?"

"What is it, Sykes?"

"These two guys look real familiar, sir." Sykes pointed to the dead man and his partner. If I was a betting man, I'd put it all down on these guys being our phony FBI agents."

Murphy's smiled. "I'll be damned," he said under his breath. "Nice work."

* * *

Will Mercer was out of the SUV and leaning against the hood waiting for Murphy and Lynn to come back. He hadn't seen the men who were in custody and his blood turned cold when he finally locked eyes with Russ. Rage boiled up from inside.

"You son of a bitch," Mercer shouted, trying to get to Russ.

Sykes saw what was unfolding and got between Mercer and Russ, grabbing Mercer and pushing him back.

"That's the guy who's been trying to kill me. He works for Carson." Murphy quickly moved in to help hold Mercer.

"Calm down. Let's think about this," Murphy said. "This man was found in the woods in the possession of a large sniper rifle. And apparently this fellow and that man shot each other." Murphy pointed to the dead man on the ground. "Your guy made out a bit better."

Murphy looked at Sykes. "What did you find on these guys?"

"The dead man had very little on him. My guess is anything he had is in the Caddie. We haven't processed that yet. But this guy," Sykes pointed at Russ, "had a small pack with some extra bullets and a cell phone."

"You need to talk to us, mister." Murphy said to Russ.

"Miller," Will said. "His name is Russ Miller."

"Okay, this is what we're going to do," Murphy said to Russ. "Agent Brewster is going to put you in custody then see what we can make of you. I think that you and that Cray fellow—you know, the dead one—were partners, and you're the one who got away from us in Salem."

Murphy watched Russ closely for a reaction to the news. Russ remained stone-faced, but Murphy noticed his eyes seemed to be more intense, almost take on a fire.

"Were you here protecting this Carson woman or trying to kill her?" Murphy continued. "It really doesn't matter either way because I have you on enough charges to lock you up for a long time."

Russ opened his mouth but Murphy held up his hand to stop him.

"Don't talk yet. We haven't read you your rights, and Agent Brewster here with the FBI will want to make sure I do everything by the book. And she's a little pissed off after the killing of her agents."

"That's right. Why don't we take care of that right now?" and Lynn began reading the two men their Miranda rights.

"Captain Murphy? Could you come here for a second?" Agent Stone said from the front of the sedan.

Murphy motioned Mercer to follow. Murphy poked his head in the window. "Yeah? What did you find?"

"Looks to me like some kind of digital tracking system." Stone pointed at a computer tablet with a digital map. "That blinking light is what was being tracked, but it's also right where we are."

"What do you think they were tracking?" Murphy asked.

"The cell phone?" Mercer offered.

"If that's the case, then these guys were definitely not working together. But we still don't know if this Miller guy was protecting Carson or trying to kill her."

"Or whether these two assholes were sent to kill both Carson and Russ," Mercer added.

"That's an interesting theory. Tie up all the loose ends," Murphy said. "Let's go check out this guy's cell phone."

Murphy and Mercer went back to the items spread out on the ground. Murphy picked up the cell phone. It looked normal. He flipped it open and scrolled down the previous calls made. Only one number had been dialed.

\* \* \*

Sully had been sitting in the chopper drinking coffee and munching on mini-powdered doughnuts when he heard the first shot. Sliding out of the helicopter, he wrenched his neck up to listen. Suddenly another burst of gunshots pierced the morning stillness.

Small arms fire. Close too.

He pulled his cell phone out of his pocket and called Russ. It went through to voicemail. Another round of shots rang out and Sully made up his mind: it was time to leave.

Once in the air, he guided his chopper toward the area of the cabin—where the shots had come from moments before. When the cabin came into view, he saw flashing lights and law enforcement crawling all over the place. Sully turned the chopper toward the mountains in an attempt to disappear.

\* \* \*

Murphy saw a helicopter coming towards them low over the trees. He grabbed for his radio.

"King County sheriff, come in."

The radio crackled to life. "Sheriff here."

"I need the chopper up and heading in an easterly heading. I have a helicopter that might be involved heading toward the mountains. Over."

"Roger that. They are in the air."

Murphy stood with Mercer and Agent Brewster around the SUV. "Okay, so what do we have? Will and I are thinking that the two thugs in the Cadillac were some kind of hit squad. It looks like they were tracking Miller. My guess is that they're the same guys who killed your agents and my prisoner down in Salem," Murphy speculated. "I think only Miller knew where to find the cabin and the other two guys used him to close in on Carson. But what I can't figure out is Miller's motive here. Was he here to protect or kill Carson?"

"And where did Carson go?" chimed in Will.

"The cabin was empty, but had been used, and her car is in the shed. So we know she was here," interjected Agent Brewster. "Did she somehow make it to that chopper? Some kind of extraction?"

"If that's the case, then she is in the wind," replied Murphy. "Maybe the sheriff's department can fly it down."

"So now what?" asked Will.

"Did we get a BOLO out on Carson yet?" asked Agent Brewster, over her shoulder.

"One was just issued," Agent Stone said, as he tagged the evidence.

Murphy watched as the paramedics loaded Russ and the man who was still alive into the waiting ambulances. He, Mercer, Agent Brewster, and the others all climbed into their SUVs and followed the ambulances, heading for the hospital in Monroe.

Agent Brewster secured an empty hall in the hospital to put the two men they had in custody. Russ and the other man were put in separate rooms down the hall from each other. Mercer and Agent Brewster sat in two chairs in the room with the suspected hitman. Murphy started in on him.

"Okay, buddy, we need to know a couple of things. Like your name. You don't have any identification on you, so we're running your fingerprints. It's just a matter of time before we know anyway."

The man stared at the ceiling from his bed.

"You know, it really doesn't matter if I know your name or not. I have you for the murder of Cray Warren and two FBI agents. I also have you for the attempted murder of Russ Miller and Sarah Carson. I mean, you are going to be in a hole so deep, you'll never see the light of day again. The FBI agents and crossing state lines make this a federal crime, which means federal prison."

The man continued to stare, though Murphy thought he saw his breathing change.

"Help me out and maybe we can get you some leniency. I can't make any promises, but I can try," Murphy said. "Just tell me who's in charge. Who sanctioned these hits? I'm going to offer the other guy the same deal. It's just a question of who is smart enough to take it."

The man remained silent but his jaw flexed as the words sunk in.

"Think it over."

Murphy rose from his chair and motioned for Mercer and Agent Brewster to follow him. They left the room and walked down the hall to the room where Russ lay.

"Nicely done, Murph," Agent Brewster said.

"Thanks, but it only counts if we get something."

"You can turn Russ," Mercer said. "He's a self-preservationist."

"Let's go have a conversation."

As they entered, they took up similar positions as they had in the first room.

"Okay, Mr. Miller. May I call you Russ?"

Russ didn't answer. He just stared through Murphy.

"As I told your buddy, you have the right to have an attorney present if you want. Do you want an attorney?"

"No," grimaced Russ.

"Okay, let me tell you what I can charge you for. First, the murder of that poor Forest Service kid out near Sisters, and the buddy of that thug who was in the woods. I also have you for the attempted murder of at least five people, including the dead guy's buddy in the other room; Carson; and of course Will here, Jeff Pennoyer, and Jessie O'Brien. Then there's illegal possession of a firearm, intimidation, bribery of a government official, illegal dumping of hazardous waste, fraud, conspiracy to commit fraud. The list goes on." Murphy watched Russ deflate after hearing the list of charges.

"Now, we have a lot of evidence against you and more is being collected as we speak. I have a number of witnesses. You remember Will Mercer, right?" Murphy said thumbing over his shoulder. "Look, we found your operation in Wilsonville and a hard drive that was left behind. Your boss recorded every phone conversation she ever had. Some of those were with you and some were about you."

"I didn't murder that Forest Service guy," Russ said, his voice barely above a whisper.

Murphy sighed. "The thing is we found two sets of fingerprints on that rifle. One belonged to your buddy. The other set, I'm pretty sure, is yours."

Murphy sat down in an empty chair. "So how about we talk? It seems to me like you were here looking for Carson. So if you were looking for her, then you weren't trying to protect her. So the question I have is, who sent you to kill her, and who sent the two goons to kill both of you?"

Russ remained silent.

"Look, we think you had a tracking device in your cell phone. They tracked you. You were double-crossed. So here it is. I'm going to make a phone call about those prints while you think it over. But the window of opportunity for a deal is closing. You sit and think about your options."

Russ looked at Murphy and nodded. Murphy stood up and walked out of the room with Mercer and Agent Brewster once again trailing behind him.

"I bet he talks," said Agent Brewster pulling the door closed behind her.

"He'll cut a deal," Mercer said. "He knows he's been hung out to dry. He doesn't have much of a choice."

\* \* \*

The same thoughts were running through Russ's mind as he combed his mustache with two fingers. He was stuck and so the question came down to how many years in prison. If he could duck the murder charge of the Forest Service employee, he could probably plead self defense for the murder of Ashe's hitman and then take the attempted murders and the rest of the charges. He was sure he could deflect some of those to others. When his mind circled back to the same issues, he realized that he had made a decision.

"Come back. I want to deal," Russ yelled.

After Murphy, Mercer, and Agent Brewster re-entered the room, Russ recounted everything that had led up to the events at the cabin, implicating Ashe, Carson, and others as the story unfolded. When he finally finished, Murphy, Agent Brewster, and Mercer were quiet. Russ lay back in his bed with a deep sigh.

"What about the guy in the helicopter?" Murphy asked, scratching an ear.

"I have no idea what you're talking about." Russ was not going to give up Sully.

"Really?" Murphy feigned surprise. "Is that how Carson slipped away? What aren't you telling us?"

"Okay, that's enough for now," Agent Brewster said. "We are going to book you and, as I promised, protect you through trial. We will be moving you back to Portland as soon as you are able to travel."

Russ nodded. "I think I'm going to need my phone call now."

"You can use the one by your bed," Murphy said.

Murphy and Lynn exited the room. Russ dialed a number from memory. The phone rang a few times, and then passed through to voicemail.

"Don't go home. They know too much," Russ whispered, then hung up.

*  *  *

Sully flew the chopper just above the treetops, hoping to blend in with the deep green of the towering fir and spruce trees. Out of the corner of his eye, Sully saw a river, not very wide, but hidden by old-growth trees that lined the banks. Sully pushed the helicopter into a dive and headed for the deck. He pulled up and leveled the helicopter as his rotors passed over the tops of the trees.

Sully followed the river east, deeper into the mountains. He expected to see a police chopper at any time, but they never appeared. Deciding to take a chance, Sully slowed the chopper and swung it 180 degrees. He slowly lifted it above the treetops and searched the morning sky. There wasn't a chopper in sight.

He spotted a clearing to the east and landed. Smorning air, he opened a compartment and pulled out a second set of numbers to replace the tail numbers that identified the helicopter. He wanted to move fast and put as much distance as he could between himself and the operation that had just gone south. His goal was to get back to his place, pack a bag, pick up Bear, and head south to California where he had a small compound for just this type of contingency. Sully noticed he had a voicemail on his phone. After hearing Russ's message, he realized he had to move faster.

# CHAPTER 36

Agent Lynn Brewster moved quickly, making calls to the judge she had dealt with earlier on the Wilsonville and Molalla properties. She explained everything while Judge Simpson quietly listened.

"Are you sure these connections are strong?" Simpson asked when she had finished.

"We have him for the murder of several people, including FBI agents. The rest, and there is a lot more, will make his guilt beyond a reasonable doubt. We have solid evidence connecting him to this sham business. We have this guy dead to rights, Judge."

"Okay, you have your warrant. Where do you want it?"

"If you could get it to the field office in Portland, I'll have Josh Benjamin coordinate the arrest."

"Now what about this Sarah Carson woman? Where is she?" asked the judge.

"We don't know. It looks like we missed her by minutes. The problem is that we have evidence that she changed her appearance. We are going to circulate the photo we have to all Washington and Oregon law enforcement, especially at the border, but I don't have high hopes."

"Let's hope you catch her, but you definitely hooked the big fish. Let's land him."

"Thanks, Judge, we will." Lynn hung up and called Josh. "Where are you?"

"We're still in Salem. What's going on?" asked a groggy Josh.

"We have Ashe. I just secured an arrest warrant from Judge Simpson. I need you to coordinate with local FBI to execute it."

"Will do. I'll call them now and be in Portland in fifty minutes. I'll let you know when it's done."

"I'll arrange for some surveillance until you get there so we don't lose him," Lynn said.

"I'm leaving now," Josh said and hung up.

\* \* \*

An hour later, Josh and Pen sat in Josh's car across the street from Ashe's office. An unmarked FBI car with two agents was parked down the block. Everyone watched the building. They wanted confirmation Ashe was inside. The street was deserted except for a couple of pigeons flitting about. Josh made the phone call. Somewhere deep inside the building a phone rang and a man answered.

"Is Peter home?"

"No idea who you're talking about," Ashe said and hung up.

Josh flashed the lights of the car and then got out. Pen and the agents followed, all converging at the building's front door.

"Jeffrey, you need to stay behind us in case anything goes wrong," Josh said and Pen nodded.

One agent tried the locked door, then pulled out a small drill and drilled out the lock. Seconds later, they were inside and heading to the bank of elevators across the tiled lobby.

Josh stood behind the two FBI agents, poised outside of Ashe's office. He tapped an agent on the shoulder, and the agent busted through the door.

"What that hell—?" yelled a surprised man, who rose from his desk.

"Mr. Ashe, we have a warrant for your arrest and to search the premises. Please move away from the desk."

Noticeably stunned, Ashe did as he was told. Then quickly, he seemed to regain his composure.

"Who the hell do you think you are?" he bellowed. "Do you have any idea who I am?" He stuck his cigar defiantly back into his mouth.

"Oh, we know exactly who you are, Mr. Ashe," Josh said. "And we also think we know what you are."

"What the fuck is that supposed to mean?"

Josh cleared his throat prior to reading the long list of charges. "Mr. Ashe, we have a warrant for your arrest on the following charges: five counts of Murder One, including several federal agents; attempted murder; conspiracy; intimidating and bribing a state official; fraud; a number of charges related to your hazardous waste program. I'm sure more will follow."

"Who the hell are you?" Ashe roared, his face turning purple.

"My name is Josh Benjamin, District Attorney. I'm assisting the FBI in this matter."

"I want to contact my attorney," he said, his voice returning to a low growl.

"Of course," Josh said. "Agent, would you be so kind as to read Mr. Ashe his rights and take him into custody? Mr. Ashe, you will be able to contact your attorney after you are booked. Now, gentlemen, I think we have some evidence to discover."

Ashe looked at the folders on his desk as he was being handcuffed.

"I'll start with those," Josh said, noting Ashe's stare.

Ashe began to struggle with the agent. "You're not gonna get away with this. I'll make sure of that," Ashe said through clenched teeth.

"Sir, are you threatening another state employee?" Josh asked, smiling. "I would suggest you reconsider the rights that you have just been read and which you acknowledged understanding only moments ago."

"Smug bastard," Ashe growled under his breath.

"Get him out of here," Josh said in a tone that was all business. "And tell Jeffrey he can come up."

"Let's go." The agent marched Ashe out of his office.

Josh watched him go, then turned on his phone and called Agent Brewster. "We have Ashe in custody and are beginning to search the office."

"That's music to my ears. Good work. Let me know what you find. We should be headed back south soon."

"Sounds good. Safe travels."

Josh hung up and looked at the folders spread across the desk. A broad smile swept across his face. Moments later, Pen joined him.

"Let's get to work," Josh said.

Pen grinned and grabbed a stack of folders.

# CHAPTER 37

Ted and Rachel had spent the weekend reconnecting. Ted served as her driver as Rachel showed him where she had grown up. Each night she was exhausted, but Ted noticed a glow that had not been there when he had first arrived. Even though she had lost a lot of weight and looked gaunt from the cancer, she was still the full-of-life woman he had fallen in love with.

It was Sunday evening, the end of his second full day and another beautiful summer night in western Massachusetts. They had just returned from Ted's first tour of the Yankee Candle store when they decided to park the car and go for a walk along the Connecticut River. The moon was rising and fireflies flashed throughout the forest and meadow that they walked along. They were holding hands, and Rachel was leaning into him. He could smell her shampoo—pine—and the leftover fragrances from the candle shop. Suddenly, his phone chirped to life.

"You should answer it. It's still early back in Oregon," Rachel said.

"You sure? It was pretty peaceful just now."

"And it will be again once you're done," Rachel said, winking at him. She broke the grasp of his hand and wandered a few steps away to give him some privacy. Ted watched her go and then pulled his phone from his pocket and looked at the caller ID.

"Dia, how are you?" he said, answering the call.

"I'm good, Ted. How are things going there?"

"Really good. It's just great being with her again."

"*Mi tio* said you told him she had lost a lot of weight?"

"Yeah, but her spirits seem good," Ted replied.

"Good, so the reason I'm calling is that we finished running the blood and tissue samples. Ted, they were dangerously high for benzene. Those cows might have died from the smoke, but they wouldn't have lasted long after. It also explains some of the stillborn calves," Dia said pausing.

"And would explain a miscarriage," Ted said finishing her thought.

"Yeah," Dia said softly. "I'm so sorry."

"Ah, yeah," Ted began, his voice catching. "Ah, any luck with your search for other people getting sick?" Ted asked, changing the subject.

"Yeah, that was the other reason I called. I've found a couple of clusters of people who look like they could be suffering from this poisoning. One of the clusters is in and around Molalla. I have about ten workers from that cluster who are sick, and they're the ones I could get to talk to me. I think it's because they are here on work permits and legal. They told me about others who left the area after getting sick. I also started to do a little digging around with the Department of Public Health. I have a friend there. They collect data on illness like this. There were some residents that also reported this kind of illness in the same areas as the migrant workers. Ted there are a lot of sick people," Dia finished.

"Wow," Ted said, the news still sinking in. "Okay, so what's our next step? Can you get the lab results and patient information together? Maybe plot the locations of the clusters?"

"Already done. I have a bunch of information to email you. What are you going to do with it?"

"I think I know just the person to send it to," said Ted, remembering the call he had received from Jessie. He recounted the call he had and what was going on back in Oregon. Ted heard Dia let out a long breath when he finished. "I know, right? This is crazy—like bat-shit crazy," Ted said.

"Yeah, okay. I'm hitting send on the email right now. Let me know when you get it. Let's get these bastards. Keep me posted."

"I will, on all counts," said Ted before he disconnected.

Ted pocketed his phone and jogged over to where Rachel was sitting on the riverbank. He told her everything that Dia had shared, holding nothing back. They cried together about the miscarriage, but grew resolute on seeing everything through.

"I want to get these people, Ted," Rachel said firmly, wiping her wet eyes.

"Me too," Ted said gruffly.

"We'll let's get back so you can check your email and call that Jessie," said Rachel, slowly getting to her feet. Ted jumped up and helped her.

The trip back to Rachel's house took less than ten minutes. Once there, Ted booted up his computer and opened up his email account. There was a new message from Dia with several attachments.

Ted quickly moved the mouse over and clicked on the first attached file. It was a analysis of the blood and tissue samples. Ted read the finding out loud.

"Okay, so the analysis we did for the cow's blood and tissue samples showed benzene as the chemical. We knew that," he said, still reading. "And the amount of the chemical detected was 500 parts per million."

"Is that high?" Rachel asked. "It sounds high."

"I'm not sure," said Ted clicking open the next attached. This attachment was a report from the United States Library of Medicine, part of the National Institutes of Health. Ted quickly skimmed the page.

"Okay, so here it says that the U.S. and Europe have established occupational benzene limits of one part per million and environmental exposure at 100 parts per million."

The statement hung in the air, as Ted digested what had just read.

"So the samples were five times the environmental exposure limit and 500 times the occupational?" Rachel asked, jarring Ted back into the present.

"Holy shit," Ted said, his mind and eyes trying to reconcile the information. After a moment, he opened the third attachment. This one was a spreadsheet that listed names of people down the left side and information of where they were working, symptoms, and current address.

"This must be the list of workers that Dia mentioned. I could probably add to this if I dug into why my neighbors sold and where they went."

Rachel, who had been reading over Ted's shoulder, dropped into a chair.

"You okay?" asked Ted turning toward her.

"No, yes, I don't know. That's a lot of information to take in. A lot of answers. Is it enough to do anything with?"

"Well, I think between the ash and water samples, and now the blood and tissue, and your illness, it would be enough to help the investigation that they are working on right now. Dia said I could send them along to Jessie. I think that's exactly what we do."

"Agreed. Maybe call her first and let her know what's coming."

"Yeah, I'll do that now." Ted said pulling his cell phone out of his pocket. He quickly dialed Jessie's number and three thousand miles away, she answered on the second ring.

"Ted?" came a sleepy voice.

"Yeah. Hey, I'm sorry. Did I wake you?"

"Oh no. It's three hours earlier here. I just haven't slept much in the last few days. So what's up?"

Ted explained to Jessie what Dia had found through the analyses of the samples and search for other victims.

"Ted, can you forward the email with the attachment?" Jessie said, an intensity coming through her voice.

"Yes, doing that now. We just thought it would be good to walk you through it first before we sent it."

"No, that's perfect. I'll give you an update once I get this information to the team."

"Thanks. Okay, I'm sending it right now," Ted said as he clicked on "send." "Let me know if you don't get it."

"I will. Thanks Ted. We'll talk soon," said Jessie. Ted clicked off his phone.

"Okay, it's done," said Ted turning to Rachel. "Now all we can do is wait."

# CHAPTER 38

Carson rode hard, fueled by the adrenaline coursing through her veins. She had no idea what was happening at her cabin, other than a full, all-out assault. As she rode, the past few minutes replayed in her mind like a skipping record.

*How had they found me so quickly?* she thought. *And who was in the assault gear? They looked like law enforcement.*

She pedaled harder. The trail ended abruptly, feeding out onto a gravel road and almost sending her over the handlebars. Braking hard, she spun the bike onto the road, turned left and kept going. The gravel road ended at blacktop. Carson again looked left, then right. The road was deserted this early in the morning. Hoping that it was south, she turned right and pedaled on.

A sign appeared a hundred feet ahead: North Bend 10 miles.

Carson covered the ten miles in a little under an hour. She was beginning to tire, feeling her adrenaline draining. Suddenly, a gas station sign appeared in front of her. The sign, though rundown, boasted a diner. Carson decide to stop.

She pulled into the gravel parking lot and walked her bike around back. Leaning it up against the building, she entered through a back door. The place smelled of congealed grease, but she was hungry. She flopped down in a booth in the back. The white-haired waitress saw her come in and approached her as she sat down.

"Good morning, hon. Coffee?"

"Please," Carson said, smiling. "Where's your restroom?"

"Just around the corner, honey. I'll bring your coffee and a menu."

Carson went into the restroom. She looked in the mirror at her new appearance. "Just keep calm. You're almost clear," she said to her reflection.

She splashed cold water on her sweaty face. It felt good. She took a deep breath, ran her fingers through her new short, brown hair, and pulled herself together. When she returned to her seat, a steaming cup of coffee waited on the table, along with a laminated menu.

The waitress came back a few minutes later. "What would you like?"

"I'll take the Farmer's Breakfast. Over easy, bacon, and wheat toast."

The waitress nodded, jotting down Carson's order in some kind of hieroglyphics on her note pad. Carson picked up her coffee as the waitress walked away. She took a sip and grimaced. She added sugar to help hide the burnt taste and looked around the diner. An older couple sat together in silence, eating their breakfast. A rough-looking man sat on a stool at the counter, hunkered over his plate, shoveling food into his mouth. Carson noticed a store that fronted the building. She left her booth and walked through the diner and into the store.

She wandered up and down the aisles, looking at everything and nothing. Her eyes came to rest on an upright display of reading glasses. She walked over and looked through the selection. Most of them were hideous, but she found a pair of low-power glasses that fit her face. She pulled out her ID and compared herself to the picture. The glasses finished off the look. She also grabbed a Seattle Mariners baseball cap. Putting it on and pulling back her hair transformed her image again. She needed people not to remember her, and the glasses and hat would help.

By the time she got back to her table, her food was waiting. It was a heart attack on the plate but good. Carson ate quickly, feeling the need to push on. She finished her meal and a second cup of burnt coffee as the diner started to fill with regulars. She paid her bill in cash and left by the back door.

The ride to the highway only took a few minutes. As she approached another gas station, she saw a Greyhound bus pull away and a thought struck her. Quickly, she ditched her bike and helmet in the bushes behind the gas station and ran around the front.

"Damn it!" she said, loud enough so several people filling their tanks could hear. She put her hands first on her head as if giving up on something, then to her face. "I can't believe this is happening today," she said in a loud voice. She had cast her line and was hoping for a bite. It didn't take long.

"Something wrong, Miss?" said a man with a large potbelly stomach and a stained, white t-shirt.

"I just missed my bus to Seattle," Carson said, without looking up, her face still in her hands.

"If you don't mind riding in my rig, I'm headed to Seattle."

Carson looked up at the man and smiled. "Really? That would be fantastic," she said, wiping away the tears she had willed herself to cry.

The man smiled back. He seemed happy at the prospect of having a woman in his rig. Carson considered herself way out of his league, and wondered if he'd have thought twice had he known she was a stone-cold killer.

"Let's go. I'm all fueled up and ready to get out of here," he said, thumbing toward his truck over his shoulder.

"What's your name?" Carson asked, following him.

"Ben. Some people call me Big Ben," he said. "What's yours?"

"Natalie. So how do I get into this thing?" Carson asked, motioning at the truck.

"Let me help you." Ben opened the door and showed her the footing to get up to the passenger seat.

"Great," Carson swung up into the seat. "Let's roll."

"Let's roll," Ben said, his excitement coming through in his voice.

Carson watched Ben trot around the front of the truck, trying to stick his chest out farther than his belly but failing. He struggled to get into the rig a bit more than Carson had. He smiled and took a couple of deep breaths, then started the truck. He eased out of the gas station and onto the highway on-ramp. Carson looked out the window, a genuine smile spreading across her face.

# CHAPTER 39

Ted's cell phone rang. It was Thursday and he and Rachel were sitting down to lunch. Their relationship had been rekindled and Ted hoped they'd be together for the long haul. They had been talking about his return to Oregon and Rachel following him a few weeks later, once they had some of the medical issues sorted out and a transfer to an Oregon doctor.

"Hello," said Ted, answering his phone.

"Ted, this is Jessie. Hi."

"Hi, Jessie. Do you need more information? Did you get the samples?"

"Yes, the samples are great. I'm also hoping to get some more information from you, but that can wait."

"Miguel told me that the police raided Green Grass."

"That's what I'm calling about—we got them."

"What?" Ted's stomach lurched.

"The vet, the farm, a guy named Ashe who ran it from Portland, his hit men—everyone. Well, almost everyone," Jessie said, rethinking her statement.

"What about Carson?"

"Well, she's the only one we didn't' get. We think she changed her appearance and went into hiding or slipped out of the country. We were really close though, minutes from getting her."

"Hmm," Ted said. What about that state guy, Crocker?"

"We got him, too."

"That's fantastic."

"Ted, I have someone here who would like to talk to you, if you don't mind."

"Sure," Ted said, still reeling from the news.

"Hi, Mr. Kameron. This is District Attorney Josh Benjamin. How are you?"

"Great. Much better now."

Rachel looked at him, a quizzical expression on her face.

"I wanted to thank you for everything you've done to help with this case. You've helped a lot of people."

"Thanks."

"I hope you can help us a little more."

"Name it."

"We want you to testify. You have first-hand knowledge of what Green Grass was doing and can testify to how those samples were obtained. We need to make sure those responsible pay and there is no room for Ashe's attorney to argue that the samples were tainted."

Josh continued. "I'd like to get access to your property for our state forensic services division to collect similar samples. They are basically Oregon's CSIs, like from the television show. If we can have them collect samples that show similar chemical concentrations then we can corroborate your results. I'd also like to talk to the folks who ran the tests for you. We need to close up any loose ends," Josh explained.

"That's no problem at all, sir. I am coming back this weekend, but if you want access to farm property before that, I can have my foreman take your staff around to the different locations."

"That's great, Mr. Kameron."

"Please, call me Ted. Mr. Kameron is my dad."

Ted heard Josh chuckle on the other end of the phone. "Okay, Ted it is. Yes, if we could get access in the next couple of days, that would be really helpful. It's been dry since the last time they recorded burning, but it's supposed to rain on Saturday."

"Say no more," Ted interjected. "I'll call my foreman Miguel and he can get you access today. I don't want any potential evidence washing away. I know that Will and Jessie have already met him and he knows what's going on. In fact, it was his niece Dia who tracked down the other potential  victims and ran the blood and tissue samples."

"Ah, okay. I'm starting to connect some of the dots here," said Josh.

"Something else. Have you arrested José Garcia?"

"Well, yes, we have both José and a man named O'Neil in custody. They were both at Green Grass when we seized everything. Why?"

"Has José said anything?"

"No, not yet, I think he is pretty scared."

"Miguel can help you. He knows José and his family well. José is probably worried about his immigration status. I'm pretty sure he wasn't aware of anything they had him doing, though. He is a really good man."

"That's our take on him too. We have some phone records that seem to show that Crocker was threatening him and that he was just a low-level employee not 'in the know,' as they say. But if Miguel could help persuade him to talk, I'm sure his status wouldn't be an issue."

"That's good to hear. I'm sure Miguel will be willing to help out. I'll call him after we get off the phone and get everything set up on that end."

"That would be really helpful, Ted. Thank you. I was also hoping that I might be able to talk to Rachel at some point. I would really like the opportunity to interview her, whenever she's ready of course. How is she doing, by the way?"

"Better, and this news will help. I'll see if she is willing and we'll be in touch soon."

"That's all I can ask, Ted. Thanks again and I look forward to meeting you. We'll talk again soon. Bye."

Rachel's eyes sparkled when Ted explained the conversation. She reached across the table and grabbed his hands and held on for a long time.

"I should probably give Miguel a call and get things set up."

"Yes, yes. Right now," Rachel said, breaking the hold. "Call him."

"Okay, okay," Ted said, laughing. He took up his cell phone again and dialed Miguel.

"*Hola*, Ted," he heard as Miguel answered. "*Que pasa?*"

"We're good. I wanted to call and update you on what's been happening. I'm gonna need your help."

Ted explained to Miguel about the status of the investigation and the need to show the state investigators where Ted had gotten all the samples. He also suggested showing them where they had buried the last cow that died.

"Okay, I got it. Is the cottage open? Or is the key in the same spot?"

"Same spot. Remember to make sure they take the water samples when the water is first turned on."

"I will."

"There's something else," Ted said pausing. "They've arrested José."

"Yes, I heard about that. I've been to see his family. What do they want with him?"

"I think it was just that he was there and worked for Green Grass. I was told he's pretty scared and hasn't said a word."

"Hmm, I'm sure he is scared," Miguel said.

"I was hoping you might be willing to help. I just talked to the District Attorney. They seem to have evidence that he didn't know anything about the operation in terms of what was being burned, but he would also be an important witness. The state isn't going to go after him or his immigration status. I was hoping you might be willing to go with the District Attorney and help reassure José."

"*Si*, of course," said Miguel. "It will also help to reassure his *esposa*."

"Thanks, Miguel. They also might want to talk to Dia, since she was the one who ran those blood and tissue samples and tracked down the others who got sick."

"Okay. I'll let her know. Do they have my phone number?"

"No, not yet. I wanted to make sure you were okay with everything first."

"Thanks, *mi amigo*. Yes, please let them know I am ready to help anytime."

They spoke for a bit longer, Ted explaining his and Rachel's plans to return to Oregon. And talking about his trip and how Rachel was doing. When Ted finally hung up, he made a quick call to Jessie, told her things were all set with Miguel, and gave her his cell phone number.

# CHAPTER 40

Several weeks had passed since the arrest of Ashe and all those involved. The news was carried nationally; the suspected damages and clean-up costs were expected to be in the hundreds of millions of dollars. The trial was set to start and the news of it ran on the front page of a number of regional papers. *ASHE GOING UP IN FLAMES* read one of the headlines.

The news was also carried in the local papers on Vancouver Island in Canada. A short trip from Washington across the Strait of Juan de Fuca, the island was a vacation spot for many Americans in the Pacific Northwest. Natalie Barton read the article while she waited for a flight from Victoria to Edmonton, and then to Turkey. She had abandoned her escape to Venezuela after realizing she had left the travel book in her cabin. She smiled when she read who had been arrested and the predictions of the trial. The paper even carried a very old, very different picture of her, describing her as still at large.

The announcement of her flight came over the intercom. She folded the paper and grabbed a new carry-on bag filled with new clothes. She took one last look at the terminal before walking down the ramp to her flight.

She would be back. She hated to lose, and there was a score to settle.

# CHAPTER 41

W ill watched as spectators and reporters filled the courtroom. It was the beginning of the second day of the trial. Jessie and Pen sat next to him, behind the government's table, where Josh Benjamin sat. Ashe had been paraded to the defendant's table, where he had sat emotionless through the first day and was now ready for a repeat performance. At one point during the first day, Ashe had locked eyes with Will and Will saw the hatred burning there.

The first day was filled with a reading of the different criminal charges Ashe was being prosecuted for and opening statements from the defense and the prosecution's team. Josh Benjamin was co-leading the prosecution with the U.S. Attorney's Office because it was a complicated case of jurisdiction between State and federal criminal charges related to murder, attempted murder, blackmail, intimidation, and then the associated criminal environmental charges. A civil suit had also been filed to compensate those injured by Ashe's actions, but wasn't scheduled to start for another month. Day two would see the beginning of the prosecution's case and the parade of witnesses.

Will was the first person called to give his testimony. Silence fell over the courtroom as he told his story. He openly admitted to his role, unknowing at first, in the disposal of the hazardous chemicals. Then he described his attempt to blackmail Sarah Carson and the multiple attempts on his life. He finished his incredible story recounting the capture of Russ outside of Sarah Carson's cabin in Washington.

311

The defense jumped on Will's admittance to his blackmail attempt and tried to call into question his character. Will shrank slightly during the cross-examination, his shoulders drooping. However, the prosecution argued that whatever the original motivation, the multiple attempts on his life canceled it all out. Josh explained Will's state of mind during that period and how it had changed and how only with his cooperation were they able to bring the defendant to justice. After an hour, Will was finally allowed to leave the stand and rejoin his friends. As he sat down, Jessie reached over and squeezed his hand. Will gave a weak smile in return and then turned to watch the next witness be sworn in.

Ed Crocker, the now-ex-Oregon Department of Agriculture employee, took the stand. Will had only ever met him once during his time as the farm manager for Green Grass. He now looked much older and was haggard; his bald spot having grown. Crocker's whole demeanor was one of a man serving a penance, as if sitting on death row. Will assumed that his pension was on the line, depending how well his testimony went.

Crocker explained how he had been approached by Sarah Carson and paid to look the other way when it came to monitoring the field burning. He disclosed that he had received more than $150,000 over the years in bribes—most of it squandered away playing craps at the nearby Indian casino. The defense tried to establish that Crocker was an unreliable witness, but the prosecution entered into evidence the recorded phone records Jessie had uncovered between Carson and Crocker and the judge overruled the objections.

"Your Honor," said Ashe's attorney. "We object to this line of questioning. It does nothing to implicate our client. All it does is implicate this Carson woman, who is not here or being tried for these crimes."

"Your Honor," Josh said, quickly getting to his feet. "We are trying to lay the groundwork and intricacies of this web of criminal activity—all leading to one Sarah Carson. We will next establish that Sarah Carson took her orders directly from the defendant."

"Overruled. I'll let this line of questioning proceed," ruled the judge.

"Thank you, Your Honor," said Josh, showing deference to the judge. "We'd like to call our next witness to the stand: Mr. Russ Miller."

Russ was brought in by a court bailiff. He was dressed in an orange prison jumpsuit and his hands were cuffed. Will watched him enter and scan the room. He stood tall and looked defiant. He was quickly sworn in and seated in the witness stand.

"Now, Mr. Miller, in all transparency, is it true that you made a deal with our office. That you are going to provide your testimony in exchange for a life sentence without the option for parole?" asked Josh.

"Yes," replied Russ through gritted teeth.

"Why would you do that?"

"I'm not crazy about the death penalty," replied Russ, deadpan.

"Understood. Mr. Miller, can you please state your full name, your employer, and your position with said employer," said Josh, turning to rest his gaze on Ashe.

"My name is Russel Miller and I worked for Sarah Carson as security."

"Security?" asked Josh. Will could tell he was playing with him. "And what kind of security would you provide?"

"Pretty much anything she told me to do," replied Russ.

"Now, Mr. Miller, do you recognize the defendant?"

"Yes, his name is Ashe and he was Sarah Carson's boss," stated Russ plainly.

"How do you know that?" asked Josh.

"She took her orders from him. She went to his office. He directed everything she did."

"Objection," cried Ashe's lawyer. "Speculation."

"Your Honor, I am confident that the prosecution has corroborating evidence that supports Mr. Miller's assertion."

"Overruled. I'll allow it."

"Your Honor, the prosecution would like to introduce Exhibit 5 into the record. It is a series of recorded phone conversations between Mr. Ashe and Ms. Carson that establishes this relationship."

"Your Honor, we object to this evidence. These are illegal recordings. My client had no idea his conversations were being recorded."

"Your Honor, although we would agree with the defense under certain circumstances, the basis for the admissibility of recordings is that one person intentionally recorded a conversation of another who was unaware. Given the damning evidence contained in these conversations initiated by Ms. Carson and implicating Ms. Carson, it is our belief that she would never have intentionally recorded them."

"Mr. Miller," Josh said turning to Russ. "Did you ever know Ms. Carson to intentionally record her conversations?"

"No, no way. That wasn't her practice. She made sure we had new burner phones every two weeks because she was paranoid of the cops. But when she was in the office, she just always used her computer to make calls because it was easier."

"Your Honor, given that the evidence in these calls implicate Ms. Carson in murder and multiple attempted murders, we submit that she was unaware that she was recording herself. Therefore, since there was no intent to deceive, we ask you to allow this into evidence."

"Okay, overruled, in that it looks to establish a relationship and not to the subject of the calls," replied the judge. "Unless there is additional corroborating evidence."

"Thank you, Your Honor. Now, Mr. Miller, you took your orders from Sarah Carson and she took her orders from Mr. Ashe. What orders did Ms. Carson give you concerning Mr. Will Mercer?"

"She ordered Cray and me to kill him."

"That's Cray Warren, who was killed while in the custody of the Salem police?"

"Yeah," muttered Russ.

"Go on," said Josh.

"Anyway, she was in contact with Ashe during that whole time, constantly having to check in with status updates. She was afraid of Ashe and didn't want to call him until we had Mercer dead."

"Did you ever take orders from Mr. Ashe?"

Will watched as Russ turned his cold stare toward Ashe.

"Yes. Yes, I did."

"And what were those orders?"

"He wanted me to find and kill Sarah Carson."

"Can you please tell the court what happened on the night in question, when the defendant told you to find her and murder her?"

Russ retold the events that took place the night he tracked down Carson and was double-crossed by Ashe. Will hadn't heard all of it before and had only pieced together the information. Hearing it all as part of a single narrative made the hairs on his neck rise.

"Holy crap," he heard Jessie whisper to his left.

"So, the defendant double-crossed you and sent his own kill squad to murder you and Ms. Carson?" asked Josh, already knowing the answer.

"Objection," said Ashe's attorney, quickly getting to his feet. "It's speculation, Your Honor."

"Withdrawn, withdrawn. Mr. Miller, when you went to find and kill Ms. Carson, was an attempt made on your life?"

"Yes," replied Russ.

"And who tried to kill you that night?"

"Two men who worked for Ashe," Russ replied.

"How do you know they worked for him?"

"I'd seen them in his office before."

"Thank you, Mr. Miller," Josh said. "I have no further questions."

Will watched as the defense mounted a weak cross-examination. Since Russ had already made a deal, he told the court everything. Finally, the defense had nothing left to ask and hadn't made any headway in discrediting Russ's testimony. Ashe sat in his chair, red-faced and smoldering with anger like a volcano in the last days before an eruption.

Finally, the judge called a recess for the day and Will and the others got up and left the courtroom.

"Josh wants to meet for a little bit. He suggests grabbing a beer at the Rogue Brewery over in the Pearl District. He wants to try to get away from the press," said Pen, reading the text on his phone.

"Free beer? I'm in," said Jessie smiling.

"Yeah, that sounds good," said Will, distracted.

"You okay?" asked Jessie, taking him by the arm.

"Yeah, yeah. It's just been a long day," said Will. Weariness sinking into his bones. "So how are we getting up there?"

"I'll drive," said Pen, pulling his keys from his pockets. "And cheer up, this thing is almost over," said Pen, slapping Will lightly on the back. "We just need to get a beer in you."

They all walked to Pen's Subaru and Pen drove the mile to the brewery. It was late afternoon on a Tuesday and the small brewery was deserted expect for the bartender and a man in the corner working on his laptop, a fresh pint sitting in front of him. The patron turned and looked at them as they entered, but Will noticed he was wearing headphones. The man quickly turned back to his computer, dismissing the newcomers.

"Let's grab that table in the back over there," said Pen, pointing to a table that would provide the unneeded privacy given the current sole patron of the bar.

"Okay," said Jessie. "We sure don't want to be overheard by all these customers," she said smirking. "Pen, grab me an IPA, will ya?"

"Sure," replied Pen. "How about you, Will? What do you want?" Pen asked as they approached the bar and looked over the tap list.

"Well," said Will smiling. "Not to jinx myself, but I think I'm safe now. I'll take a pint of their Dead Guy Ale."

"Well played, sir," said Pen, chuckling. Pen ordered the beer, including one for Josh, and paid the bartender. Will picked up Jessie's beer and his own and they walked over to where Jessie was sitting.

"Here you go," said Will, setting Jessie's beer down in front of her.

Will took the chair across from her and took a long drink from his glass.

"Ah, that's better," he said, closing his eyes.

"It seems to me to be going really well," said Jessie. "The trial, I mean."

"I agree. Will, your testimony was great. And then I think Russ really put the nail in the coffin," replied Pen.

"Thanks," said Will, shyly. "Yeah, it went okay."

Just then, Josh walked through the front door, waved to them, and walked over.

"Hey, gang," he said warmly. "This one for me?" he said motioning at the full beer and empty seat.

"All yours," said Pen.

"Will, your testimony was spot on today," said Josh, sitting down and reaching for the beer.

"Thanks. I was worried when the defense went after me."

"Ah, they had to. But even they knew that the man who was testifying wasn't the same one who had been part of that mess in the past. Maybe that head injury of yours recalibrated your brain or something. Anyway, today was a good day of testimony. The only time I was nervous was about the recorded phone conversations, but that worked out."

"So, what's on the docket for tomorrow?" asked Jessie.

"So tomorrow we call on Ashe's thug to testify as to what Ashe ordered him and his buddy to do. Then we have some top-notch chemists and an industrial hygienist to testify about benzene. Should make for an interesting day," Josh said.

Taking a sip of beer, he continued, "But, I was thinking that before we do that, maybe I could call Jessie up as a witness. I was talking to the U.S. Attorney about it. We want to make sure Jimmy gets his day in court too. Since Cray is dead and he pulled the trigger, and Carson is on the run and she gave the order, we need to find a way to connect the murder back to Ashe. So, if I call you to the stand, Jessie, I'd want you to testify to Jimmy being in the fire tower and the phone conversation you had with Russ right after he was murdered. You'd have to testify that you recognize his voice from the phone call you had that night."

"I can still hear his voice over the phone. I'll testify."

"So how are you connecting it back to Ashe?" asked Pen.

"Well, we established that Carson took orders from Ashe and Russ took orders from Carson. Jimmy was killed because they thought he was you, Will. They don't get off because they made a mistake. Ashe ordered Carson to kill you, so anyone who was killed in that process is on him," explained Josh.

"Got it. So, after Jessie and the scientists, what's next?" asked Pen.

"Next, we put a face to the repercussions of the benzene poisoning. Ted and Rachel will be testifying. I think that they'll be enough, but based on the list of other poisoning victims, we could continue to call witnesses until the defense cries 'Uncle'."

"Can't wait," Jessie said, her eyes twinkling.

The four of them sat around the table and talked about the case and plans for life after it was all over. They ordered a second round and chatted about a lot of nothing. Will appreciated the escape into the mundane. He was still trying to figure out what he was going to do next.

Day three of the trial sealed Ashe's fate. Jessie's testimony linked Russ to the killing of Jimmy, allowing that murder to be tied back to Ashe. Blood, water, and ash samples were introduced, showing lethal benzene levels that were connected to the chemicals being destroyed at the farm. Finally, the veterinary practice was exposed for how it covered up the deaths of cattle and manipulated the data and information.

Will, Jessie, and Pen were back in the seats they had been in since the trial began. The door to the courtroom opened and two people entered, catching Will's eye. His mouth dropped open. Jessie noticed and followed his gaze to see a tall man escorting an overly thin woman to a seat near the back.

"That's Ted Kameron," Will whispered.

"And Rachel?" Jessie asked.

The prosecution wasted no time calling Ted to the stand to testify. Ted struggled through some of his testimony, his anger and nerves raw. He fixed his stare on Ashe and explained his role in the case. He explained how his neighbors had moved away or had been intimidated to sell their land. He described the ash that fell like snow and covered the cottage, and how some of his cattle had died in the fields.

Josh next called Rachel to the witness stand. She exuded a quiet strength, even though her body had been ravaged from recent chemotherapy. She spoke of the ash, the coughing, her health prior to living in the cottage, and her miscarriage. Will was impressed with how succinct and matter-of fact she was. It was clear to him that she was carefully controlling her emotions—a mix of anger and sadness.

When Rachel finished her testimony, a hush fell over the courtroom. Quietly, Josh said that he had finished with his questions and the judge gave the defense the opportunity for cross-exam. Ashe's attorney, standing with his eyes focused on the floor, said they had no questions. Rachel was helped by the bailiff back to her seat next to Ted. It was clear she was leaning heavily on the man escorting her.

Josh stood. "Your Honor. I have twenty or so more witnesses whom I can call that will describe the same kind of suffering and illnesses as a direct result of the defendant's actions. However, if the defense would stipulate that they agree with the testimony and have no objection, we can save both the victims and the court from having to relive and hear the pain and anguish they suffered."

Ashe's attorney whispered softly something to Ashe, who nodded almost imperceptibly. "Your Honor, the defense agrees."

"Then the State rests its case."

"Does the defense have anything to submit for evidence or anyone to call as a witness?" asked the judge.

"No, Your Honor."

Will watched and listened as the prosecution and defense gave their closing statements, the defense trying in vain to pin everything on a rogue Sarah Carson. Finally, the judge called for a recess until he was ready to render his decision and dismissed the court.

Will watched as a once-intimidating Ashe, now diminutive in appearance, rose from his table and was led out of the courtroom by federal law enforcement. Josh had explained that there would be a period when the judge made his decision and that then they would schedule a sentencing hearing.

The experience was surreal and Will, though knowing in his heart that they had won, felt empty inside. In part, it was because he had been on an adrenaline high and tense for the last few months—from the first day when they had run him off the road in the mountains. With the trial ending, he really had to figure out exactly what he would do next.

Jessie grabbed him by the arm and shook it brightly. She was smiling ear to ear and her eyes were on fire.

"We did it," she said. "He's gonna go away for a long time."

"Well, that's the plan anyway," interjected Pen, trying to add a hint of caution about getting their hopes up too high.

"Come on, Pen, they basically threw in the towel after Rachel's testimony," Jessie shot back.

"True, very true," replied Penn. "Ashe is screwed."

"Let's get out of here," replied Jessie. "I need some air."

They all walked out of the courthouse, Jessie leading the way and taking Will by the arm. They walked across the street to a bench in Lownsdale Square, a few acres of greenspace with benches and sidewalks. Will sat down heavily, tired. He looked up across the park and his eyes came to rest on the giant statue of an elk that stood on a pedestal in the middle of the road, forcing the lanes to go around it.

"Penny for your thoughts," said Jessie.

"Oh, I don't know. Just seems somehow unsatisfying," said Will, trying to give words to his feelings.

"Yeah, I get that," said Pen. "It can be like that with these kinds of trials. Everyone knows what the result should be, but you have to keep waiting for it. But I'm in Jessie's camp. We totally got him."

Will smiled. "We did get him, didn't we?"

"Hell, yes. We did," said Jessie, helping to lift the mood. "So we need to celebrate. Where are we going?"

Pen's phone buzzed and he looked at the screen. "Josh just texted. He wants to take us all out to dinner to celebrate. I think he's pretty excited."

"Free dinner on the State's dime. Sweet!" replied Jessie. "Tell him we want to go to Jake's. I've never been there, but it's a Portland staple."

"Will do," Pen said, tapping the text out on his phone.

"So, Will, what are you going to do now?" asked Jessie.

"That's the million-dollar question. I've been thinking that I might head back to northern Minnesota. Back to the Boundary Waters, the end of the road. I need some time to figure out what I'm gonna do next."

"Why don't you do that here?" asked Jessie.

"I think I just need some time to heal and someplace really familiar might help. Right now, Oregon has a lot of memories that I need to sort through and then try to figure out the rest of my life."

"Okay," Jessie said. "I understand that. But here's the thing. Remember you have us and we're here for you. And you need to promise to come back and visit, or we might just have to hunt you down in another wilderness. And I am relentless."

"I think we all know that," said Pen smirking. "And Will, if you don't come back, I'm gonna have to deal with Jessie all by myself, and that's not really fair."

At this, Will chuckled. "Okay, I promise. I promise. I'll come back for a visit. But right now, I feel my stomach growling. Let's head to the restaurant."

They got up together and started walking in the direction of Jake's. The sun was starting to set and the buildings cast their long shadows across the street. Will felt lighter as he walked with his friends. Regardless of Ashe and everything that had happened, he finally started to feel like he was turning a page in his life and it was a blank one ready for him to start the next chapter.

The End

# ACKNOWLEDGMENTS

I wrote this book over eight years ago and have been honing it and pursuing its publication. As it is my first thriller, I learned a lot from the authors and agents I met along the way. I owe a debt of gratitude to everyone who helped me with your advice, willingness to read earlier drafts, and reach out to your friends to help me get to this point.

Thanks:

- To my publisher, Kira Henschel at HenschelHAUS Publishing and Three Towers Press for taking a chance on a new author.

- To my family for their support and for allowing me to disappear for a few hours every week to document Will Mercer's world.

- To Shannon Jamieson Vazquez of SJV Editorial for providing the first editorial review and positive feedback.

- To the number of readers (friends and colleagues) who read earlier drafts and provided both constructive feedback and encouragement. Those helped me get through the dark clouds of the rejections.

- To International Thriller Writers and its annual festival that gave me exposure to authors and agents, who helped me better understand the genre and industry.

- To all the small coffee shop owners who allowed me to sit in their establishments and write.

# ABOUT THE AUTHOR

M. Stone Mayer was born in southeastern Massachusetts and grew up running around the forests of New England. Stone, the youngest of six children, attended the University of Massachusetts, Amherst where received a B.S. in Wildlife and Fisheries Biology. Upon graduation, Stone moved around the country working as a seasonal biologist, including Fire Island National Seashore in New York and Jamestown, North Dakota—two very different places. Stone headed back to UMass to complete his M.S. in Wildlife and Fisheries Conservation before setting off to Portland Oregon to pursue his J.D. in environmental law at Lewis and Clark Law School. Combining these two professions, Stone has been working in the environmental policy, planning and compliance sector for the last 20 years. Stone has moved around the country living in a variety of different places including Denver, Colorado; Ashland, Wisconsin; Kansas City, Missouri, Portland, Oregon (twice); and finally landing in Northfield, Minnesota.

Throughout his travels, Stone has continued his passion for writing, one he developed at an early age. His debut novel *Ashes to Ashes* took over ten years to write, as it was done in two-hour increments on weekends when he could hide away at a local coffee shop. He drank a lot of coffee and has a favorite coffee shop in each place he's lived. Stone tries to weave the places that he has explored and experiences he has had into his writing to create a deep and stirring sense of place that he hopes resonates with the reader.

www.mstonemayer.com

Made in United States
North Haven, CT
15 June 2024

53665464R00203